Anne Baker trained as a nurse at Birkenhead General Hospital, but after her marriage went to live in Libya and then in Nigeria. She eventually returned to her native Birkenhead where she worked as a Health Visitor for over ten years. She now lives with her husband on a ninety-acre sheep farm in North Wales. Her previous novels, *Like Father, Like Daughter*, *Paradise Parade*, *Legacy of Sins* and *Nobody's Child*, are also available from Headline.

Merseyside Girls

Anne Baker

headline

First published in 1995
by HEADLINE BOOK PUBLISHING

First published in paperback in 1995
by HEADLINE BOOK PUBLISHING

20 19 18

ISBN 0 7472 5040 5

Typeset by CBS, Felixstowe, Suffolk

Printed and bound in Great Britain by
Clays Ltd, St Ives plc

HEADLINE BOOK PUBLISHING
A division of Hodder Headline PLC
338 Euston Road
London NW1 3BH

This book is for my daughter Christine

BOOK ONE
1939

CHAPTER ONE

July 1939

'Goodness knows what you all get up to,' Celia Siddons complained. 'You should live at home where your father can keep a proper eye on you.'

Having three daughters all at an age that attracted male attention weighed heavily on her, and now it seemed with good reason.

It was Saturday afternoon and her middle daughter Amy had come home for an hour. She was sitting at the table in the narrow slit of a kitchen.

'Why all the fuss?' Amy folded up the newspaper she'd been scanning. 'Doesn't the news give you enough to worry about? It seems war is almost on us.'

Celia found Amy the most difficult of her daughters, the most questioning, and the one most likely to guess why she was such a bundle of nerves over this. She saw her own hand shake as she peeled potatoes for Alec's dinner.

'Come and sit down, Mam, and have your tea before it gets cold.' It wasn't like Amy to be so considerate. 'You're never off your feet.'

'I don't know why you had to find our Katie that job.'

Celia knew she shouldn't keep on like this, but she couldn't help it. Already Amy's dark blue eyes were following her thoughtfully. She was the one most like Alec. She wore her black wiry hair in one thick pigtail down her back.

'Why does she have to be a nursemaid? We should never have agreed to it. Should have insisted on her getting

3

a job where she could live at home.'

'Katie's all right. Better if you thought about getting blackout material.'

'I've bought enough for three windows. It cost one and six a yard, and they've run out of curtain hooks at Woolworths. Goodness knows what'll happen to us if there's another war.'

'There will be. There's an article about evacuation in the paper, and Pa's being sent on an anti-gas course.'

Celia's eyes went to the two gas masks taking up space on the shelf next to the cake tins.

'It's all a terrible worry, and now this business of Katie on top.'

She heard quick, light footsteps coming up the yard, and immediately her stomach was churning again. The back door burst open.

'Hello, Mam. Hello, Amy. Any chance of a cup of tea?'

Katie was the youngest and the prettiest, and the most innocent. The daughter most likely to get herself into trouble. Her thick dark hair curled about her head and shoulders, and though it seemed almost black, a shaft of sunlight coming through the window was burnishing it to bronze at this moment.

Celia knew she sounded unaccountably vicious: 'What's this I'm hearing about you, you little madam?'

'What, Mam?' Katie immediately looked wary. She'd found the teapot under its knitted cosy on the mottled blue enamel gas stove, and was already pouring herself a cup.

'Leave that a minute. You've been seen walking in the park with a young man.'

Katie started to add milk to the cup.

'Listen when I'm talking to you.' Celia couldn't stop herself shouting like a fishwife, nor from studying Katie's face for signs of guilt. Her daughter's widely spaced midnight-blue eyes were staring back in shocked surprise. The blue pinafore dress she wore was exactly the same shade.

'Who saw me?'

'Does that matter?'

Katie was guilty all right, she could see it in every line of her slender body. It infuriated her more to see Amy wink at her younger sister.

'Winnie Cottie, who else?' Winnie Cottie lived next door. 'I saw her curtains twitch as I came in just now.'

Celia straightened her lips into a hard line. 'You know I don't speak to her. Pa's forbidden it.'

'Doesn't stop her speaking to you, Mam. Not if she's got something to say that'll wind you up.'

Celia never ceased to be amazed at the things Amy seemed to know by instinct.

She burst out: 'Winnie said to me as bold as brass: "I see your Katie's courting though she's hardly out of school. Her young man was being very forward." Going behind our backs. Letting the family down. You know how your father feels about that.'

'Why are you so worked up about it?' She could see Katie's tongue moistening her lips.

'Mam worries about us.' Amy gave her a sympathetic smile, and poured more tea for herself. 'Let me explain it to her, Mam.' She tilted her chair back on two legs.

Celia wondered what was coming. Amy's eyes were more alert than Katie's and she had none of her sister's innocence.

'Katie, Mam sees us daughters as a big responsibility, and she takes it very seriously. Isn't she always telling us that family honour must be upheld? So must our good name, and we mustn't lose our good character. That sort of thing?'

Katie nodded. 'All the time.'

Celia didn't like the way Amy could joke about serious things. There was a wicked gleam in her eyes as she said: 'Mam, for a long time I believed you were telling us we mustn't steal, because it would embarrass Dad, him being a policeman.'

Amy giggled and went on: 'In the last year or so, I realised I was mistaken.'

Katie's eyes were watching her sister with rapt attention.

'What Mam really means is beware of men. Especially those who want to put their arms round you. Make very sure you don't produce a child before you are wed. That's what she's afraid we'll do.'

'Amy!' Celia protested. 'For goodness' sake! Such talk from a daughter of mine. If your father were here . . . You're shameless. I don't like to hear you being so crudely outspoken.'

'There you go again. You don't say what you mean. Unless you do, nobody understands.' She laughed.

Celia felt the blood rushing to her head. Amy could be so uncouth, and she'd never seen Katie look so beautiful, so vulnerable.

'Mam is afraid that one of us might fall into that trap. Particularly you, since you are so fetching. Just put her mind at rest, will you?'

Katie said in a clipped, awkward voice, 'I was going to ask if I could bring him home to meet you and Pa.'

Celia couldn't stop herself: 'So it's gone that far?' Her face was screwing up with foreboding she shouldn't let them see. 'Well in that case, the sooner the better. You'd better bring him.'

Amy said slowly: 'So our Katie's got a boyfriend. So what? It's hardly the end of the world.'

'In the park too. I hope you know it isn't safe, young lady. Keeping company at your age.'

Katie's lips broke into a smile. 'He's lovely, Mam.'

'That's for us to decide,' she said sharply. 'Your pa and me. You're only sixteen, far too young to know anything about that. Perhaps next Sunday? You won't have to work?'

'No, Sunday will be fine. Can you come too, Amy?' Katie implored. Usually Amy didn't, if she knew Pa would be around.

6

'All right, if you want me. I've got a half-day.' Amy was a student nurse at the hospital down the road, and was wearing her uniform dress with a navy cardigan on top. 'Yes, I'd like to meet this boyfriend of yours.'

Katie said: 'I'll help you, Mam. Get the tea ready, and all that.'

That brought a grain of comfort to Celia. Not the actual help Katie was pledging, but a well-brought-up girl should offer. Perhaps, after all, they'd raised her well enough.

'Our Nancy is bringing Stan for tea,' she told them. Nancy was her eldest daughter and engaged to be married. Stan came to tea every fourth Sunday. Celia knew and trusted him. Nancy was the least of her worries. She wished the other two were more like her.

'Ask your boyfriend too. We'll all be here.' She sighed heavily. 'What's his name?'

'Jimmy. James really, I suppose. James Shaw.'

Celia crashed down her cup and rushed to the living room. She had to get away, blot out Katie's face so rosy with hope and love. It brought a rush of unhappy memories. She could remember when she'd felt just the same about a man, and look where it had got her.

'That was terrible.' Katie let her pent-up breath hiss slowly out. She closed the kitchen door so Mam couldn't hear her.

'You have stuck your neck out,' Amy whispered. 'You know what Pa's like. He'll give your Jimmy Shaw a hard time. Ask all sorts of embarrassing questions. Whatever made you do it?'

'I had to, didn't I?'

'Why? You could have said Winnie Cottie makes up gossip if there isn't any. Or she could have seen you talking to anybody. You didn't have to admit he was your boyfriend.'

'I did really. Everything stands still until I do. I need their consent to get engaged, to get . . .'

Katie didn't say married, but she knew she'd left the word

7

hanging in the air as clearly as if she had. Amy's wide-awake eyes were searching her face. Katie went on hurriedly.

'I can't put it off, Amy. They'll hold it against me if I keep going out with him without telling them.'

'He's keen, is he?'

'Very, and oh, Amy, I do like him.'

'They'll say you're too young.'

'But Jimmy isn't.'

By Sunday morning, Katie felt almost as nervous as her mother. She wasn't looking forward to introducing Jimmy to the family.

There was hardly space enough in the tiny kitchen for them both to work together, but her mother believed in thrift, and if Katie wanted to bake cakes for tea they had to go into the oven at the same time as the joint for dinner. She hadn't been able to escape from her mother's endless questions.

'How long have you known him?'

'Quite a long time.' For Katie, it was an effort to stay calm. She was stretching the truth. It was only a few months.

'I thought the Brents didn't allow you to have followers?' Her mother's voice was sharp with suspicion.

'They don't.' And it had made her nervous to see Jimmy hovering in the park beyond their back garden fence, waving to her. Signalling to her to come out. Miming that he was prepared to wait.

'He doesn't come near Park Road West.' That much was true, the park was handier and he could sit on the grass.

'Then you don't see much of him?'

'I can't.' That was stretching it again.

Why should the fact that she had a boyfriend make everybody suspicious and nosy? And why should it be forbidden? She found it hard to talk about Jimmy. What she felt for him was too new, too different from the way she felt about everybody else. Even Amy and Nancy, to whom she felt close.

If she said Jimmy made her feel wonderful, lifted her until

she sparkled with excitement, it would only increase this unaccountable anxiety her mother had about him.

'You're too young to be keeping company,' her father had said, 'hardly out of nappies.'

Alec Siddons was a police constable and had a way of rocking back on his heels and delivering his opinion as though it were a verdict. Once he'd made his judgement, that was it. He didn't allow any appeals.

'Treats us all as petty criminals,' Amy had whispered behind her hand. It didn't bode well for a satisfactory outcome, but Katie wouldn't even think of that yet. She dared not.

'Mother! Please,' Katie implored, as she watched her basting the joint. 'He's lovely. Brown curly hair, ever so thick, and such a wide smile. You'll like him.'

'What's his job?'

'He's a ship's officer, merchant navy. Third officer, quite a gentleman.'

'We'll see about that.' Her mother's tone sounded as though she didn't believe it. 'How old is he?'

'Twenty-five,' she breathed. 'A real man.'

'Good gracious, he's far too old for a slip of a girl like you. I hope you know what you're doing, young lady. Don't you let him get you into trouble.'

Katie wanted to scream. That was all her mother ever thought about. That men could get you into trouble.

'Can I open a tin of salmon for tea? There's a big one in the cupboard.'

'We're not made of money, Katie. Surely a slice of cold mutton with salad? We had boiled ham for dinner yesterday, so there's some of that left too. It'll be plenty.' All morning, Katie had felt the tension sparking across the kitchen. Both of them were on edge.

Katie kept thinking to herself: It's got to be all right. Jimmy will make a good impression. Please make them like him. Too much hung in the balance.

She wanted them to accept him. Then accept an engagement

9

and get a wedding date settled. She had already transgressed the rules her mother had laid down, but Jimmy was casting such a spell on her, she couldn't help herself. She loved him.

Her parents, though, were tight-lipped with disapproval. She was afraid they'd already made up their minds he was unsuitable.

'It's different for our Nancy. She's twenty-four and old enough to be thinking of marriage, and she's making a wise choice. Silly at your age. Enjoy your youth while you can. Marriage isn't all a bed of roses, you know.'

Katie had intended to train as a nurse as soon as she was old enough, like Amy and Nancy. But compared with being Jimmy's wife, that was as nothing.

The aroma of roasting mutton still hung in the air from Sunday dinner, but as soon as the dishes were cleared from the living room table, Katie rushed to the front room to put a match to the fire that was permanently laid but rarely lit. The room felt dank and airless, unlived-in. She looked round, seeing it with fresh eyes, as Jimmy would see it.

The wallpaper was busy with overblown pink roses that faded to beige where the afternoon sun touched the wall opposite the bay window. A large picture of a stag at bay in the Scottish Highlands hung over the mantelpiece.

She felt jumpy as she started to prepare for tea, pulling out and extending the gate-legged table, putting the aspidistra on the windowsill. Their best damask cloth had been so heavily starched and firmly ironed that it stood up in neat rectangular folds she couldn't smooth out.

She carried in the food from the kitchen, while her mother unlocked the china cabinet and laid out the Royal Doulton tea service that had been a wedding present from her father's family and was only brought out on special occasions.

She was glad when Amy came home in the middle of the afternoon. She'd had her dinner at the hospital and was vague when asked where she'd been since.

The afternoon was crawling, but in fifteen more minutes

Jimmy should be here. There were butterflies in Katie's stomach as she ran upstairs to the bedroom she had shared with Amy all her childhood. Still did, if they were both home for the night. In the spotted glass on their dressing table, her cheeks looked flushed. She flicked her powder puff over them to reduce the colour. Took out her lipstick, but decided against it. Pa might send her back to wash it off if he noticed.

As she went downstairs again she heard him rustling his newspapers in the living room. He called: 'Is tea ready?'

'Yes, Pa, but we're waiting for the guests to come,' Amy answered from the kitchen.

Katie felt on tenterhooks now. She watched her mother take off the pinafore that covered her mauve Sunday dress, check her thin, colourless face in the mirror, and pat her wispy grey hair into shape. She seemed a faded shadow of herself.

This was the worst part, waiting for Jimmy to come. He should be here by now. Had he gone somewhere else first and forgotten the time? Or, and she went cold at the thought, had his nerve failed him at the last minute?

'It makes me nervous, the thought of being inspected,' he'd said when she'd invited him. 'I'm being vetted to see if I'm good enough for you.'

'I'll be nervous too, but you will measure up, Jimmy, don't worry,' she'd assured him.

To know Jimmy was to like him. He had that effect on everybody. Edna, her friend, thought he was charming too. Katie had told herself a hundred times that her family would take to him just as she had, but she had expected him to be here on time.

She made herself join the rest of her family in the living room. She perched on the edge of a bentwood dining chair because the table where they usually ate their meals took up most of the space, leaving room for only two armchairs.

Her father sprawled on one of them, his feet up on a footstool. He'd scattered newspapers all round him on the floor.

'Every paper says war will definitely come. Start stocking up on food, Celia. It'll all go scarce. Remember last time?'

'I'm doing my best. Buying up tinned food.'

The lived-in shabby room seemed overfull with so many of the family at home. Her mother talked of getting a carpet square to cover the cracked lino but said they couldn't afford it yet. She wanted to replace the two Rexine-covered armchairs too, though Pa said they were very comfortable.

Katie was beginning to fret. Her father's newspaper rattled down again. He stretched to look at the clock on the mantelpiece. 'This boyfriend of yours is late.'

'You did tell him six o'clock, didn't you, Katie?' Her mother's nervous eyes met hers. Seeing Mam all twitchy like this was making her worse.

'He'll be here any minute now,' Amy said firmly from behind one of Pa's newspapers. 'Just be patient.'

'It shows poor manners not to get here on time,' her father grunted, but he didn't get to his feet. Katie closed her eyes and willed the doorbell to ring.

But she couldn't sit still for more than two minutes. She went back to the front room, poked the fire up and put more coal on. The temperature still seemed ten degrees cooler than in the living room.

She couldn't stay away from the window and kept flicking up the crisp white nets to look out. On the other side of the main road stretched the leafy green acres of Birkenhead Park, lush now in midsummer but dripping with moisture on this rainy afternoon.

Another half hour dragged by. For Katie, each minute seemed like ten. It helped that Nancy was late too and Jimmy wasn't the only reason for delaying Pa's tea. She stood with her forehead pressed against the glass, hoping Jimmy would come first.

'I'm getting hungry,' her father grumbled from the living room.

'Pa, we can't invite people for tea and then start without

them,' Amy said with more assurance than the average nineteen year old could muster.

Alec Siddons had an enormous appetite and believed in eating well and often. From an early age Katie knew that the food in her home was better than at the homes of her friends. Her mother was always cooking. She couldn't remember a time when there wasn't cake in the tin.

Often her father would come off his shift with a large piece of ham or beef, or two or three dozen eggs, almost as though he didn't trust her mother to keep the larder properly stocked.

'Took a turn through the market,' he'd say. Sometimes it was on his beat. 'Eggs were down in price,' or 'I fancied a bit of ham.' And his large ruddy face with the moustache several shades lighter than his black wiry hair would beam round the kitchen.

Her mother liked him to bring such offerings home because it meant her housekeeping would stretch further.

'We aren't waiting much longer,' Alec growled irritably. 'Our Nancy knows what time we have tea.'

Katie watched a car drive past. There was an elderly couple on the other side of the road. Where could Jimmy be? She realised she was biting her fingernails and clasped both hands determinedly behind her back.

A blue and yellow double decker bus was drawing to a halt a few yards further down the road. She implored the powers that be that Jimmy would get off. Instead, it was her eldest sister Nancy who jumped from the platform and turned laughing towards her fiancé Stanley Whittle who followed. Katie felt her spirits plummet. Moments later, the back door slammed and Nancy breezed in.

'Sorry, Mum. I know we're late.' Nancy laughed excitedly.

'What time's this to come home for your tea?' Alec demanded angrily.

Nancy's face glowed in the dark hall. She was small and dainty in her flowered cotton dress and she moved like

13

quicksilver. 'We've been to see the curate and made some big decisions.'

'And kept us waiting while you did it,' her father complained.

She went over to kiss his cheek. 'Sorry, Pa. Then we went to tell Stan's parents and we had to wait for a bus. You know how few run on Sundays.'

Alec patted her arm. Nobody stayed angry with Nancy for long. 'You're here now and, anyway, we're still waiting for Katie's boyfriend to come.'

'I'm so looking forward to meeting him, Katie. Fancy you having a boyfriend too.'

Katie wished she was more Nancy's build. Nancy was her half-sister, and she and Amy bore little resemblance to her. How could they, with a mountain of a man like Alec Siddons for a father?

Nancy's complexion took a tan better and her hair was lighter; a mid chestnut brown with golden highlights. Her hazel eyes shone with goodwill for everyone.

Stan Whittle stood awkwardly behind her. He was a collector for the Prudential.

Amy had whispered that he reminded her of Pa and looked old before his time. He rode the same sort of big black bike and wore bicycle clips on his trousers, and a bowler hat with a collar and tie when he was working.

Amy had smiled and said she wouldn't hanker to spend the rest of her life with him, but Nancy thought he was absolutely wonderful.

'The tea looks lovely.' Nancy inspected the table. 'You've worked hard Katie, Victoria sandwich and chocolate cake and scones.'

'She was busy all morning,' her mother said.

Katie was on her feet again and lifting the front room nets, pulling the beige velvet curtains back as far as they'd go. Her mother had got into the habit of keeping them half drawn since they'd had the new carpet square in here last year. She was afraid the sun might fade the vivid red and brown of its geometrical design.

Her father demanded: 'What's happened to this lad of yours?'

'Perhaps he's lost his way,' Nancy suggested. She always thought the best of people.

Katie was grateful, though she knew that wasn't possible. They'd walked in the park opposite too often. She'd pointed out her parents' house in the red brick terraces that faced it.

Alec said with another burst of irritation. 'We can't wait any longer. This fellow has no thought for anyone else. Quarter to seven, I'm hungry.'

The kettle had been hissing softly on the kitchen stove for half an hour. Her mother went to make the tea.

In desperation, Katie went to the window one last time. Still no sign of Jimmy. She felt the tears sting her eyes and resolutely blinked them away. She must not let anybody see how much she cared. She felt terrible, it seemed Jimmy was letting her down. Perhaps after all he didn't love her as much as she loved him?

As her father settled himself in the chair nearest the fire, Katie crashed together the place setting she'd set out for Jimmy and stacked it on the upright piano.

'Not the sort of man for you, Katie,' her father said dourly. 'Accepting an invitation and then not keeping it. No manners. All the trouble we've gone to and then this. Drop him. He isn't going to do.'

Her teacup smelled of dust and disuse. The cold mutton was sticking to her throat. Katie sprinkled vinegar on her lettuce to help it down. Around her, she heard the chink of cutlery on plates and knew everybody else was eating heartily. Especially her father.

Katie felt she'd spent all day preparing this feast, working herself up for nothing. Getting Jimmy here was the first essential.

'Perhaps it's just as well,' her father said with his mouth

15

half full. 'There's no hurry for you to get married, not at your age. Let's get Nancy off first. One wedding in the family is enough to cope with at a time.'

His gaze went to Nancy. 'And we've promised you we'll put on a good show, haven't we?'

Nancy smiled at Stan. 'I'm so excited, Pa. We've finally decided on the date. We're going to be married on December the sixteenth. Stan says he can't wait any longer.' They'd been engaged for three years.

Katie saw the way they were looking at each other, and it stabbed into her. She was pleased for Nancy, of course she was. Everybody had known for ages this was coming. It was what she wanted for herself and Jimmy.

She chewed determinedly. It would do her no good to be envious of Nancy. Though Nancy had an engagement ring flashing fire on her finger and her mother had spent months sewing ivory slipper satin to make her wedding dress. She would gladly settle for fewer trimmings than Nancy was going to have.

'We'll have a week's honeymoon in London,' Stan said. 'And come home in time for Christmas.'

Out of the corner of her eye, Katie saw a shadow through the net curtain, there was somebody on the front step. That second, the doorbell pinged and she felt her stomach turn over. She was aware, as she ran to open the door, that her family's interest in Nancy's wedding plans had ended abruptly.

'Jimmy! Thank goodness. Come in.' Through tears of relief she could see him smiling at her. She wanted to throw her arms round his neck but was only too aware she'd left the front room door ajar.

'Darling Katie.' She knew his voice would carry easily to the tea table. He made a move to kiss her but she stepped back in embarrassment.

'Am I a little late?' His gaze captured hers, playing games and not allowing her to look elsewhere. He was wearing his best grey suit with a fancy yellow waistcoat and was clutching a pot plant. She could see pink azaleas in full and glorious bloom rising above the fancy wrapping paper.

'Yes, a little,' she said hastily, but her spirits were rising. Everything could still be all right. He looked wonderful. 'Come in.'

The hall was narrow and dark and made claustrophobic by the heavily striped wallpaper. Once the stripes had been brighter and lighter, but the years and coal fires had darkened them to oppressive bars of nigger and tan.

The only furniture was an oak hall stand. A large policeman's helmet set on its narrow table top, as though on a pedestal, dominated the gloomy hall. A policeman's tunic seemed the largest garment dangling from the pegs. Her father meant these trappings of the law to catch the eye of everybody who came to the door.

As a child Katie had not been encouraged to bring other children home, and those she did didn't come twice. The hall intimidated them.

'Is this the prison?' they'd all asked. 'Your father locks people up, doesn't he?'

The steep stairs with a central strip of brown drugget held in place with brass stair rods added to the aura of a bridewell.

'Good Lord!' Jimmy's smile faded as his eyes took in the helmet. 'Is your father a copper?' The tone of his voice left no doubt where the police force came in his estimation.

Katie was rigid with tension. She would have preferred her father not to hear that.

She hung Jimmy's elegant white macintosh over her father's tunic, and put a finger across her lips before saying: 'In here.'

Hastily she pushed the door wider and five pairs of eyes were examining Jimmy minutely.

'This is Jimmy,' she announced. He must see they had started to eat without him and realise how very late he was.

'Pleased to meet you.' Her mother was on her feet. He

pressed the pot plant into her hands. 'How kind. Thank you.'

'I'm so sorry I'm late.'

His arrival caused a general disturbance. Katie retrieved his place setting from on top of the piano and introduced her family. Amy got up to bring another chair from the living room, and everybody shuffled closer to make room at the table.

Her mother was looking round for somewhere to put the plant. She found a spot for it beside the teapot on the hearth. All were ill at ease.

'How are you, Mr Siddons?' Jimmy put out his hand. It took a few moments for her father to grasp it. His whole manner showed reluctance.

'You'd better come and sit down, lad, so we can finish our tea.'

'Thank you, sir. Very kind of you to invite me.'

'Katie did tell you six o'clock?'

'Yes. I say, I am sorry. Entirely my fault.'

'We did wait,' Katie told him.

'You're not fond of the police then?' her father asked, lifting his wiry eyebrows.

'Oh yes. I've always had great admiration for the job you do. I was just surprised, that's all. I thought Katie said you worked in the town clerk's office.'

Katie propelled him to his seat. 'That's Edna's father,' she hissed, aware that this wouldn't endear him to her father either.

'Got lost, did you?' her father asked stiffly. 'We'd given you up. Couldn't wait any longer.'

'Er – no. I was walking across the park and saw two elderly ladies looking quite distressed. They had a Sunbeam Talbot. I couldn't hurry past.'

Tight-lipped, her mother was putting the last of the meat on a plate, Katie piled on the last of the salad. 'Do start, you've a bit of catching up to do.'

One by one, the others were putting down their knives and

forks. Katie was the only one with anything left on her plate. She ate even more slowly to keep him company. She could see her father eyeing the trifle.

'I'll have a little of that,' he said.

'We all will in a minute, Pa,' Amy told him.

Jimmy went on with bubbling good humour, as though determined that Alec wouldn't get him down. Katie could feel herself being won over. She was achingly aware of his presence. She looked everywhere but at him, afraid to meet his gaze. Compared with him, Stan Whittle was a dull old stick who hardly opened his mouth.

Jimmy had a deep gurgling laugh and a voice that could change its note from tease to seduction in seconds.

'These ladies said: "Please could you help us? We've got a puncture." I had to change the wheel for them.'

'That took an hour, did it?' Alec asked sourly.

'Well, I might have been five minutes late already, but the wheel had never been off. I thought it would defeat me.' Jimmy beamed round the table. 'But I managed it eventually.'

'Managed not to get your hands dirty too,' Pa said. 'That was clever.'

'They offered me old gloves,' he said quickly.

'And clever not to mark that fancy suit. Changing a wheel's a dirty business on a wet afternoon like this.'

'I wasn't quite so lucky with my mac.'

'Right then,' Amy said loudly to change the subject. 'You'll have trifle next, Pa?' She started serving out generous helpings.

CHAPTER TWO

Katie shuffled on her chair. She wished Pa would stop baiting Jimmy. Surely nobody could resist him when he was like this? The devil was dancing in his brown eyes as he beamed round the table. His wavy brown hair was flopping over his forehead. He was on top form this afternoon.

'You don't come from this part of Birkenhead,' Alec Siddons mused at him. 'I've never seen you before.'

She saw Jimmy give him a strange look.

'I know most people around here. By sight. It's part of my job.'

'Of course. I come from Liverpool,' Jimmy said easily.

'Oh, what part?'

'Er . . . West Derby.'

Katie gritted her teeth. The inquisition was starting again.

'How do you come to be here, then?'

'I was paid off in Birkenhead at the end of my trip,' he said. 'I'm in the merchant navy. Went home with another officer for a few days, he lives in Upton.'

'And you've never gone home? Not when your parents live so close?'

'My father's dead, sir. Beyond my reach, I fear. My mother is staying in Ipswich. She comes from that part of the world.'

There was brief respite while Celia cut the cakes and handed them round. Then Alec started again.

'So, how long have you been here?' Jimmy's eyes met Katie's. She knew this was leading somewhere and hoped he did too.

'Quite a while. Decided to stay for a bit.'

She knew her father was used to getting more exact answers. He asked testily: 'How long is quite a while?'

'About six months now, I suppose. I've been at sea for six years. I needed a break.'

'Glad you can afford it. Many wouldn't be able to. The merchant navy, eh? Then our Katie will be on her own a lot. It'll hardly be a normal marriage.'

Katie saw Jimmy blench at the word 'marriage'. His gaze shot nervously to hers and away again. He recovered quickly.

'I'd like a shore job. I'm looking. I don't want to leave Katie, of course I don't.' He flashed a smile in her direction.

'Then your prospects aren't good. No job. How do you propose to keep a wife? Our Katie can't keep you on what she earns.'

Katie cringed. She saw Jimmy swallow hard.

'Of course not, sir. I could get a sea-going job easily enough.'

'But you've just said you don't want that. Jobs aren't easy to come by in this part of the world. Not without a trade. There's a lot of good workers on the dole.' The cakes were being neglected, the tea was growing cold in the cups.

'Where do you live? Do you have a house?'

'Lodgings at the moment, bed and board. More convenient while I'm on my own. Park Road South.'

'Not convenient for a married man. You'd pay double to keep a wife in lodgings. So you haven't a house, either?'

Katie saw her father's face twist into a grimace of disbelief. His imperious gaze swept to her and away again.

'I'll get one.'

'How did you meet our Kate?'

Jimmy smiled in her direction again. They'd discussed the answer to that question. She'd seen this as a hurdle they'd have to get over. There must be no hint of a pick-up; that

21

would immediately detract from his chances.

'Edna Ritchie introduced us,' Jimmy said, with a smile at her mother.

'She's another nanny that I know,' Katie put in. 'We meet when we take the children to school.'

'And how did you meet Edna Ritchie? I mean, if you aren't from these parts.'

Katie kicked herself for not foreseeing this, but Jimmy's smile didn't slip.

'I've known her for ages. We're related vaguely – some distant cousin on my mother's side.'

Katie knew that wasn't true; it made her curl up inside. What had seemed a mere glossing-over of the truth had led to a downright lie. The ease with which it slipped off Jimmy's tongue scared her.

The meal was over and they began clearing away. Abruptly, Alec got up from the table and went back to the living room, leaving the door wide open. Katie began to breathe again, believing the worst was over.

But as Jimmy came down the hall with what remained of the chocolate cake, she heard her father call to him: 'I want a word with you before you go.'

He put the cake on top of the pile of plates Katie was carrying. She hovered as he presented himself at the door.

She could see her father standing stiffly with his back to the fire. He was a big man, inches above the police force's minimum required height of five foot ten, and he was broad too, with shoulders like those of an ox.

He had developed a habit of rocking back on his heels as he spoke, to give his words more authority. Twenty years of cautioning naughty boys and cyclists who ignored stop signs had honed a naturally authoritarian manner, so that even the most streetwise lout took notice. His voice boomed round the house.

'You do understand that I have to be very particular about

the people my family take up with? Being in the police force, I mean.'

Katie felt the strength drain from her legs. He'd expect her to drop Jimmy. Never see him again. That much was evident from what Pa had already said.

She heard the clatter of dishes being washed in the kitchen. Nancy, tea cloth in hand, looked at her full of sympathy. Katie turned her back, not wanting to miss anything Pa said.

'I'm not a criminal.' Jimmy was still in a joky mood. 'No previous convictions at all, honest.'

'I didn't mean you were.' Katie heard the irritation in Pa's voice. 'It's just that you don't come from these parts, and you can't afford to get married. Think of getting a job before you think of marriage, lad. It makes sense that way round.'

Her father was a handsome man, his black hair, blue eyes and fair skin showing his Celtic origins. Katie couldn't understand why he should look in his prime while Mam looked faded and so much older. He had strong opinions about everything, and dictated the way his family lived. Mam had no more say in things than she and Amy.

'Yes, sir, I realise that, of course.' Jimmy was trying to soothe him now by being polite.

'Besides, there's a war on the way, and you'll be called up and in the trenches before you know what's happening to you. What's the point in tying Katie down if that's going to happen?'

'I don't know about the trenches. By all accounts this will be a very different war.'

'That's beside the point.' Alec's irritation boiled over. 'A war will change everything and Katie is very young. Her mother and I don't approve. You're too much a man of the world for such a young girl. She needn't think of marriage for several years yet. Better if she doesn't. Get herself trained for a job first.'

'We weren't thinking of marrying immediately.' Jimmy's

voice was smooth. To Katie, his words were the worst treason. She felt her spirits plummet.

'I'm telling you I'm not happy about you marrying our Kate at all.'

'Not even if we're prepared to wait?'

'Not even if you wait for ever. No, I won't give her permission to marry and it'll be a long time before she doesn't need that.'

'Sir, I do ask you to think again.' Jimmy was floundering. She'd never seen him so put out.

'I've made up my mind and that's it, lad. You can go now. Good night.'

Jimmy turned then and saw her standing in the gloom of the hall, still balancing the cake on the pile of plates.

'I'll see you back to Park Road West, Katie.' He sounded choked and angry. 'You are going back tonight?'

'Yes.' Katie rushed to the kitchen and slid her burden on to the table. Amy's eyes were full of horror.

'Not so fast, young man. I'd like Kate to stay a few minutes longer,' her father said coldly. 'There's something I have to say to her too.'

'Then I'll wait,' Jimmy offered.

'That won't be necessary.'

'No trouble.'

'I'd prefer you to go now, if you don't mind. Amy will be walking some of the way with Kate.'

Jimmy blinked. Her mother had come to the kitchen door. 'Thank you for an excellent tea,' he said to her. 'I enjoyed it.'

Katie cringed. Polite words, but everybody knew they weren't true.

'Tally-ho then, Katie.'

She felt the hall swing round her. Jimmy was being ousted. 'I'll see you out,' she choked. She couldn't look him in the eye. Even he had the message now.

At the door he hissed: 'I'll wait for you at the bottom of Ashville Road. What's got into him?'

She nodded in silent misery. What was she to do now? She loved Jimmy, yet to meet him in Ashville Road was going directly against her father's command.

'Come here, Kate,' her father's voice boomed out. Slowly she dragged herself back to the living room door.

'I forbid you to have anything more to do with that fellow. We know nothing about him except that he's got a silver tongue. He's kissed the Blarney Stone, that one. You're out of your depth with him, Kate. He's got no job, and no business to be thinking of marriage.'

Katie quailed. She didn't know anybody who dared to disregard his commands, unless it was Amy. Pa towered over most people, and his manner had military force behind it. He expected to be obeyed and most of the population of Birkenhead did so.

'You can forget about him. He'll not make a decent husband. No thought for anyone but himself.' Her father was bristling again. 'Late for such an important occasion. Looks shifty. You should be able to see through the likes of him.'

'Big-headed too, thinking he can walk into a job when he wants one, and he didn't explain why he stays in Birkenhead. Did he jump ship or something?'

'Of course not,' Katie was stung to answer. 'He could get himself on another. He's quite sure he could.'

'Then the sooner he does it and gets away from here, the better. You're not to see him again, do you hear?'

Katie swallowed on the ball of rebellion that was rising in her throat. 'Yes, Pa.'

Amy slammed the front door behind her as she left with Katie. Their house was the last in a shiny red-brick terrace of ten, built in the Edwardian era. As they passed the matching bay window of the house next door, they both looked at it closely.

'Winnie Cottie's watching us.' Amy nudged her sister. 'Bet she knows exactly who's been to our house for tea.'

'And why,' Katie added miserably. 'And the outcome.'

'Paul's seen us too.' Amy lifted her hand in a discreet wave as they passed the window next to Winnie's.

Paul Laidlaw, who lived there, was a relative. His father, Jack, was Alec Siddon's first cousin. The cousins had been brought up together by Alec's mother, which should have made them more like brothers, but the Siddonses had not been on speaking terms with the Laidlaws for the past decade and Alec had forbidden all of them to have anything to do with their cousins.

The window was open a few inches at the top. A strong, clear voice was singing, rising without effort above the crashing piano accompaniment.

'Sounds more cheerful at Paul's,' Amy sighed.

They crossed the road and walked along by the park railings. Dusk was only just gathering. The rain had stopped and all was soft blue twilight.

'Hard luck about Jimmy.' Amy took Katie's arm companionably. 'Pa did exactly the same thing to Nancy. He turned down two of her boyfriends before Stan Whittle came on the scene and got the thumbs-up. Things have worked out all right for her this time.'

Katie sniffed hard. Pa had turned a searchlight on Jimmy. He'd brought out facets of his character she hadn't seen before. Perhaps he did have faults, but she loved him, and anyway she was committed. Totally committed. The thought was numbing.

'That's why I've never taken anybody home. I'm not going through all that, or putting some defenceless fellow through it. I wouldn't, unless I was deadly serious.'

'We are deadly serious,' Katie said, trying to keep her voice even.

She saw her sister turn to study her face, but Amy went on: 'Pa's having no say in what I do, it's none of his business. You'd be better waiting till you're older and can do the same.'

26

Katie made an effort to put her own affairs out of her mind. 'I thought you liked Paul Laidlaw?'

Amy laughed. 'Pa's made up his mind about all the Laidlaws. He wouldn't even ask Paul to tea.'

'Paul's keen on you though.'

'Not like your Jimmy. He's not trying to persuade me to marry him. Haven't come across anyone who is, yet.'

Katie saw Amy's wide-awake eyes studying her again and shivered. She was almost sure her sister had guessed. She was frightened and Amy seemed to sense it. She felt a comforting arm come round her.

'You're too pretty, Katie. Never been gawky like me.'

'We are alike.'

'Yes, but the Siddons features have come out better on you.'

'You like Jimmy, don't you?' It was important to her that Amy did.

'Ye-es.' Amy was guarded. 'He's handsome. Nobody would dispute that.'

'But?' Katie forced herself to ask.

'A bit of a smoothy, don't you think?'

'No.' Katie rounded on her fiercely. 'What makes you say that? I think he's lovely. He was trying so hard to be pleasant to Pa.'

'He could have made more effort to arrive on time.'

'He was worried. About being vetted.'

'All the more reason to be punctual. He put Pa's back up. Couldn't have done anything worse than keep him waiting for his tea. Jimmy's too charming. He can turn it on like a tap.'

'No,' Katie protested. 'He isn't like that at all.'

She knew from Amy's silence that she didn't agree. 'Dresses a bit fancy too, doesn't he? Bit of a dandy.'

Katie felt hopelessness descend. She couldn't look at her sister. She'd known Jimmy might fail to impress Pa, but she hadn't dared think about it. What was she to do now?

Then she remembered: 'Jimmy said he'd wait for me at the bottom of Ashville Road.' She had to tell Amy because she was bound to see him. Ashville House, the nurses' home, was halfway up the road through the park.

'You're not carrying on with him? Not after Pa's forbidden it?'

'I've got to, Amy.' She knew she sounded desperate. 'He's going to marry me. He's just got to.'

Amy stopped dead in her tracks. Katie felt fingers bite into her arm as she was pulled round to face her sister. 'You don't mean . . . ? You aren't expecting?'

Katie couldn't say anything. Amy's horrified eyes were six inches from her own.

'You're acting as though you are. Otherwise why all this fuss? Why the rush?'

'Oh, Amy, what am I going to do?' It came out with a choking sob and the tears she'd been holding back all day flooded out. 'I am. That's the trouble, I am.' She felt relief that she'd said it openly. She'd kept it to herself too long.

Amy's arms enfolded her in the middle of the pavement, but there were few people about to see at this time of night.

'You poor love. I did wonder . . .' Amy's breath was coming out in shocked gasps. 'You are . . . sure? Quite sure? What about . . . ?'

'I've never been very regular, but there's been nothing for the last two months. That's got to mean . . . Yes, I'm sure.' It had been on her mind for weeks. The sooner she married Jimmy the better. That was the only way to put it right.

'Good God, Katie!' Amy was angry now. 'After all Mam's warnings. The risks . . . Why didn't you say no?'

'I did say no. Of course I did. I said no twenty times.'

'But you eventually gave in?' Amy wailed. 'Why?'

'I told you, I love him.'

Katie shuddered. They had not got gradually to the stage where the act of love came naturally. Jimmy had been persuasive, asking for it before she was ready to give.

28

He had said: 'If you truly loved me, you would. That would be proof.'

'I do love you.' She loved him too well. Enough to put his wishes before her own.

'You don't show it, Katie.'

Of course she'd wanted to show it. She wanted him to love her in return, and was afraid that if she didn't let him have his way he'd leave her for another who would. She couldn't remember him ever saying so, but somehow the threat seemed there in his manner.

Amongst the bushes in the park, late on summer evenings, with the wide sky overhead. Katie had been a little shocked by his wild excitement. There would have been no way of stopping him then, even if she had changed her mind.

'I could have a baby,' she'd whispered afterwards.

'No, it's perfectly safe,' Jimmy had assured her. Katie was afraid he was wrong about that.

'So you risked all this for a few minutes' pleasure?'

Katie was trembling. If there had been pleasure in it that first time, it had not been hers. And it had left her overcome with guilt and terror.

Amy snorted with indignation. 'I never agree with Pa on principle, but this time he's right.'

'We'll get married.'

'You can't without Pa's permission. Oh, for God's sake, Katie!'

Katie could only groan. 'What am I going to do?'

Amy walked along slowly, thinking, then she said: 'You'd better see Dr Poole, for a start.'

Katie flinched at the thought.

'And you'll have to tell Pa.'

'I couldn't!'

'Mam then, you'll have to. Sooner or later they're going to find out anyway. Tell them, then they'll be all for it. You'll see, they'll have you and Jimmy married in double-quick time.'

Katie couldn't speak. The thought of telling them appalled her.

'Do you want me to do it?' Amy offered gently. 'Better if you do it yourself though.'

Katie swallowed hard. 'I'll do it. But only if you're there to hold my hand.'

They went a few more steps in silence. 'He does want to marry you?' Amy was hesitant.

'Yes, yes, he said so.' Katie shivered. It seemed that Amy shared her doubts about that.

'Mam will blame me,' Amy said. 'Say it's all my fault. I found you the job with the Brents and persuaded them to let you take it. Mam will be quite certain this wouldn't have happened if you'd stayed at home.'

Katie said: 'Here's Jimmy.' They had reached the bottom of Ashville Road. Jimmy was stamping his feet impatiently, his hands pushed deep into the pockets of his smart white macintosh. 'Don't say anything about . . . Don't let on I've told you.'

Amy shook her arm impatiently. 'The more you talk about it the better. Make him see how worried you are. Don't let him forget what's happening to you.'

Then Jimmy was smiling at her. 'That was a turn-up for the books – forbidden to see you. What are we going to do now?'

Katie was blinking back her tears when she heard footsteps thudding on the pavement. They all turned.

'Amy, hang on a minute.' Paul Laidlaw was running towards them. 'Wait for me, I was beginning to think I'd never catch you up.'

He caught hold of Amy's arm and swung her away towards Duke Street without stopping to be introduced.

'Bit of luck for us.' Jimmy smiled and nuzzled Katie's cheek. 'That fellow turning up to take Amy off our hands.'

Katie was left gulping for air. Though she was glad that at

last she was alone with Jimmy, she couldn't quite banish the feeling of hysteria. 'Wasn't it awful?'

'Dreadful! But I love you, Katie. That's what's important.' Jimmy's voice was warm with sincerity. 'We mustn't let what's happened frighten us off each other.'

'Of course not.' Katie knew she had to push her father's reaction to the back of her mind.

'I couldn't bear to lose you,' Jimmy soothed. 'Your parents are too old to remember what love is.'

'You told Pa you weren't thinking of marriage yet.' Katie knew her tone was accusing. 'But we were. "Just as soon as we can arrange it," you said.'

She saw Jimmy's gentle smile. 'I know, love, but I had to say that. I was hoping that at least he'd agree to a long engagement. Then when we told him about the baby, it wouldn't seem such a big step to bring the date forward.'

Katie began to relax. Jimmy was doing his best.

'Let's go into the park.' He took her arm. 'We can sit down there and talk.'

All the gates to the park were locked at night, but there were one or two places in the railings where the bars had been forced a couple of inches apart so that a slim and supple person could squeeze through.

Jimmy found the place. 'Don't bend these branches back too much. Don't want to make it obvious that we get in here.'

Katie felt safer because she knew they had the park to themselves.

It was not just a public garden with an acre or so of stiffly laid-out flowerbeds. It stretched for two hundred acres with Ashville Road running through the middle. There were two lakes, complete with swans and ducks.

Jimmy said, 'Did you know that the man who designed this park designed the Crystal Palace afterwards, and that Central Park in New York was copied from the same design?'

'How do you know that?' Katie asked impatiently. Every

inch of it was familiar – she'd played here throughout her childhood – but that was news to her.

'Read about it in the library.'

They reached the lake in the upper portion of the park and sat down on a wooden bench. The water rippled with silver, and the Chinese bridge looked very romantic in the blue summer darkness. The ducks and swans were not to be seen; she thought they must be asleep somewhere under the bank.

Katie shivered. It was here that she had first met Jimmy. He'd been sitting on this very bench.

The day had started like any other, a busy day spent looking after the children. She was fond of her charges. Bernard, the elder, was seven and had started full-time school. His father took him there in the morning but it was one of her duties to collect him at dinnertime, give him something to eat, and walk him back by two o'clock in time for the afternoon session. Then she had to pick him up again at four.

In fine weather, it was a pleasant walk across the park several times a day, with two-year-old Daniel in his pushchair. She found the children well behaved and rather sweet.

She met regularly with Edna Ritchie, a trained nanny who was several years older than her. Edna had three charges, one of whom attended the same school as Bernard, and she and Katie had become friendly. Katie felt that knowing Edna made her job even pleasanter. Better for Daniel, too, to have a playmate. On fine days they would linger in the park, sometimes staying until it was time to collect the children from school again. Katie took a ball so the little boys could kick it about on the grass.

Edna's employers dressed her with some formality in a brown gabardine coat and hat and a brown-striped dress. She'd been at school with Nancy and thought she was doing very well for herself.

Little Daniel was fond of feeding the ducks and if there was any stale bread in the house Katie took it with her to help keep him amused. She and Edna usually sat on the bench nearest the duck pond to gossip, Edna rocking baby Isabel in her pram while they both kept an eye on the toddlers. One day, Jimmy was occupying their usual park bench.

It was a blustery afternoon at the beginning of the summer. She and Edna sat down on the next bench. Katie had seen his thick glossy hair blowing in the wind and knew that his eyes were following her. Edna noticed him too, and said he was wonderfully handsome.

The following day, he was there again with his own supply of stale bread, most of which he divided between their two charges.

It seemed rude not to talk to him. He insisted they sit on the bench he occupied. He moved to sit on the grass facing them. He amused them so well they forgot to watch the time and then had to race behind their prams to the school gates.

After that, they saw him regularly at the lake. Only if it was raining would he not come. They walked past it anyway, just to see. If Jimmy wasn't there, they talked about him. How he was always full of bubbling good humour, always with a joke to crack.

But Katie was careful not to appear too friendly when she had Bernard with her, because at seven years old he was getting worldly-wise and might tell his parents.

It was only when Edna's charges caught measles and couldn't come to the park that she began to see Jimmy on her own. Almost on her own, for little Daniel was always playing close, if not climbing all over her.

'We should see more of each other,' Jimmy told her. 'It would be more fun without that child. Don't you ever come for a walk in the park at night?'

'No. They don't like me going out except on my evenings off.'

'Surely once you've put the children to bed?'

'No, I'm supposed to listen for them, in case they wake up.'

'Do they?'

'Daniel cries a lot in the night. That's why they want me to live in. I sleep in the next room and it's my job to get up in the night to soothe him.'

'They've got proper nurseries? A big posh house?'

'No. It's a bigger house than ours but nothing special, not like where our Nancy works. Their mother owns a dress shop in Birkenhead. She goes to work so she needs me to look after the children.'

'When are your evenings off?'

'I get Sunday because Mrs Brent's home then, and a half-day alternate Thursdays when the shop's closed. She has her hair done the other Thursday, but I can get off in the evening.'

'It's Thursday tomorrow. I'll take you to the pictures. Deanna Durbin is on at the Ritz. How about it?'

Katie's heart leapt with anticipation. 'I'd love to.' She'd never been taken out by a boy before. Not that Jimmy was a boy, he was a man in his prime. He emanated strength and masculinity. His brown eyes wouldn't leave hers.

In the cinema, the best in Birkenhead, Jimmy bought tickets for the most expensive seats, on the front row of the balcony, and held her hand throughout the performance. He pretended not to believe her when she told him she was only sixteen.

She felt he was taking her into a world of luxury. He'd brought chocolates with him and insisted on buying ice cream for her in the interval. She loved Deanna Durbin's pure, sweet voice.

Even back at the bus stop, it wasn't quite the prosaic world she knew. Not with Jimmy bending his head to hers in order not to miss anything she said. She clung to his arm; he smelled wonderfully masculine, of cigarette smoke and hair pomade. They rode only a few stops, passing the magnificent main gates to the park. The hospital was brightly lit still. She could see a nurse hurrying up the ward and thought of Amy, but of course she wouldn't be there now. The night staff would be on duty.

'I'm going to be a real nurse,' she told him. 'Not just a nanny.' When she was eighteen she would start her training.

They turned up Ashville Road, which had no street lights and was shaded from the silvery moonlight by tall trees. Jimmy slid an arm round her waist and pulled her closer. He'd known about the bent railings from the beginning and had taken her into the park itself.

Now she could see the lights of Park Road North through the trees, and the glow they cast up in the sky. She wrenched her mind back to the present. 'What are we going to do now we can't get married?'

Jimmy took her hand between his own. 'We still can. We can go to Gretna Green.'

'Can we?'

'Why not? Other people do in our position. We won't need anybody's permission there.'

'I mean . . . Oh! That would be wonderful.' Katie clung to him in relief, unable to believe he'd thought of a way of getting round her father. 'You're sure it's possible? It would be legal?'

'Yes, I was reading about that too in the library the other day. It's both legal and possible.'

Katie felt lifted on a wave of joy.

'I won't let your father break us up. I love you too much for that.' Jimmy nuzzled her cheek. 'Anyway, I feel married to you already.'

Katie laughed. She'd said that to him, more than once, and she truly did.

'Here's what we'll do, Katie. I'll look for a job. We'll have to get some money first, but as soon as that's arranged, we'll go off to Gretna Green.'

'I do love you, Jimmy. You think of everything.' She could feel his breath against her cheek, his arm around her waist pulling her closer. She moved away.

'The grass will be wet tonight, it's been raining,' she whispered.

35

He was spreading his mac on the ground. 'We won't feel it through this.' He kissed her and urged her down on to it. He'd taught her to enjoy his lovemaking over the last weeks. She felt the tiny hairs on the back of her neck pull erect. Her flesh tingled.

She was comforted and reassured that he'd thought of going to Gretna. It meant he wanted to marry her as much as she wanted to marry him.

'Just as soon as we can,' he whispered. 'We'll get married, just as soon as we can.'

CHAPTER THREE

Celia Siddons was glad to hear the front door slam behind Kate and Amy. The foreboding she felt was growing. Kate had upset Alec and given them all a bad day. Celia had wanted them gone for the last hour.

'We've got to go too, Pa.' Nancy was reaching for Stan's coat on the hall stand. 'I've got to be back early tonight. Stan and I wanted to talk about our wedding, but we couldn't, not with you going on at Katie's boyfriend like that.' She chuckled. 'I thought you were a bit heavy handed. Look, Pa, we want to fix up about the reception.'

Alec was frowning. 'I thought you had.'

'We've booked the church hall, Mr Siddons,' Stan said, holding Nancy's coat out for her. 'But we've got to decide what we're going to do about food and drink.'

Nancy smiled. 'We want to get it all organised.' There was an undercurrent of contentment about her. 'I'll come back another night to talk about it. Wednesday?'

'No, nor Thursday either,' Alec said. 'I'll be working overtime. And I've got a lecture to attend on Friday. Civil defence preparations.'

'You're never in, Pa.'

'The police will have new and important duties if war comes. They have to take precedence over your wedding,' but he was smiling, humouring her. 'How about Friday afternoon?'

'Fine, I'll come then.' Nancy went over to his chair and kissed him. 'You all right, Mam?'

Celia felt her daughter's lips, warm and loving, touching her cheek, then Nancy's hazel eyes were smiling into hers. 'December the sixteenth is the magic date,' she laughed. 'But you won't forget that?'

'Course not. We've all waited a long time for this.' Celia followed them to the door, wanting Nancy to stay. Waiting to see her turn and wave before closing the door.

Even Nancy couldn't banish the sinking feeling from her stomach. She felt almost ill as she tiptoed past the living room door with the stack of plates the girls had washed.

'Celia?' Alec straightened up in his chair. 'Why don't you leave that now? You'll have plenty of time tomorrow.'

He made her jump and she felt the precious plates slip in her fingers. Gripping them tighter, she said: 'I just want to put the best service away, dear.'

She wanted it all back in the cabinet in the front room. She wanted to remove every sign that the terrible tea party had taken place. She went back for the cups and saucers.

As she swept up the hearth she called: 'Would you like to sit in the front room tonight? It's nice and warm in here now.'

She heard Alec grunt and his newspaper crackle. She didn't know whether that meant yes or no. She'd put everything neatly back in its place but she still couldn't sit down, she felt too much on edge.

She got out her mop and bucket and wiped over the red quarry tiles of the kitchen floor, though they hardly needed it.

'Come and sit down.' Alec's voice, full of irritation now, came from the living room. She'd have to do what he wanted. 'If I'm staying in with you tonight, you may as well come and sit with me.'

She went in. 'You don't think our Kate will see him again, do you, Alec?'

'She'd better not. She'll feel the weight of my hand on her backside if she does. She's not too old for a good spanking.'

Celia knew she ought to feel relief. Kate would be all

right now. She wouldn't dare flout Alec's authority. Amy might, but not Kate. Alec had seen that fellow off.

But Alec's violence frightened her too. He had such strong opinions and delivered them so forcefully. It made her realise he'd be just as ruthless with her, if he discovered what she'd done.

She got out her sewing which she kept under the sideboard in a large cardboard box that had once held Sunlight soap. She had to do something to take her mind off Jimmy Shaw.

'You're not going to start sewing now?'

'I need to get on with it, Alec. Now our Nancy's set the date. There isn't all that much time left.'

'I thought you'd finished her dress?'

'I have.' She thought of Nancy, bright-eyed with excitement, sweeping round this room in all her finery. Preening in front of the looking glass, trying to see herself. Then rushing upstairs to have a better view in her wardrobe mirror. That had been back in the spring.

'I do wish she'd chosen white velvet. It would have been warmer for her, but she hadn't decided on a Christmas wedding then.'

'Warmth, Mother, is the last thing our Nancy's likely to worry about.' Even Alec sounded indulgent.

'And her slipper satin was reduced in the July sales. Was it last year, or the year before?'

'They've been planning it a long time.'

'Over three years,' she agreed. But that had pleased Alec. He had strong moral values. He believed it right and proper for a bride to wear white, but only a virgin bride who could honestly wear the symbol of chastity and purity. 'Only sensible for Nancy to qualify first and save up for it.'

As she spread pieces of peach-coloured taffeta across her knee, Celia thought of the greater prosperity all those years of self-restraint would give Nancy. She was beginning to feel better. Alec had got over his anger, his mind was on Nancy now; she'd calmed them both.

'What's that then?'

'A bridesmaid's dress for Kate. I want to tack it ready for sewing. Good job they didn't choose blue. In mid-winter it would have made them look like ice maidens.'

'Oh, Kate! In too much of a hurry, that one. She'll have to be satisfied with being a bridesmaid this year. Can't afford to have them all marrying at once, can we? Not if they want a big do.'

'Nancy's got everything organised.'

'You have too, Celia, with all this sewing.'

'It's just the wedding breakfast. I don't want Nancy to worry. You did talk about getting caterers . . .'

'They won't come cheap. Better if we can do it ourselves.'

Celia sighed. She knew that meant most of the work would fall on her. 'I've a lot to do between now and Christmas. I want to bake the wedding cake next week.'

'Perhaps I can fix up some help. I'll see what I can do.'

'It was you that promised Nancy a big do.'

'She deserves it, and she'll have it. Have you seen the guest list the pair of them have drawn up? Every Tom, Dick and Harry in town.'

Celia got up and went over to the sideboard, where Stan had left the list. She ran her eye down the names and was suddenly gasping. She felt beads of perspiration stand out on her forehead. The name Victor Smith stood out as though it had been written in red ink.

Seconds later, she was telling herself she was a fool to be knocked sideways like this. Smith was a very common name, and Victor wasn't rare either. Stan Whittle had several Smith relatives. It didn't mean it was him. She mustn't even think it. But her head was suddenly throbbing with the new threat she hadn't foreseen. She felt queasy.

Alec said: 'At least Nancy does everything right. Not like the other two.'

When she had left school, Nancy started working in a

chemist's shop in Grange Road. She soon settled down and found the work pleasant enough. The pills, potions and ointments interested her.

One Sunday, she was standing at the bay window of their front room with Amy, watching the nurses walk past on their way to Beechwood, another nurses' home overlooking the rugby ground on the far side of the park.

'I shall be a nurse when I grow up,' Amy said importantly, tossing her thick black plait over her shoulder.

All the family knew that the nearby hospital, and the many student nurses in the vicinity, had fascinated Amy from a very young age.

'Are you going to spend all your life working in that shop? Why don't you become a nurse?' Amy wanted to know. 'Once you're trained, you could get a job on a passenger liner and sail round the world. P & O were advertising in the *Echo* this week. That sounds a lot more glamorous.'

'Perhaps I will.' Nancy knew she was drifting. Nursing seemed more interesting than the chemist's counter. She had turned it over in her mind for weeks before doing anything. Somehow, it didn't seem possible until she saw the appeal. Birkenhead General was a voluntary hospital and was appealing for funds to build an extension to commemorate the Coronation of George VI and Queen Elizabeth.

There was an exhibition of photographs of the hospital outlining its history in the public library. Amy insisted they go to see it. The land had been donated by the benefactor who had provided the land for the park, the money to build by Henry Laird.

It was one of the first hospitals in the country to use trained nurses. It had started training its own in 1918 and there were pictures of the nursing school, which took four intakes each year. Matriculation was asked for, but girls who did not have that might sit an entrance examination.

'Go on,' Amy urged. 'Try the entrance exam. You're not stupid. It would give you a good reason to leave home. You

41

know Mam, she wouldn't agree to you going otherwise.'

Two of the nurses' homes were further away from the hospital than their own house, but the rule was that all student nurses had to live in.

'Apply, why don't you?'

Nancy did, and started reading all she could about Florence Nightingale and Edith Cavell. There were no questions about either in the entrance exam she took with two other girls, but a fortnight later she had a letter offering her a place in the next school intake.

Her mother thought she was silly. 'You get better pay at the chemist's.'

'But as well as pay, I get a room in the nurses' home, my uniform and my keep.'

Celia sniffed. 'What's the point of that? You've got a room here. Your pa and I . . . Well, we'd rather you stayed with us.'

Nancy felt a niggle of guilt because she wanted to go. Mam expected her to be in at night by nine thirty; Nancy thought that too early now she was eighteen. She couldn't get to the first house at the pictures because she had to come home for tea after the shop closed. The second house didn't finish until ten thirty or later, so she couldn't go to that either.

None of the other girls she worked with had to be in so early. Boyfriends didn't believe her, and thought she was just making excuses.

'You've enough sense to see you'd be better off,' Amy had said.

Victor Smith. The name hung in Celia's mind, taunting her with unwanted visions of the past. She'd thought she'd pushed all that behind her but the name on Nancy's wedding guest list had brought it bursting back to life.

She could see him now in her mind's eye, a youngish man, with medium brown straight hair and a wide smile. Victor always had a laugh or a smile. He'd been a happy-go-lucky sort of person.

Alec had the list in his hand now and was counting the names. She felt a terrible urge to snatch it from him. When he looked up at her, Celia held her breath, quite sure he was going to ask 'Who is Victor Smith?'

He said: 'What about another cup of tea? And I'll have another slice of that chocolate cake.' He tossed the list back on the sideboard. 'Stan Whittle's got a big family.'

Celia rushed to fold up the peach taffeta and put the kettle on again. She watched Alec bite into the cake. He was a good man. He'd never done anything wrong, but that raised her anxiety further because it put him above reproach.

'I like to sleep well at nights,' he'd told her many times. 'I've nothing on my conscience. I see too much of people who have. The villains, the lazy and the inadequates of this world.'

Celia felt a wave of guilt wash over her again, though she didn't think he counted her in any of those categories.

She wanted him to think well of her. She prided herself on coming from hard-working stock and never being idle. For him she kept the house spotless and the table groaning. She did her utmost to keep him happy.

But it hadn't stopped her worrying. She was afraid he'd discover what she'd kept from him all the years of their married life. Afraid the same thing would happen to her girls. She'd tried to protect them from that. She wouldn't wish it on her worst enemy.

Alec put the wireless on for the late news. There was speculation that Germany meant to invade Poland. War seemed to be creeping closer, tightening the tension.

'Stan could be called up if war comes.' Alec ran his fingers through his wiry hair. 'Our Nancy won't like that so soon after getting married.' He chuckled. 'Be good for that Jimmy Shaw though. Somebody will find him a job.'

'I'm going up to bed.' Celia rushed upstairs, wanting to

get away from Alec and all the talk of war.

Through the bay window of the front bedroom she could see the yellow lights of the road and the lush green of the park beyond.

Everybody told her how pleasant it must be to have a house overlooking the park, but Celia couldn't bear to look at it. Nobody knew better than she did how girls could be led astray in the park. It had been her downfall.

She sank down on the edge of the double bed and stared at her reflection in her dressing table mirror, wondering how she had managed to produce three attractive daughters. She was stick-thin and gaunt. She ate sparingly because too much rich food made her indigestion worse. Her features looked pinched and sharp and she could do nothing with her hair. It was wispy and thin and faded; more grey than anything else now. She'd had some hard years in her life and had not always looked after herself.

Celia shuddered again at the thought of war. She remembered the last one only too well and was terrified at the thought of another. Since she'd seen Victor Smith's name on the guest list, she was terrified she might see him again too. It had been 1914 when she'd first met him, a corporal in the Pioneer Corps.

Her mother had recently died and her father was unwell. She was living at home with him in Brassey Street, and working for a family called Travers who lived in one of the big houses on the other side of the park. An ideal job, she'd thought, and an easy and pleasant walk across the park to get to work.

The town's Victorian benefactors had intended the park to bring a touch of grandeur to the town and provide a place for exercise and fresh air. A broad road ran round it, a distance of three to four miles. The main entrance, a triple arch with added Ionic columns, was on Park Road North.

The hospital and the Laird School of Art were opposite,

and close by was the mansion known as Royden House. All were built of stone in a grand style. Large villas for the middle classes had been built on Park Road West and Park Road South. Now, all were smoke-blackened with age.

After the turn of the century, and totally out of character with the splendour of the other buildings, terraces of shiny red-brick villas had been built along Park Road North, smaller houses to accommodate the growing number of prosperous workers. Behind them ran the railway, and beyond that, artisans' dwellings stretched back to the docks.

Celia remembered crossing the park on a warm late autumn afternoon. In the distance she could hear the thump thump of drums and the sound of marching feet. A brass band was playing, and instead of going straight home she strolled closer to see it. In the early days of the Great War, feelings of patriotism ran high. Military music heightened them, as well as making feet tap.

At the time, Celia had thought them heady days. War had brought a fever to life. Men in uniform, especially those in hospital uniform or with armbands showing that they were recovering from war wounds, were fêted as heroes. Men still in mufti were being sent white feathers and called cowards.

The band was marching towards her along the carriage drive that circled the park, the sun glinting on their shiny instruments. Behind came soldiers in their full dress uniform of red jackets, carrying flags fluttering in the breeze. The gathering crowd was loving it.

Celia felt a surge of pleasure. She stopped on the grass verge to watch them march past. The crowd threatened to engulf her, so she stepped backwards to give them more space. She felt a bump as she collided with someone and couldn't mistake the swift painful intake of breath.

'Sorry,' she said, spinning round. Victor Smith was doubled up with pain, cradling the arm he had in a sling.

45

'I've hurt you, I'm so sorry.' Celia was distressed that she'd added to his suffering. He was wearing a hospital armband on his uniform of rough flannel. 'Is there anything I can do?'

'No, I'm all right, really.' He sank down to the grass, his brown eyes gazing up at her. 'Yes, you could stay with me. Keep a lonely soldier company for a while.'

She sat beside him. The band had passed, even the boys straggling behind had gone. The tune had changed. The strains of 'Pack Up Your Troubles' were drifting back, as he started to tell her about himself.

'The bullet just missed my heart. I was glad to have it all the same. Got me out of the fighting. It was hell, pure and absolute hell.' His eyes showed his fear. There was a haunted look about him.

'All those posters about how England needed me. I was daft enough to believe them and join up. Nobody would, if they knew what they were letting themselves in for.'

Celia warmed to him. 'My fiancé was killed at Mons in the first month. He was in the Pioneers too.' She'd thought she would never get over it.

He told her that before the war he'd worked at Cammell Laird as a shipwright. At the time he'd thought that a hard life for little pay, but compared with the fighting it had been a picnic. He was dreading going back.

'On sick leave now, but I don't know for how long. I keep telling them my shoulder's very painful.'

Vic was not a particularly handsome man. He was of average height, with brown hair, but he had an engaging smile and exuberant high spirits that lifted everyone who came in contact with him. Celia felt exhilarated. She stayed with him in the park until gone five o'clock, when she had to go back to work.

He said: 'I want to see you again. When can I?'

She told him how she had to be at the Travers' house by eight o'clock in the morning, in time to cook their breakfast.

She prepared and served their lunch, and then went home for the afternoon, returning between five and six to cook and serve a light supper for them at seven.

'I'll meet you when you come out,' he told her.

'I have to go home. My father . . .'

'Just to walk you home,' he grinned. 'Then I'll see you again tomorrow. Might as well enjoy myself while I can.'

Three days later Victor was telling her he'd fallen in love with her at first sight. And how could she help but feel very much in love with him? He swept her along on a wave of outings and pleasures. To the cinema and the music hall, rides on boats and buses. He took her to his home, a pleasant house in Tranmere where he lived alone. He said he'd been lucky enough to have it left to him by his father.

He was living for the moment, doing his best to drain every ounce of pleasure from life, quite sure that he was going to be killed when he went back.

All the same, she should never have let him make love to her. She'd grown up in a hard world, with strict rules that must never be broken. She'd understood the taboos well enough.

'There's a war on now,' he'd persuaded. 'All that stuff's going by the board. The world won't be the same after this. Let's have a bit of fun while we can.'

To Celia, it seemed a long time since she'd had any fun at all. He made her laugh, she was thrilled with him. She needed the comfort of his kisses too. He was generous with his money. Generous with everything. Love had been her gift to him in return. For who could hold back from a man destined to die for his country?

Celia couldn't believe that everything could change so quickly. Within a few short weeks her bubble of happiness had burst.

'I think I'm having a baby,' she'd whispered. She hadn't allowed herself to be too upset. She expected Victor to offer marriage. After all, he kept telling her how much he loved her, and she loved him too. He already had a house; she couldn't see any problem.

Celia was shocked to see the colour drain from his face at her words. The arms he'd wrapped round her fell away. It took him so long to say anything, she felt her confidence ebbing away.

'I'm married. Already married,' he choked, not looking at her.

That had stunned her, left her gasping. It took only seconds to realise the awful predicament she was in.

'Where is she? Why isn't your wife living with you?'

'She went back to Glasgow, to stay with her family. She comes from there.' He buried his face in his hands. 'Then one of our sons was taken ill. He's in hospital, so she stayed on to be near him.'

'You have children too?'

'Two boys.'

'Then why aren't you there with them?'

'I meant to go, until I met you. I was just waiting to be discharged from hospital here.'

'There's nothing to keep you now,' she said coldly. 'Go.'

'Celia, I can't leave you like this. I do love you.'

She'd shaken off his hand, wanting nothing more to do with him.

'Look, I'm sorry . . .'

'Sorry! What's the good of being sorry now? You should have said you were married at the start. You persuaded me. Told me you loved me and it would be all right. Well, it isn't all right.'

She wanted to cry. She'd been very silly to be taken in by his talk. What made it worse was that she was old enough to know better, over thirty. When Arnold had been killed she'd resigned herself to being an old maid. Victor had offered another, unexpected, chance of finding love and happiness. Now the vision she'd had of her future was shattered.

'Celia . . .'

'I'll never forgive you for not telling me sooner. This would never have happened if you had.'

She never had forgiven Victor Smith.

Alec came heavily upstairs. 'Aren't you in bed yet?'

Celia began taking off her clothes as quickly as she could. The years she'd spent alone had left their mark. She could see the ravages on her face and knew only too well what they'd done to her mind.

She couldn't help watching Alec in the glass. He had a good colour in his cheeks. He looked strong and healthy, his flesh was rounded. He was still in his prime.

She was eight years older than Alec and had never told him that either. She knew now that it might have been better if she had. Instead, she'd made a false declaration on their marriage certificate and now the years were beginning to show. She looked every year of the fifty-four she'd lived.

Her age wasn't the only thing she'd lied about. She'd never stopped worrying about the other false declaration she'd made, about being a widow, but she'd had to. Alec had such strong ideas about right and wrong. He'd never have loved her enough to propose marriage if he'd known Nancy was illegitimate. She thought she'd ruined her chances of marriage when she'd had Nancy and decided to keep her.

She pushed away the fading sepia photograph on her dressing table. She'd told everyone it was of her first husband. Once, it had had a frame of painted wood, but seeking to please her, Alec had given her a silver one as a gift.

The confident smile of a handsome young major taunted her nightly. Years ago, she'd been in service with his parents. His name was William Travers. Well, she was almost sure the picture was of William. There had been two sons; the younger was Thomas. Both had been killed in the First World War. She had another picture of William playing with a spaniel in the garden. She'd been very fond of that dog, it had spent a lot of time in the kitchen with her. Having two

49

pictures of the man seemed to add a ring of truth to her story.

She got into bed quickly and put out the light. Alec was already settling down to sleep, but she was too full of forebodings tonight to drop off quickly. She wasn't sleeping well anyway. The horror of those early years was bringing a nasty taste to her mouth.

She'd been asked to leave her job once her condition had become obvious. Nobody wanted to employ a woman of loose morals.

She'd been lucky she had a home to go to. But her father had been sinking over that year, and when he died his pension went with him.

Celia knew she'd only escaped the workhouse because she had the family home. What little money her father left went to pay a few months' rent.

She'd had the baby in a home for unmarried mothers, going in six weeks before it was due and staying for a month afterwards. If she'd had no home to return to, it would have been longer.

Celia found that like the others, she was expected to work a nine-hour day. They were told hard work was good for them, even if they were in the last stages of pregnancy. The home took in laundry to keep them busy and help defray the cost of their keep.

Fallen women, the sisters at the home called them. Women who had lost their character. Women who needed to mend their ways and be trained to do a decent day's work. Some did housework, cleaning and cooking; Celia went into the steamy atmosphere of the laundry. She found the home totally humiliating.

She knew of young girls who had been turned out and disowned by their own families. She heard of two who had drowned themselves in the river, and others who had tried and failed. She told herself she was tougher than that, though the shame was hard to bear.

When her daughter was born, she called her Nancy, and

thought the worst was over, but the rule was that the babies must go for adoption. Celia, though, had no one else in the world to love, and the last thing she wanted to do was part with Nancy.

When the adoption papers were put in front of her, she refused point blank to sign them. Celia believed she was only allowed to have her own way because she had an address to take the baby to.

She also knew that she could only afford to keep the house on for a few more weeks unless she found a job where she could have Nancy with her.

She'd thought she stood a good chance of getting a post, because girls were leaving domestic service for better-paid war work. She applied for countless positions, describing herself as a widow, but nobody wanted a cook or housekeeper with a young baby taking up her time and energy.

Celia's money was running out and she was beginning to feel desperate when she was offered a job in an orphanage. The matron said that her baby could join the twenty-two others in the nursery during the hours she worked, and be looked after that way.

Matron's husband had been killed fighting in the trenches. Celia knew it was sympathy for another in even more difficult circumstances that had led to her being offered the job. With two young girls to help her, she cooked for thirty toddlers and fifty children of school age, as well as the staff.

It had seemed a reprieve, though she was almost dropping with fatigue at the end of the day when she was free to take Nancy back home. Miraculously she was able to survive. She counted herself lucky. It became easier as Nancy grew older.

In her loneliness she gave all her love to her daughter. Nancy responded by being a loving and biddable child and was always happy. Celia found her delightful. So did the staff at the orphanage, who were never tired of holding her up as an example to the more difficult children they had to cope with. They all indulged her.

'You'll spoil her,' Celia protested. But nothing could spoil Nancy. She seemed to flower with all the attention.

Celia took a lot of trouble with Nancy's clothes, making them all herself. She took her to a decent hairdresser, so that her golden-brown hair was cut to enhance its natural wave. She was determined that Nancy wouldn't look deprived even if she was fatherless. She was a charming little girl.

'Why isn't my daddy here with us?' Celia could hear Nancy's childish treble again, as clearly as if she was with her now.

'He's in heaven, darling,' she'd replied. She couldn't tell her the truth: Nancy could blurt it out to anyone, and she wouldn't understand, not yet. 'He's watching over us from there. He was a soldier and was killed in the Great War.'

'Was he a brave soldier?'

'A very brave soldier, a hero.'

Celia didn't know what had made her go on embroidering more and more details, unless it was Nancy's never-ending questions. She wanted to know everything she could about him.

'Show her a photograph of her father,' the matron had advised one day. 'Let her see what he looked like. That will settle her curiosity.'

Celia looked through her collection of old photographs. There was one of Victor Smith taken with her on New Brighton beach. She couldn't bear to look at it and had thrown it behind the fire.

The younger of the Travers' sons had had ambitions to be a photographer. He'd had a dark room in the attic. She came across several photographs of the Travers family that he'd given her.

She'd shown Nancy the picture of William Travers in his uniform. Told her he was her father. But Victor Smith was not the officer and gentleman she'd described to Nancy.

Celia had had an affiliation order drawn on him for Nancy's

maintenance. She'd been glad of the few shillings a week the army deducted from his pay. Once the war ended, though, she had received nothing more. She'd lost touch and didn't know whether he was dead or alive.

She hoped he was dead. He'd done little to help her. But she was very much afraid that he hadn't died for his country after all.

It had left her frightened of men, yet wanting one to be a father to her daughter.

CHAPTER FOUR

After her first month at the hospital, Nancy knew she'd made the right move. Even the split shifts didn't put her off. Starting at seven-thirty every morning and finishing at eight at night seemed prodigiously long at first, though she was allowed to have three hours off during the day. She was settling down and knew she was going to be happy in her new job.

When she first saw Stan Whittle sitting with his mother outside Sister's office, waiting his turn to be admitted, she'd completed two years of her training. He was a lanky young man with brown hair and serious eyes.

Later, Sister had summoned her to put him through the rest of the process. Nancy had shown him to one of the bathrooms, put in the plug and turned on the taps.

'A bath?' he asked, looking awkward. 'I've just had one this morning before coming.'

'I'm afraid it's the rule here.' Sister liked to be sure all her patients were clean before allowing them between hospital sheets. 'Would you mind taking another? Then put your pyjamas on. Have you brought a dressing gown?'

'Yes. Do I have to get undressed and into bed straight away?'

'I'm afraid that's another of our rules – so your mother can take your clothes home.'

'Ugh, I feel too well; it's as if I'm here under false pretences.'

'We'll soon change that,' Nancy chuckled. She knew that

the patients being admitted were on tomorrow's list for orthopaedic surgery. She was curious about Stan Whittle. 'What are you coming in for?'

'Hurt my knee playing football. Torn cartilage.'

When he was sitting up in bed, she took his mother in. She was plump and kindly. Nancy spent more time talking to her than she needed to, making doubly sure that she knew hospital visiting times and the number to telephone to enquire about Stan.

For the rest of the morning she was conscious of his dark eyes following her up and down the ward. There was an intensity about his interest that kindled a spark in her. When Sister went to lunch she took the opportunity to study his file to find out all she could about him.

At twenty-six, he was six years older than she was. He lived quite close, in Haldane Avenue. He'd had no other illnesses. She was lingering at his bedside now, making opportunities to talk to him. When the time came for her to go off duty, she would have preferred to stay talking to him rather than take the evening off.

Nancy saw his serious eyes light up the following morning when she came on duty. Already she felt drawn to him. The other nurses thought him rather staid and dull. She was pleased to be given the job of accompanying him to theatre for his operation.

'I was hoping it would be you,' he said sleepily, having had his pre-op half an hour earlier. 'You've come to hold my hand?'

'Figuratively speaking,' she said.

'You will be staying with me?' He seemed a little anxious.

'Yes.'

He tried to smile then. 'See they do a proper job. You won't want a boyfriend who limps.'

That made her laugh but it warmed her too. The anaesthetist joined them at that moment and started to talk to Stan.

Nancy thought she must be falling in love. She'd had a few boyfriends before, but none for whom she'd felt so much so soon.

His recovery was routine. She couldn't stay away from his bed. He told her he was studying for insurance examinations: he was determined to make something of himself. When he was able to start moving round the ward, he seemed to follow her.

The two weeks he was likely to spend on the ward were passing far too quickly. Nancy didn't want him to be discharged. She was afraid it might be the last she'd see of him. Other patients had been very friendly while they were on the ward, but once they'd gone, she'd never heard from them again.

The day before he was due to leave, Stan said to her: 'You aren't planning to cut me off now I'm restored to health?'

Nancy knew she was glowing with pleasure.

'You'd cause an immediate relapse if you did. If I can get tickets for the theatre, will you come with me?'

'I'd love to,' she smiled. From that moment she'd known where she stood with Stan.

He'd met her outside the hospital to find out when she had an evening off, and then bought tickets for *Chu Chin Chow* and took her over to Liverpool. He held her hand throughout the performance, Nancy spent as much time looking at him as she did at the stage. She'd been planning to get a job on a liner and see the world as soon as she was qualified. Once Stan proposed, all she wanted to do was to settle down with him.

Alice Peacock had been admitted to hospital so many times that many of the nurses knew her. She was eighty-five and had been diagnosed as diabetic late in life.

The new private block hadn't been built when she'd first started coming, and the few private patients were nursed in small side wards on Ward Three, where Nancy was working.

'You're like a sunny morning,' she told Nancy when she

went in to give her her insulin. 'You brighten up everything around you.'

Nancy laughed. 'Even when I come to stick needles in you? That's a very nice thing to say.'

'I know I have to have the needles. You always look content, as though life is kind to you.'

'I suppose it is,' Nancy smiled.

'And that makes you very kind to patients like me.'

'I hope we all are, Mrs Peacock.'

'Would you do something for me?'

'Of course. What do you want?'

'A little errand when you go off duty.'

Nancy paused doubtfully. 'You want me to buy something for you?'

'Yes. Now where's my handbag? In the wardrobe I think. Would you get it for me?'

'It depends what you want me to buy,' Nancy said, suspicious now.

'Just a box of sugared almonds, dear. I do hanker so for something to suck.'

Nancy smiled. 'I'm afraid I can't do that. You know you aren't allowed sweets.'

'One wouldn't hurt me. Not just one little one.'

'Absolutely not, and don't you ask anybody else to do it. Sweets will make you ill again.'

'You're not as kind as you look.'

'You don't look naughty at all, but you are. Golly, yes, positively devious.'

'Life is being very unkind to me at the moment.' The old lady's face wrinkled into lines of discontent.

'It is hard to be denied your little luxuries, I'm sure. I'd be glad to buy you books or magazines, or . . .'

'My family bring me more than I can read.' She sighed. 'I shall be glad to get home again.'

'You won't be able to eat sweets there either,' Nancy told her firmly.

Another nurse said at dinner: 'Alice Peacock? I remember her. A dear old thing with a face like a prune. Obstinate as an old donkey at times but her mind was as clear as crystal. How is she?'

'Frail and rather shaky now,' Nancy said. Alice was one of her favourite patients.

Her family seemed close-knit. While Alice was in hospital, one of them came every day to sit with her for an hour or so. Nancy liked them all and usually stopped for a word with whichever one was there.

Bill Frampton was head of the family, a solicitor running the family firm of Metcalf and Frampton. The Metcalf connection had long since died out. His sons James and Toby were also solicitors and were the third generation of the family to work in the firm. It employed six solicitors and numerous legal clerks and secretaries.

Both of Alice's grandsons interested the nurses until they learned that James was married, at which point all the attention switched to Toby, the younger one. He was ruggedly built and had straight hair streaked with shades from corn colour to gold. He came regularly in the evenings to read to his grandmother.

On the day Nancy heard she'd passed her final examination and was entitled to call herself a state registered nurse, Alice was almost ready to be discharged for the sixth time.

'What are you going to do now you're qualified?' Bill Frampton asked her. He looked a formal and dignified man with thick, straight silver hair.

Amy had been asking her that too. 'Nancy, you're a drifter,' she'd said. 'Get yourself organised or you'll go nowhere.'

Nancy had no plans to further her career. She wanted to marry Stan Whittle and settle down as his wife, but like Amy, Stan believed in planning. He'd explained long ago that they would have to save up and work hard to get their home together before they could think of marriage.

'I'll stay on here for a while,' she'd smiled. 'Matron lets

us know that having enjoyed the advantage of three years' training at this hospital, we can repay our obligation by staying on a further year as a staff nurse.'

'Do you want to?'

'I want to save up to get married. I'm engaged, you see.'

'You don't have to stay? You haven't signed a contract to do so?' He adjusted his heavy horn-rimmed spectacles. Behind them, his grey eyes looked at her kindly.

'Oh no, it's voluntary. Some go straight on to do midwifery.'

'Would you consider coming to work for us?'

Nancy felt a trickle of interest. 'Private nursing?'

'This is the sixth time my mother-in-law has been admitted to hospital to be balanced. My wife, Mary, is a diabetic too.'

'Yes, I know, I've nursed her too. I'm glad to see her so well now.'

'Neither of them has learned to give their own injections. I can't persuade Mary to try. Nor does she seem to be able to keep to her diet.'

'It's not easy for people diagnosed late in life.'

'Mary was only fifty.' Bill Frampton tried to hide a smile. 'She thinks a nurse living with us is the best solution. She said she'd like you.'

Nancy's heart lurched. It was nice to feel wanted. She hadn't expected to be offered such a job. It appealed to her. She smiled.

'If you would come to us, I'd be prepared to offer a little over the odds as far as salary is concerned. Alice is eighty-five and needing more help generally. She's always kept chocolate and biscuits in her room; now all her little indulgences are forbidden and she doesn't really understand why.'

Nancy was pleased. She'd have the patients she enjoyed and be rid of those she found hard work, and the promised increase in salary would be very welcome.

'We'll be taking Alice home tomorrow. Would you like to

come and see where we live? The room you'd have, that sort of thing?'

'Yes please,' she said, but she had already made up her mind to take the job.

'You've got the right personality for a nurse,' he told her. 'You cheer us all up.'

Nancy radiated contentment. She felt she could afford to wait for marriage. The promise of greater happiness in the future added sparkle to the present, and the present was bringing its own share of pleasures.

It wasn't a job that would enhance a nursing career, but she knew that as far as Stan was concerned, a girl's career and paid employment ended on her wedding day.

The Framptons lived in Vyner Road. The following Sunday afternoon Nancy and Stan cycled up there. It was winter and already dusk when they reached Thermopylae Pass.

'It's beautiful up here,' Nancy said, stopping to admire the view. Far below, myriad lights sparkled, in the houses and on the roads, but the fields she knew were there were grey velvet.

'A different world,' Stan agreed.

'I can't believe it's possible that I'm to come and live up here.'

'Only temporarily. We couldn't afford anything in this district.'

'I'll get it out of my system before we get married,' Nancy laughed. 'You know anywhere with you would be great.'

They found Henshaw House. Nancy propped her bike against the garden wall.

'I'll go back to the pass and wait for you there,' Stan said. 'I don't feel I can hang about their front gate for you.'

Nancy walked slowly up the short drive, the cuban heels of her best shoes sinking into the white gravel. The house seemed long and low and large. Light spilled out from many of the windows into the garden shrubs. It was a welcoming house.

Toby Frampton let her in, the light glinting on the blond streaks in his hair. He greeted her as though she were a family friend. Warmth enveloped her as soon as the front door closed behind her. The hall was wider than any she'd seen before, the carpet soft underfoot.

He led the way to the drawing room. Nancy looked around her in amazement. A large fire blazed in a long stone grate. Comfort was the word that came to her mind. Her gaze settled on a mahogany cabinet displaying china.

'Are you interested in Crown Derby?' Mary Frampton asked. She was a big woman who carried herself well. Shoulders back, bosom out. Her grey hair had been recently set in deep waves close about her head. Her grey eyes were gentle like Toby's, her dress staid and rather plain. 'My mother has collected it all her life.'

Alice Peacock greeted her in a very friendly fashion. Nancy had never seen anything as sumptuous as the old lady's bedroom. It was huge, with velvet curtains drawn against its three large windows, a pale green carpet and delicate French furniture.

Mary Frampton led her up more stairs. 'I'm afraid your room is up on the attic floor. I hope you don't mind? Hilda's room is across the landing. There's just the two of you up here.'

Nancy thought her room large and very comfortably furnished. She went to the window. She could see lights shining in the distance.

'The views are good in daytime.'

'Lovely now at night,' Nancy said. 'I like the room, it's better than any I had in any of the three nurses' homes.' It was better than her little box room at home as well.

She met Hilda Redway, the live-in housekeeper. Hilda was a dark-haired, attractive woman in her mid-thirties, who asked Nancy's advice about diet for her two patients over the next few days.

'I think you'll be happy here,' Hilda whispered

earnestly when Mary Frampton went to speak on the telephone. 'I am. The Framptons are very easy to please. Good employers.'

Nancy was delighted with everything. She told Mary Frampton so, and that she would give the required month's notice at the hospital straight away.

She walked slowly down the drive, marvelling at the Framptons. They were blessed with every material comfort and in addition seemed to have a charmed and happy family life.

She thought Toby and James very fortunate to have such parents. They were kindly and thoughtful for others, whether family or not. They were not looking for trouble, like Pa with Amy and Kate, nor were they anxious and weary like poor Mam. Nancy thought it would be a wonderful house to live and work in. She knew she'd enjoy her new job. Then, in a few years, she'd marry Stan and live happily ever after.

The following day, Nancy went home to tell her parents. They were just finishing a meal.

'Private nursing? Should be a nice change, and you won't have to work so hard,' Mam enthused.

'Frampton, did you say?' Pa barked at her. 'William Frampton, a solicitor?'

'Yes.'

'He's a member of the Watch Committee. I'm not sure I think it's a good idea.'

'Why ever not?' Nancy asked.

'The Watch Committee is in charge of police affairs. It brings it too close to me.'

'What difference does that make?'

'Don't tell him I'm a policeman. I'd rather he didn't know.'

'I already have. He asked about my family and what you did.'

Pa was pulling a face. 'He could take a dislike to me.'

'He's the sort of man you'd approve of, Pa. Upright. Transparently honest.'

Pa pursed his lips. 'He can afford to be.'

'I'm sure he'd never do anything he didn't believe to be right.'

'If she's going to get more money, Alec,' Mam said diffidently, 'it would be a pity not to take the job.'

'I've already said I will,' Nancy said, cheerfully.

Nancy moved into Henshaw House, and discovered there was a daily cleaning woman and a daily gardener as well. She thought the atmosphere very relaxed and friendly at first.

It didn't take up much of her time to attend to what she considered her main duties: giving two injections twice each day, and regularly checking her patients' sugar levels. She consulted with Mary Frampton about what they should eat and made sure they had the right amount of everything.

She spent a lot of time with Alice, who was doing very little for herself. She helped her wash and dress, read to her and played bezique with her. The old lady ate most of her meals in her room upstairs, but every evening Nancy helped her down to the dining room for dinner. She and Hilda ate with the family too, unless there were guests.

She'd wondered how Mary Frampton filled her days, if she didn't have to cook and clean and look after her mother.

'She plays bridge,' Hilda told her with a smile. Nancy found that three like-minded ladies came one afternoon each week and the card table was set up in the drawing room.

On three other afternoons Mary Frampton set off to play bridge in other houses. Nancy found that if one of the ladies was unable to come, she was required to play in her stead.

The ladies, in their smart frocks and large diamond rings, took the game very seriously. They did their best to teach her the rudiments and loaned her books to help her understand the rules. Nancy quite enjoyed it, but didn't feel she was ever going to reach their standard.

If Hilda could sit with Alice, Mary Frampton occasionally took Nancy to her friends' houses to play. Nancy was amazed that this was now considered one of her duties.

The other thing that filled Mary Frampton's time was organising dinner parties. She set the table and sometimes cooked a special dish herself. Nancy helped her choose food that she too could eat, and laid down strict rules about quantities.

Hilda did the rest of the cooking and waited on table. On evenings when there was company, Nancy helped in the kitchen and had her meal there with Hilda. She got on well with her.

Hilda always had knitting on the go when she wasn't cooking. Nancy asked: 'Is that a baby's bonnet you're making?'

Hilda laughed and spread out the piece of pink angora for her to see. 'I'm making a pair of knee-cosies for Alice. She says they help her rheumatism.' She promised to knit a cardigan for Nancy when she'd finished them.

Nancy didn't see much of Bill Frampton. He was at work each weekday, and he and his wife often went out in the evenings. She didn't see much of Toby either.

It took her a little time to discover that there were undercurrents of disagreement in the family. She hadn't realised that Bill Frampton was impatient that his wife couldn't manage her illness better.

'I can quite see why Alice can't manage it,' she heard him say, 'but it shouldn't be impossible for you. You're competent at most things. Why not this?'

'You know I've always been squeamish about medical matters. Injections just set my teeth on edge. I hate having them.'

'You could at least try,' he insisted.

'Goodness, Bill! We've got Nancy here to do all that.'

'She could teach you. You'd be independent then.'

'I couldn't do it, and that's the end of it.'

It made Nancy realise that Bill Frampton didn't expect to employ her for ever, that she mustn't bank on it being a permanent job. She was quite pleased to find that Mary couldn't even look at a syringe. She didn't press her to do so.

In addition, Nancy could feel a strained atmosphere between Toby and his father.

'Don't they get on?' she asked Hilda in the kitchen one day.

Hilda pulled a face at the question. 'It's like this. James can do no wrong. Toby keeps putting his foot in things.'

'In what way?'

'James has been working in the firm for four years and has taken on a lot of important clients. He was married a few months ago to the daughter of a family friend. His father is delighted with everything he does.'

'And Toby?' Nancy had already discovered that Hilda loved a good gossip.

'I heard his parents talking. They think he's having trouble trying to follow such a good act. Having second thoughts, you know.'

'About joining the firm?'

'Well, I'm not sure that he wanted to in the first place.'

'He's a solicitor, isn't he?'

'Yes, but I don't know that he finds the work all that exciting. He did a few months with another firm for wider experience, and they had some connection with an office in Lisbon and were looking for people to work there. I think Toby was tempted.'

'So how long has he been with Metcalf and Frampton?'

'He started back in the summer.'

Katie had cleared away the children's lunch and folded back the gate-legged table in the playroom. It was a school holiday, but it was raining too heavily to take them to the park. She was setting out the pieces of a jigsaw puzzle to keep Bernard occupied when the front doorbell rang.

Amy was standing on the doorstep, her dark blue eyes glinting with determination.

'It's my afternoon off,' she announced. Katie was surprised to see her. She very rarely called at the Brents' house.

'Come in.' Katie was not overpleased. She sensed what was coming.

'Yes, come in,' Bernard said delightedly. Both he and Daniel had scampered to the door with Katie. She led her sister to the playroom. Amy surveyed the toy-strewn floor.

'Somewhere more private?' she suggested.

Katie's spirits sank. 'You get on with your jigsaw, Bernard, and Daniel is going to paint me a picture. Amy and I are going in the sitting room for five minutes, all right?'

The Brents' sitting room was immaculately tidy. Amy sat down on the velvet sofa. Katie sat as far away from her as she could.

'I'm worried about you, Katie.'

'No need. I'm all right.'

'You're expecting, but you're doing nothing about it. You can't just ignore it. It won't go away.'

Katie tried to explain: 'I know that. Jimmy's trying to get a job, then, when we've got enough money, we'll go to Gretna Green.'

Amy's expression told her she didn't believe it would ever happen. Not if Katie left it to Jimmy.

'I've saved a little. I'll let you have it if it's money you need.'

Katie stifled a sigh.

'It's more than a month, Katie, since you told me. Time is going on. When does Dr Poole say the baby's due?'

Katie shook her head. She hated to see Amy's eyes assessing her abdomen.

'You mean you haven't been to see him?'

'Not yet,' she admitted.

'You ought to be under medical supervision.'

'You would say that, you're a nurse. I'm all right.'

'That's not the point, and it's no good feeling embarrassed about it now.'

'I'm quite well.'

'You've got to do something.' Katie knew she'd exasperated her sister. 'I'm the only person you've told, and I don't like that. I want to help you but I don't know how. If you don't tell Mam, I'll have to.'

'I don't see . . .'

'If it's permission to get married you want, she'll see you get it. She'll run you and Jimmy to the altar so fast his feet won't touch the ground. It'll save you the expense of going up to Gretna, can't you see? And she's got to know sometime, as has everybody else. You can't keep it a secret.'

There was a scuffle at the door and her two charges fell into the room, giggling together. Katie picked up the damp painting that had fallen paint-side down on to the carpet square.

'You know your mummy doesn't like you coming in here,' she chided. 'She likes one room tidy when she gets home from work. Come into the kitchen, Amy, I'll make a cup of tea.'

Katie felt that the children had delivered her from Amy's lecture, but she had to agree, Jimmy was dragging his feet unnecessarily.

'What's it to be?' Amy wanted to know as she was leaving. 'Will you tell her, or shall I?'

'Let me talk to Jimmy first,' Katie pleaded.

'I'll give you a week, Katie. If you've done nothing by then . . .'

'I'll let you know. Don't say anything, not yet.'

Katie felt sick with indecision, but Amy was right. She was in a mess. She had to do something.

'I haven't seen Edna for ages,' Katie said to Jimmy. 'I used to see her every day at the school gates.'

'Neither of you goes near the school now. It's the summer holidays.'

'We used to do the same things. I often met her at the lake or taking the children for walks on Park Drive. I do miss her.

'I caught a glimpse of her the other day the far side of the tennis courts. I shouted and waved but she seemed to rush away. I think it was her. I've never seen anybody else with a brown pram like that.' Katie had the feeling that Edna was avoiding her.

'I think she's jealous of you,' Jimmy said.

'Jealous? Why should she be?'

'Katie, I didn't want to tell you this.' Jimmy was suddenly serious.

'Have you seen her?'

'Yes, it's a little embarrassing.'

'Go on. What happened?'

'I met her by chance near the lake. You were late coming out that day. She threw herself at me, Katie. Put her arms round my neck and all that. I didn't quite know how to deal with her.'

'Edna did?'

'She said she'd fallen in love with me. Well, I had to tell her I loved you. A bit embarrassing all round. I'm not surprised to hear she's avoiding you.'

Katie sighed. She was not surprised. Hadn't Edna agreed that Jimmy was the most handsome man they'd ever seen? She was sorry, though. She needed a friend now.

CHAPTER FIVE

Police Constable Alec Siddons let himself out of his back door into a cool grey morning. It was spitting with rain and more was forecast. He was fed up with the weather, it hardly seemed like summer. His heavy boots scraped on the damp concrete of the yard as he crossed to the shed.

Inside, his black bicycle leaned against the wall. He unhooked his trouser clips which he kept swinging on the crossbar and put them on. They made his boots seem larger. Then, adjusting his voluminous black rain cape he wheeled his bike out.

Some sixth sense told him he was being watched, and he glanced up to the bedroom window of the house next door. Winnie Cottie's face was pressed against the glass.

Alec shivered. She made his flesh creep, the way she stood staring down at him in silent condemnation. She was always doing it. He must stop her from baiting him.

He raised his clenched fist and waved it at her, to show he didn't care. He was rewarded by the instant alarm on her face. She jerked back and the net curtain fell into place.

He'd never liked Winnie. Even as a child she'd kept close watch from her windows on what he did, and had been quick to tell his mother. And she'd always favoured Jack.

He turned away in a rage. Damn Winnie Cottie! She was trying to frighten him, still trying to sow seeds of doubt, raise his anxiety level. But they both knew she'd already done her best to get him into trouble.

Winnie had known too much, but she'd had no proof, and

she'd made the mistake of talking to Sergeant Peachey and no one else. If she'd put it in writing and posted it to the top brass she could have finished him.

But she hadn't. She'd tried and she'd failed. It had taken him years to get over Randall Cottie's death. Every detail was still burned in his memory.

They'd put the best brains in the force on the case, tightening his tension. Those had been the worst weeks he'd ever lived through. Down at the station he'd been made to repeat his story, God knows how many times, but he'd never varied it. He'd kept calm, occasionally adding a few words about how much he owed to Randall. How much he admired him. About him living next door, and suggesting that Alec choose the police as a career too.

Even now he couldn't suppress a shudder. He could hear Winnie's voice still: 'They're giving you a bit of rope, Alec, just enough to hang yourself. It'll all come out one day.' Then her laugh had cackled out, making her sound like a mad woman. She'd known too much. They'd hanged the wrong man for it, but he was a killer anyway and deserved all he got.

But it was all a long time ago, and there was nothing she could do now. He was a fool to go on fearing Winnie Cottie.

Out on the street, he pushed off with one foot and swept the other leg over the bar with practised ease. He had to pedal hard. As he turned the corner, rain blew in his face and the squally wind flapped at his cape. It was probably going to rain all this shift.

He hated seven till three and getting up at the crack of dawn. Seven till three indeed! He had to be on parade at the station by six thirty to get his orders, and officers weren't paid for that time.

He was soon panting. What he really needed was a car instead of this old bike. A car was the only thing that would make life worth living on a day like today.

He'd put himself to a lot of trouble to pass the examination in Morse code in the hope that now they were putting two-way wirelesses in cars he'd be given that duty. Night patrol would be bearable in a car.

The exam qualified him to be in control of a wireless station, and a warm cushy shift in the station at Well Lane would suit him down to the ground, but that didn't come his way either. He seemed to be passed over every time.

He still had to pound the beat. On mornings like this he fantasised about winning a huge sum on the horses. Throwing up the job, riding round in his own car and never having to worry about money again.

A wedding in the family meant a lot of expense. Nancy and her mother were all set on having a posh do. Well, he wanted it too. He wasn't all that keen on Stan Whittle but Celia liked him and it was time Nancy settled down.

Finding the money wasn't going to be easy. He'd make Jack pay his whack. He'd see him about it today. No point in putting that off.

At the station there was the usual huddle of young constables laughing and chattering amongst themselves. They acted like boy scouts; he couldn't be bothered with them. All busy beavering away for promotion, hoping to be noticed by the top brass.

He'd had no promotion and it rankled. Men half his age were getting it. Only this week, he'd heard that John Barber, only thirty-three, was being promoted to the rank of inspector.

He'd put himself out for promotion time and time again. He'd taken his education exams and got a top grade. He was qualified to render first aid.

He'd even had a citation and an award of two pounds for rescuing a woman trying to commit suicide in the Mersey. He'd been given a medal and a certificate for that, but had been passed over again.

He'd even managed to achieve a fair number of convictions. Though not as many as he could have had. And where had it got him? Nowhere.

* * *

The morning routine ground on. There was the usual standing to attention to get their orders. The usual over-officiousness of the station sergeant. God how he hated it all.

He was bored to death with traffic duty and pounding his beat. Another four years and he could get out on pension – if only he could find another job. He wanted to. He really wanted to, but what other job would give him the opportunities that this one did to pick up a little more on the side?

He was out on his beat with the rain blowing in his face again. He was stopped by a man who wanted to report that his bike had been stolen from outside a church. Unsecured of course. It seemed its owner had expected God to keep it safe while he was inside. Alec had to stand about in the pouring rain taking down the details.

Then he had to go on treading the pavements with the rain coming down in sheets, and cars and buses spraying him with water as they drove past.

The one duty he didn't object to was inspecting licensed premises. It was an offence to sell liquor out of hours and to allow too much singing and merriment in hours. The poor licensees had to protect themselves against police inspections or they'd have their licences withdrawn and find themselves out of work. He knew several landlords who were prepared to stand him a drink when he came round, in order to guarantee that they'd be let off with a caution if they were caught breaking the rules.

Alec had planned to get out of the wet and have an hour of relaxation before he had to report in to the station. But halfway through the morning, he saw a car skid into the back of a lorry waiting at traffic lights. He couldn't avoid doing something about that. Nobody hurt much, but the car couldn't be driven afterwards. It caused a hold-up that took him ages to sort out, resulting in frayed tempers all round. It barely left him time to throw down a double brandy at the Lighterman's Arms.

He went back to the station for a break and something to

eat after that, and sat at a table by himself in the canteen with his sausage and mash. He didn't think much of it. Didn't think much of anything they served there. The buzz of conversation rose and fell around him, but he liked to keep himself to himself. It gave him time to think about Nancy's wedding. He was fond of her, always had been.

He'd first seen Nancy one hot afternoon twenty years ago, when he'd gone to the orphanage to question some of the older boys about petty pilfering from nearby shops.

The front doorbell had been broken. He'd rung several times without an answer. Then he'd wheeled his bike round to the kitchen and Celia had let him in. She'd been a good-looking woman then. Rather aloof, with cool blue eyes and a shy manner.

Afterwards, when he went back to collect his bike, she'd been leaving, with Nancy swinging on her hand. He'd stopped for a word, then pushed his bicycle and walked part of the way home with them.

Nancy had been an attractive child with a mop of brown curls. Outgoing and talkative for one so young. She'd been wearing a pretty pink dress and told him that her father had been an army officer, a hero killed in the war.

He'd been touched; he remembered even now the surge of sympathy he'd felt. He'd wanted to take her dead father's place. Now he knew that Celia was a war widow, reduced to straitened circumstances through no fault of her own, he wanted to help her too.

He'd been young then, and idealistic. It wasn't the first time he'd fallen in love, but he'd never loved anyone more than Celia. To have Nancy too seemed a bonus. It didn't take him long to propose. He hadn't realised, though, how cold Celia was. How little she showed her feelings.

He warmed at the thought of Nancy. She'd climbed on his knee and put her arms round his neck from the beginning. She always rushed to the door to meet him when he came home from work. He'd wanted another child straight away, one of his own so that they'd have a real family. He'd chosen Amy's name for her. Both he and Celia had expected the new arrival to be like Nancy. Prettier and more loving if that was possible, and equally well behaved. Even more rewarding because she was part of both of them.

Amy had not been like that.

He remembered the thrill he'd felt when lifting the newborn baby into his arms. Remembered how he'd congratulated himself on producing a child who looked so very much like him.

Amy had his dark, almost black hair, rough and wiry as a terrier's. She also had his dark blue demanding eyes and knew exactly what she wanted. And from the first, she'd been determined to get it.

He said proudly to Celia: 'Another lovely daughter. We can try again for a son as soon as you feel like it. We'll have a big family, Celia, a happy family.'

Once home from hospital, Amy began to drain Celia. She had a voracious appetite and Celia, who was doing her best to breast-feed her, lost confidence in her ability to cope.

Celia had endlessly compared the two children, to Amy's detriment. During the day Amy slept far less than Nancy had, and demanded twice the attention. Nancy had slept through the night from an early age. Not so Amy, and once awake, nothing would settle her but another feed. She was constantly wakeful at night and disturbed them all.

Within a few months Celia was exhausted and ill. The broken nights were difficult to cope with, and Alec too felt worn out by the demands Amy made on them.

Even sweet little Nancy didn't take immediately to Amy. She was a five-year-old who had had her mother's full attention up till then. Now the dark squawking bundle took up most of Celia's time.

Alec arranged for Nancy to start school immediately, to ease the burden on Celia. Nancy even learned to be a little difficult herself at times.

Celia complained that Amy led her a right dance. She learned to crawl at a very early age and after that Celia couldn't turn her back on her for five minutes. She started walking at ten months and was doing it alone and with confidence a month later.

Amy never wanted to be cuddled as Nancy had. She would fight her way out of Alec's arms if he tried. So he tried less and less often.

She didn't show love as Nancy had. She was too busy scaling stairs or climbing on tables, and more than once had whisked out of the door and down the street the minute her mother's attention was elsewhere. She was fascinated by water and left taps on and plugs in, flooding the bathroom several times. She put shoes down the lavatory and blocked that.

She moved the fireguard on the one occasion Celia had forgotten to hook it to the wall, and lit a fire on one of their Rexine armchairs. She broke countless dishes and took her own toys and Nancy's to pieces to see how they worked.

On her first birthday, Celia had said: 'I don't think we'll go in for that large family after all. We don't need any more like her.'

'Thank goodness for that,' Alec said. Another child was the last thing he wanted. 'Absolutely no more children.' Celia was less loving towards him and neither of them had much energy for anything.

As Amy grew older she became even more of a handful. She was speaking in sentences at eighteen months and was always alert and looking round for more mischief. At two she had terrible temper tantrums if she didn't get her own way. By three years of age she could argue the case for getting whatever she wanted.

Celia didn't have a moment's rest from the moment Amy was out of her bed in the morning until she went back to it at night.

And Amy brought out the worst in all of them. Sweet-natured Nancy had to fight to maintain the superiority of her five-year seniority. Alec knew that Celia dreaded the school holidays, when the girls could fight like cat and dog.

Celia also dreaded the confrontations she knew would come if she insisted Amy do what she was told for a change. Alec knew that Celia gave in for a quieter life.

'There are times,' he told her, 'when I wonder why I feel so much more love for another man's child than I do for my own.'

Katie was unplanned and unwelcome. For Celia, it came as a shock to find herself pregnant again. It precipitated something of a crisis in their lives.

Celia became withdrawn and weepy and told Alec she dreaded going through it all again and having another active, wilful child like Amy. She had a difficult pregnancy, never feeling very well.

Alec had tried to jolly her out of her depression. 'It might be a son. Surely you'd welcome a son?' He even pretended that he would.

'I'd rather have a miscarriage. I'm praying for it.' But that didn't happen.

Katie was born at home, and when she was put into Celia's arms, she'd said: 'She looks like Amy.' Alec could hear the horror in her voice.

'Just a sisterly likeness,' he'd tried to reassure her. 'Her hair is silkier, curlier too.'

'She is prettier.'

And Katie didn't clench her lips with the same determination that Amy had. She smiled more as she grew older, she laughed more. In many ways, Katie was like Nancy, though Katie reached out for life more.

Alec had been left with a feeling of resentment for Amy. She'd soured Celia, turning her into a cold woman. He blamed her for ruining his home life. It had been more comfortable before she came.

Neither he nor Celia took much interest in Katie, but she

was happy enough. She was mothered and treated as an outsize doll by her older sisters.

Alec was thankful when it was time to go off duty. Rain was still lashing down and the town had been dead all afternoon. Time had seemed to stand still from the moment he heard the one o'clock gun, and the highlight of his afternoon had been escorting a stray dog to the dogs' home.

He collected his bike and decided to call on Jack Laidlaw on the way home. For once, with his usual rotten luck, he'd been given a different beat and hadn't been able to get to see him in working hours.

He freewheeled down the hill to Woodside, the train, bus and ferry terminus. The café stood back to the left of the ferry building.

It had been his father's, and had been called the Woodside Refreshment Room for as long as Alec could remember. Recently the name had been painted out. The new red and gold lettering called it Jack's Caff. To catch a glimpse of that through the driving rain made him boil with indignation. What had been good enough for his father should be good enough for Jack Laidlaw.

Not that Jack had managed to change anything. Family, friends and customers knew it as the Refreshment Room and couldn't be persuaded to call it anything else. Alec couldn't even think of Jack, let alone visit the place, without feeling het up. Jack was his cousin, and a first cousin at that; their mothers had been sisters. Jack's mother had died in childbirth, and Alec's parents had brought the boys up together. Alec knew that Jack ought to seem more like a brother.

The café provided cooked food all day, with good-value hot dinners, and was patronised by bus and ferry crews, railwaymen and the travelling public. Today, the windows were steamed up so he couldn't see inside.

Alec braked, and muddy water sprayed up his trousers. Rain coursed down his face, dripping down the neck of his tunic. He could do with a cup of tea. More than do with one, he was parched.

He was disappointed to find that Jack's car wasn't parked in its usual place. He'd know the old grey Ford anywhere, because it always towed a small trailer. Just a box on wheels really, in which to transport goods from the wholesaler to the café.

It might mean he wasn't in, but not necessarily, since his son Paul drove it too and had another café nearer the docks.

Alec leaned his bike against the building, and lifted his cycle cape carefully from over the handlebars so that the rain collected there didn't splash on to his boots. He let it pour off over the step.

The wooden building was raised on blocks; Alec went up the two red cement steps to the door. Inside, the scent of crisping bacon made his mouth run with saliva. There was no sign of Jack, only Vera, his second-in-command, with a young girl.

Alec leaned against the counter that ran along the back. Beside him a glass dome displayed sausage rolls, meat pies and sandwiches. In another, further along, he could see scones and cakes.

They all looked fresh and appetising. Just what he needed for Nancy's do. It promised to be quite a thrash. Fifty there'd be at the very least, and it was up to him to make sure there was a good spread in the church hall.

He'd get a barrel of beer in at home and Celia could make cakes and sandwiches. They'd ask a few of their closest friends back to the house afterwards, when the bride and groom had gone on their honeymoon.

Once he'd been made to feel welcome in this café, and Jack had given him free tea and free meals, but those days were long since gone. He slapped down three pennies on the scratched oak counter. He'd have a cup of tea, no harm in that.

The free posters from the Great Western Railway Company

that decorated the walls had not been changed recently. The views of Rhyl and Prestatyn were curling back over their drawing pins. Behind the counter, the tea urn hissed softly like a train waiting at the platform.

'Is the boss in?' he asked Vera as she pushed the tea towards him. The word 'boss' stuck in his throat. By rights, he should have been boss here.

'No, gone to the wholesaler's. Back soon.'

So it had been a wasted trip, though the tea was good and hot. Plates were coming across the counter loaded with eggs and sausage and black pudding, making his stomach rumble in anticipation.

Alec sat down, keeping his eyes peeled. They were all told they must wear uniform whenever they went out, and act like policemen at all times. He sometimes allowed himself to transgress that rule: the uniform drew the eye too much. There were a few faces here he knew, but only one real villain, who was tucking into ham and chips.

Rain was blowing under the door, making a dark patch on the bare floorboards. Rivulets ran off raincoats on bentwood stands, wet footprints were everywhere. The atmosphere was clammy and smoke-ridden. Alec drained his cup and got up.

Outside it was still pouring down, but he was pleased to see Jack Laidlaw backing his trailer up to the kitchen door round the side.

He walked over to him. 'Glad I've caught you. I want a word, Jack.'

The lean lines of his cousin's face screwed up with distaste. It didn't help that Jack had always been better-looking than he was. That now he wore a new trilby, and owned a car in which to keep dry.

'You're not on the fleece again? You're sucking me dry, Alec.'

'That's the last thing I want to do.'

'I told you last time there'd be no more. I've got to live too.' Jack's sour expression hardened to a scowl.

'It's a long time since I asked for anything.'

'A piano, not more than a month ago.'

'Two months at least, and you refused point blank.'

'You've got a piano, and none of your girls play it. What do you want another for?'

'It's a bit of help with our Nancy's wedding I want this time, and it's not until December the sixteenth. Catering for fifty.'

'I hope you're expecting to pay for it?'

'I'd expect a discount, seeing it's from you.'

Jack's cold gaze was surveying him. 'Provided you pay in advance, I'll give ten per cent discount.'

'Not enough, Jack.'

'Fifteen, then, it's my last offer.'

'Come on, temper the wind to the shorn lamb. Your pies and sausage rolls would go down a treat. And a ham and a couple of turkeys. Right time of the year for turkeys. Cold, I thought, with a bit of salad for the ladies.'

Alec stationed himself between the car and the kitchen door. 'And perhaps a barrel of bitter, if you want to be generous.'

'I don't,' Jack said shortly, getting out of the car. He pushed past Alec and ran for the door, where he knew he'd be safe from further conversation.

'I'm counting on you, Jack,' Alec shouted. He was sweating now under his cape. Damn Jack Laidlaw. He'd done Alec down, cheated him out of his birthright, after all the Siddonses had done for him.

Alec couldn't remember how many times he'd wished Jack had died along with his mother. Then he would have been left to enjoy what was rightfully his.

He'd had enough for today, he felt like a drowned rat. Celia would have a hot meal waiting for him when he got home.

Katie felt stiff with worry. The weeks were passing and

Jimmy hadn't managed to find work. The trip to Gretna Green was as far off as ever.

'I'll get some sort of a job with shipping,' he'd said at first. 'It's what I know best. There are plenty of jobs where I wouldn't have to be away from you.'

The following day he showed her a letter of application he'd written to the Mersey Docks and Harbour Board, and the reply. They didn't need more staff.

'What about the Irish boats?' Katie suggested. 'Or those going to the Isle of Man? You'd be home most nights and never far. Surely that's your best bet? That's your line of work.'

'I've tried both,' he assured her.

'The ferries then?' The Mersey was being crossed by ferry boats all day; from Liverpool to New Brighton, Wallasey, Birkenhead and Rock Ferry.

'Bit of a comedown for me, with my experience.'

'Surely anything?' Katie knew she was pleading. She was growing desperate. What she wanted was for him to say: 'Let's get married anyway. Something will turn up sooner or later. If not, I'll have to do a few trips deep sea to get us on our feet.' He'd been so sure he could get that sort of work.

'I'll try the ferries,' he said, but his tone told her he didn't hold out any great hope. 'I've got to get a job of some sort soon.'

'There are dredgers working in the Mersey,' she said. She knew because her father had said so. 'And pilot boats and lighters and all sorts of jobs you could do.'

'I'm trying, Katie. Really I am. I'm as desperate to get to Gretna Green as you are.'

'I've saved a little money,' she said. 'If we pool what we've got, perhaps we could go there first.'

'I couldn't use yours, and anyway it'll cost quite a lot,' Jimmy said slowly. 'I think we need to live there a few weeks before we can be married.'

Katie stifled the cold feeling of doubt. The problem was

on her mind the whole time. She couldn't get away from it.

Katie knew that Amy always meant what she said. It took her a week to accept that, one way or another, her mother was going to be told. Katie wanted to discuss it with Jimmy, but could not.

Jimmy didn't know she'd told Amy, and she knew he'd be dead against her telling anybody else. He'd try to talk her out of doing anything, but he was doing nothing, and Katie wanted things to move.

She couldn't concentrate on her charges. Her mind kept going off into reveries about Jimmy. He'd got himself a good job, they were packing to go to Gretna. She was only too aware that they were daydreams.

The week was almost up when she met Amy by chance in Ashville Road. 'I'll tell Mam myself,' she told her.

'On your own?'

'Be there, Amy, will you?'

Once the time and date were fixed, Katie was in a flat spin trying to work out what she would say. She couldn't stop biting her nails, she didn't feel ready to say anything.

Her heart was in her mouth as she let herself into the back yard of her home. Her mother's unwelcoming face peered through the window, and before Katie had undone the straps to get Daniel out of his pushchair, Celia had come to the back door.

'What are you doing here at this time? I've got your father's dinner to get on.' Celia's hands were floury, and she was wearing a flour-dappled apron. 'I didn't expect you today.'

Katie shivered. She didn't usually come home when she was looking after the children. She felt her mother's questioning eyes rake her face.

'Hello, Mam.' She carried the child indoors and sat down with him on her knee.

Amy smiled reassuringly from the kitchen table, where

she was drinking tea. Katie was glad she'd come as promised, but the moment was on her. She opened her mouth to say what she'd rehearsed. Her mother had turned her back and was rubbing lard into flour.

Nancy came bounding downstairs. 'Hello, Katie.'

'I don't know what you're all doing home this morning,' Celia grumbled. 'Under my feet when I'm trying to cook.'

Katie swallowed hard. She hadn't expected Nancy to be here and for a moment it threw her off balance.

She told herself it was better to have Nancy here too: she could rely on her sympathy. Anyway, they'd all have to know. No point in putting it off.

'Mother,' she said, 'I've something I have to tell you.'

That brought Mam swinging round from her pastry, her face drawn and anxious. As though she knew something terrible was coming before a word of it passed her lips. Mam came to stand over her.

Katie hugged little Danny closer. 'I need to marry Jimmy. I'm having his baby.'

She half saw the flash of her mother's arm as she raised it. The smarting slap cracked against her cheek. Katie's head jolted back, hurting her neck. She hadn't expected that.

'I'm sorry, Mother.'

'You fool, you stupid little fool.' Katie could feel her cheek stinging. 'You've ruined your life. Do you realise that? There's nothing I can do to help you. Nothing anybody can do. When? When's this baby due?'

Katie shook her head numbly. All her life she'd wanted to earn her mother's love but she only ever seemed to deserve treatment like this. Her troubles were not hers alone. She'd let the whole family down.

'Some time in February, by all accounts,' Amy said for her.

'Throwing yourself away on a con man like that Jimmy Shaw. What sort of a life do you think you're going to have with him?'

83

Katie could see shock in Nancy's eyes, but there was sympathy there too.

'That a daughter of mine should come to this! Didn't I warn you? What do you expect me to do about it now?'

Katie tried to pull herself together. 'I want permission to get married. Tell Dad. I want him to change his mind.'

'He'll have to, won't he? All our hopes for you dashed. We wanted you to have a decent life. How could you?' Katie had never seen Mam so venomous, so intense.

It was Nancy who came and lifted Daniel from her knee and handed him to Amy. Nancy who put her arms round her slumped shoulders, as though she knew how she was hurting inside.

'You can wear my wedding dress first, Katie,' she said. 'You'll make a lovely bride.' That was what brought the tears flowing down Katie's face, not her mother's venom.

'She'll be having a shotgun wedding, not your sort at all. They won't be able to afford it. It'll have to be the register office.'

Amy had made fresh tea for them all and was leading her mother into the living room.

'It'll be all right if you really love each other,' Nancy soothed. 'At least you won't have to save up for years, like me and Stan. You may be short of money to start with but there'll be compensations.'

Nancy's sympathy made Katie cry more. 'Mam's mad at me.'

'She wants us all to save up until we can afford to run a house of our own. Don't worry if you have to do it differently. Sometimes I wish Stan and I had gone straight ahead. Saving drags on for ever.'

Her mother had recovered a little by the time Katie left. 'You'd better tell that fellow of yours to get it all fixed up as soon as he can,' she said. Her face looked grey. 'The neighbours will have plenty to talk about; no point in making it even more obvious.'

Katie wanted to get out of the house as soon as she could. Amy stood up to leave at the same time.

'Couldn't stay any longer,' Katie choked as she fastened Daniel back in his pushchair. 'Mam really went off the deep end.'

The back door was firmly closed now. 'She's frightened,' Amy said. 'Some bee in her bonnet. You know what Mam's like. Good job Nancy happened to be home. She'll look after her. She's better at sympathy than I am. Look on the bright side, Katie, you've got your way. You'll get permission to marry. I was right, wasn't I?'

'Yes, but it was awful, and there's still Pa. What's he going to say?'

Celia couldn't sleep. She'd been worried about Katie for a long time, half expecting trouble from her. Now she knew for certain it was coming, and the prospect appalled her.

She could see Katie's face before her now, innocent and childlike, yet telling her bluntly that she was having a baby. Celia took a deep, shuddering breath. She wished now she hadn't gone for Katie the way she had, slapping her face and raving at her. Sheer terror had made her do it. She knew only too well what Katie must be feeling.

It was what she'd dreaded most. A daughter in that same dire state. Celia knew she'd only survived because her father had died and she'd been able to take over his house and its contents. Katie would have no advantages like that.

She'd had to steel herself to tell Alec. He'd gone berserk, just as she'd known he would.

'That Jimmy will have to marry her,' he'd raved. 'The little slut. The stupid fool. We're having no more to do with her, Celia. She's no daughter of ours after this.'

It had left her quaking. That was how Alec would treat her if he ever found out the truth about Nancy. Only he would be even worse, because he'd feel he'd been cheated.

Victor had left her in the lurch. When it came to the

crunch, she wondered whether Jimmy would treat Kate the same way.

She hoped fervently that he would, although things looked bad either way. He'd make Katie a rotten husband, but if he refused to marry her, trouble would explode.

Celia pushed down the eiderdown. She was sweating. She lifted her head to see the clock. It was three in the morning. A shaft of moonlight was coming through the curtains, lighting up the photograph she'd told Alec was of Nancy's father.

She couldn't cope with Katie's trouble and she was scared stiff it would bring her own to light. That was the worst part, knowing that she had hidden the same secret. She felt responsible for Katie's downfall. She'd always had this foreboding that history might repeat itself.

She turned over in bed gently, so as not to disturb Alec. He was snoring like a motorbike revving up, but then, unlike her, he had a clear conscience.

Celia felt another niggle of guilt. She'd never loved Alec, but she'd tried to be a good wife. She had kept her part of the bargain, working hard for his comfort, but she didn't trust him. After all, he was a man.

CHAPTER SIX

Katie had arranged to meet Jimmy that night after she'd bathed the children and put them to bed. She'd told Mrs Brent at supper that she needed to go out for an hour.

Jimmy met her at the park gate. It was a relief to feel his strong arms round her. She hadn't recovered from the morning's trauma and Mam slapping her face like that. It had left her feeling she was balanced on an emotional knife edge.

'I've told Mam,' she blurted out.

'You didn't need to. Not yet.' Jimmy had straightened up.

'She's got to know sooner or later. It was awful. I thought she was going to have a heart attack.'

Jimmy sighed. The hard look left his eyes. 'You poor love. I'm sorry it had to happen like this.'

'She said she was ashamed of me. That it's a dreadful thing for the family.'

'Nonsense,' Jimmy said stoutly, and bent to kiss her.

'She said to tell you to fix up the wedding as quickly as you can.'

She desperately wanted to hear him say that he loved her, that they would be married immediately.

His arm round her waist seemed to stiffen. 'It's not all that easy, though I want to, of course. We'll do it, Katie, I promise you, but I'll have to find a job first. We'll need money.' She'd never seen Jimmy so serious.

His lips fastened on hers again, his arms were tightening round her.

Katie pushed him off. 'We've got to make definite plans. In a few months' time . . .'

'Let me kiss you, Katie. It'll soothe you after the horrible things that have happened today. Then we'll be able to think clearly.'

Katie knew it wouldn't have been her way, but she couldn't hold out against Jimmy. She needed him too badly now.

Despite herself she was persuaded. Jimmy was a loving and passionate man. She could feel the desire burgeoning in him as he led her towards the thick shrubbery. It built in her too. This need to have love, to be cared for.

She loved Jimmy and he loved her. They'd have a happy marriage. She didn't doubt that. It was just that, in her family, a wedding took so very long to arrange, and she couldn't wait much longer.

Winnie Cottie climbed stiffly out of bed, hating Sundays. She was late getting up – it was already nine thirty – but what did it matter? What did anything matter any more? She had all the time in the world.

Outside in the road, a couple walked by, she could hear them laughing together. A bus whined to a halt at the bus stop a few yards further down the road. A child passed on a bike. There was life out there.

Winnie listened. Indoors, the silence was heavy and still, reminding her that she was alone. Quite alone. She reached for her corsets and began to dress.

She had tried to maintain an illusion of normal life. Randall's clothes were still in the wardrobe; his brushes on his tallboy; his slippers under the bed. Even the book he'd been reading was open on his bedside table. Nothing had changed in sixteen years. Except that she was growing older.

They'd been so happy together through thirty years of marriage. Randall had been looking forward to retirement, making plans. He'd been a gentle person even though he was a policeman. What had he done to deserve such a violent death?

The shock was still vivid in her mind across all those years. Even now, this minute, she could feel herself quivering.

She still couldn't believe he'd been snatched away from her without warning. She felt washed up, like some piece of flotsam no one wanted. Alone.

Anger was hot in her throat. She'd tried to tell them they'd got the wrong man but they wouldn't listen. They thought it was turning her mind, that she was deranged.

She knew who to blame, whatever they told her. She hated Alec so much it hurt. Her gnarled hands clenched and unclenched. He wouldn't get away with what he'd done, she'd get even with him. She owed that to Randall.

She'd met him in the road soon after it had happened, on her way back from the shops.

'Don't think your secrets have died with Randall,' she'd said with venomous fury. 'He told me what you were up to. I know all about you, Alec Siddons.'

'I'm not up to anything.' He'd tried to carry it off, but he looked guilty.

'I suppose you think you're safe, poor Randall dying like that, but you're not, because he told me everything. You wouldn't have lasted another month if he hadn't been killed. I suppose you're laughing about that.'

'Of course I'm not. I'm very sorry, Winnie.' His sympathy rang false. It made her want to scream. 'I admired him, he went out of his way to encourage me.'

'Encourage you? That was his big mistake.'

Alec Siddons had walked on, trying to shake her off, but she'd followed. Shouting louder than ever so he'd hear, and so would anybody else who had a window open.

'He didn't know what a rotter you were then. You're telling everyone he was killed by the burglars he disturbed. That he was run down by their getaway car. But nobody stood to gain more than you from his death. You know more about it than you're saying, don't you? Randall was out of luck, having only you with him then.'

Alec had turned back to her, his face furious.

'I can have you charged for saying things like that,' he'd hissed. 'It's malicious slander, nothing more.'

'I've been in to see Sergeant Peachey. I've made a statement. I told him you're accepting money from thieves on the understanding you won't produce enough evidence to bring charges against them. I know what you do. You'll get what's coming to you.'

She'd watched the colour drain from his face, and knew she'd caught him on the raw. She could see the effort it was costing him to stay calm.

'I know you're upset, Winnie. It's a terrible thing to have happened to Randall. It's bound to leave you feeling angry and confused.'

That had made her see red and she'd shouted, just before he'd let himself into his own house: 'They're giving you a bit of rope, Alec, just enough to hang yourself with.'

Even Sergeant Peachey had treated her as though she was having mental delusions.

'I know how upset you must be, Mrs Cottie,' he'd said in the same placating manner. If it had been Randall saying these things, she knew they'd have taken notice of him.

Randall had thought Alec lucky to have survived that far, yet nothing had come of her complaint against him. She found it hard to believe his luck still held. She'd had a sympathetic letter from someone high up in the force. It said they had enquired closely into her allegations but believed that Alec Siddons had behaved in an exemplary manner.

'The Devil looks after his own,' she muttered to herself, as she stood in front of her mirror to put her hairnet on.

Memories were all she had left and they brought cold despair. Worse, within her was this terrible need for revenge, a burning urge, a hard core nothing could soften.

Winnie went stiffly down, one stair at a time, her hip

troubling her, into the brooding kitchen. Everything was exactly where she'd left it, clean and neat and tidy. What was there left in life for her?

She lit the gas under her kettle. On the windowsill, a blackbird pecked at the crust she'd put out last night.

She must pull herself together. Get rid of this dreadful resentment. She'd have some bread and marmalade. Go to church as she usually did. Get out and about, it was the only way to shake her bad moods off.

That same Sunday morning, Paul Laidlaw shook the clean sheet out of its folds and started tucking it round his mattress.

His mother was sure that she did all the housework to the satisfaction of her family. But Paul had know for several years that if he wanted his sheets changed regularly, he'd better see to it himself.

From the front room below he could hear his mother playing the piano with more than her usual verve. The house was pulsating with the music from *Snow White*. The dancing school his sister attended was putting on a show, and she had the leading role. Paul loved being at home, it was a jolly place.

The volume was softening to pianissimo and Fliss's voice took the lead. It was her favourite song, 'One Day My Prince Will Come'. He thought it romantic yet very suitable for one so young. She had a lovely voice, soaring, strong and crystal-clear. Fliss was just fourteen and about to leave school.

Paul was captivated, lifted by her singing. He stopped to listen in spite of wanting to hurry through his chores. Fliss really had talent. His mother's voice took over. She too, had a good singing voice.

Paul looked round his room and decided it would do for another week. He went downstairs. His mother's imprint was on the house: lots of gilt mirrors and clocks and fancy ornaments.

Everything she wanted for the house his dad bought for

her. Fitted carpets, a new three-piece suite, a new piano. She'd have had a baby grand if there'd been space enough in the front room for it. Dad could never do enough for her.

'Like this, like this,' she was saying to Fliss, and then with her auburn head tilted back, her voice traced the path she wanted Fliss to follow. Myra Laidlaw had lots of fine and rather frizzy hair that stood out like a halo round her head.

Once his mother had been very ambitious for herself. The tale was family folklore now. She'd earned her living as a cook in the Refreshment Room, but she'd sung at the Floral Pavilion in New Brighton in summer shows and appeared in pantomime at the Neptune Theatre in Liverpool. Somehow, she'd never quite managed to move from amateur shows to the wholly professional.

His dad said once: 'I made her marry me, and then with you children to look after it was no longer possible.'

'Now I'm fat and forty, it's too late for me,' she'd laughed. She was forty-two now. 'The years of good living are beginning to show. Nobody wants a chanteuse with a figure like mine. I'm overblown. Past it.'

'Nonsense,' his dad had laughed. 'A full-blown rose perhaps. One with every beautiful petal on show. A man of my age doesn't want buds.'

Dad said she was buxom, but everyone else said fat. Paul thought she was inclined to dress herself with too many frills and furbelows and fur collars. She had big eyes that dominated her small face, and was such a jolly person that everybody was drawn to her.

Mam still knew exactly what she wanted from life. Her ambition had been transferred to her daughter. She wanted to see Fliss singing professionally, and all her energies went on achieving that object.

Paul knew it worried his dad that she was firing Fliss's ambitions; winding her up to reach for what might prove impossible for her too.

'Fliss is still a child,' he demurred.

'With all her future before her,' Mam said enthusiastically.

'If we play our cards right,' she told Fliss, 'you can do it. I'll help you. I'm sure you'll be a great success.' Mam was absolutely determined, and now Fliss was totally hooked on the idea too.

She had the same big laughing eyes and pink cheeks. The same shock of flyaway red hair, though Fliss's was a darker red with no sign of Mam's ginger tint. She was well built for her age and danced with tremendous vim and vigour.

'A real chip off the old block,' Mam said with satisfaction. 'I had nobody to help me, but I'm here to give you the push when the time comes.'

In the meantime, she was teaching Fliss the piano. Fliss had passed most of her exams and could play well. She was also learning to play the accordion. She went to dancing classes – tap and classical ballet.

'One never knows where a child's talent will surface,' Mam explained. The dancing school put on shows and it was all experience for Fliss.

Mam was always stitching costumes for Fliss, and was certain that success was round the corner. Her stage name was to be Felicity Lane. Lane had been Mam's maiden name.

Fliss had met a boy at dancing school, called Yves Fellipi. He was of French extraction and a year older than her. His black hair and dark skin were the perfect foil for Fliss's looks.

He was strong on ballads and operetta, and they sang duets. They'd been billed as the new Jeanette MacDonald and Nelson Eddy, but he was versatile and could sing comic songs and play the banjo too.

Mam thought him a talented youngster. His mother was pushy; she'd danced professionally in her youth, and might have a bit of influence. She was trying to get a booking for them on Blackpool Pier.

Paul had seen them in an amateur show, Fliss with her

hair piled on her head to make herself look a little older, Yves wearing a false moustache, which he complained about because it interfered with the way he opened his mouth. Mam thought Fliss could do worse than team up with Yves.

Paul headed into the kitchen. His father was shelling peas at the table. He had his shirtsleeves rolled up, showing his pale, sinewy arms, just as he did at the Refreshment Room. He wore an apron over his best Sunday waistcoat.

'Just about organised now,' he grinned. Paul pulled up a chair and set about helping him.

No one ever suggested to Mam that she neglected her duties. Paul knew his dad went out of his way to compliment her on the way she kept house. A little palace, he called it. They all thought she made it a happy place.

Mam maintained that she always cooked a dinner for them on Sundays when they were all at home, and sometimes she did. This morning he'd heard Dad put the big piece of prime ribs of beef into the oven and mix up the Yorkshire pudding.

Dad thought it helped if Myra didn't have to cook much. Well, it stood to reason, with all that food about in the cafés, they didn't want big meals when they came home.

Long ago, in the school holidays, Mam quite often used to take him and Fliss to the Refreshment Room for their dinner, and then perhaps they'd take the ferry to Liverpool for some shopping, or a matinée at the theatre. In the summer she took them on to New Brighton for donkey rides along the beach, or to visit the funfair there.

And ever since Paul could remember, Dad had brought cakes home, to save Mam the bother of making them. Now Paul was doing it himself.

'Joan does them better than I do,' she admitted. They all loved Joan's cakes.

This afternoon, he knew his father would take Mam out somewhere in the car. He couldn't do enough for her.

When they were younger, he and Fliss had been included in these excursions, but now they went their own ways.

Today he'd arranged to meet Amy.

With the last peas in the pan, his father was heading to the front room. Paul was setting the living room table when he heard Fliss fingering her accordion.

Mam encouraged her to sing every type of song. She was quite vehement about the need for this.

'Fliss, you never know quite where your niche will be. You've still to find it.'

Paul liked to hear her sing children's songs, like 'The Teddy Bears' Picnic'. She was good at Shirley Temple songs, too, like 'The Good Ship Lollipop', and 'Animal Crackers'.

'But she's growing up,' Mam said. 'Aren't you, Fliss? The time for songs like those is almost gone.'

Paul heard the accordion wheeze and falter, then suddenly burst into 'The Lambeth Walk'. Fliss's voice soared above it, deep and strong, almost contralto. Not the voice of a child at all. She sang fast, she could inflect laughter and real joy into her voice. It was a style all her own and Paul loved it. She did the popular songs of the moment this way, and he thought nothing suited her better.

Mam and Dad took up the last verse with such gusto, they almost raised the roof. Though poor Dad had a voice that sounded like a cinder being crushed under a door. Even worse than Paul's own.

Neither he nor Dad were able to do much to help Fliss, but they were behind her all the way. The whole family was pinning its hopes on her.

Paul was heading to the front room to join in when the doorbell rang. He went to answer it instead. Their next-door neighbour, Winnie Cottie, was on the step.

'It's only me,' she said in a voice that always sounded apologetic. She surprised him by sliding an egg into his hand.

Winnie was a small, shrivelled woman of seventy, who seemed smaller than ever now her shoulders were rounding with age. She dressed in a style that had been fashionable in the early twenties. Long grey coat topped with a grey silk toque like the one Queen Mary wore. She always carried a large crocodile handbag. Randall had been a sailor before he was a policeman and had brought the skin back from Africa for her. He'd had it made up with a heavy gilt clasp, and years of wear had improved its patina.

'Come in, Winnie,' his father said, before Paul could open his mouth. 'We were just having a bit of a singsong with Fliss.'

'I heard you outside on my way back from church. You've got the window open.' The accordion scraped and wheezed to a halt. Myra put her head out into the hall.

'I brought back the egg I borrowed on Friday,' Winnie told her, her wizened face deadly serious. She swung to Jack with an explanation. 'I'd started making pancakes for my tea before I realised I was out of eggs.'

'That's what neighbours are for,' he told her.

Paul knew that his father was fond of Winnie. Jack had known her all his life. He'd been brought up in the Siddonses' house with Alec, and Winnie had always lived next door.

Paul thought there was something unnerving about Winnie. She had wrinkles like tram lines; deep tracks running from nose to mouth that made her look frighteningly miserable.

'Come and sing along with us,' his father said heartily, leading her to an armchair. 'Let our Fliss cheer you up. How many times do I have to tell you? You're welcome here any time, when you feel like a bit of company.'

Winnie was lonely, of course, she'd been a widow for as long as Paul could remember. He'd heard the tale of Randall Cottie's death many times; it had passed into legend in the road.

'What shall we sing next?' Fliss was asking, her eyes shining. 'Would you like "Run Rabbit Run"?'

Winnie's grey toque seemed to nod. 'I'm glad you bought this house,' she said. 'You're good neighbours.'

'Makes up for the other side, eh?' Myra asked.

'He's no gratitude, that one,' Winnie sniffed.

'Run rabbit, run rabbit, run . . .' Fliss led them into the refrain. Winnie's voice was a melancholy squeak that was easily drowned by the rest of them.

Half an hour later Myra turned from the piano to say: 'Take your hat and coat off, Winnie. Stay and have some dinner with us.'

'I don't want to push myself . . .'

'You aren't. Come on, say yes and I'll set another place at the table. One more won't make any difference, we've got plenty.'

'You're very good to me, Myra.'

Paul could almost see the old lady unbending. The haunted look had left her face. Poor devil, she was spending too much time on her own, it was turning her mind.

She tucked into roast beef and Yorkshire pudding as though it was the first decent meal she had had in a week. She even seemed pleased that she had the washing-up as an excuse to stay with them a bit longer afterwards.

Katie had hoped that arrangements for her wedding would gather momentum now, but Jimmy still hadn't found a job, and he seemed reluctant to do anything until he had. Going back home again had been a nightmare. Mam had been hollow-eyed and grey-faced.

Pa had been cock-a-hoop and crowing. 'What's the matter? Is your lover from Liverpool dragging his feet? Is he finding out I'm right, he can't just walk into a job when he feels like it?'

Katie had cringed, it was too close to the truth.

'You're a little slut. I hope you're not thinking of moving back in here?'

'No, Pa. Not now.'

'Letting us down like this after all we've done for you. You married now, then?'

'No. You know I can't be. You have to sign.'

'Don't let that hold things up. Your mam wants it done. You're to come home every Sunday so we know what's going on. Do you hear, Kate?'

She was meeting Jimmy in the park as often as she could. The Brents were getting used to her going out for an hour or so most evenings, after she'd put the children to bed. These were the best times, when Jimmy held her close and they strolled in the moonlight.

Katie closed her eyes and sighed. 'Mam's on at me every time I go home. She keeps asking: "When's it to be then?"'

Jimmy's hand tightened on hers reassuringly. 'It'll be just as soon as I can fix it.'

'Dad's worse, he's on at me the whole time.'

'He's giving you a hard time?' Jimmy's brown eyes were full of sympathy. 'You shouldn't have told him anything.'

'And they want you to come to tea again. To talk over the arrangements.'

'I'm not keen on that, Katie. Don't fancy doing it again.'

Katie didn't either. 'They're horrible about you.'

'We can manage our own affairs. We don't need help from them. They won't give it willingly and they don't like me. No, I don't want your dad involved with us. We're independent. All you need is permission to marry and he's said he'll give that.'

'They say you should take me to meet your mother. They can't understand why you have no contact, it worries them. She's back from Ipswich now, isn't she?'

'Yes, but my mother's as bad as yours. I've told you we don't get on very well.'

'Marriage is such a big step. Shouldn't she at least meet me?'

'Maybe you're right. West Derby's quite a long way, but perhaps I can take you one Sunday.'

'I'd like that,' she said shyly. 'I've just got to tell Mam a date, Jimmy.' She stole a glance at him. He'd quickened his pace, and his eyes were fixed on some point a hundred yards ahead. 'Besides, I'd feel better if I knew exactly when.'

'Of course you would. So would I.' He sounded impatient. Sometimes she had the distinct impression that Jimmy felt he was being trapped into marriage. That he was putting off the evil day as long as possible. He'd spoken of it with much more joy before she'd told him about the baby.

'Just to get a ring on my finger. I'm afraid it will show . . . Mr Brent has very strict ideas. He'll not want me to stay working there. He's like that.' Katie knew she was going on about it too much, but it had to be said.

Jimmy's lips had straightened into a thin line. 'Say a date then, Katie. What about two months from now? October? That still gives me time to find work.'

She swallowed. She'd wanted him to say: 'Let's go down now to the register office and find out how soon we can. The sooner the better as far as I'm concerned.' But two more months, she could stand that as long as she had a definite date.

She felt cold, desolate. Don't be such a fool, she told herself. He had said October.

The next day, as she watched him walking towards her in Park Drive, she knew immediately that he was more cheerful. There was more spring in his step and he was smiling at her over the last twenty yards. It buoyed her up.

'Any news?' She couldn't wait to ask. Hope was bubbling up inside her that he'd got a job at last.

'I've got something for you.' Jimmy's old sparkle was back. 'A present.'

'Have you got presents for us too?' Bernard's treble interrupted. Daniel looked up hopefully.

'No, and not so much a present for Katie, more a surprise,' Jimmy said easily, bringing out a small box from his pocket and opening it to display a ring. 'I thought, since we've set a date, we are engaged.'

'Oh!' Katie felt a rush of delight. It seemed to cement his intention. Marriage suddenly seemed closer. 'It's very pretty.'

The pushchair stopped. Jimmy took the ring out of the box and slid it on her finger. 'A garnet. It's not new, a Victorian ring.'

'I love it.' She laughed out loud.

'I hoped you would.'

'It's beautiful. Have you been down to the register office?'

'Not yet, I wanted to get you a ring first. You deserve it, Katie.'

'We could go now,' she suggested nervously. It wasn't easy to go as far as Hamilton Square with two young children, but it wouldn't be impossible if Jimmy would take Bernard's hand. They could get a bus, though she wasn't supposed to take them on buses.

'I've got an appointment to see a man in the Lairage about a job,' he said quickly. 'Three o'clock, so we can't do it now. But there's no desperate hurry, I understand they only need a few days' notice.'

When he'd gone and she'd had time to think, she knew that she'd have preferred him to arrange their wedding, and that he ought to have kept his money for the essentials they'd need. The ring was lovely, but it was a luxury they couldn't afford.

CHAPTER SEVEN

Paul Laidlaw looked round his café feeling torn between hope and despair. His father had wanted to open this place for him. Trade in the Refreshment Room had been picking up after the recession.

'It's the right time to start another venture,' Dad had said.

'What if there's another war?'

'Then you'd have to go and fight. I wouldn't want it then, not unless Fliss . . .'

Fliss was due to leave school this summer, but she'd never shown much interest in the café; she had big ideas about going on the stage.

'I wouldn't bank on Fliss being able to manage a café. Not down here with dockers for customers.'

When Neville Chamberlain had come back from Germany in September last year, bringing 'peace for our time', Dad had been convinced. He'd signed the lease the following week while all England basked in relief.

But the threat of war was a big worry again and this time it looked as though Neville Chamberlain would not be able to stop it coming.

From the first, his father had voiced doubts about the position of the new café. Though it was near Park Station, which was on the underground line to Liverpool, it was round a corner and out of sight of people using the station and the busy parade of shops there. It was close to the docks but not on the main streets used by lorries delivering goods.

'Customers are prepared to walk a bit further if the food is

101

good. Once they know you're there.'

That it was within easy walking distance of home was a plus factor, and it was also far enough away from the Refreshment Room not to draw trade away from it.

His café looked fresh and smart. Paul could still smell new paint when he opened up in the mornings, but he was waiting for customers with mounting frustration, and the returns were disappointing. He wanted it to be always full of customers like his father's place.

'It takes time,' his father had reassured him. 'Be patient.'

The premises consisted of two shops knocked together. One had been a bakery: bread and cakes had been made there since before the First World War, but it hadn't made much profit and the lease had been on the market for years. The ovens and equipment were old-fashioned and the shop very small. The old bakery now served as Paul's kitchen, while the next-door shop had been turned into the café's seating area. An archway in the wall connected the two; Paul and Jack called it the Bakehouse Café.

The shop door pinged. It made him spin round, hopeful of custom. Amy was smiling at him and tossing her thick black plait over the shoulder of her uniform gabardine.

'Tea please, Paul, and a cake.' She sat down at one of the green tile-topped tables she'd helped him choose.

'I'm glad you've come,' he told her. 'I need cheering up.' He liked the way Amy dropped in on him.

The week he'd opened, he'd asked: 'Don't you have any friends you could bring? I need customers.'

One afternoon he'd had twelve nurses in for tea and cakes because one of them was celebrating a birthday. A few continued to come in for off-duty snacks.

'They love your cakes,' Amy had reported. 'But the restaurant in the Ritz Cinema is thought to be more of a treat. It's posh there, and handy for the big shops.'

Paul went behind the counter where kettles simmered on a hot plate and the new green and white crockery was piled high. He made two pots of tea and took them both back to Amy's table. He had plans to install a tea urn later when the expense could be justified. He was very anxious to make a success of the place.

'Joan,' he called into the bakery, 'come and have a cup of tea with us.'

'It's black Monday,' he told Amy now, sitting down with her. 'On top of my other troubles, Joan has just given notice. I don't know how I'll manage without her.'

He'd done his best to keep the trade from the bakery. Cakes were still being made in the old ovens; his father had kept Joan on to do it. Now in her early thirties, she'd been working in the cake shop for seven years and knew the business backwards. Paul knew that having Joan had made things easier for him.

'Which cake do you want, Amy?' The cakes were set out each morning in the windows and sold over the counter of glass shelves which he'd kept in place.

Amy chose a chocolate eclair. The new fluorescent lights sparkled on pink, white and chocolate icing, decorating fairy cakes and buns. Joan also made Cornish pasties, sausage rolls and jam tarts, and all manner of cakes filled with cream. She also made six different sorts of sandwiches. The greater part of her output went to satisfy the appetites in the Refreshment Room.

The scents were always delicious because she was baking all day. Paul had wondered many times if the display of delicious morsels was what was needed to attract dockers in to partake of his all-day breakfasts and hotpot lunches.

This morning he'd heard Joan humming softly in the bakehouse.

'You sound happy,' he'd said, going in.

'Yes. Got some good news.' She was grinning up at him. 'Good news for me anyway. I'm getting married, Paul.'

'Congratulations. When?' He'd tried to seem pleased for her sake. He didn't want to be a killjoy, but already he was wondering what he'd do if she could no longer work for him.

'Soon. He comes from London. A sailor, of course. He wants me to live there when we're married.'

That had made him even more anxious. The problem was more immediate than he'd supposed. 'Not good news for me, Joan. I'll miss you here.'

'You'll get somebody else.'

Paul was worried. How was he going to replace her? Joan did all the cooking, was happy to serve behind the counter in the shop and wait on the tables too, if he wanted to pop out for an hour. She was honest and trustworthy.

Joan came out to join them. She had a smudge of flour on her nose.

Paul watched her pull out her diamond engagement ring to show Amy. She was wearing it round her neck on a chain to keep it clean.

Amy admired it. 'I hope you'll be very happy.'

Joan had trained as a chef but she'd wanted a job that didn't mean split shifts and working every evening. Paul's main trade came at lunchtime, and he closed at five thirty.

'You'd better show me all your cooking secrets before you go,' he said.

'Oh come on, boss,' she teased. 'You can make scones and sausage rolls as well as anybody.'

Running the café had its advantages. If he and Amy were going to the pictures it was a convenient place to meet. When closed, it gave them privacy. While he waited for her he kept his books up to date.

Often he brought her back here for a cup of tea before he walked her up to Ashville. Sometimes he cooked a meal for her and they ate together in great style. He'd be content if only he could find a good worker to replace Joan, and if only trade would pick up and give him a decent turnover.

His father came up every afternoon to take fresh cakes to the Refreshment Room. Today he brought Alec Siddons with him.

'A big order for you, Paul.' Uncle Alec rubbed his hands importantly. 'Our Nancy's set the day at last. I want you to see to the catering.'

'You'll be transporting what you want up to the church hall yourself?' his father was asking.

'Be easier if you did it for me,' Alec said easily. 'We'll have other things on our mind that day.'

'I could do it,' Paul offered.

'I'll have to charge for delivery, Alec. And only if you pay in advance,' Jack said, adding, to Paul, 'He's come to see what Joan makes, to make his choice.'

Paul had shown Alec what they had in the shop and then ushered him into the kitchen with his order book in hand.

It was an order well worth having, but he was worried that they might not be producing the same goods by then. With Joan gone, standards might drop.

His father said softly behind his hand, 'Take nothing out of the shop until you've got his money.'

Amy Siddons hurried across the wet car park in front of the General Hospital and headed for the nurses' cloakroom. It was five minutes to five and the evening shift was gathering there in the bowels of the hospital. It was as noisy as a parrot house.

Amy stripped off her hat and coat, parted the line of nurses sitting squeezed on a long row of shoe boxes, and hung her outdoor clothes behind them. The boxes were the only seating provided, though one nurse perched on a washbowl.

At least half a dozen other nurses were changing in the cramped space and Amy had to forage for her own apron. She fastened it round her waist with a safety pin, which she then covered with the navy belt that matched the collar and cuffs of her dress. She used two tie pins to hold the front bib in place. When she was qualified, she would be allowed to replace one of these with the hospital badge, an elegant oval depicting St Luke in enamel on silver.

She enjoyed the perpetual companionship of living and working with girls of her own age. The buzz of chatter was mostly about boyfriends.

The last thing any nurse here wanted was to reach middle age and be in charge of a ward. They all knew that would turn them into sour and carping old maids, like the present ward sisters.

The general aim was to have as many boyfriends as possible until one signified he wanted sole rights. To have a good time, to be treated to shows at the Ritz Cinema and the Argyle Music Hall, and the theatres in Liverpool. To be taken out to gorge on cakes at the Ritz Restaurant.

If a partner could not be produced for the hospital dance at Christmas, it represented a loss of face. To reach the age of twenty-one and be qualified, with no engagement ring, was total failure. Every girl's goal was to get a good husband.

In the last free minutes, nurses were taking frenzied drags at their cigarettes, gearing themselves up for action after an afternoon lazing before the fire in the nurses' home.

The fug of cigarette smoke was enough to make Amy's eyes smart. Occasionally some sister would come and throw the window open, but usually the fug thickened as the day wore on.

At one minute to five precisely, the ends of all cigarettes were carefully scissored off over the waste bin, and the remaining inch or two re-inserted into the packet.

With thirty seconds to go, the cloakroom emptied. A posse of chattering nurses swept up the main staircase towards the wards. Amy went along the corridor to the casualty department. Another second-year nurse by the name of Madden followed a few feet behind.

Sister Steele was returning from her afternoon tea break ahead of them. They followed her to her office. It was part of the ritual, to hear about any patients who had been detained.

'There's two, both in the women's ward. Mrs Ada Mary Hoskins, aged forty-one. Complaining of abdominal pain and vomiting. Raised temperature and pulse rate. The surgical registrar is coming in to see her. Nil by mouth, in case she goes to theatre tonight.

'And Julie Annette Caine, aged nineteen. Ingestion of aspirin. Thought to have taken ninety tablets. Stomach washout given. Her mother is with her and will take her home shortly.'

The casualty department was part of the new extension. So new that the opening ceremony was still a few months ahead. On the floors above, the new wards had only just been fitted out. Already, the scent of disinfectant was sharp enough to catch the throats of those unused to it.

The department consisted of a long hall with a bench under the frosted windows into which were set sinks and sterilisers. Syringes were visible in glass dishes, covered with purple spirit. The fluorescent lights sparkled on glass and steel.

Only two patients waited for treatment on the row of chairs up the middle. Amy picked up the top card, and pushed the other towards Madden. Her patient was a ten-year-old street urchin, who demanded: 'What you going to do to me?'

The boy's mother smiled nervously. 'An Alsatian, it was. Shouldn't be allowed to roam the streets. Should be put down.'

The words 'dog bite' and the treatment had been written on the card by the casualty officer.

'It doesn't mean an injection, does it?' the lad persisted tremulously.

Amy had discovered the hard way that with children it was better to give the least painful treatment first. She cleaned the circle of puncture holes made by the dog's teeth and applied silver nitrate.

'Archie, isn't it? That didn't hurt, did it?'

'No, but I can't stand an injection. I don't want it.'

Amy drew it up, carefully keeping her own body between the syringe and the boy.

'Right, could you take his pullover off, Mum? And roll up his shirt sleeve.'

'I'm not having it! Mam, tell her I'm not having it.'

'Let your mother hold your arm. Like this. Now, Archie, here's Father Christmas coming through the door. What's he bringing?'

'He isn't,' the child said. 'Ooh!'

'There now, I've done it, and it hardly hurt at all.'

'Yes it did. It still pricks. And it's only the ambulancemen at the door.'

The double doors had crashed back and a stretcher case was being run in. Amy went to help.

'Road accident,' the ambulanceman told her. The young police constable with them grinned at Amy; she thought he rather fancied himself. Sister had been off duty last time he'd been in, and he'd had the cheek to ask Amy for a cup of tea.

Amy wanted nothing to do with policemen. She saw them as hard men like her father, and advised her colleagues that the ultimate failure of ending up on the shelf was better than ending up with one of them as her mother had done.

'How many hurt?'

'Three. This one's bad; one with leg wound and fractured tib and fib, the other just minor abrasions.'

'Into the back.' Amy followed the trolley towards the men's ward.

Sister joined them at the door. 'What's the matter with this one?'

'Not sure. He's unconscious.'

'I can see that,' she said sourly. He was finding it difficult to breathe. 'Get the oxygen, Siddons.'

Amy wheeled the oxygen cylinder to the patient's bed. While Sister fed a nasal catheter into his nose, Amy was taping it in position on his cheek.

An abrasion on his forehead was covering his face with blood. She looked at him closely for the first time and froze.

'I know him,' she gasped. 'He's my father's cousin!' A ball of cold horror rolled through her gut.

It was Jack Laidlaw, Paul's father. She felt sick, but she turned back the scarlet blanket to see more of him.

'Help me get his clothes off. Cut them,' Sister ordered. 'Up the seams.' Amy hacked at the strong twill with her scissors. They needed sharpening again.

'Madden, get some water and clean him up.' But it was Amy who sponged the blood from his face.

The abrasion was no more than a minor cut, he'd caught his ribs on the steering wheel and had more abrasions on one hand. The injuries were slight, yet he seemed in a bad way. Amy had seen him often from a distance: his skin was usually clear and pink, but now he was grey and sweating.

The casualty officer, a young man just out of medical school, was listening to his heart. 'Don't like this one,' he said.

'What's the matter?' Sister never showed much faith in the abilities of new housemen. She treated them more roughly than she did the student nurses.

'I don't know. Heart sounds are weak and irregular.'

'What's your diagnosis?'

He shook his head.

'How about blood pressure?'

'Low and falling.'

'Cardiac infarction?'

He swallowed. 'I'm not sure.'

She gave up on him. 'Better call in the medical registrar.'

Amy could hear the policeman questioning the remaining victims on the other side of the door. 'What caused the accident?'

'He did. Ran straight into me.'

'Yes, it was the fellow in there.'

Paul was fond of his father: Amy was afraid he would be devastated.

Amy saw Paul in the doorway, looking anxiously round him. He was tallish and slenderly built, with a thick thatch of straight brown hair like his father's, and Amy had always thought him good-looking. This evening, he looked very young and vulnerable, though he was four months older than she was.

He caught sight of her. She was used to seeing his face light up with vivid charming smiles when he did so. Today it did not.

'How is he? Is he very poorly?'

'He's unconscious I'm afraid. He hasn't been able to tell us anything.'

She could see desperation in Paul's brown eyes. Amy wanted to give him a comforting hug, but his mother's frightened face behind him stopped her.

Amy had hardly spoken to Myra during the ten years of the family feud. She was seeing her close to for the first time. The aura of jollity and enjoyment she associated with her was gone. She'd put on weight and her once bright ginger hair had faded and showed grey in places. Her face was still dominated by her big eyes.

Amy noticed the tears spilling over. Instinctively, she hugged her instead.

'It's such a shock for you, Auntie My.'

Myra Laidlaw screwed a damp handkerchief in her fingers, and huddled lower in the fur coat Jack had bought her for her birthday.

'You can sit with him, we're waiting for another doctor to come to see him. I'll show you. Where's Fliss?'

Paul answered: 'She's at her dancing class. I've left a note on the kitchen table for her. She'll come down later, I expect.'

Amy shuddered at the thought of Fliss going home to an empty house and that note.

110

'I'll let the casualty doctor know you're here. He'll come and have a word with you.'

She tried not to hear Paul's sharp intake of breath as he caught sight of his father, nor his mother's audible sob.

Madden had bandaged the slight grazes of one accident victim, and he'd been sent home.

The other had had a back splint put on his leg by the ambulance crew. Sister had given him morphine to deaden the pain but he still moaned softly.

Amy removed the temporary dressing, and winced at the fractured ends of tibia and fibula sticking out through a great gash in his leg. She dabbed iodine liberally over as much of the unbroken skin of his foot and leg as she could, and covered it with a sterile towel.

Sister and Madden had already removed his clothes and dressed him in a white theatre gown and turban. He was drowsy. Amy was pulling a thick operation sock on to his good leg when the theatre porter arrived with the trolley.

'Hang on a sec,' she said. An envelope, labelled with the patient's name, waited on his locker. It already contained his watch and his wallet. She whipped out his false teeth and put them inside too. His clothes were neatly folded into a pillowcase. She checked that he had a label on his right wrist and piled his belongings and his notes on to the trolley with him.

'Haven't you got him ready yet?' Sister was asking impatiently.

'Ready now, Sister. Who is to go to theatre with him?'

'I can't spare anybody. He'll be going up to Ward Two, they're sending a nurse. Just take him, Siddons, and get back as soon as you can.'

Amy found the nurse gowning up in theatre. She pushed the patient's notes and belongings into her hand and hurried back.

Paul met her as she crossed the department, his face anxious and frightened.

'Amy, come quick,' he gasped, grabbing her arm.

Her heart turned over; she guessed what had happened before she reached Jack's bedside. The oxygen was whistling out of the cylinder but his chest was no longer moving. He'd stopped breathing. Myra was clinging to the screens Amy had drawn round his bed.

She called to the casualty officer and barely had time to take the bedclothes off Jack Laidlaw's chest before the houseman was there trying to resuscitate him. Amy shot into the department to draw up a heart stimulant. She jabbed the syringe into the flesh of Jack's thigh, but she knew by then that it wouldn't be any use.

She took the Laidlaws out of the ward and found them seats. She felt sick as she went to turn on the urn to make some tea.

Jack Laidlaw was not the first patient to die on her by any means, but he was the first person she'd known outside the hospital to do so. And he was family. It made a difference. It would make a very big difference to Paul. She wondered about the business. Paul would have to take charge of it now.

Amy's heart turned over again when she saw Fliss Laidlaw at the door, looking lost, her big eyes, so like her mother's, staring out from under dark red hair that glistened with health.

Amy saw the flash of recognition on her face, and then Fliss was coming towards her, moving with the coiled-up energy of a dancer.

'I'll show you where your mother is,' Amy said, but for once Myra seemed oblivious of Fliss's needs. It was Paul who put his arms round her to tell her the news. He'd always spoken of his dad with affection. Amy knew she wouldn't feel as bad if it was her father who was dead.

Amy found Paul's grief very hard to bear, and Fliss's sobs made her own eyes sting. By the time she had the tea ready, Sister had moved the Laidlaws into her office. Auntie My stared at the tea cup as though she didn't know what it was.

'It'll make you feel better,' Amy urged. 'Drink it.' She knew it wouldn't still the aching loss she must be feeling, but what else was there to say?

'He's gone.' Auntie My's big eyes reflected horror. They were red and swollen now and her nose had red patches at the nostrils.

'Yes, I'm afraid so.'

'What am I going to do? Without him?'

'It must seem very cruel. To have him snatched away so suddenly, without warning.' Amy had to blink hard herself. 'All you can do is remember the good times you had together. Try to be grateful for them.'

'You're very kind, Amy. A good girl. To see you grown up like this, and a nurse . . . Your father . . . It's a pity we haven't seen eye to eye all these years.' Myra sighed and dabbed again at her nose. 'I expect he's very proud of you. Your mother too.'

Amy smiled as though she agreed. The last thing Pa was was proud of her. He was spoiling for a fight as soon as she set foot in the house. She could feel his dislike like a wall. Now she'd grown up she could admit to herself that what she felt for him was hate. He was horrible to Mam too, treating her like a slave.

Amy couldn't get what had happened to Paul's father out of her mind. When eight o'clock came, she went home instead of walking up to Ashville with the other nurses. She could see the living room light on as she went up the yard. Her mother had hung the blackout curtains behind the blue chintz that had been up for as long as she could remember but she hadn't drawn them.

She paused at the living room door. It was a tableau she'd seen a hundred times. The wireless was tuned to a play. On one side of the fire, her mother was hemming the bridesmaid's dress for Katie. Pa was dozing on the other.

Celia looked up. 'Aren't you going to take your coat off, Amy?'

Amy went over to the wireless and switched it off. Pa grunted irritably and opened his eyes.

'What did you do that for? I was listening.' He half rose to his feet to turn it on again.

'Jack Laidlaw is dead,' she said. 'He was in a road accident. Died soon after he was brought in. I thought you ought to know. He is your cousin.'

Her father's mouth dropped open. The colour drained from his face. 'I don't believe it. He can't be!'

Amy stared at him in disgust. 'Suit yourself, Pa. It doesn't alter the facts.'

'Good God! I saw him this afternoon. Spoke to him.'

'Well, you won't speak to him again,' she retorted. Then she paused, frowning. 'I thought you hadn't spoken for the last ten years?'

'Only by way of business, otherwise I wouldn't,' he said quickly. 'Ordering food for Nancy's wedding, that's what I did. He crashed his car, you say?'

'Yes. They think he might have had a heart attack while driving. No visible injuries sufficient to cause death. There'll be a post-mortem to find out.'

'Poor Myra.' Her mother looked stunned.

'Poor Paul too,' Amy said. 'I'm going in to see him now, whether you like it or not. I think you ought to forget this stupid feud of yours and get round to see Auntie My. She is a relative, after all.'

'Only by marriage. I can't see it need make much difference.' Her father's face was flushed.

'I thought your quarrel was with Uncle Jack?'

'Well, yes, it was.'

'He can't fight you from the grave, Pa. As far as the rest of us are concerned the feud is over. We aren't children any longer, having to do as we're told.'

'When did you ever do as you were told?' Pa growled.

'I'm going round there as often as I please. Auntie My will want you to come too, Mam. She'll need a bit of support. It's come as a dreadful shock.' She turned on her heel and marched out.

Paul answered her knock on his back door. He looked at her with bleary eyes, led the way into the living room, slumped down at the table and put his head in his hands. Amy pulled out the chair next to him and put an arm round his shoulders.

'I can't take it in,' he choked. 'It's going to mean a lot of changes. And the business, it's all up to me now. How am I going to manage two cafés?'

'You can't be in two places at once. You'll have to get somebody to help you.'

He groaned. 'Easier said than done. I'm sure Vera could run the Refreshment Room, but she isn't the sort who'll take responsibility. She won't want to.'

'There's Fliss. Only the other day you said she was better at baking cakes than you'd expected.'

'It's only a month since she left school, and you know she's spent two weeks of that in Blackpool, singing in a summer show on the pier. Working in the café is just filling in for Fliss. Now she's had a taste of singing professionally, she's all fired up and can't think of anything else.

'Dad was talking of sending her to commercial college, so she'd have something to fall back on if she didn't make it, but Fliss and Mam, well, they've got stars in their eyes. They can't think about commercial courses or working in the café.'

'She's working there now, isn't she?'

'Yes, she was helping Dad, but I can't rely on her staying. She'll be off like a shot if she gets half a chance. Yves's mother is trying to get them a booking in a variety show at the Argyle next month. I need somebody to manage the café, and there's no way Fliss could do that yet.'

'She'll want to help now your dad's gone.'

'Perhaps. Joan's leaving at the end of the month, and I've no one to replace her. I haven't got much time left.'

Amy felt full of sympathy.

'Where do I find somebody I can get on with? Somebody honest I can trust to handle money and run the cake shop?' Paul sighed. 'And the place is hardly paying its way.'

'Would it be better to close it down?'

'Can't do that. Dad signed a lease for fourteen years. He made me a partner in the business so I'm committed to pay the rent whether it's open or not. I could put it on the market, but who wants to buy a café when there's a war round the corner? I'm in a mess, Amy.'

'You could put Fliss in the cake shop to keep an eye on things.'

'I'll have to, as a stopgap, but Mam's built up her hopes. I can't expect her to stay if her chance comes up, can I?'

'Not if that's what she cares about.'

'To be honest, Dad wanted her to have her chance too.'

Amy put an arm round his shoulders, pulled him close and kissed him. 'I wish there was something I could do to help. It's a terrible time for you.'

'It's Mam I'm worried about. Dad thought the world of her. Couldn't do enough to please her. Always bringing little presents home for her. She's really going to miss him.'

'Your father wanted to take care of you all,' Amy said slowly.

'Not me, I was pushed out to do my bit. He expected it of me. But Mam and Fliss, yes. He looked after them.'

'Hand and foot,' Amy agreed. 'And brought you up to do the same.'

'Looks like I'll have to get on with it. I hope I'm going to cope.'

'Course you'll cope, Paul. Where are they? Your mother and Fliss?'

'In bed. The doctor's been and given them both a sedative.'

'I'll make you a cup of tea. Didn't he give you anything?'

'No. He thinks I should be able to cope too. But what will happen if war comes and I get called up?'

BOOK TWO
1929

BOOK TWO

CHAPTER EIGHT

Spring 1929

Amy knew it had been burned into her memory, the night Pa had forbidden her to speak to the Laidlaws.

'You're not to set foot in that house again.' Her father had glowered round the tea table at his family. 'None of you.'

'But I like playing with Paul,' she'd said, biting into her bread.

'I'm telling you not to like him in future.' Pa had rounded on her fiercely.

'Auntie My's taking me to see Fliss dance at the Little Theatre next Saturday.'

'Drop him, and Fliss too.'

'She said she'd teach me to play the piano. I like going there,' she persisted.

'Amy, don't you understand plain English? I've said you're to have no more to do with them. You're not going to see Fliss make an exhibition of herself. Not ever again. Fliss, what a silly name.'

'It's Felicity,' Nancy had murmured.

'Of course it's Felicity. I told Myra it was stupid before she had her christened,' Pa had growled. 'Too fancy. Too theatrical.

'Do you know what she said? "And what's wrong with that? It's a pretty name, and anyway, she could end up with it in lights." Myra's getting above herself.'

Amy tried to say how much she loved Auntie My.

'Celia, you're not to go near them either. You don't have

to put up with Myra thinking she can do better than the rest of us.'

Amy could still remember the feeling of outrage building up in her.

She said mutinously: 'Just because you've fallen out with Uncle Jack doesn't mean Paul and I have to fall out too.'

'It does if I say so.'

'That's not fair.' Amy felt as much at home next-door-but-one as she did here. Now she felt her whole family turn against her.

Pa glowered at her. 'I'll tan the hide off you if I find you still playing with those Laidlaws.'

'If Pa doesn't want you to play with them, you mustn't,' Nancy said primly. 'I won't.'

'Amy, you're not to go round to their house again. Stay away from them,' her mother had added.

Amy and Paul saw each other every day at school; they were in the same class. They whispered together in the playground about Pa's orders. They had no intention of breaking off their friendship, they were agreed on that. But they must be very careful to hide it from their families.

Paul had told her how he'd heard his father getting up one Saturday morning. How he'd shot out of bed and dressed himself quickly and run downstairs to the kitchen.

'Will you take me with you, Dad? I want to help you in the café this morning.'

His mother had turned round from the kitchen table and smiled.

'Funny how easy you find it to get up on Saturday mornings, when I have so much difficulty getting you up in time for school.' She was wearing a brown dressing gown printed with orange whorls that matched her auburn hair.

'Since you're up and ready,' Dad grinned, 'I suppose you can.'

'Wouldn't you rather stay here with me and Fliss?' Mam

asked. 'It's going to be a nice day, I was thinking of packing a picnic lunch and taking you both to Eastham Woods to pick bluebells.'

Paul hesitated. He knew she didn't like him going to the café. 'I could go and be back in time for that,' he said. 'Can Amy come too?'

Dad said: 'Let him come for a few hours. He's a help to Vera in the kitchen now.'

'It's against the law for a child of his age to work. He's got to be at least thirteen. Alec's been quoting chapter and verse at me. Local Authority by-laws. You could get into trouble if he's seen in there.'

'He's my son. I can take him there if I want to.'

'Not according to the law.'

'That's how I learned the trade. I used to go down and help from the time I was eight. There was nothing I liked doing better.'

'Times have changed, Jack.'

'Who is going to see him in the kitchen, for goodness' sake, Myra? He can stay out of sight if anyone comes, and he can come home on the bus when he's had enough.'

Myra laughed. 'Well, I suppose it'll be all right. What do you do to make him love that place so much?'

'He takes after me, Myra. As noticeably as Fliss takes after you.'

Paul studied his father's handsome, good-natured face as he shook Force flakes into a bowl and added milk, and wondered if he'd be like him when he was grown up.

He knew his mother was ambitious for him. She had ideas about him being a teacher. Her uncle had been a school-master.

'It'll be a better life for you,' she insisted. 'Your father has to work very hard for his money.'

'But at least I'm my own boss, Myra.' His father winked at him. 'It's not a bad life.'

'I'd rather work in Dad's café,' Paul said with all the

123

determination of his nine years. 'School isn't very exciting. I don't want to be a teacher and spend all my life in one.'

'Do you find the café exciting?' Mam had asked him.

'A little bit exciting.'

'It isn't when you have to spend every day working there. I should know because I did. I had to marry the gaffer to get out of it.' His mother giggled like a schoolgirl. 'When you're grown up, what job would you find absolutely gripping?'

'I'd like to fly an aeroplane. Be a pilot.'

Dad laughed at that: 'You do your best at school then, son. See if you can get to the grammar school. Then perhaps, one day, you might just be able to become a pilot.'

Myra said: 'We've never had a pilot in the family.'

Dad grinned at him. 'In the meantime, it won't hurt if he comes to learn the trade.'

Paul loved the ride down to Woodside in the rather battered Ford van his father had owned since the early twenties. It had a wooden body with running boards, and needed two jerks on the starting handle to get the engine going. His mother kept urging him to sell it and buy a car instead.

His father was proud of his café. As he unlocked the door, he said: 'A right little earner, Paul. Do you know why?'

Paul shook his head.

'It's the position, here in this busy place. There's always plenty of people passing the door.'

There were ten tables covered with new oilcloth in a red and white gingham pattern. One was usually upturned on another in the corner to make more floor space, and only lifted down to cope with the dinnertime rush. Four chairs were pushed under each.

The crockery was thick and plain, the cutlery cheap with a shortage of teaspoons. The atmosphere was clammy and smoke-ridden, covering the windows with steamy moisture. They had green frilled curtains made by his mother. She had been talking at breakfast of making new ones to match the new oilcloth.

Paul went through to the hot kitchen behind the café. Vera had already arrived.

'I've come to help you again,' he told her. She was a motherly woman in her fifties with an inch of straight grey hair showing beneath her white cap. She did the cooking and made up the orders as they came in.

'That'll be lovely. He's learning fast, Jack. You're a great help to me, Paul. And your dad's saving money by not having Polly in on Saturdays.'

Saturday was not such a busy day for Vera. Many of their regular customers worked a half-day and went home to eat afterwards. There were more people travelling to Liverpool to shop, but they wanted cups of tea and cakes rather than hot meals.

'You've got to arrange it all nice on the plate now, ducks,' she said. 'Like I showed you last time.'

With his tongue clamped between his teeth in concentration, Paul struggled to do his best. The hardest part was to get the orders right. No good putting out egg and bacon if they asked for sausage and egg.

His father was behind the counter in the café, taking orders. He came in and said: 'A special for Constable Siddons.'

'Can I do that?' Paul asked, getting a plate from the pile warming in the slow oven. 'What's a special?'

'A bit of everything. You keep out of sight, son. Don't forget Uncle Alec is a policeman. He can be a bit officious. Better if he doesn't see you here.'

'He won't lock me up?'

'No,' his dad laughed. 'If he locks anyone up, it'll be me, but better if he doesn't know you're here.'

'He won't come in the kitchen, will he?'

'Probably not, but you can hide in the cupboard if he does.'

Paul laid out two slices of bacon and a fried egg. He arranged two sausages on the side and a slice of black

125

pudding, added some fried tomato and then set it off with triangles of fried bread.

'Looks great,' Vera praised him. 'Toast now, on another plate.'

The door swung open as she took the special out to the counter. Paul heard Constable Siddons's familiar laugh and then his voice boomed, 'Beautiful, I'll feel better with that inside me.'

Paul felt quite grown up because he'd earned praise for his work. He was making up sausage and scrambled eggs for two customers when he saw the cart backing up to the kitchen door. Of the driver, high on his seat at the front, only his trouser legs, tied over his boots with string, were visible through the window.

'Somebody's coming,' he said to Vera, and heard her passing the news on to his dad when she took another order into the café.

'Dick's here, bringing the vegetables.'

Paul opened the door. The old grey horse brought her foot down heavily on the stones, sending sparks flashing from her shoe. Dick, Vera's husband, a small, wiry man, was opening up the cupboards under the seat and bringing out trays of eggs. Then he began humping sacks of potatoes into the pantry. A sack of onions followed. Two boxes of tomatoes. Paul half listened to his father bargaining about the price of mushrooms. Vera came to the back door to ask Dick to pick up a packet of tea on his way home.

They all heard Constable Siddons call out in the café: 'Jack, are you there?'

Paul was aware then of his weighty footfall coming behind the counter.

Vera's hand steered him rapidly into the broom cupboard and pushed the door to. A mop bucket took up most of the floor space; there was barely room for his feet, and the door wouldn't quite close. He had to hold it tight against the toecaps of his school shoes. Through the inch gap, he could

126

see Amy's father inspecting the contents of Dick's cart. He opened up the cupboards under the driving box.

'What's this then, ham? Thought you were supposed to be a greengrocer? And bacon and beef?'

'Expanding me business. That's what I'm doing.' Dick was a small, slight fellow with a furtive manner. He wore a greasy waistcoat which didn't match his trousers, a celluloid collar and a twisted tie. 'It's perfectly legal.'

'Meat pies?'

'Yes.' Paul could see them, all neatly wrapped and boxed.

'A vanload of meat pies and sausages was stolen last night. Purbright's pies they were. Like these you have here. I shall have to ask you to come to the station with me to sort this out. I have to caution you that you don't have to say anything, but if you do, it may be used in evidence against you.'

Paul heard Vera's gasp of horror.

'Where did you get them?'

'My wholesaler.' Dick's voice was indignant.

'Who might he be? You have receipts? You must have.'

Paul leaned forward. Through the back door, he could see Dick rifling through a pile of papers on his cart.

'These are for potatoes and onions,' Uncle Alec's voice boomed. 'Those are for lettuce. What about the pies and hams? Whole hams, very nice. Is this goods vehicle yours?'

'Yes.'

'Then you can be charged with failing to keep current records, too.'

Paul heard his father cough. He knew he was ushering them back into the kitchen. The back door slammed. He could feel the tension from inside the cupboard. He peeped again. Vera's plump cheeks were sagging with fear.

'Go behind the counter and serve instead of me,' his dad ordered her.

'Don't let him get Dick,' she choked. 'They'll put him inside again.'

127

'Go on,' his dad barked, pushing her towards the café. 'You shouldn't let your husband do these things.'

'Please,' she implored. Paul heard the swing door flip backwards and forwards as she went through.

There was a moment's silence, then his father's voice said: 'Alec, let's not be hasty about Dick.'

Uncle Alec had not relented.

'You'd better think of your own position. Could be you're receiving stolen goods. I'll have to ask you to come with me too.'

'Good God! I didn't know they were stolen. I've been buying from Dick Frisby for ages.'

'You must have known he had form. It's common knowledge.'

'Damn it, Alec, I'm your cousin. You aren't going to see your own family prosecuted?'

Paul shivered and involuntarily moved one foot. His heel clattered against the mop bucket, but the men didn't seem to notice.

'Can't you give Dick a second chance?'

'Second chance? He's had umpteen chances. He's been in and out of prison for the last decade. Surely you knew that?'

'He's Vera's husband; I thought I was doing them a favour. Giving him custom. Helping him go straight.'

'You haven't done yourself any favours. I'll have to book you. It's my job, you know that.'

Constable Siddons was rocking back on his heels, his tone self-righteous. Paul was half choking with horror.

'Come on, Alec. You've been eating here several times a week for nothing. I'm family. Surely you owe me something? Is it too much to ask that you forget you ever came here this morning? That you saw nothing?'

'For you I might, Jack, but Dick Frisby is a known crook.'

'Look, guv, I don't want to go back inside.' Paul could hear the crackle of pound notes accompanying Dick's voice.

He was holding his breath, unable to believe his own ears. He was sweating; the cupboard was hot and airless. The mop gave off a rank odour.

Through the gap he saw the wrinkled hand holding out the bundle of bank notes, and a larger hand, plump and covered with tiny black hairs, take them.

'All right then, let's say I didn't come here this morning.'

The café door swung open, and Paul heard Vera's heavy footfall, followed by the slam of the oven door as a hot plate was taken out and the scrape of a metal spoon in the scrambled egg pan.

'Who's that?'

'My wife.'

'That's right, I told you. Vera's worked for me for years.'

'Got to be careful. The fewer people know about this the better. It's just between us then.'

'Vera won't say anything. Of course she won't.' Paul heard the tea urn hiss and splutter in the café as Vera turned it on.

As soon as Constable Siddons had gone his father was locking the back door.

'Bloody hell,' Dick spat. 'That was a close shave. I'm still shaking.'

Paul came out of the broom cupboard, glad to be able to move again. 'What happened, Dad?'

His father slid on to a chair. 'Get us some tea.'

Paul went behind the counter and filled two cups. Normally he was forbidden to go near the tea urn; his mother was always reminding Dad how dangerous it was to allow him near steam and boiling water. He was very careful not to spill any as he took the two cups back to the kitchen.

'What's happened, Dad?' he asked again. He'd never seen his father so upset.

'Never you mind, son. The less you know about this the better.'

'He's a bent copper.' Dick was wiping beads of sweat

from his forehead. 'I didn't know. I thought I was going behind bars again. Bit of luck there.'

'Cost you a pretty penny,' Vera sniffed. 'I can't see much luck about that.'

'What's a bent copper, Vera?' Paul asked.

'Get away with you. None of your business.' But Paul thought he knew all there was to know.

His father looked shocked, but Paul felt even worse.

'You'd better go home, son,' Jack Laidlaw said a little later. Paul felt the penny bus fare being pressed into his palm. 'There's a bus in now.'

His mother was in the kitchen when he got home, packing the last items into a picnic basket. Fliss was jumping up and down with excitement and wearing a new summer dress. They were almost ready to go to Eastham Woods.

Kate and Amy had come round earlier and had been invited to go too. In the pleasure of the moment, Paul pushed from his mind what had happened at the café. He didn't think it so momentous that it would change anything in his life.

It was a lovely spring day. Paul could remember the sunlight coming through the branches to dapple the bluebells underneath, and the haze of blue spreading as far as the eye could see. He remembered Amy as she'd been that day, holding a great armful of bluebells she'd picked to take home for her mother.

In the late afternoon, they got off the bus only a few yards from their house. They were all dawdling, tired now; his mother had organised games for them, and he'd had to run hard to beat Amy. He felt replete with sun and fresh air.

Paul saw Uncle Alec striding towards them with a face like thunder. He wore a fawn pullover instead of his uniform but the sight of his anger brought the events of the morning flashing back into Paul's mind. He could feel himself stiffening.

'Myra, I'll thank you never to take my children out again. You've no business to do this.'

'Why? I often do. What's the matter? We've had a lovely day, haven't we, Amy?'

Alec snatched his daughters' hands and began to tow them away. 'You're not to do it again. Not ever.'

Kate dropped her bluebells all over the pavement. Both little girls pulled back, stooping to pick them up, acting as anchors on Alec.

'We aren't late back, are we? I told Celia between four and five. It's our usual time.'

'Myra! I don't want my children playing with yours. Is that clear?'

'Oh come on, Alec, what's biting you? I've done nothing I haven't been doing for years.'

'Jack's gone too far this time. I don't want anything more to do with either of you. Stay away from Celia and keep your offspring away from our house. All right?'

'Well, no, it isn't. I don't understand what you're on about.'

'Just a minute, Pa,' Amy said, much hampered with her own flowers and the fact that her father had locked one of her hands in his. Paul bent to help. Fliss was already doing so.

'Come on, you two.' Alec almost jerked Amy off her feet. 'I've no doubt, Myra, that Jack will tell you his version. I've got to be fussy about who I keep company with.'

Paul couldn't breathe. He knew why this was happening but he couldn't get a word out. Things were worse than he'd supposed.

He and Fliss were given the task of putting the bluebells in vases. He dragged the job out long after Fliss had grown tired of it, listening to Mam banging dishes on the living room table for their tea.

Alec Siddons had put Mam in a bad mood. He couldn't remember ever seeing her like this before. She was always happy, ready with her jokes and her hugs. Never moody and

131

silent like this. When his dad came home it was worse.

'Alec accused me of receiving stolen property,' Dad said. 'He wanted to take me in, charge me.'

'No! You weren't, were you? Receiving . . . ?'

'No!' Dad caught Paul's eye, and he shrank back against the sink. 'Well, I don't know. Perhaps . . . But I didn't know the stuff was stolen.'

'You shouldn't . . .'

'I should have had more sense than to trust Dick Frisby. Vera's all right; I wanted to help her, and look where it landed me.'

'You know what Alec's like.'

'He's jealous of everything I have. He's always been like this. Wasn't normal even as a boy. He always wanted to do better than me.'

'You said he saw you as a rival?'

'A rival he had to dominate. Alec always made it clear that it was his home and his parents who were looking after me.'

'I thought you said you had a happy childhood?'

'On the whole, I did. Of course, it would have been better if my mother hadn't died, but my father used to come to see me regularly and take me out.

'Usually he took Alec along as well, on fishing trips and to football matches, but he was my dad, he belonged to me.'

'Alec told me once that your family sponged on his.'

'I know my aunt was paid to look after me. I saw the money changing hands. I received love and kindness from her and Uncle. They couldn't have done more for me. They treated me and Alec like brothers. We're almost the same age . . .

'But Alec resented me being there. All I ever wanted was to get on with things my way, but he always had to interfere.'

'He didn't want his father to sell his café to you.'

'He'd already joined the police. He'd said he didn't want to go into the business. I know my uncle let me have the

Refreshment Room at a very reasonable price, and he let me pay for it from its earnings.'

'And Alec was furious about that?'

'Haven't I said? Like a raging bull. He's afraid now that I'm earning more from the café than he's being paid by the police.'

'Are you, Dad?' Paul asked.

'Never you mind.'

'Did you live in Amy's house, Dad?'

'Yes, I've told you I did. I spent my childhood there. It was rented then, but my uncle bought that house with the money I paid him for the business, and willed it to Alec. So Alec has nothing to complain about. Neither I nor his dad did him down.'

'He's a jealous man,' Myra said. 'Don't I know?'

'Jealous because his parents showed affection for me, but they always had his interests at heart.'

'Why do we live so close, then?' Fliss wanted to know.

'That's another story,' Jack said with a sigh.

Paul found that tea was not the comfortable family meal it usually was. Mam and Dad were touchy and kept going over and over the grievance with Alec Siddons.

For once, he and Fliss were put to bed early and without much ceremony. It was a warm evening and with the windows open, Paul could hear his parents talking in the living room below. He strained to hear what was being said, but he was just out of earshot. He felt a burning curiosity to know more. What he knew already had whetted his appetite.

He'd never heard any criticism of the Siddonses before. He'd thought the two families were close. They were related and ought to love each other, and Mam was very open about everything. Dad often laughed, and said she opened her mouth too wide, but she hadn't about this. Paul knew they were continuing to discuss what had happened. He crept out of bed and sat halfway down the dark stairs.

The living room door was open. He could see Mam sitting back in the red velvet armchair, the lamp behind her head shining through her halo of ginger hair. Her big eyes were flashing anger at Dad.

'There are times,' she said, 'when I could shake Celia till her teeth rattle. She runs round after Alec like a fool, yet she neglects those poor girls. It's all I can do to stop myself telling her to pull herself together.'

'She seemed all right with Nancy last time I was there.'

'Oh, it's Nancy this and Nancy that, but never a thought for the other two. They wear Nancy's cast-offs. I don't believe Amy ever had a new dress until I bought her one for her birthday. Celia just ignores them. That's why I take them out and make a fuss of them here. They wouldn't have any sort of a life if I didn't.'

'Come on, Myra, admit it. You like mothering them.'

She snorted with disgust. 'Half the time they don't get enough to eat. Celia only puts a meal on the table when Alec's at home. I've heard Katie say she's hungry and seen Amy go foraging in the pantry for her. I've told Celia she makes far too much fuss of Nancy.'

'What did she say to that?'

His mother mimicked Celia's voice: '"I can't help it, Nancy's such a lovely child." Well, she is, nobody's disputing that, but it's pitiful to see Katie. She treats Amy like a mother. I was round there the other day when she fell down in the yard and grazed her knee. She ran to Amy for comfort, not Celia. And it was Nancy who washed her knee and put iodine on it.

'There's something the matter with Celia. Her mind's been turned. To be so stinting with affection for her own children.

'You know what little Amy said to me the other day? "I wish Mam liked me more. She thinks I'm naughty on purpose, just to annoy her. I do try to be good, so she'll like me better, but I'm not as nice a person as Nancy, am I?"

134

"'I think you're a lovely little girl,' I told her. "You're always very good when you're round at my house."

"'But Nancy is nicer? Than me and Katie?'"

"'Nancy is nice, but not nicer. I like you and Katie very much." It sort of pulled at my heartstrings. God love her, she's only nine.'

'You encourage them to come round here,' Jack said. 'You'll have to stop.'

'I've tried to make them feel welcome. Celia gives the impression she's just putting up with them at home.'

'Amy asked if she could have a Saturday job when she's older.'

'I suppose you said yes?'

'I'll have to tell her I've changed my mind if she gets round to asking again.'

'She's very independent. Self-sufficient.'

Paul saw his mother pull herself upright in the chair, and heard her say with increased venom: 'Remember the time before Katie was born? I told you about it. Celia whispering desperately that she didn't want another baby? That Amy had stretched her mothering instincts beyond breaking point? I think that's why she's opted out of bringing Katie up.

'She put her straight on the bottle, didn't even try to feed her herself. I went in to see her when Katie was a few days old and found Nancy giving her a bottle. The two of them were slithering about on that Rexine chair in the living room.

'Alec, useless as ever, was reading his newspaper on the other. Hoping somebody was going to wait on him.'

His mother snorted with indignation. 'If you could turn your hand to a bit of housework when the babies were born, there's no reason why Alec couldn't do the same. I went straight upstairs and said as much to Celia.

"'Nancy loves doing it," is all Celia said. "She gets up early to give the baby a bottle before she goes to school, and demands to feed her again as soon as she comes home. She can change her napkin too."

'"You can't leave it all to Nancy," I told her. "She's only eight years old."

'"There's a lot to do with three of them, you know," was all she could say. "Washing and ironing, cleaning and cooking. Alec says he can't do everything."'

'Does he ever lift a finger?' asked Jack.

'Of course he doesn't. As they grew older, I used to watch Amy playing with the baby and it seemed to me that she and Nancy took her over. Celia's always been too busy running round after Alec.'

CHAPTER NINE

'What's your dad done to mine?' Amy demanded of Paul. He filled his cheeks with air and let it whistle slowly out.

'You'd never believe.'

She stared at him. 'Course I would, if it's true.'

Paul shook his head slowly and pulled a face.

'I've got to know,' Amy told him indignantly. 'What's Uncle Jack saying? Pa would never do anything wrong. He's very particular about that.'

'That's what you think. Just listen to this.'

When he'd finished he said: 'That's brought your eyes out on stalks, hasn't it?'

'Pa's always been awful to me, horrible. I should have known he'd be awful to others. He just pretends . . . But I know what I'm going to do.'

'What?'

Amy had seen it as a game at first. 'We'll play at being detectives. Following Pa about town. If what you say is true and he's sort of blackmailing your dad . . .'

'Course it's true, I saw him doing it.'

'You're saying he does it to other people too.'

'Well, my dad thinks so.'

'We'll find out. We'll soon see what he's really doing if we follow him.'

'When he's working, you mean?'

'It'll have to be weekends and school holidays.'

'But he goes on his bike.'

'Nancy's got a fairy cycle. She'd lend it to me if I asked.'

'What about me?' Paul said.

'Could we manage with one bike? I could sit on the seat and you could pedal. We've done it like that before, haven't we?'

'Only in the park. Better not about town. I've asked for a bike for my birthday.'

'Mostly he says he walks. Let's try without bikes. If he's working next Saturday, how about then? I'll find out first.'

'What shift is he on?'

'It's seven to three this week.'

'We've got to start at seven?'

'That'll be easiest. We know he goes to the station to start. He'll go down on his bike. He has to get there half an hour earlier to go on parade and get his instructions. We can go down on the bus and pick him up when he comes out.'

'It could be quite boring,' Paul said. 'And there aren't many people about at that time. He might see us.'

'That makes it more exciting,' Amy said. 'If it is boring we can always go down to the Refreshment Room.'

They waited round the corner from the main police station, hovering between Hamilton Street and Brandon Street.

'They don't start prompt at seven,' Amy grumbled. They had a long wait, but at last they saw policemen coming out. They didn't find it difficult to follow Alec Siddons. His huge bulk topped with his policeman's helmet made him easy to pick out at a distance. He walked slowly, ponderously.

There were few people about to begin with and it all seemed rather dull. The most exciting thing he did was to unlock a small box on a telegraph pole and use the telephone inside.

'It's a fixed line back to the station,' Amy said. 'I heard him telling Nancy about it. He has to keep reporting in. Tell them if anything exciting is going on.'

'Definitely nothing exciting. He doesn't actually do very much,' Paul said in amazement. 'Just walks about in the sunshine talking to people. Not a bad job.'

'It's different on wet days,' Amy said. 'He complains about the rain. Says it's a dreadful job and gives him rheumatism.'

'Better than being shut up in the café all day. On sunny days I'd rather be out.'

'It's going to be fun,' Amy said. Though seeing him like this scared her. He was the official arm of the law here. She had no doubt he felt his own importance. He held his shoulders back and his head high. She was afraid he'd turn round and see her and then there would be trouble. She'd be in for a belting when she got home.

They watched him climb the steep steps into the covered market, and followed once he disappeared inside, picking him up again as he walked ponderously down one of the aisles. Amy clutched at Paul and giggled, hanging back when Pa paused to talk to somebody.

'We've got to try and creep close enough to hear what he's saying,' Paul insisted.

'He'll see us,' Amy protested, dragging him back.

'This way.' Paul pulled her into a parallel aisle. The market stalls were set out on a grid system. They could check on his progress at regular intervals. Amy felt safer.

She saw her father leaning against a stall, having a cup of tea and a sandwich. They hung about round the corner near a crockery stall until its owner shooed them away.

'Did he pay for it?' Paul hissed, but they didn't know. He might have done without them seeing.

Their first stroke of luck came when he paused at a butcher's stall. Poultry, still with feathers on, hung above the front of it. But although they could get quite close, it was impossible to hear anything against the background noise of the market.

The owner came out from behind his counter to talk to him. Under his straw boater, his face didn't register any pleasure. Amy could hardly breathe for tension as she saw Pa indicate a large fowl. The butcher wrapped it up and put

139

it into a brown paper carrier bag.

'Wait for it,' Paul murmured beside her. 'Is he going to pay for it?'

This time they were both quite certain that he did not.

Alec strolled on, swinging the carrier bag, out into Market Street at the back. Amy watched him pick his way between the horses with their heads in nosebags while their carts were being unloaded on to trolleys. Then he was threading his way through the unemployed who hung about to pick up fruit and vegetables discarded by the traders because they were faded or damaged.

'We've seen enough,' she said, feeling suddenly tired of the game. 'Let's go home.'

'You'll be having chicken for dinner tomorrow,' Paul said. 'Your dad got that for nothing. I told you he was up to something.' He seemed to have more enthusiasm now for what they were doing. 'This is what I call real detective work.'

'Perhaps he did buy it.' Amy felt full of doubt again. Pa was always congratulating himself on his high ideals. 'Put it on the slate or something.'

She was very surprised when Pa didn't bring the carrier bag home, and it was roast beef for Sunday dinner after all.

Paul's appetite had been whetted. 'Let's play detectives again,' he suggested, a week or so later.

'Perhaps we're getting it all wrong,' Amy said, undecided. 'Perhaps Pa's just doing his job.'

'You said you were sure he was up to something when you didn't get chicken for dinner.'

Amy had been disappointed. 'That butcher must have asked him to deliver it to another customer somewhere on his beat. It could be as straightforward as that.'

'He picked out that chicken. You saw him choose it.'

'Then he chose it for someone else.'

'The only way we'll find out is by following him again,' Paul said victoriously.

'All right, then.'

They trailed behind him often enough to learn the different beats. They learned where the fixed line phones were too, and Amy felt a flicker of pride that Pa didn't realise they were following him.

'He goes out a lot by himself,' she said. 'After work, and he never says much about where he's been or what he's done. Except that he's going out for a drink.'

'Perhaps he is.'

'We could go and see.'

The first time Amy did it alone. She'd been playing hopscotch with Nancy and Katie on the pavement outside their house when Pa came out dressed in his moleskin trousers and Harris tweed jacket.

She could hear Fliss singing and her mother playing the piano in their front room, but she had no way of letting Paul know what she was doing. She let Pa get a hundred yards down the road and then left her sisters to follow him.

He went to the Queen's Arms on the corner of Park Road East and Conway Street. There was a group of unemployed hanging about on the pavement outside without the price of a pint, and several children waiting for their parents.

Amy caught the sharp smell of beer in her nostrils as another customer let the door slam behind him. Pa was doing exactly what he'd told Mam he was going to. She went home to play more hopscotch.

Then, a few days later, Mam sent her and Katie down to the greengrocer's on Duke Street.

As they went into the shop, Amy recognised another customer who was being served. She wore a large grey hat, and under it her grey hair was kept in place with a hairnet.

'Hello, Mrs Cottie,' Amy said, as the woman put her change into her crocodile handbag and tried to pick up several shopping bags.

'Are you two going to buy a lot?' she asked.

'Just a pound of onions for Mam.' Amy was standing

back because Katie was just learning to ask for the shopping and count out the money.

'Then I'll wait for you. I shouldn't have bought five pounds of potatoes as well as this other stuff. Too much to carry all at once.'

'We'll give you a hand.'

'Good girl, Amy. You help me and I'll give you a halfpenny to buy a few sweets between you.'

'Thank you, Mrs Cottie, but Pa says we must do it for nothing.'

'Does he now?'

'He says we must tell you it's a kind thought, but being a policeman's children we mustn't accept. We mustn't expect payment for every little job we're asked to do.'

Amy was surprised when Mrs Cottie brayed with laughter. 'That's a good one!' She guffawed until she had to dab at her eyes. 'He might tell you that, Amy, but he doesn't do it himself. He'd accept a backhander, you can bank on that.'

Amy thought about it all the way home. It seemed Mrs Cottie was saying the same thing as Paul.

Amy felt Grand National fever building up. It was the high spot of the racing year on Merseyside.

The day before the race, when school was over, Mam asked Nancy to fetch her a dozen eggs from the grocer's in Duke Street. Amy went with her and as they waited in the shop, they heard other customers holding forth about a horse called Dingley Domino that was a dead cert to win the National.

When Pa came home from work he was more jovial than usual, because he'd put half a crown in the sweep being run at the station and drawn a horse called Dingley Domino.

'It's going to win,' Nancy assured him. 'Everybody's saying so.'

'An Irish filly, jumping on top of its form,' Amy added.

He laughed at them. 'I'd like to see it.'

'So would I,' Mam said wistfully.

The next day was Grand National Day. Amy had already agreed with Paul that they would play at being detectives again.

Pa had a day off and came down to breakfast wearing his best moleskin trousers and rough tweed jacket, which meant he was going out.

He seemed in no hurry to go. He spent an age sitting round reading the paper and then putting a polish on his best shoes.

'What time d'you want your dinner?' Mam wanted to know.

'You eat when you're ready, I don't know when I'll be back. Maybe late.'

'Where you going, then?'

'I told you, I'm going racing at Aintree.'

'You never did.' Mam drew herself up indignantly.

'I'll get something to eat while I'm out.'

'That's going to cost. I could cut you some sandwiches.'

'No, there's a few going from the station, I said I'd go with them. They'll want a hot meal.'

'Lucky for some,' Mam said, with a sniff.

Amy went to her bedroom to get her coat. Mam made her hang it there to keep the hall stand tidy. She knew Paul would be watching for Pa passing his house, but it wasn't as easy for him, because he didn't know what was happening.

She was putting on her outdoor shoes when she heard the front door slam, and realised Pa had already gone. She shot out after him. If he was going to Liverpool, he'd walk down to Park Station and get the train.

She drew back from the door with a jerk. She could see Pa standing at the bus stop. Perhaps he was going into town to meet up with his friends from the police station first?

She hesitated. It hardly seemed worth following him, because why would he tell Mam he was going to Aintree if he was not? And she wouldn't be able to go anyway, she had no money for fares.

She had to make contact with Paul. They'd agreed a signal. A quick rat-a-tat on the front door knocker, then she'd scarper round to the back entry before she was spotted. But Pa would be able to see her do that from the bus stop.

She went straight to the back entry. Paul's bedroom was at the back, but she could see no sign of him at the window. She was about to give up when Paul came shooting out of his back gate.

'Your pa's getting the bus. He's going in to town.'

They ran down the entry, into the next side street, and then doubled back so they could peer round the corner into Park Road North again.

'There's two buses coming together and they're both going to Woodside,' Paul said, a quiver of excitement in his voice.

'I'm going to stop the second one and get on. I'll keep it waiting while you make a dash for it. We mustn't be seen together.'

'I've got no money.'

'I have, Dad's just given me pocket money for helping in the café.'

The first bus was crowded. Amy watched Pa climb on. Then she ran and caught the second one. Paul pulled her down on the seat nearest to the door and they both craned their necks at the bus in front.

'We'll get off where he does,' she said.

He rode all the way down to Hamilton Square. They jumped off when their own bus pulled up behind his. The crowds were thicker here, making their way to Aintree, but Amy was still scared that Pa would turn round and see them together.

They hung back, watching him stride jauntily into the underground station. They followed warily and peeped in. The crowd behind them surged forward, taking them inside, and the hot scent of the underground was in Amy's nostrils. When the crowd parted for a moment she spotted Pa near the bookstall, by a placard announcing special trains going to Aintree.

'He's meeting somebody,' Paul said.

He was advancing on a plump woman wearing a bright green costume with fancy scolloped edging and a very frilly blouse. Amy could see her smiling at him. Pa took her arm and kissed her cheek.

'Who is that?' Paul whispered.

'I don't know.' Amy was aghast.

'Have you got an auntie?'

'Only Auntie My. I've never seen this woman before.' She had a lot of yellow hair showing round her face, topped with a big green hat with artificial flowers round the brim.

'I know Mam wanted to go, so why is he taking her instead?' Amy thought of her mother. Alongside this brightly dressed woman, Mam seemed drab in her apron. 'And who can she possibly be?'

'I thought you said he was going with a party of policemen?' Paul's brown eyes were wide with amazement.

Another thought occurred to Amy. 'I wonder if Mam knows about her?'

Summer 1929

Amy was eating stew and potatoes at the living room table with the rest of her family. Dinnertime in the Siddons home was varied to suit Alec's work rota. Today it was one o'clock.

'School holidays are far too long,' Celia complained. 'I'm absolutely exhausted. Children round my feet all day. There's no peace.'

'Can't be that bad,' Alec grunted unsympathetically. 'Anyway, only another week and you'll have all day to yourself again.'

Celia sighed. 'Nancy needs new shoes. A new skirt too, she can't go to work in a gymslip. She's got to have more grown-up things now she's got a job.'

'I need new shoes myself,' Alec said. 'We could go down

145

Grange Road tomorrow and fix both of us up.'

'I've only got one pair,' Amy reminded Mam. 'I need new shoes.'

Her mother continued to eat her stew.

Amy pushed back her chair and pulled one foot up on her knee to show the sole. 'Look, there's a hole here, I can put my finger in it, and both shoes let in water.'

'For goodness' sake.' Alec frowned as he helped himself to more pickled onions. 'I can't afford to outfit everybody, not all at one time. I'm not made of money.'

'Amy can have Nancy's old ones. She's grown out of them but they're still good. Same with the gymslip.'

'What about me?' Katie wanted to know. 'I'm going back to school next week.'

Her mother rounded on her. 'Thank goodness for that.'

'I need new shoes.'

'She doesn't,' Celia told Alec impatiently. 'Her shoes are perfectly all right.'

The next morning, as soon as breakfast was cleared away, Amy watched her parents getting ready to go into town. Nancy put on her best red coat with a black velvet collar. Amy hoped she'd consider that too juvenile too, she'd always admired it.

'I want to come,' Katie said. Amy knew she didn't stand a chance because she was wearing the same dress she'd had on for the last few days. It was printed with scarlet poppies and was now none too clean.

'No,' Alec said. 'We can't be doing with you. You'll be whining the whole time for new shoes.'

'You stay here with Amy,' Celia said.

Amy intended to go out herself. 'What time's dinner?'

'One o'clock. Your pa's on afternoons.'

'If you're going out, see that you're back in time if you want any,' Pa added.

From the front window, she and Katie watched them go. Nancy was wearing her matching red hat with a turn-back brim of black velvet. She was walking between Pa and Mam, linking arms with both of them. They seemed a complete and happy family without her and Katie.

Amy turned away when they got on the bus. She'd arranged to meet Paul. He'd promised to take her for a ride on the ferry.

She was finding the long school holidays rather dull and longed to go somewhere different. Paul was always being taken on expeditions by his mother but Celia took her nowhere. She'd been very envious when Paul told her about a family trip to Morecambe.

To please her, Paul said they'd go on the ferry, that it was a lovely thing to do on a hot day. Today was not hot, it was cool and overcast, there was even a hint of rain in the air. Amy didn't care. She still wanted to go.

'I'm going out too,' she told Katie, and saw her little sister's big blue eyes fill with dismay.

'Nobody cares about me. Can't I go with you?'

Amy almost said no.

'Where are you going?'

'It's a secret. I've been planning it for ages.'

'I won't tell anybody.'

'You will, you'll let it slip out. You're too young.'

'No, Amy, I promise I won't. I don't want to stay in by myself.'

At nine years old, Amy knew the risk she was taking. The last thing she wanted was to trust little Katie with her secret.

'I'm big now. I won't say a word to Mam.'

'Or Pa, or Nancy?'

'Not even Nancy?'

'Not Nancy, not anyone. Cross your heart now.'

'I promise. I promise never to say a word to anyone.'

'I'll flatten you if you do.'

'I won't, Amy.'

'And I'll never let you into any more secrets as long as I live.'

'I've promised, haven't I?'

'Get your money box and a knife. It costs money.'

Katie brought it down from their bedroom an instant later. 'Where are we going?'

'On the bus to Woodside.' She saw Katie's eyes widen with pleasure and amazement.

'But Mam doesn't pay for me on the bus. I still look under school age.'

'Then we're going on the ferry. We'll have to have the money ready, you might have to pay for that.'

'I'm not supposed to spend this. What will Mam say?'

'You promised not to tell her.' Amy looked at her sister doubtfully.

'Mam knows I've got threepence, Amy. I'm saving up for a doll like Nancy's.'

'If she asks, tell her I took twopence out of your money box and we spent it.'

'On sweets?'

'If you like.' Amy fiddled the knife into the slot until she managed to withdraw two pennies. 'Get your coat,' she said. 'It's time we went. We're meeting Paul.'

'Cousin Paul, who we mustn't speak to?'

'Yes, I speak to him, but you mustn't say his name. It mustn't pass your lips in this house. You promised now.'

'Is this your secret?'

'Yes, and you mustn't breathe a word of it, or Pa will kill me.'

'I won't. Will he kill me too?'

'Yes, if he knows Paul's taken you out.'

'But where is he?'

'He'll meet us. His dad takes him down to his café with him. He helps him for a few hours but he says he can go when he wants to.'

The Refreshment Room stood on a cramped site to the left of the ferry buildings. The front windows had misted up and Amy could see no sign of Paul. She went warily into the narrow entry towards the kitchen door, ready to duck and run at the first sight of an adult.

Paul was washing up at the sink in front of the window. He signalled that he'd seen her and she ran back to where she'd left Katie and grabbed her hand. Giving the front of the building a wide berth, she took Katie into the ferry building. A few minutes later, Paul joined them. He frowned at Katie.

'You didn't say you were bringing her. She wasn't part of the plan.'

Amy watched Katie's face crumple, and knew she was afraid of being left behind now.

'I had to bring her. Mam left her with me. She won't be any trouble, will you, Katie?'

Katie was shaking her head so vigorously her dark curls danced.

'I suppose it's all right.' Paul led the way through the turnstiles. He'd been on the ferry lots of times with his mother. Half fare for children was a penny each. Amy pressed a coin into Katie's hand and they each paid for themselves.

'Doesn't it smell wonderful?' Amy laughed. 'Disinfectant and wood, old rope and tar.'

The ferry boat *Upton* was just coming alongside the floating landing stage when they reached it. Amy felt a surge of anticipation.

'This is lovely, a wonderful secret.' Katie was jumping up and down with excitement.

It was a mild grey morning without wind. The Liverpool waterfront was hazy in the pearly mist, and out to the Irish Sea was the dark bulk of a trans-Atlantic liner. A foghorn echoed eerily from upriver. White seagulls whirled in their wake.

Amy gloried in the boat. Under Paul's direction they explored every inch of it. They sat in the saloon for a short time and smelled the hot oil from the engine room.

Amy liked it best on the top deck overlooking the bow. She clung to the rail and looked down at the flat, oily waters of the Mersey creaming along the sides of the boat. She could see the tide running in fluttering currents. There was the taste of salt on her lips.

'All the seats on this deck float if the boat sinks,' Paul told them. 'They're life rafts too.'

'Will it sink?' Katie asked anxiously.

'Not today.'

There were lots of ships to watch on the river. The ten-minute journey to Liverpool was over much too quickly to please any of them.

They got off and walked along the St George's landing stage, then up to the pier head, where there were twice as many trams and buses as on the other side of the river.

'It's the boat ride I like,' Amy sighed happily. She could see another ferry coming over, and they queued up and caught it back to Birkenhead. Standing against the rail, Paul pointed out landmarks on the south bank.

When it was edging alongside the landing stage and the passengers were standing up ready to disembark, Katie said: 'I don't want it to be over yet. I like riding on the boat.'

Amy looked at Paul; she liked it too. But they had no more money.

'We could hide,' Paul suggested. 'I've thought about how to do it, when I've been with Mam. The only place passengers pay is going through the turnstiles at Woodside. If we don't go through, we can go backwards and forwards as often as we like.'

'Let's try it,' Amy said, taking Katie's hand. 'Where can we hide?'

'On the seaward side. Behind those seats. Crouch down on deck so we can't be seen. Nobody comes to look.' With Katie between them they squeezed between the ship's rail and the seat. Amy huddled low, feeling very daring.

Katie giggled. 'Ssh,' Paul warned as the gangways came rattling down to crash on the lower deck and the passengers pushed their way off.

Further upriver a ship hooted and a little coaster chugged past on its way out to sea, black smoke curling from its tall, thin funnel. It was all very exciting.

As soon as all the passengers had disembarked, others started coming on.

'Sit on the seat,' Paul commanded. 'They're coming up on top, and we don't want to look suspicious. Keep your heads below the backrest for a bit.'

'It's easy,' Katie crowed as the boat cast off for another round trip. Amy grinned at Paul. It was.

'We'll do it again and again, until we've had enough,' Paul whispered. 'This is smashing.'

Amy laughed out loud. It was wonderful. They were just starting on their fifth round trip when she heard the one o'clock gun being fired. For almost two hundred years it had been the traditional time signal to shipping on the Mersey, and it could be heard all over Birkenhead and Liverpool.

She straightened up from the rail in dismay. 'We're supposed to be home for dinner at one o'clock. I forgot about the time.'

Katie pulled a face: 'Pa will be cross if we're late.'

'We'll be very, very late. He'll tell Mam not to keep any for us. Probably eat it all himself.'

'Will she let him do that?' Paul asked.

'He does whatever he wants. He leaves for work about quarter past two. We won't go home until he's gone.'

'I'm hungry,' Katie said. Amy felt empty herself now she'd thought of food.

'It's a pity you can't come to the Refreshment Room and eat a proper dinner like you used to,' Paul said angrily. 'It's this silly feud. I'll get a few sandwiches and bring them out to you. Dad won't mind, he'll think they're for me.'

The sun broke through the grey clouds at last, and it felt warm. Katie was running from one side of the deck to the other. She took her coat off because she was hot.

Amy watched the ferry come alongside the Woodside

151

floating landing stage for the last time, and they got off as soon as the gangways were in position. The need for food was driving them now. They went through the turnstiles and Paul said: 'You two wait here, in the ferry building. I'll try and get you something to eat.'

She watched him hurry away. They examined the two machines with chocolate bars inside and looked at all the posters. It was draughty waiting in the doorway and the sun had gone in again. Paul was taking longer than Amy had expected. Beside her, Katie shivered. Amy noticed then the scarlet poppies on her dress.

'Where's your coat!' Her voice was sharp with anxiety.

She watched Katie's face screw up in alarm. She was almost in tears. 'Oh gosh! I've left it on the boat.'

Amy dragged Katie back to the turnstile. Should she leave her here alone and run back to the boat? But she hadn't even one spare penny; she needed what she had left for the bus. If she went back to the boat, they'd have to walk home from here and it was a long way. There was no guarantee that the boat would still be waiting either; Amy thought she could hear it casting off. It could be halfway to Liverpool by now.

'It's only your old coat,' she said. 'The one you play out in.'

'What's Mam going to say?' Katie began to cry.

'It's been mine and Nancy's. It was nearly worn out. Don't worry about it. Look, here's Paul coming back.' He was holding a bottle of pop with a straw in it and had some sandwiches in a paper napkin.

'We can't stay here,' he hissed urgently. 'Come on, over to the railway station. Mam's in the Refreshment Room. She's taking Fliss over to Liverpool shopping. I don't want her to see us together. 'Specially not sharing these sandwiches.'

Amy felt ravenous; she was almost dragging little Katie. Paul found an empty seat in the station and she was able at last to sink her teeth into a ham sandwich.

'I ate some chips while I was in there. These are for you, and I've got you a pork pie each as well.' He was fishing the food out of his pockets as he spoke.

Amy felt better now she'd had something to eat. Even Katie cheered up as they watched a train getting up steam before setting off to London.

'What are we going to do now?' Paul wanted to know. 'Shall we trail your pa again, since we're in town?'

Amy couldn't think of anything else. Neither she nor Katie wanted to go home just yet. 'He won't start till three o'clock.'

When she turned round to look at the big station clock she saw that it was already twenty minutes to.

'By the time we walk up to the police station,' Paul said, 'we'll not have long to wait.'

They climbed the hill slowly, stopping to drink water from the ornamental drinking fountain on the way.

Pa was coming down Hamilton Street from the station, stepping out ponderously. They waited the other side of the Town Hall to let him get on his way.

'He'll see us.' Katie hung back, afraid. 'He'll half kill us.'

'Not if we're careful. We've done it before and he didn't even know.' Amy took her hand. 'You do what I do. We'd make good detectives when we're grown up,' she giggled to Paul.

'I would. Girls can't be detectives. I asked Uncle Alec once, he said girls can work in the office but they don't do proper police work.'

Amy sniffed. 'I'm beginning to find this game a bit of a bore.'

'We're learning our way round town, aren't we?' Paul jabbed her in the ribs. 'Better than just playing in the park.'

They were on their way up Argyle Street South when pa came to his first check-in and stopped. They watched him from round an adjacent corner. As soon as he put the phone back and started locking up the little box, Amy could see that something was different. His movements had more purpose.

It came as a shock to find him coming rapidly towards them instead of continuing on his beat. She fled, panic-stricken, dragging Katie with her. Paul passed them, his feet pounding on the pavement. Fifty yards from the corner, outside a public house, beer was being unloaded from a dray. With that and two carthorses to shield them from view, they saw Pa briskly crossing the road without a glance in their direction.

They ran back then, afraid that they had lost him, but Alec's height and uniform made him easy to pick out. He was heading towards Grange Road, the main shopping street.

'Something must have happened,' Amy breathed, 'to make him double back like this.'

Soon it became obvious: a small crowd was gathering on the pavement outside Martin's the jewellers.

'They've had a break-in,' Paul breathed.

'A brick through the window,' a woman with two loaded shopping bags told them, excitedly. 'I saw them do it. Grabbed handfuls of stuff and then scarpered. All over in a minute.'

'Got away, they have.'

Shoppers were hanging about to see the outcome. Amy watched from further down the road, feeling safer in the crowd.

'Your pa's just making sure nobody pinches anything else.'

Amy could see him standing in front of the broken window, feet apart, shoulders back, a stance she recognised only too well. Other policemen were arriving and going into the shop.

'We're not going to know what happens next,' Amy mourned. 'I'd love to go in and hear what the jeweller is saying about it.'

'Let's go,' Paul said. 'Your pa's got nothing else to do

but look about him. Wouldn't do to be seen, not together like this.'

'This is real police work,' Amy breathed. 'It is interesting when something happens. Pa's doing a good job, guarding what's left in that window display.'

Paul put his hand on her arm. 'Your dad's moving people along. Come on, we don't want him to see us.'

Amy saw Katie shoot off in a swirl of scarlet poppies, and when Pa's voice blared out loud as a foghorn, she realised they'd caught his eye too.

'Katie! What are you two doing here? You've no business . . .'

Amy felt rooted to the spot, and went hot then cold. Pa's malevolent eyes were picking her out in the crowd, burning like two angry fires.

CHAPTER TEN

'Amy, who said you could come into town?' Pa bellowed across the street, his words audible to all. 'And bringing Kate down here? You should have more sense. She'll get run over if you don't watch out.'

Amy couldn't move. This was a disaster, Pa finding out what they were up to.

'Your mam will be looking for you. Get yourselves off home, this minute.'

The taste of terror was on her tongue. She could see his face turning puce.

'Wait till I get home, I'll give you what for. I'll tan the hide off the pair of you.'

Amy looked for Paul, but he was nowhere in sight. She didn't know whether to be glad or sorry. She could feel Katie cowering against her and felt for her hand. The next instant, the little girl was clinging to her, crying noisily. Amy felt the eyes of the crowd on them.

'Better do as he says and take your little sister home, love,' a woman told her. Amy fled, her face wet with tears of terror, dragging Katie with her.

She pushed through the crowd and had left it well behind when she heard Paul's voice calling her name. She slowed to a brisk walk. He caught her up.

'I'm in the most awful trouble,' she sobbed. 'We didn't go home for dinner and we've lost Katie's coat. Now Pa's seen us watching him.'

'No, Amy.'

'He'll thrash us,' Katie added, between choking sobs.

'No, he thinks he caught you looking round the shops, that's all,' Paul insisted.

'You're sure?' Amy couldn't think straight.

'Certain, and he didn't see me with you. He doesn't know everything.'

'If he knew all the things we've seen him do . . .' Amy shuddered. 'Him taking another woman out.'

'He won't even think of it,' Paul comforted.

'I don't want to go home,' Katie cried. 'I'm never going home.'

'We'll have to, sometime,' Amy told her. They were heading back to Woodside where they could catch the bus.

'It's starting to rain. I'm getting wet.'

Amy opened her own coat and pulled Katie closer, wrapping it round her shoulders.

'What'll Mam do to us? She'll be awfully cross.'

'Probably send us to bed without any tea, to punish us.'

That made Amy cry louder. 'I'm hungry again.'

Amy had a terrible sinking feeling. She was tired now and wanted to get home but she was scared of going. Katie was shivering and the rain was making her thin dress cling to her small body.

'I can get you more food from the café,' Paul soothed. 'Come on, let's run, the rain's getting heavier.'

It was coming down in sheets by the time they reached the Refreshment Room.

'Dad's not here,' Paul said. 'His van's gone.'

'I'd love some chips,' Amy said, as the scent of cooking food reached her. 'Shall we wait in the ferry building?'

Paul was looking at Katie's bedraggled frock. 'Stay in the entry for a minute. The café's slack at this time. Vera will be on her own. I might be able to let you in through the kitchen door. It's always warm, and there's places to hide. Perhaps I can get you something hot to eat.'

'Chips?' Katie asked.

'Maybe.'

Amy stood in the entry, feeling Katie shiver. After a few minutes the kitchen door opened and Paul was beckoning them in. Once inside, warmth enveloped them. Katie came out from under her coat. Amy shook the rain off it.

'In here.' Paul bundled them into a small room. There were sacks of flour and sugar, and shelves laden with tins of custard powder, jams and jellies. They sat together on some unopened sacks.

It seemed only moments before Paul was back with two plates piled high with sausage, black pudding, bacon and chips.

'Chips have been waiting a bit too long,' he apologised, bringing them cutlery and tomato sauce. 'It's what's left over.'

'It's all hot,' Amy breathed. Nothing had ever tasted better. She could hear Paul washing up at the kitchen sink and felt reasonably safe. Katie was eating as though it was the first food she'd had all day.

Paul came back with two plates of spotted dick and custard. 'Vera says Dad's coming back to cash up, about half four,' he told her. 'You'd better eat that up and go before he gets here.'

It seemed that Paul had barely had time to slide their plates into his washing-up water before they heard a van backing up the entry. Paul, suddenly agitated, put his head round the door of their storeroom.

'Dad's here,' he hissed. 'Keep quiet.' He snatched Katie's spoon from her hand and pushed it at Amy. 'I'll let you out when the coast's clear.'

Then the door snapped shut and the light went out. There were two gratings above the top shelf that let a little grey light into their hiding place.

'It's all right,' Amy whispered to Katie and after a moment or two, as her eyes grew accustomed to the dark, she could see her eating her pudding with her fingers.

It was more difficult to hear anything now the door was closed. Once, Amy heard Jack Laidlaw's voice and she thought she heard the back door slam. Even Katie heard the key turning in their storeroom door. It made her clutch at Amy's coat for comfort. Amy thought she heard the van drive off, but she wasn't sure. Then there was silence.

'What are we going to do?' Katie beseeched her.

'Wait for Paul. He'll come back and let us out.'

They settled down on the soft sacks and very soon Katie fell asleep.

Amy was even more scared of going home now. Goodness knows how late they were going to be. Good thing Pa wasn't going to be home until after eleven. As if they weren't in enough trouble without this.

It had been a dark, damp afternoon. Celia Siddons had dozed off on the chair in front of the fire she'd lit in the living room. She hadn't meant to rest, but after a morning spent trailing round the shops with Alec and Nancy, she'd just drifted off.

When she'd woken up she'd made a cup of tea. Nancy had come down from her bedroom and they'd both listened to a play on the wireless. Ever since she was small, Nancy had liked sitting on a cushion at her feet and resting her head against her mother's knee. Celia ran her fingers through her daughter's silky brown curls from time to time. This was how she liked things to be. Just her and Nancy.

Children's hour came on, and by then she felt mesmerised. Arthur Ransome's books had been a firm favourite with Nancy all through her childhood, and her attention was still captivated at fourteen. Celia relaxed and closed her eyes again. The six o'clock news came after that. They listened to most of it, though Nancy was growing more restless. 'What are we having for our tea?'

'A boiled egg each?' Celia suggested. 'You can make us some toast.'

She liked Alec to work the afternoon shift. It meant she had time to herself and she didn't have to cook another meal. It would be after eleven when he came in. He wouldn't go to bed on an empty stomach, but all she'd need to do was cut him a sandwich and fill a flask with tea before she went to bed.

Hopefully, she'd be asleep before he got in. She put two eggs on to boil, and after a moment's deliberation put two more in the pan for Alec's sandwiches. She could hear Nancy spreading the cloth on the living room table and setting out plates and cutlery.

'Put the apple pie on the table, Nancy, and the sponge cake,' she called.

When she looked up, Nancy was standing in the kitchen doorway, frowning.

'Mam, where's Amy? And Katie?'

Celia straightened up against the stove. She hadn't given them a thought since dinnertime. She'd been cross with Amy then when she hadn't come home. Now she felt the first niggle of concern.

'It was at breakfast,' Nancy said slowly, 'when we last saw them.'

'They'll be playing somewhere,' Celia said, trying to shut out the feeling of guilt that was rising in her. 'Not outside in all this rain.'

'At Patsy Bream's?' Nancy suggested. 'Amy goes to her house sometimes.'

'Put your coat on and go and see,' Celia said. 'And if she's not there, there's that other girl from Aspinall Street who's always calling round here.'

'Jean Hersey. I'll try her house too.'

When she'd gone, Celia turned out the gas under the eggs and went upstairs to the room Amy and Katie shared. It wasn't very tidy but the blankets had been pulled straight on the bed as she insisted they must. She could see nothing unusual. None of their clothes had gone. She'd been silly to

160

even think they might have run away.

No, everything was in its place. They were wearing their play clothes. She counted up the hours since she'd last seen them. More than nine. She couldn't believe that in all that time she'd hardly given them a thought. Now she felt a frisson of alarm.

She couldn't sit down. She backed up the fire, fiddled with the tablecloth. Cut two slices of bread.

She was listening for Nancy. At last she heard her running up the yard. She knew she was alone before she opened the back door. Her heart lurched sickeningly.

What was Alec going to say? They were troublemakers, those two. For the first time ever, she wished Alec was at home. She felt helpless, but he'd know what to do next.

Amy was woken by the scrape of the key turning in the lock. She felt stiff and uncomfortable and was blinking in the sudden light. Paul's face came round the door white with anxiety.

'I'm sorry, Amy, I'm sorry. Dad came back early and started switching everything off and locking up.'

'It's all right.'

'I nearly told him he'd locked you in the storeroom, but I hesitated and somehow it was too late then. He took me home in his van but he had the keys in his pocket. I had to wait my chance to get them. I know I've been ages.'

'I've been to sleep. What time is it?' Amy yawned and rubbed her eyes.

'Half past eight. Mam had tea ready and I had to sit down and eat it. I was on tenterhooks the whole time.'

'We'll still be able to get home before Pa.'

'I didn't know whether I should go round to your house. Tell your mother you were all right. She'll be worried stiff.'

'I hope you didn't? She'll tell Pa.'

'No, I knew that would get you into more trouble. It's this stupid feud. Dad could have taken you home if it hadn't been

161

for that. It was only when he decided to take us all to the music hall and went up to change that I was able to take the café keys from his pocket. I had to pretend I didn't want to go.'

Amy giggled. 'Poor Paul, you missed a treat.'

He laughed too. 'I had visions of you being stuck here all night.'

'It's Sunday tomorrow and you don't open. I did think of that.'

'Dad usually comes for an hour or so to check the stores for re-ordering, and a woman comes to give the place a thorough clean. You'd have been found.'

Amy shook Katie awake. The little girl didn't know where she was and started to cry again when she remembered the dire trouble they were in.

Paul buttoned her into a coat of his sister's that he'd brought.

'It's lovely,' she said. 'Better than the one I've lost.'

'You can't keep it,' he said, as he locked up carefully behind them. 'It's still raining. I brought it so you wouldn't be cold.' They sat on the bus for ages before it pulled away from the terminus.

'Your mam will be tearing her hair,' Paul said. Amy didn't want to be reminded.

It was gone nine o'clock when they got off the bus. At the back gate, she stripped Fliss's coat off Katie and handed it back to Paul.

Amy was filled with dread as she walked up the yard, holding Katie's hand tight in hers. As they went into the kitchen, the house seemed unusually quiet.

'Mam?' she called.

The living room was empty too and a half-eaten meal remained on the table. Amy's heart sank. It showed Mam's state of mind that she hadn't cleared away before going out. She always insisted on doing that immediately. The fire had died away too.

'They're out looking for us, Katie. Best thing is to go to bed straight away.' Katie was folding up anyway, it was past her bedtime.

'Mam even forgot to lock the back door; she must be in a fearful tizz. Just as well, or we'd have had to wait in the shed.'

Amy draped her wet coat over the kitchen table where it would be seen straight away, and kicked off her wet shoes in the doorway where Nancy would surely fall over them.

She had to help Katie undress, she was nearly out on her feet. It was always Amy's job to see that Katie washed herself properly and cleaned her teeth before climbing into the double bed they shared, but she'd never known a bedtime as bad as this.

They huddled together. Katie felt cold but she was soon soundly asleep. Amy lay awake in the darkness, too scared to relax. Surely there weren't many places Mam could look for her and Katie? She couldn't think what could be keeping them so long.

Just when she was beginning to feel drowsy, she heard the front door open and voices in the hall. Amy slid out of bed, felt for her slippers and went down to get it over with.

'They're home,' she heard Nancy say before they saw her coming slowly downstairs in her flannelette nightie. Mam's face was working with rage as she came closer.

'Where the hell have you been until now?' Mam's hand came slicing at her face. The blow jolted her sideways, stinging her cheek.

She'd never seen Mam thunderous like this before, but she could see her shaking with fear too. Behind her Nancy was aghast.

It hurt to speak. 'I'm sorry, Mam.'

'So you should be. I've been out of my mind. Have you no consideration for anybody?'

Nancy hurled herself at Amy then, throwing her arms round her warmly, half crying with relief.

'Thank goodness you're back safe and sound. And Katie too?'

'Yes, she's all right.'

'You'd no business taking her with you.' Mam had slumped against the hall stand, her head in her hands.

'I'm sorry, Mam.'

'Where have you been?'

Amy could only shake her head numbly.

'Your pa will have to deal with you when he gets home. I've got a raging headache. You make me ill.'

'A cup of tea?' Nancy suggested. 'For us all.'

'Not for her! She doesn't deserve it. Go back to bed, Amy. It upsets me just to look at you.'

'Mam, I'm sorry to cause . . .'

'Do you know where me and Nancy have been?' Mam's face was frightening now, ugly with rage and anguish.

Amy shook her head in despair.

'Down to the police station to report you missing. You wicked girl!'

Amy gasped as she realised the full awfulness of that. Mam had reported her missing to the police, when Pa had seen them in the afternoon.

'Wait till your pa comes home. He'll deal with you then.'

Amy ran back to bed to lie there cold and quaking. Katie had woken up, and clung to her for comfort. After a little while they heard Nancy creep up to bed, then Mam's loving murmurs coming from the little bedroom Nancy had to herself. Mam always spent ages saying good night to her.

Both Amy and Katie knew that Mam loved Nancy more. They'd seen the way she touched Nancy, kissed Nancy, smiled at Nancy. They knew she and Pa indulged every whim Nancy had, favouring her in every way.

Tonight, Katie pulled the blankets over her head, to shut Mam's whispers out. Normally Mam would come to their bedroom door and say, 'You're in bed at last? Good night, girls,' and click off the light. There were never kisses for them. Tonight, she didn't even come near their room. Katie pushed the blankets away from her face.

'Why doesn't Mam love us?'

'She doesn't love me because I'm naughty,' Amy whispered. She knew she'd been a difficult and devious child. Both Mam and Pa had told her that. She knew she threw tantrums, she couldn't stop herself. She knew this made Mam angry and more likely to slap her than kiss her.

Everybody expected her to be difficult, so if she wasn't happy with things, she was. It had made her grow up with a determination to get what she wanted from life. Her wants were more desperate than Nancy's. She'd been disappointed more often.

'Nancy loves us,' Amy comforted. When she was behaving badly, Nancy would come and put her arms round her. Nancy seemed full of love and always shared the treats she was given between the three of them without being asked. Nancy was never stinting; nobody could feel jealous of her.

Five years younger, Amy had trailed behind her through early childhood. More recently, she'd fought Nancy's battles at school as well as her own. Nancy never felt the need to fight for anything. What she wanted was always given to her.

Katie dozed, but Amy was still awake when Pa came home. She heard Mam meet him in the hall, then Pa was making a noise like a raging bull. She closed her eyes, waiting for him to come up, but he didn't. Instead she heard the front door slam as he went out again. She was stiff with tension as she realised he'd gone to ring in to tell the police that she and Katie were safe.

The waiting seemed endless but his heavy footfall sounded on the stairs at last. When he switched on the central light in their bedroom, he was icy with rage. Amy wanted to pull the bedclothes over her head.

'Get up,' he shouted. 'The trouble you've put us to.' She could see the strap in his hand. He flicked it threateningly. 'Right, I want to know what you were doing in town?'

'Just looking round, Pa.' Paul was right, he didn't know they'd been following him.

'Until nine o'clock at night?' The disbelief in his voice was unmistakable. 'In the pouring rain?'

'We went to Liverpool, too, on the ferry.' Amy had decided that was the best part to own up to.

'Liverpool! You could have got lost there, anything.'

'We didn't go to the shops, just back and forth on the ferry a few times.'

'Without paying the proper fare?' The strap swung down to bite into her legs. The flannelette did nothing to cushion it.

'How many times do I have to tell you? Honesty is expected of me and my family. You bring disgrace on me when you do things like that.'

'I'm sorry, Pa.'

'You took Katie out without a coat. She could catch pneumonia from walking round in the rain all day. You had no business to take her at all.'

'Katie wanted to come.'

'She won't want to again, not when I've had a go at her. It's no good pretending to be asleep, young lady. You're going to stand up and take your medicine too.'

The strap flicked through the air and landed on Amy's legs again. She winced.

'All the trouble you've caused. You know your mam went down to the station and reported you missing? She was beside herself. The desk sergeant put out a call. You had the whole Birkenhead force looking for you. What a waste of time and public money. It's about time you had a bit of discipline.'

The strap continued to whistle through the air to slash her legs.

'If it was up to me I wouldn't let you out of the door again for a week, but that would punish your mother too. Give her more of a headache because you get on her nerves. It'll take

166

her a bit to get over this. All the worry you've given her.'

Amy was praying for the strap to stop; her legs felt raw.

'You're never to miss another meal. Is that clear? I'll thrash you to within an inch of your life if there's any more trouble like this.'

'I won't, Pa, I promise.'

'Causing trouble at work for me. I'm a policeman, for heaven's sake, and I've got problem children. I don't want it said I've no control over the likes of you.'

He was lifting Amy up by her nightdress until his face was three inches from her own. He was so livid with rage she couldn't look at him.

'You're not to get on a bus, tram, ferry or train without prior permission. You're forbidden to go into town at all. You're a damn nuisance, always have been. But I'm having no more of it. Is that clear?'

To drive it home, Pa brought the strap against her legs with all his strength a few more times. Amy could stand no more and started to scream.

He started on Katie then. Amy pulled her pillow over her head to shut out Katie's screams, but her punishment was over much more quickly.

She clung to Katie for what seemed hours after that. Neither of them could get to sleep again. Their legs hurt too much.

Pa didn't allow them to sleep in the next morning. He was at their bedroom door, still sounding angry, telling them what to expect if they weren't down for breakfast in ten minutes. Amy's legs felt stiff and sore. At the table, the atmosphere was terrible. Mam pushed bread and marmalade at her without speaking.

'Am I allowed out this morning, please?' Amy wanted to know as soon as she'd helped wash the breakfast dishes. She felt she had to get away from them.

'Where are you planning to go?'

'To the park, Pa.'

'You're not to take Kate. She's to stay with Nancy,' he told her. 'Yes, you go. We can all do without your company this morning. You're not to go into town, and you're to be back in time for dinner.'

Nancy whispered that Amy could borrow her fairy cycle if she wanted it. Nancy had lost interest in it, she was hoping for a full-size bike for her next birthday.

'Thanks,' she whispered gratefully. It was Sunday and a fine morning. She'd go for a ride round the park to cheer herself up.

As she wheeled the fairy cycle out of the shed, she could hear Paul in his own yard. She pushed the bike into the entry, closed the back gate and tapped on Paul's as she passed. He followed her to the park where she told him what had happened and showed him the scarlet weals on her legs, two of which were still bleeding.

'Amy, they're terrible! He's a brute to do this to you.'

'My legs feel stiff, it hurts to pedal.'

'My dad never canes me.'

They rode round Park Drive. Amy sat on the seat holding her feet wide, while Paul pedalled standing up. Soon, they realised they had a puncture in the back tyre.

When they looked closely, Paul pointed out the head of a nail deeply embedded in it.

'We'll have to walk home,' he said.

Amy pushed her fingers through her dark wiry hair in despair. 'Pa will be cross. He hates mending punctures. Complains even when Nancy gets them.'

'We'll fix it,' Paul said. 'I know how. Do you have a repair outfit?'

'Pa keeps that sort of thing in our shed, but you can't come to our yard. Pa's on afternoons, he'll probably be at home now. Can't upset him again. He'll be livid if he sees us together.'

'I don't tell my mother I'm out playing with you, but I

think she guesses,' Paul said. 'Dad explained to me that it would be wiser if I didn't.'

'So where can we mend Nancy's bike?'

'I'll go round to Billy Owen's and see if he'll let us do it in his yard. You go home and get the puncture outfit first.'

Amy let herself quietly into her own back yard. Washing that hadn't dried yesterday flapped on the line, obscuring the view from the living room window. She opened the shed door, went in, and pulled it closed behind her.

The shed seemed airless on this early autumn morning, the window almost opaque with dust and cobwebs. A pile of rusting paint tins occupied one corner, a stepladder another. Her father's big heavy bike leaned against one wall. Above it were three shelves; every inch of each was covered with domestic oddments.

She knew exactly what she was looking for. A small orange oblong tin, containing rubber patches, rubber glue and French chalk. Pa also had two levers for taking the tyre off if she could find them; if not, Paul might be able to manage with dessert spoons. Only it was harder to borrow those from somebody else's house.

Amy sorted through used and hardening paint brushes, sheets of half-used sandpaper, a hammer and a saw, a broken bicycle pump. There were some screws in a jam jar. Her foot encountered other jam jars in a cardboard box on the floor.

She remembered helping Nancy to pack them. They'd meant to take them back to the grocer, who allowed them a halfpenny for each. Mam had seen them doing it and stopped their fund-raising expedition. She'd said she wanted them for when she made jam and pickles.

There was something small wrapped in newspaper, pushed behind the plunger they used for unstopping the kitchen sink. Amy pulled it out. There seemed to be two smallish boxes inside the parcel. She unwrapped it to see what they were.

Suddenly her heart was pounding in her throat. She was holding two expensive black leather boxes. She prised one open. Inside, on black velvet, a bejewelled watch sparkled in the dim light. Gold and diamonds, on a very pretty gold bracelet. Printed on the inside of the lid in gold lettering was the name and address of Martin's the jewellers.

Amy felt she was choking. She looked inside the other box: it contained a necklace of gold and pearls.

She knew immediately where they'd come from. Her dad had taken them when he was guarding the shop after the robbery. This was proof. Paul was right. Her father was a bent copper.

Yet only last night he'd called Amy wicked, complained she was letting him down by not paying on the ferry. And all the time he was thieving. Really thieving. If she had been in any doubt, the newspaper they'd been wrapped in bore yesterday's date.

She was shaking with terror. If Pa came out and found her looking at these things, he'd half kill her. She wrapped the boxes up again, hoping they looked as though they hadn't been touched.

She had to get out of the shed before he came. She was searching madly then for the puncture outfit, and managed to put her hand on it after only a minute. Cautiously then, she opened the shed door to see if the coast was clear.

The washing still flapped gently in the breeze. From the open kitchen door she could hear martial music coming from the wireless. Amy slid quietly back out to the entry. With the back gate shut behind her, she took to her heels and ran. Impossible now to believe what she'd seen. It was the most beautiful watch in the world.

Mentally, she compared it to the chromium-plated watch on a moire strap that her mam wore. Brown metal showed where the chromium was wearing off. Mam complained it didn't keep good time.

Amy wondered if Pa was keeping the watch she'd just seen for Mam's birthday present. She wondered how he dared do such a thing. He always said he wanted to sleep well at night with an easy conscience. But his conscience shouldn't be easy.

Pa's high ideals were just a front. She thought him very lucky indeed to get away with all the bad things he did. She didn't have luck like that. She was usually found out.

BOOK THREE
1939

CHAPTER ELEVEN

August 1939

Katie and Jimmy no longer met every day at the lake. He said it was no fun while she had the children with her. 'Especially Bernard. It'll be different when he goes back to school.'

Katie wanted to see him, but she knew Jimmy was right.

'Who is that man?' Bernard had asked several times. His piping voice seemed to carry all over the house. She didn't want his parents to hear.

'Nobody important.'

'We see him every day. He walks with us.'

'Not every day, just some days.'

'He always talks to you.'

Katie felt shaken; this would certainly cause her employers to question her.

'It's just someone who says hello to us because he sees us often in the park,' she choked.

'He brings bread for us to feed the ducks.'

'He's only being kind, because he likes you.'

Arthur Brent was the sort of father who lifted his children on his knee every evening to discuss the events of the day with them.

'What did you do at school today, Bernard? Did Katie take you to feed the ducks?'

Katie listened to the boy's replies with bated breath. She was afraid that sooner or later, Bernard would tell his father she was meeting Jimmy. Arthur Brent had strict views about followers. Besides, he'd think she wasn't paying enough attention to his boys.

She continued to take the boys to the park, but if they met Jimmy it was as though by chance. Sometimes there was a game on the cricket field and they would sit on the grass to watch and Jimmy would come across them. The children soon got bored with cricket.

It scared her when Jimmy sometimes called it off. 'I'm going down to Cavendish Wharf to see about a job,' he'd say. Or, 'I hear they're taking on workers in the Wallasey docks.'

Katie felt she had to go on meeting Jimmy despite the risks. Another fear was growing in her, that he wasn't trying as hard as he made out to get a job. All the papers said jobs were getting easier to find as the country mobilised for war.

Katie shivered. She didn't think deeply about war: there was nothing she could do to prevent it coming, and her own problems were crowding it out. The summer was ending with threatening dark clouds.

Alec sat at a desk in the main office, scowling down at the paperwork he had to do. It was all such deadly routine stuff. Milk tickets stolen from a doorstep. A few packets of cigarettes stolen from an automatic machine in a shop doorway. He was fed up with the job and all the overtime he was expected to work. Nothing was going his way.

He knew he was feeling more sour than usual this morning. Last night he'd gone to see Freda. He'd been going every week or so for the past couple of years. She'd been a very obliging girlfriend.

'I've put it about the neighbours that you're my brother,' she'd laughed with her mouth open, showing her bad teeth. 'Next door wanted to know why a copper was calling so often. Bob says you'll get him a bad name.'

'Course I won't. It's a good thing to have a policeman in the family. Make you seem respectable.'

Freda lived in one of the small streets behind the Town

Hall, which was handy for the central police station but difficult if he was supposed to be covering a beat on the other side of town.

If he thought he could get away with it, there was no better way of passing the odd hour on a wet day than going to Freda's, but mostly he went when he came off duty at eleven. Sometimes before he went on at eleven.

He fancied Freda. She was thirty-three but looked younger when she dressed herself up. Her figure was well fleshed out and she had good legs, but her blonde hair came from a bottle and she didn't do it often enough to keep the roots from looking black.

She was a bit of a tart – even the kindest would have to say that – but a good-hearted tart. He wasn't too keen on Bob, her husband, but Freda knew how to give a man a good time when she wanted to.

'I was hoping you'd come tonight,' she'd said, as soon as she saw him on the step. She rushed him into her untidy living room. The welcome was giving Alec a feeling of warmth until he saw her face twisting with anxiety.

'Bob's in a bit of bother again. He said to tell you he needs help.'

That pulled him up short. 'What's happened?'

'He got caught doing a shop in Grange Road West last night. He was with Ned Morris. They were taken to Slatey Road station.'

Alec felt his confidence lurch. 'Slatey Road? I can't do anything for him. Only on my patch here. Bob knows that.'

'But you've got to. With his record he could go to prison.'

Alec tried to think. 'What sort of a shop?'

'Coins and stamps specialist. For collectors. Menzies, you know the place?'

He nodded. 'What happened?'

She sighed. 'Ned knows another dealer. He had a customer for some special stamps. They went in and asked for them. When the shopkeeper handed them over for them to see, they walked out with them. That's all.'

Alec stared down at her.

'Well, Bob snatched a frame displaying coins too.'

'How were they caught?'

The shopkeeper let out a yell and this fellow was just coming in. He stopped them. Rotten luck, wasn't it?'

'A *policeman* was just going in? They were caught red-handed, with the stuff on them?'

'Yes.'

'Do you know his name? The name of the policeman?'

Freda was searching behind the clock on her mantelpiece. She found an envelope. 'Bob wrote it down for you. Sergeant Birtwhistle.'

Alec felt a cold shiver run down his spine. 'I can't do anything.'

'But last time you got him off.'

'I was the arresting officer then. It was just a question of not disclosing all the evidence.'

'But that was the deal . . . Ned had cased the shop. He said it wouldn't be difficult.'

'I told Bob to stay away from Ned Morris. He's always in trouble.'

'Yes, well he didn't.' Freda was opening the envelope and drawing out two five-pound notes. 'He told me to give you these, for Sergeant Birtwhistle. To buy him off.'

Alec felt his blood run cold. 'I can't do that!' She didn't know what she was asking. For him to offer ten pounds to Birtwhistle, a senior officer, to suppress evidence against two well-known petty thieves . . . He felt weak at the prospect. If Birtwhistle was honest and took it the wrong way, he'd be dismissed from the force.

'He'll take ten, won't he?'

'How do I know?' Birtwhistle was young, clean-cut and honest-looking. 'On second thoughts, I don't think he'll accept a bribe. I'm not touching this.' Alec waved the two fivers away. 'Bob can try it himself, if he wants to, but I'm not having anything to do with it.'

'That's rotten of you, Alec.' Her eyebrows lifted. They'd been plucked into a high, thin line. 'You made the deal that you'd help him. And now he needs help you're refusing, though I've been paying you for the last two years.'

Alec was turned to stone. He'd been quite proud of the fact that he could pull a girl as young as Freda. They'd had some good laughs and some good times too.

'I thought you liked me.' His pride was hurt.

Her laugh was contemptuous. 'I did it for Bob, you know I did. Keeping you sweet, he called it. An insurance policy, so when he got into trouble you'd get rid of the evidence and keep him out of jail. And now you say you won't. You're not playing fair.'

'You said you liked me.' He had to swallow back his indignation.

'All part of the service.'

'What?' Suddenly, he was choking with rage. 'You bitch!'

'Come on, Alec. You're not that green. What could make me fancy you? You're old and fat, and you get breathless in bed. You're not as wonderful as you think.'

Alec lunged at her, but she dodged back. She was light on her feet. Light enough to dance circles round him.

He knew he was shouting: 'You're on the game then, is that what you're saying?'

'Course I'm not. I'll have a thing or two to say if you try charging me with that.'

He took another swipe at her.

'Don't get nasty,' she taunted him. 'I told Bob you looked the sort that would. You're the one reneging on the agreement, not me.'

He cornered her at last. Anybody would get nasty with a hussy like her. He could see fear in her eyes now; he'd got her where he wanted her.

'Bob will be livid when he hears about this. You've had more than your fair share from me. You owe us, Alec. Not the other way round. Don't you forget that.'

What she was asking was impossible.

'I don't owe you. You're a nasty-minded harlot.' He could feel the heat pulsating through his body.

'All part of the service,' she'd said. That cut deep. He'd been fond of her. His fingers fastened round her throat. He'd squeeze until her eyes popped out. He'd show her . . . He heard a gurgle in her throat. She was pushing at him like one possessed.

Suddenly he realised what he was doing. He thrust her away from him, frightened at what he'd so nearly done.

She was coughing and choking. She looked up at him from the floor where she'd collapsed.

'Bob'll get you for this,' she wheezed. He saw the tears of terror in her eyes before he slammed out of her door.

He'd pedalled home feeling both scared and angry, and had spent a sleepless night tossing and turning.

He was afraid that Bob Hood would turn nasty and open his mouth too wide. There was no guarantee he wouldn't, not when Alec had scared the pants off Freda and nearly throttled her. And the Hoods were the sort to bear a grudge.

There was still Sergeant Peachey. If he could, he'd see Alec was all right. After all, he'd saved Peachey's bacon once.

Peachey had beaten up a thief called Riddle, and then said he'd only raised his fists in self-defence, that Riddle had hit him first. Alec had altered his evidence to corroborate Peachey's story. He'd done him other favours too.

'Only fools get caught,' Peachey had said. 'We've got to be sensible about what we do.'

Up to now, Alec thought he had been. With hindsight, he wished he hadn't gone for Freda's throat.

By morning, he'd worked himself up into a panic. He wasn't going near Slatey Road and Sergeant Birtwhistle. He wasn't going to mention the case to anybody except Peachey or show any interest in Bob Hood. The best thing for him to do now was to keep his head down and hope it would blow over.

'He's been charged,' Peachey told Alec. 'Case won't come up for months.'

Alec sighed and started on the two letters he had to write to owners of property because he'd found their premises unsecured.

Women were a disappointment to him. He'd hardly miss Freda, because he still had Olive, and she was a much better class of woman.

Women never lived up to their first promise. He knew several in the force who shared that feeling. Even Celia had turned out to be a bit of a disappointment. He'd expected an officer's widow to have more style; more dress sense and somehow more class. He'd thought her a catch at first. Enough to make Jack feel envious. He'd wanted to show her off. He'd been proud of her and Nancy.

Alec sucked the end of his pen and looked round the bleak, bare walls. He hadn't expected Celia to be so cold. She'd seemed eager enough to marry him, but once the ring was on her finger she'd been more interested in keeping house than she was in him. These days she looked exhausted, half dead, with no energy for anything. Not that she denied him anything but there was no enthusiasm in what she did. It was as though she saw it as her duty. It was a good thing he still had Olive Driscoll.

Paul looked round the Refreshment Room. He still felt shocked at the way he'd been catapulted into running it as well as the Bakehouse.

Without his father, Paul knew he had to spend more time here. Vera was a good worker, and she'd been here so long that everything was second nature to her, but she didn't like being left on her own for long.

He'd moved Lena, the young girl who'd helped Vera, to the Bakehouse, but she wasn't happy because it was further for her to travel to work. She'd given in her notice.

He was finding it impossibly difficult to run both without Joan and his father.

He'd said as much to Amy. Practical as ever, she'd said: 'Your mother could help. It's no good her lying about on the sofa in tears.'

'She's very upset, Amy. It's knocked the bottom out of her life, Dad dying so suddenly like that.'

'Aren't you upset? It's changed everything for you too. She'd be better if she had something to think about apart from herself. She's wallowing in her own loss.'

'It seems cruel to ask her now.'

'Nonsense,' Amy retorted briskly. 'It would do her good.'

'She's not worked in the café since she married Dad. I don't think she could now.'

'She'll have to, Paul. If she wants it to survive, she'll have to.'

'She isn't the sort to go out to work. She thinks a woman's place is in the home, looking after her family. It's a man's place to bring in the money.'

'Ask her again,' Amy said. 'You'll have to keep at her. She's not herself. She's gone to pieces since your dad died.'

Paul had chosen what he thought was a good moment and asked her. Myra sighed, and said perhaps she ought to give it a try.

It was midday and the place was filling up with customers. Vera did a very good hotpot, and chips were served with everything. He was watching the door for his mother.

He set out bottles of Daddy's brown sauce and tomato ketchup and added salt and pepper shakers in clear glass with red Bakelite tops. Customers were beginning to bang them on the tables, a sound as familiar as the hoot of river traffic. In the clammy atmosphere, getting the salt to come through the hole was a perennial problem.

There was an aura of success about the busy atmosphere, yet he felt he was barely holding the family business together.

It was imperative that he made a profit, his mother relied on it to live.

There were other problems: Joan had kept the Refreshment Room stocked with cake and sandwiches but it could sell more than was being produced now. He'd had to start buying in buns and teacakes.

At last, his mother's anxious face peered round the door. The fug of cigarette smoke made her grimace. He went to meet her, divested her of her fox-fur-collared coat. He went to hang it on the bentwood coat stand, but she demurred. He knew she didn't want it to come in contact with the heavy work coats that hung there.

'Come into the kitchen and say hello to Vera. Then perhaps you'd like something to eat before you start?'

'I don't know, dear.' Her nose wrinkled at the sight of two plates overflowing with ham and chips which he whisked off the counter and placed in front of customers. Her appetite was not what it used to be.

'Hello, dear.' Vera's face was damp with perspiration, he could see one rivulet running down her cheek. 'Lovely to see you here.'

He'd told Vera to be welcoming. She was dolloping helpings of hotpot on to thick white plates. He took them into the café and slid them in front of the men who had ordered them. They had to be nippy here to keep up with demand.

As he went back through the swing door he heard Vera say: 'Terrible thing to happen to Jack. I was devastated, I can tell you.' At home, Paul knew, that would be enough to bring tears to his mother's eyes.

He said hurriedly, 'I'm trying to persuade Mother to stay and help us.'

'Jack was a lovely man. The best. A good boss.'

'We know all that, Vera,' Paul said pointedly.

'He was on top of the world the day it happened. Laughing and joking. Until Alec Siddons came, that is.'

'Was he here that day?' Myra asked.

'Yes, they had a row. I could hear it going on outside the kitchen door. It really upset Jack.'

'Good gracious,' Myra said.

'Enough to give anyone a heart attack, I'd say.'

'Dad brought him up to the Bakehouse that day,' Paul put in quickly. 'He ordered stuff for Nancy's wedding. Dad seemed perfectly all right then.'

'It was when they came back. Alec Siddons started shouting at him, they had a row.'

'What about?' his mother asked suspiciously.

'I don't know, do I? Only that he was always coming round pestering Jack. Upsetting him, always on his back. Late on in the afternoon, Jack went to the wholesalers. That's when it happened.'

Myra's face was grey with anguish. She was backing towards the door. This was not the time he'd have chosen to tell her that.

'I don't think, Paul . . . It's too fresh . . . too upsetting.'

Katie wheeled Daniel's pushchair past the shops and Park Station and carried on down Duke Street towards the entrance to the docks. Each time she came to a street that crossed Duke Street she paused. At last she found what she was looking for, tucked just round the corner and smart with green gingham curtains. The freshly painted sign read: 'The Bakehouse Café'.

Katie had chosen to come today, because Bernard had gone on an outing with the cubs. She was wearing her engagement ring, though usually she did not while she was working, because she didn't want the Brents to see it.

The ring was a little large for her finger and she twisted it round and round as she rehearsed what she wanted to say to Paul.

The door pinged as she pushed it open. She saw light green linoleum stretching away in front of her, clean and new, without a mark. Katie started unstrapping Daniel from his chair. When she looked up, Paul was standing over her.

'Hello, Katie.' A smile lit up his face. She thought him attractive but not nearly so handsome as Jimmy. She'd wondered whether he would be prepared to help her.

He was Amy's boyfriend, but that was a secret supposedly kept from everybody else. Katie, though, had hardly spoken to him for ten years. She told herself now that he had no quarrel with her.

She said: 'Do you mind if I bring the pushchair in?'

It was only when she saw him hesitate that she remembered Amy saying she'd persuaded him to choose light green lino to brighten the place up. And that Paul was sorry he hadn't taken his father's advice instead and had something darker. On wet days the pale colour showed every dirty footprint.

'Come on, then.' The pushchair was imprinting muddy wheel marks on his lino. Hurriedly Katie jammed the brake on and left it where it was. After all, the café was empty but for her.

'Strange,' he said when she sat down, 'Amy usually chooses that chair. What can I get for you?'

'Tea, please. A cup of tea.' She pulled Daniel on to her knee and let her eyes linger over the cakes. The scent of baking coming from the back was making her mouth water.

'Cake to go with it?'

'No, no, thank you.' Katie knew she was going to need every penny she could get her hands on.

'Please,' Daniel said. 'Cake, please.'

'No, you won't eat your tea when you get home,' she told him firmly. Paul was clattering cups behind the counter.

'This is an unexpected pleasure,' he said, bringing two steaming cups back to the table.

Katie wanted to say her piece before another customer came in.

'Paul, can I ask a favour of you?'

'Try me,' he said, but he was no longer looking at her. He didn't seem keen.

She made herself say: 'Has Amy told you . . . about me?' She felt the colour run up her cheeks.

He nodded, trying to sip his tea, but it was too hot.

Katie went on: 'She's told me about you. That you need someone to work here.'

'Yes? Aren't you happy looking after him?' He was staring at Daniel.

'Oh yes, I don't want the job for myself. For Jimmy, my fiancé. We want to get married, you see, but he can't get a job.'

Paul was looking at her in surprise. 'I thought Amy said he was in the merchant navy? What would he want with a job here?'

'He doesn't want to go away to sea and leave me.' Her voice was coming out half strangled. 'He's not been able to find anything . . .'

'There's a war coming, Katie. He won't be given any choice. Either he'll go back to sea or they'll have him in the army.'

She knew all that, she'd said as much to Jimmy: 'Why worry about having to go away? You'll probably be forced to, anyway. Take a seagoing job and be done with it.'

'Katie, I need somebody who's used to this sort of work. Baking cakes, waiting on tables.' Paul's brown eyes were kindly when she met them.

'Oh, but he can do that. He told me his parents had a transport café out on the East Lancs Road. He grew up helping in it. Says he knows all the ropes.'

'Well, that's different. I do need somebody. Somebody I can trust . . .'

Katie felt a surge of joy. 'Can I tell him?'

'Tell him to come and see me. We'll talk about it.' Paul was frowning thoughtfully. 'I can't afford to pay him much, and we could both be off fighting a war within weeks.'

'It'll be a start for us.' Katie felt on top of the world. If Jimmy could get this job, there was nothing to stop them being married. 'Thank you, Paul.'

Katie bubbled with excitement as she walked briskly towards Jimmy's lodgings. She wanted to let him know.

He'd pointed out the house in Park Road South but had never taken her there, nor encouraged her to call. For important news such as this, she was sure he'd be pleased to see her.

'He's out,' his landlady said brusquely. Her hair was screwed into metal curlers. The door started to close.

'Can I leave a note? It is important.'

'All right,' she said grudgingly. 'Where is it?'

'I haven't written it yet. Would he have paper and pencil in his room?'

'I don't know, I don't touch his things. He wouldn't like it.' The woman was indignant.

'I'll come back with it,' Katie said quickly. She was smiling as she turned away. Even that encounter couldn't dampen her pleasure at the news. She knew one thing: she wouldn't want to move into his lodgings with him. Not with that dragon for a landlady.

She pushed Daniel home and carefully wrote her note, enclosing it in an envelope. That afternoon she walked all round the park, and when she didn't meet Jimmy, called again at his lodgings. He still hadn't returned there. She wondered what he was doing.

They weren't meeting so frequently, Jimmy said it wasn't safe. Katie had arranged to meet him two days hence on her Thursday evening off. She hoped by then that he'd have been to see Paul and would have the job fixed up. Every time she thought of it, she felt warm with happiness.

She had arranged to meet Jimmy outside the Ritz Cinema. As she waited to cross the road, she could see him standing on the steps in his navy blazer and yellow waistcoat.

She caught his eye and he waved to her, then grinned. Katie knew before she reached him that he had the job.

'You've got it, then?'

He laughed out loud and pulled her arm through his. 'Thanks to you.'

His wavy brown hair flopped over his forehead, and Katie felt her heart turn over with love. Everything was going to be all right after all.

'Now we can get married,' she said. 'Nothing to stop us, and we don't have to go to Gretna Green.'

'We'll have to save a little,' he said, cautiously. 'We'll need so many things.'

'But we can get married now?' Katie was suddenly scared. Panic was rising in her gut. She was afraid it was all going to be snatched away from her just when it had seemed within her grasp.

'Of course,' he grinned. 'I'll go down to the register office and fix it up. Paul said I can take an hour off work next week.'

Relief flooded through her. 'What date?' Katie asked eagerly.

'Soon,' he said. They'd reached the cashier's kiosk; Jimmy was paying for their seats.

'Good, we've no reason to put it off any longer.'

Katie couldn't concentrate on Greer Garson and Robert Donat, though it had been she who'd wanted to see the film *Goodbye Mr Chips*.

Her mind was on her wedding outfit. A new suit, she thought, she'd seen a wonderful one in Robb's. Perhaps she could find something similar but a little cheaper. She must look round the shops. Or perhaps Mrs Brent . . . Once she had a firm date for her wedding, she would ask her. Dark red was the colour she wanted. Suddenly the future looked rosy. The great black cloud of uncertainty had gone.

When Katie was not with Jimmy, she thought about him all

the time. She could close her eyes and feel his lips on hers and his arms tighten round her.

The trouble now was that it was taking longer than she'd expected for Jimmy to arrange their wedding. Her peace of mind was ebbing again. She didn't know where she was with Jimmy. He promised things but didn't do them, yet even to think this made her feel disloyal. She had only to see him again to be certain of his love.

Katie felt she was swinging from implicit trust to suspicion. She knew Amy didn't like him, neither did Mam. She felt she shouldn't be swayed by their opinion, but it crowded into her mind when she was low.

She knew now why every book, every play and every film was about love. It was an obsession. Katie was drawn to Jimmy; nobody else could make her spirits soar with delight.

It was another week more before he said: 'It's all fixed, Katie. Just as you want it. We're going to be married.'

'When?' Katie felt heady with joy.

'Twelve o'clock on January the twentieth.'

She felt her pleasure evaporate, leaving her shivering. He was smiling at her as though bestowing a great gift, he was expecting her to be pleased.

She tried to gulp down her disappointment that he'd arranged it for so far ahead.

'You said November . . .'

'Yes, Katie, but we've got to have a little time to get everything organised,' Jimmy explained. 'We must look for a small house to rent now, and get some furniture together.'

Katie shuddered. It all sounded so logical, the sort of thing Mam would have said in different circumstances.

She knew better: she'd spent last week scanning newspapers and walking up strange streets looking for 'To rent' signs. She could find something to suit them, if only he'd agree. She wouldn't need months for that.

'Nancy will be married before me.'

'She's been planning it longer,' Jimmy said. 'Just be patient, love. It'll come.'

'The baby . . .'

'We'll still be in time. February, you said?'

'But it will show . . . I'd hoped before it was obvious . . .'

'Katie, you're still as thin as a rake. Positively sylph-like in shape. Look at your waist. Not the merest sign as yet.'

She wasn't even sure it would be February. 'Perhaps not, but by January . . .'

'We'll need so many things for a baby, they'll have to be saved for.'

Katie gulped. He made her feel she was being ungrateful. Now the date was set and she was wearing an engagement ring, all she had to do was to be patient. January would soon come.

And now she could go to the café and have a cup of tea with Jimmy any time she wanted to. She convinced herself that everything would be all right.

CHAPTER TWELVE

Amy didn't yet feel comfortable in the Laidlaws' living room. In size and fitments, it was an exact replica of the living room at home, but it seemed sumptuous in comparison. It had been forbidden territory for so long, it was unfamiliar. There were so many frilly cushions on the settee of uncut moquette that Amy had to move them to make space to sit down.

'Auntie My,' she said gently, 'it would be a good thing if you helped Paul in the business.'

'I couldn't, dear.' Myra's voice was soft; she rarely raised it. 'I've tried. Really I have.'

'You worked in the kitchen there once, you could do it again.'

'I never fitted in.'

'But Paul said you were the cook.'

'I was, yes, for a year.'

'Then you're a trained cook?'

'I suppose so, but I should have been working in a top hotel. I specialised in party dishes and high-class cooking.'

'I didn't know that.' Amy pushed her thick black plait over her shoulder.

'I've never been interested in cooking, to tell the truth. It was just a way of earning my living. Something to fall back on. What I really wanted to be was a singer. You know that.'

'Then what made you go to the café in the first place?'

'Your father suggested it.'

'Pa? You knew Pa first?'

191

Auntie My's big eyes showed concern. 'It's all water under the bridge now. I was engaged to your pa once, believe it or not. I just wanted a job. Any job to tide me over to the next gig. He fixed it up with your grandfather. That's where I met Jack.'

'Gosh! You might have been my mother.'

'If things had turned out differently.'

'What made you change your mind?' Amy felt she knew already. Pa would never have been an easy man to live with.

'Jack believed in taking care of a woman and showing his love.' Auntie My smiled tremulously. 'Alec expects love to be showered on him. He wants a woman to wait on him and gives nothing in return.'

'You chose the better husband?'

'Not a hard choice.'

'You have to make another choice now, Auntie My. I came round to persuade you to go back to work in the business. To help Paul.'

'Did Paul put you up to this?' she said with impatience.

'No, it was my idea. But we talked about it some time ago.'

'I don't think Paul should be talking to you about the business,' she said stiffly.

'He's nobody else to discuss it with, Auntie My. You haven't been interested. He's afraid the profitability is going down.'

'He'll soon get the hang of it. His father thought highly of him.'

'We all think highly of him, Auntie My, but he's struggling to run two cafés, and he needs more help.'

'You know nothing about it, Amy. Even less than I do.'

'But you could learn.'

'Not now, I couldn't. It's too long ago. I wouldn't know where to begin.'

'Of course you could. Paul's working all hours to hold the

business together while you're at home alone. Surely you're bored?'

'I'm not bored, Amy.'

'He needs somebody he can trust. If you don't want to cook you could man the till, do the ordering and the accounts. I know it wouldn't be easy to start with, not after all this time, but if you want the income to live on . . .'

'I need the income,' she retorted indignantly. Her big brown eyes searched Amy's doubtfully.

'Then you'd better get down there and find out how to run it.'

'He's taken on a young man to help, Katie's fiancé. Fliss says he's running the café, that he's managing fine.'

Amy sighed. She remembered Paul saying: 'I'm surprised Jimmy's interested. He'd earn a lot more if he went back to sea. I can't afford to pay him much, but he seems keen to have the job. He must be very much in love with Katie to want to stay here with her this badly. Fliss has taken to him too, and he's doing everything that's needed. You're wrong about him.'

Amy didn't think so. She wished she liked Jimmy more; she was worried about Katie. She said firmly: 'If war comes, and it almost certainly will, Jimmy Shaw will get called up. Paul too.'

'No! Paul couldn't possibly go. It wouldn't come to that. He couldn't be spared.'

'Don't bank on it,' Amy said sharply.

'It's years since I went out to work.' Myra's lack of confidence showed in her voice.

'I beg of you, Auntie My, give it a try before it's too late. Go now, while Paul can show you how to run it.'

'I don't know . . .' Anxious eyes looked into hers. 'You really think I could?'

'Yes.'

'Perhaps, when I feel a little better. I don't think I could do it now. Such a loss . . . it's all too raw.'

'You'll feel better if you do. You'll be helping Paul when he needs it desperately. It'll put your mind on other things.'

'You're just like your father,' Myra said impatiently. 'Think you know what's best for everybody.'

'This has nothing to do with my father, but I *can* see what's best for both you and Paul.'

On Sunday, Katie went home to tell Pa that at last the date had been set for her wedding. She knew Mam wouldn't approve of it being such a long way off, but at least she had a date to give them.

She'd been going every Sunday as Pa had ordered, but she dreaded the visits. She'd given up going for her tea and arrived as late as possible so she didn't have to spend so much time there.

It was late in the evening when she let herself in through the back door. As she went to the living room, she crossed her fingers that Nancy and Stan would be here too. If they weren't, Mam nagged and Pa was increasingly nasty. To hear their suspicions about Jimmy hacked at her peace of mind.

Nancy's curly brown head turned to smile at her. Her family were listening with anxious concentration to the wireless. The nine o'clock news was on. Relieved, Katie pulled out another chair at the table. Stan was not here tonight.

She was getting used to the way people turned on their wirelesses for every news bulletin.

'Have you heard?' Nancy's face was white. 'They've announced that conscription for men between the ages of eighteen and forty-five is to start on September the first. Stan will be called up.' Her voice was frightened.

Katie's mouth was suddenly dry. 'What about Jimmy?'

'He'll have to go too,' Pa retorted.

'They say the Reserve and the Territorials have already been called up,' Nancy whispered.

'What about your wedding?' Katie had a sensation of panic. If Nancy's wedding couldn't take place, perhaps her own was not as certain as she'd supposed.

'They won't send Stan away that quickly,' her mother said. 'Or they'll give him leave. Lucky you're all right, Alec. Forty-six last birthday. You've just missed it.'

Katie heard Neville Chamberlain's voice tell them they were 'in imminent peril of war'. She felt gripped by the tension that was holding the country in thrall. War had been creeping closer all this year, but she'd been so wrapped up in her own problems, she'd been almost oblivious of it. Now it was almost on them.

The news ended, Pa switched off the wireless and her mother took up the bridesmaid's dress she was to wear for Nancy's wedding. Katie took the opportunity to tell them that her wedding date had been arranged. Her parents could no longer see that far into the future. Their worries were for themselves.

When Nancy went to the kitchen to make a pot of tea, Mam said: 'I hope you'll be able to fit into this in December.' Katie saw she was eyeing her abdomen. She got up and went to help Nancy.

A week later, Katie was home in the morning to hear Neville Chamberlain's broadcast to the nation. He said that a state of war now existed between Britain and Germany.

'I can remember what it was like last time,' her mother said in horrified tones.

'Everything will get scarce. Food will be rationed. Lay in a good stock while you can,' Pa advised.

'Stan Whittle's got his call-up papers,' Celia said. 'Our Nancy's out of her mind with worry, what with the wedding and everything else.'

Katie closed her eyes and prayed that both weddings would be able to take place as arranged.

'I'm drawing up your insulin, Mrs Peacock. Which leg would

you like it in today?' Nancy made a point of talking to her all the time she was in her room.

'I'm not going to like it at all. It's the right leg's turn, I suppose.'

'Are you ready?' Nancy turned back the bedclothes.

'As ready as I'll ever be.'

Nancy flicked the needle into the geriatric flesh.

'Good one today. You didn't hurt a bit,' the old lady told her.

The words they used hardly changed from day to day. It was a ritual they went through. Nancy felt she was almost speaking the lines of a play.

She looked out of the window at the large, well-kept garden and knew she'd drifted again in the last three years. She'd settled down here with the Frampton family in the long, low house behind high hedges in Vyner Road. It hardly seemed like a job now. The amount of nursing required of her didn't fill the day. She was spending more and more time reading to Alice, who could no longer see to do it for herself.

Officially, Sunday was her day off, but she always gave her two patients their injections and left instructions about their meals before going out. Usually, she saw to Alice's comfort too, just as she did every other morning.

If she wanted to go shopping, Bill Frampton would give her a lift into town after lunch. Often she carried out small commissions for members of the family. If she wanted to spend the evening with Stan, or go home to spend an hour with Mam, she felt free to go, merely telling Mary Frampton when she would be back.

When Hilda Redway, the housekeeper, was ill with shingles, Nancy nursed her and took over some of the cooking. She was happy to do the flowers and sometimes a little ironing, or sew on the odd button if required.

In return, she felt the Framptons treated her almost as one of the family.

Like everybody else, she'd felt the growing tension of

war. She'd listened to the news bulletins on the wireless with the family, shared their anxieties about their two sons, James and Toby.

When war burst into her life, she couldn't accept the changes that came overnight. They left her feeling upset and angry.

The blackout clamped down immediately. Cinemas and theatres closed, spectator sports like football were banned.

Stan was called up and sent to Aldershot for training. He was not the only one, but it didn't make it any easier for her to bear. She missed his company. She believed, though, that he'd be able to get leave for their wedding at Christmas.

It didn't help that Bill Frampton had applied for exemption for his two sons, claiming they were needed to run the family business. Toby was not pleased to find his call-up had been deferred.

Cinemas reopened after a fortnight and gradually everything else started up again.

It gave her a sense of unreality to see sandbags stacked outside the hospital when she passed it, and barrage balloons filling the sky. There was talk she scarcely believed of the park railings being needed to help the war effort.

Everybody carried their gas mask about with them. A gas attack was thought to be very likely. She even saw Katie tying the children's to Daniel's pushchair for walks in the park. Katie had been concerned that the Brent children might be evacuated and she'd lose her job, but in the end the Brents decided to keep the family together.

At home, Celia started making Nancy's wedding cake, using sugar and dried fruit gathered together thriftily over several weeks. Nancy felt it brought life back to normal. She didn't believe the war would stop her wedding taking place, not after all the time they'd waited, and the effort she and Stan had put into arranging it.

She would have liked to start looking for a house, but if Stan were not to be with her, it seemed more sensible to stay on with the Framptons and continue to save.

It came as a shock to find he was given three days' embarkation leave at the end of November. It was only when he'd gone to France with the British Expeditionary Force that she cancelled her wedding arrangements.

She felt frightened when she thought of Stan being in France. She couldn't allow herself to think that he might not come back to her at all.

Gingerly, Fliss Laidlaw pushed her toes out of bed and stood up.

She'd kept waking up in the night. Once she'd gone to the bathroom thinking she might be sick, and that if she could it would rid her of this heavy feeling in her stomach. But nothing would come up and she'd gone back to bed shivering, with perspiration on her brow.

Fliss drooped over her dressing table, looking at her reflection in the mirror. Her cheeks were unusually pallid. Her dark red hair looked too heavy for her small face. She tied it back in one thick bunch. Dad had thought it a more appropriate style for the café.

She hadn't felt well all week. Even now her head ached and she felt hot and heavy. She'd been a bit queasy yesterday and had a dull ache churning around in her abdomen.

She felt more like staying in bed, but she had to go to work. Paul needed her, she couldn't give him more problems now. Mam stayed at home, refusing to lift a finger in the business, and she knew what Paul thought of that. Fliss dressed herself slowly, and began to feel a little better.

Mam was making more effort about the house. She was up before them in her dressing gown. She had set the table with a brightly printed cloth, and insisted they ate a proper breakfast before going to work. Dad had never wanted to. He preferred to open up and start work and have breakfast at the café when he'd thoroughly woken up.

Fliss managed to eat half her boiled egg, though the scent

of food was making her feel queasy again. When Mam went to the kitchen to put more hot water in the teapot, she swapped her egg for one of Paul's empty shells.

'Are you all right, Fliss? Well enough to go to work?' Paul's concerned eyes were on her.

'Yes, I'll go,' she said. 'Probably feel better if I'm busy.'

'Something's upset your tummy.'

Her mother heard that as she came back to the table. 'Goodness knows what you eat in that café,' she fussed.

'It's all good food, Mam.' Paul was brusque.

'It doesn't seem like it. Fliss, you ought to go to the doctor if you aren't well.'

'If I'm not better by tomorrow, I will.' She knew Jimmy didn't do very much in the Bakehouse. She had to do what she could to help.

'You can always walk back home if you feel worse,' her mother said.

Paul drove her to the café. The first job was always to load his trailer with the trays of cakes and pastries she and Jimmy had prepared late the previous day for the Refreshment Room. Fliss helped carry them out.

'Where's Jimmy?' Paul asked testily. 'He should be here to do this. He very rarely is.'

Fliss started setting out the displays of sausage rolls, pies and cakes both in the window and in the glass-shelved counter.

Paul had decided not to continue making bread on the premises. Now the bread van arrived and Fliss took delivery of rolls and sliced loaves, carrying them through to the kitchen. When she thought of all the work that had to be done this morning, she felt overwhelmed, hardly knowing where to begin.

Jimmy was nearly an hour late. By the time he arrived, she'd sold some rock cakes and made tea and bacon sandwiches for three men. She felt exhausted, as though it was already the end of the day.

'Hello, Flissy old girl.' When he arrived, Jimmy was all

charm, rubbing his hands in the doorway. 'Got the sausage rolls cooked yet?'

'No, but I've got the fairy cakes in the oven. They'll be five more minutes.'

'Pity, I could just do with a sausage roll now.' Jimmy shot into the shop and brought one back from the window display.

'Don't open the oven,' Fliss reminded him crossly.

But she was too late, he already had. 'Just want to warm it up. Makes it taste fresh again.'

'You'll ruin the fairy cakes. They won't rise properly,' she objected.

He opened it again a minute or two later, to take his sausage roll out.

'Your cakes look all right. Look great, in fact.' His teeth bit into the flaky pastry.

'Fliss, do you mind if I just pop out for an hour? There's something important I want to do. You can manage, can't you? I'll be back well before lunch, before things start to get busy.'

Fliss forgot her troubles when she started making the big pan of scouse. She went on to make a batch of scones, then rock cakes. By the time she had them in the oven she felt drained and dizzy. She knew she was ill. The vague symptoms she'd felt yesterday and in the night were getting worse.

She wished now she'd gone to the doctor this morning. Or, at the very least, stayed at home with Mam, who would know what to do now.

She had to keep going until Jimmy came back. She couldn't just close the café in the middle of the morning.

Somehow she managed to cut a few sandwiches and serve four cups of coffee. She wished Jimmy would come back to help.

Six men came in and sat down. She made herself go over to take their orders, hoping they wouldn't want chips because she hadn't yet got round to making them.

The door pinged open again, and Jimmy was smiling at her. 'Everything under control?'

'Just about.'

'Three scouse and three sausage, egg and chips,' one of the customers called.

'Sorry, no chips today.'

'Why not?' Jimmy demanded. 'You'd better get started, you know how popular chips are. We could do fried bread, gentlemen, if you don't want to wait.'

Fliss retreated to the kitchen. 'You'll have to cook,' she said. 'I feel dreadful. I'm sick. I want to go home.'

'For God's sake, Fliss. Not now, just when we're starting dinners. Dish up the scouse while I get the sausages going.'

'I put some sausages in the oven, just put some eggs on.'

The smell of food was making her want to throw up. Her stomach felt distended now and the stitch in her side had become a throbbing pain.

She struggled on, feeling dazed. She knew she was getting the orders mixed up. She broke a plate and spilled tea, and every so often she doubled up over the kitchen table in agony.

Paul sat at a corner of the table in the Refreshment Room kitchen and tucked into a late lunch of egg and chips. He and Vera took it in turns to take their break.

He used to sit here, listening to the voices and the clatter of crockery in the café, and wonder uneasily if he would manage to run the business as well as his father had. Now that war had come, his problems had multiplied. He was worried stiff.

He'd had his call-up papers at the beginning of September along with everybody else, and had had to make a formal application for deferment. He'd applied for Jimmy Shaw's call-up to be deferred too. He couldn't afford to lose any more staff. The business was a valuable family asset; if he went in the forces he was afraid it would collapse, and then his mother would lose her livelihood as well as her capital.

Some of his school friends had volunteered before conscription had come. Others had joined up since, and Paul felt he ought to go too. In the last war, white feathers had been sent to men like him. He wondered how long it would be before his generation started receiving them. How different things would have been if Dad was still with them.

The swing door slammed back. Vera's huge frame swept from stove to table as she dished up two large helpings of sausage and chips. She said before he asked: 'The rush is dying down.'

Paul sighed, war was bringing changes on the home front, yet few guns were being fired. It meant he had to keep rethinking his strategy. It was harder to get the ingredients he needed; sugar was already scarce. There was talk of rationing for everybody and an allocation of food for businesses like this.

He'd already reduced the varieties of cakes and pies being made to simplify things for Fliss and Jimmy. Now it seemed that even if Joan had stayed on, that would have happened sooner or later.

Inevitably, it must mean he would have less to sell, and then there would be even less profit.

Paul finished his cup of tea and stood up. In the café Vera was wiping down the oilcloth on the tables. Only four customers remained; there was often a lull at this time of day.

'I'm going now,' he told her. He went every day to see how busy Jimmy and Fliss had been over the midday period. He would empty the till and bring back to the Refreshment Room as many trays of cakes and pastries as he could.

'We've run out of everything today,' Vera reminded him. The glass domes were empty. 'Output has fallen since Joan went.'

Paul winced. He didn't need to be told that. The travelling public liked his cakes; without them trade might fall off.

There were no customers in the Bakehouse when he arrived. As the shop door pinged, Jimmy's head came out of the kitchen.

'Thank goodness you've come,' he said. Paul had never seen him looking worried before.

'What's happened?' He followed Jimmy into the kitchen. Fliss was slumped at the table with her head in her hands. There was a half-finished cup of tea beside her. In front of Jimmy's seat was a collection of empty cups and plates.

'Fliss is sick. Quite bad. I was just wondering whether to shut up shop and take her to hospital.'

The word hospital sent shivers of fear down Paul's spine. He hadn't given Fliss a thought all morning. Now he felt a flush of guilt.

'Fliss? You're feeling worse?' He touched her shoulder and she lifted a grey face contorted with pain.

'Yes, I feel terrible.' Her breath came in a shaky gasp.

'Come on,' Paul told her. 'I'll take you to the hospital. You should have gone as soon as you started to feel worse. I'd no idea you were this bad.'

'Get her hat and coat,' he said to Jimmy. Together they helped her out to the car.

Paul was horrified. He'd never seen anybody as sick as this. Fliss seemed to fold up on the seat beside him. She hardly answered when he spoke to her, but she groaned softly from time to time. He drove as fast as he could.

The General Hospital was only minutes away. Fliss was a dead weight in his arms as he moved her from the car into the casualty department.

A nurse he didn't know helped him take her to a bed round the back. 'Is Amy Siddons here?' he asked.

'No, she's off this afternoon. Back at five. She's a friend of yours?'

'My cousin. Hers too.' He nodded towards Fliss, who was now flat out on the bed with her eyes closed.

Moments later, he found himself sitting where he had last

time, when his father had been brought in. He wanted Amy, he wished she was here now. The nurse came back with cards to be filled in. Fliss's name and address was the easy part.

'She's in too much pain to say much to us now. Can you tell me how long she's felt like this? Exactly what symptoms have you heard her complain of?'

Paul did his best. He felt guilt-ridden that he'd allowed her to go to work this morning.

The nurse had only just gone when the sister was summoning him into her office. He recognised her from his last visit, and it made the blood pound in his head. He asked: 'Do you know what's the matter with my sister?'

'The houseman thinks appendicitis. There's a surgeon operating in theatre now. He'll come and see your sister between cases.' Her large headdress of fine voile crackled with starch when she moved.

'When did she last eat or drink?'

Paul had no idea, but he remembered the half-empty cup he'd seen beside her.

'She'll probably go on the end of the list this afternoon.'

'So soon?'

'She's wasted a lot of time getting here, I'm afraid. Can you sign the operation form for her?'

She pushed it in front of him. Paul felt that the afternoon was taking on a nightmare quality.

'For a minor, like your sister, we need a signature from a relative before we can operate. To give us permission. Are you over twenty-one?'

'I'm twenty.'

'Oh dear. Then I'm afraid your signature won't do. What about your parents?'

Paul shifted uncomfortably on his chair. She'd been so immediately recognisable to him, he couldn't believe every detail of his last visit wasn't clear in her mind too.

An apparition wearing white rubber boots and a long

white rubber apron appeared at the office door.

'I'll do the girl as soon as you can get her ready, Sister.' He was easing back the green cotton cap that covered his hair; his face mask had already been dragged down round his throat.

'She can't wait by the look of her. I've only two more left to do on my list.'

'Appendectomy?'

'Yes. I've written up her pre-op, give it straight away.'

'I'll fetch my mother.' Paul stood up. 'We only live up the road.'

'She will be in?' Sister seemed anxious. 'We must have her permission.'

'Ten minutes,' he croaked. 'It won't take more than ten minutes.'

He went running back to his car. The trailer made it difficult to turn round in the car park. He shot out of the hospital forecourt and into the traffic moving up Park Road North.

It seemed only seconds before he was gripping the draining board in the kitchen at home and trying to convey the urgency of it all to his mother. She kept moving round the kitchen.

'I want you to come to the hospital with me. You've got to sign for Fliss to have her appendix out.'

'Where we were last time?'

'Yes, I'm afraid so.'

'Whatever made you take her there? I couldn't go, Paul! I'm not over the other . . . It's all too raw . . .'

'You must. It's urgent.'

'Besides, I've got a fruit cake in the oven. Both you and Fliss like fruit cake. It'll be another hour.'

'I don't care if I never see another cake, Mother. And right now it's the last thing Fliss wants.'

'Paul, I don't feel well enough to face that place again. Why don't you fetch the form? I could sign it here.'

Paul gasped. No doubt he could have brought the form if

he'd thought of it, but he hadn't. He strode to the stove and turned off the gas, then snatched his mother's old coat from a peg behind the back door.

'Get this on, and come. There's no time for such selfish fancies, Mother. The doctors are afraid her appendix will burst. Give a thought to somebody else for a change. Surely you care what happens to Fliss?'

As he was towing her down the yard, she said: 'Wait, I can't go like this. I've still got my slippers on.'

'They'll do,' he said angrily. 'You're going by car. What does it matter what you've got on your feet?'

He couldn't get over his mother's selfishness, couldn't stop himself carrying on at her. 'I can't give permission for them to operate on Fliss. They count me a child. You have to do this. Just sign your name on a form. For God's sake, Mam, you must feel capable of that.'

CHAPTER THIRTEEN

Paul felt he was reeling. His mother didn't speak to him on the short ride back to the hospital. She seemed so changed from the fun-loving woman she used to be. He could see anger in her eyes and her jaw was clamped firmly shut. He took her arm as she got out of the car, and felt her shiver as they went through the door into the casualty department.

They were ushered straight to Sister's office. Within moments the form was signed.

'Can we see her?' his mother asked.

'She's drowsy with the pre-op, Mrs Laidlaw, and she'll be going to theatre any minute. Better if you don't. Have you brought her things?' Sister Steele looked from Paul to his mother. Paul swallowed, he'd forgotten.

'Nightdresses, toothbrush, slippers, that sort of thing? Never mind, she won't need them yet.'

'I'll fetch them,' his mother said grimly.

'Tomorrow will be soon enough.'

Paul could understand the unwanted memories this must bring back for his mother. He hurried her out and drove up Park Road North, swinging the car and trailer round in the road's ample width to pull up outside the front door.

'I can't come in,' he told her. He was harassed and beginning to feel pushed for time. 'Too busy. I've got to get back. I've asked a girl to come in and see me about a job, and thank goodness I have. I'll have to take her on, whatever she's like. I've got to have somebody to do the work.'

His mother turned a grey face to him. She said stiffly: 'I'll take Fliss's place. You're right, I should do more to help with the business. Do you want me to come now?'

Her sudden capitulation left him gasping. He didn't think he could cope with her there this afternoon. He wasn't on an even keel himself.

'Tomorrow morning,' he choked. 'Thanks, Mam.'

Paul felt his head buzzing as he sped back to the Bakehouse. It was playing hell with him: the emotional impact of Fliss's sudden illness, the worry about the business.

There were no customers in the Bakehouse. Jimmy was in the kitchen, wearing an apron and cook's cap. 'How's Fliss?' he asked.

Paul gave him an update, finishing with, 'I wish you'd done something sooner. You must have seen how ill she was.'

'What was I supposed to do? Close this place up? There's no telephone here and I've no car.' Jimmy was defensive.

'You could have phoned from the underground station round the corner. It's only two minutes away. You could have rung me, or for a taxi to take her home.'

'She didn't ask me to. Didn't say anything.'

'She wasn't too bad when I dropped her here this morning. When did she start to feel worse?'

'I don't know. She told me she was fine when I asked, and she seemed all right. She was cooking.'

'If only you'd sent her home when she began to feel worse. It isn't as though it's far.'

'I was busy working too,' Jimmy told him sharply. 'I didn't notice until she folded up.'

Paul sighed. He wasn't taking to Jimmy Shaw. He wasn't managing the café well, and he didn't know as much about the business as he pretended. But Fliss liked him and wouldn't hear a word against him. Undoubtedly he had a way with women. He had wrapped Fliss as well as Katie Siddons around his little finger.

Paul watched him fill one of the large wooden trays with

scones and rock cakes. He couldn't dispense with Jimmy's services, whatever the man's shortcomings. Not many wanted to work in a café, not when they could be earning better money in a munitions factory.

'These are for the Room,' Jimmy said.

'What about the fairy cakes?'

Jimmy indicated a couple of batches on wire cooling trays. 'Not iced yet.'

'They haven't risen. What happened?'

Jimmy shrugged. 'Fliss wasn't at her best today.'

'No point in icing them. I'll take them, Vera can use them in trifles tomorrow. What else is there? Sausage rolls?'

'That's all. Like I said, Fliss wasn't at her best.'

Paul strode into the shop with a couple more trays, and took most of the stuff on display. He knew he could sell it at the Room. Here, he probably would not. He managed only three trays in all. Usually there were six to take down at this time of day.

On the drive down to Woodside he worried about Fliss again. He couldn't see her spending her life working in the business. She'd complained that her hair smelled of cooking. Perhaps if she could learn to type and do shorthand she could go in the Wrens and be secretary to some admiral. It was rumoured that women would be called up soon.

Then he was telling himself not to be so stupid. Fliss was only fourteen. She wouldn't be called up until she was at least eighteen. Surely this war wouldn't carry on longer than the last?

Hazel Spence, the girl he'd asked to come in and see him, was waiting when he got back. He sat her down at a quiet table and got them each a cup of tea. He liked the look of her. Sixteen, not too young, and yet some time before she'd be likely to be called up.

Paul had intended to start her at the Refreshment Room. His father had always had a girl there as well as Vera; there was more than enough work for them all to do.

But now he'd need to replace Fliss. He couldn't let his mother go to the Bakehouse and cook all day. It made more sense to bring her here. He wanted Myra to learn how to do the ordering, get used to cashing up and keeping the books. Do what he did, in case he had to go and fight.

With his mind made up, he told Hazel he'd like her to work at the Bakehouse. She seemed pleased to get the job.

It was later than usual by the time he'd got both cafés locked up for the night. He decided to call in at the hospital on the way home. He wanted to talk to Amy. She'd explain exactly what was happening to Fliss.

He went to the casualty department. The row of chairs up the middle was full. There were patients standing, a baby crawling at their feet. Amy was bandaging an ankle, her cheeks flushed. He went over to her.

'How's Fliss?'

'We're a bit busy, Paul.'

'I can see. I just wanted to ask . . .'

'I don't know, haven't had time to find out. Fliss isn't here. She'll be up on Weightman Ward now.' She'd pinned her heavy plait up under her cap, but it was coming loose.

She led him to an internal door. 'First left, up two flights of stairs and left again. Ask Sister about her.'

Paul hesitated. He'd wanted more comfort from Amy.

'I'll see you when I get off at eight o'clock,' she told him. 'Will you be home then?'

'Depends on Fliss.'

'She won't be able to talk to you yet. Don't expect it.'

It scared him to find they'd put her in a side ward by herself.

'Bad news, I'm afraid,' Sister said. 'She's had her appendix out, but it had burst before they opened her up.'

'It's serious then?'

'Yes. She isn't round from the anaesthetic yet, and she'll be very poorly tomorrow.'

When finally she led him to the door to peep at Fliss, Paul

caught his breath. He was afraid his sister was dying. She was lying flat without a pillow, and had a drip running into her arm. Her face was paste-white against the mop of dark red hair. To Paul, who was used to seeing her robust and well, she looked like fragile china.

'She will get better?'

'I hope so.' Something in Sister's manner frightened him, and he felt suddenly rigid. 'We'll have to see how she goes on.'

It had gone eight thirty when Amy rang the front door bell and he went to let her in. She kissed his cheek in the darkness of the hall, and he almost fell over the case his mother had packed ready to take down to the hospital.

'Come into the living room,' he said.

'Hello, Auntie My.'

His mother had not moved from her chair. She'd been staring blankly ahead of her since he'd arrived home.

Now she said: 'A terrible thing to happen to poor Fliss.' She sounded like the prophet of doom.

'Is she very bad? Oh God, Amy, I know she is.' Paul had taken in that much from the sister. 'Tell us what her chances are.'

'It's like this.' Amy was fidgeting, her dark blue eyes wouldn't look at him. 'Fliss had acute appendicitis, an infection. Her appendix burst before they could take it out, so all the germs are sloshing around in her abdominal cavity. The surgeon cleaned up what he could and left a drain in. That lets the fluid run out, but of course, it's full of germs. A frequent outcome is peritonitis.'

'She can die of that?' his mother flashed out, terrified.

The look on Amy's face was enough to answer that. 'She could recover too.'

'What does it depend on?'

'How well her body fights off the infection. There are medicines she'll have to help her.'

211

'Oh God, Amy!' It was Paul's turn now to look terrified. 'She's always been so fit.'

'That's a plus. Her strength might help to pull her through.'

'I knew she shouldn't have gone to work this morning,' Myra said. 'You shouldn't have let her.'

Her words did nothing for Paul's conscience. He already felt as guilty as hell over this.

'You mustn't blame yourselves,' Amy said fiercely. 'Infections can blow up much more quickly in some people than in others. They can't be predicted. Fliss has been very unlucky.'

'We must all hope for the best, I suppose,' Myra said.

Paul was glad she was coming to the Refreshment Room with him in the morning. It would give her less time to worry on her own.

'I'm pleased you're taking my advice,' Amy told her.

Paul hid his smile at that. He knew it wasn't Amy's advice that had changed her mind, but the shock Myra felt at finding out how ill Fliss was. That and guilt, because she hadn't wanted to go down to the hospital to give permission for the operation.

Fliss seemed to hover between life and death for a long time. Then, as the weeks dragged on, very slowly she began to pick up. Paul breathed a sigh of relief.

His mother was still trying to find her feet at the Room. She got on well with Vera, which he found a blessing. She was helping on the counter during busy periods, but was having difficulty grasping the ordering and buying of ingredients, and terrible trouble keeping the books up to date.

He heard that his call-up had been officially deferred for six months. So had Jimmy Shaw's. He decided he must find another woman to work at the café.

'Winnie Cottie might like to,' his mother suggested.

Paul was not keen. All his life he'd thought of Winnie as

being old. 'Too old,' he said now.

'Too old for National Service,' his mother retorted. 'She's seventy, and she used to ice cakes in Fullers.'

'Icing sugar's off for the duration.' He hadn't had any recently; the fairy cakes were now sold plain.

'She'll be more reliable than a young girl. Shall I ask her?'

Paul sighed. He had to give his mother her head. He could see her being left to run the whole thing from the beginning of March, when his deferment ran out.

As time went on, the turnover of the Bakehouse continued to fall, whereas that of the Room continued to grow. As food became scarce, more people ate meals out. People seemed to have more money to spend.

Jimmy and Hazel were making fewer cakes. 'Not our fault,' Jimmy told him. They were always short of some vital ingredient. Everybody was having to tighten their belts. They were using more baking powder, artificial sweeteners and egg substitutes in their cakes. Powdered egg made reasonable scrambled eggs, and was now regularly served on toast.

Paul wondered again whether it was worth keeping the Bakehouse open. He put the lease on the market with two agents, but they told him there was little or no interest. Paul knew he could not expect it with so many men being called up, and more well-paid jobs available in munition factories. The civilian population were told to expect a gas attack or to have high explosives dropped on them. Most expressed surprise that it hadn't already happened.

A café was the last thing anybody would want. Paul was afraid it would make a loss this year.

Katie pulled Daniel's chair closer to the glass-topped table, so he wouldn't spill the mug of weak tea Jimmy always provided for him.

Now that winter had come and the park was a less attractive place to linger, she was making a habit of calling in to see

Jimmy most afternoons before she collected Bernard from school.

Today, Daniel was more interested in the coloured paper streamers festooning the ceiling than in his drink.

'For Christmas,' Katie told him. 'Looks very festive, Jimmy. You'd hardly think there was a war on.'

'Paul saved them from last year, except for the holly, which Hazel brought,' Jimmy said, sliding two more cups of tea on to the table. 'Have a cake?'

'No thanks.'

Jimmy was just biting into the first of the three mince pies he'd helped himself to when she saw Paul's car pulling up outside.

'Oh hell,' Jimmy muttered. 'I was afraid he'd come while you were here.' He pushed the rest of the pie into his mouth. 'He's late today.'

When Paul came in, Katie saw the censorious look he gave Jimmy's mince pies. She asked: 'How's Fliss?'

'Not much change.'

Fliss had been in hospital for almost three months now. The progress she'd begun to make in November had not been maintained.

'Her wound is still leaking quite badly. She won't be coming home for Christmas.'

'Poor Fliss.' Katie knew how she'd hate to be incarcerated in hospital with no idea when she would be well enough to go home.

'She's in the new wing, on Weightman Ward, and had a bit of excitement when the wing was officially opened. Viscount Leverhulme spoke to her for quite a while. She's everybody's favourite. There was cake for tea and a special supper.'

'I'll go in to see her next Wednesday afternoon.' She'd been two or three times already. Amy had asked her to, because it was difficult for Fliss's immediate family to visit on weekday afternoons. Either Paul or Auntie My made a

214

point of going, but it was hard to spare two full hours. And it was no fun for Fliss to see other patients having visitors when there was nobody at her bedside.

'What can I take her for Christmas? Soap and talc?'

'Mam has bought her stuff like that.'

'A book then?'

'Yes, she's plenty of time for reading.' Paul sighed. 'First Christmas of the war. None of us have much to celebrate.'

'Not our Nancy.'

Katie found it hard to believe that Nancy's wedding had been postponed. She'd thought that was certain to take place as arranged.

'Mam's decided the top layer of her wedding cake will become the family Christmas cake. It frightens Nancy, makes her think Stan won't come back at all. That she never will get married.'

Katie felt that Nancy's problems and the war generally was giving her family something different to worry about. It took their attention off her. Mam nagged less when she went home.

'War is bringing uncertainty to everything,' Jimmy said, wiping the last crumb of mincemeat from his mouth.

'Not everything,' Paul retorted. 'It guarantees a lot of things. We've all been issued with ration books, so rationing is definitely coming, and we'll be called up in March, Jimmy.'

Katie was shocked. 'I thought you said Jimmy had been deferred?'

'He has, until March,' Paul told her. 'I won't apply for a further period for him. I've told him that. The job doesn't justify it.'

Katie felt as though she'd stepped under a cold shower.

'You didn't tell me.' She swung round on Jimmy, and saw an embarrassed flush run to his cheeks. 'I thought deferment meant for the whole war.'

'I got six months' deferment too, Katie,' Paul told her. 'Mam wants me to apply to have it extended, but I don't know. I'll see how she's managing. If she can cope, I'll go.'

Katie felt icy inside. 'I wish you'd told me,' she whispered to Jimmy.

'I didn't want to upset you.'

That gave Katie another rush of misgivings. Though she'd known for some time that Jimmy didn't tell her everything, she'd thought things were going along well for them. Yet he'd never mentioned he'd have to leave her in March. She knew now that she couldn't rely on what he did say.

She was having second thoughts about Jimmy. She didn't really trust him, yet what choice did she have? Soon nobody would want to employ her. Somebody would have to support the baby when it was born, and her too. Katie could think no further ahead than her wedding day.

Jimmy didn't mention marriage much, but when Katie did, he assured her that 20 January would come. It was only six weeks off now.

'Everything will be all right,' he said easily.

Amy was afraid the first Christmas of the war would turn out to be something of a damp squib. Nobody was in the mood to celebrate, but said they were going through the motions for the sake of the patients, or for the sake of the children, or just because it was Christmas. She found very little in the shops she could give as presents.

The nurses scrounged coloured paper and cotton wool, and made decorations. They toured the wards singing carols on Christmas Eve. They put together a concert and enacted it on every ward on Christmas Day, just as they always had. Amy felt she'd had a good time.

She ate turkey for the nurses' Christmas dinner, and danced afterwards on a stone floor in the outpatients' hall, made slippy with French chalk from the hospital stores. She invited Paul as her partner and there was even a live quartet. She enjoyed that too.

The New Year started badly but nobody had expected

much of 1940. It was announced that rationing of basic foods would start on 8 January.

'I've been given an allocation of rationed foods for the business,' Paul told Amy as he drove her into Birkenhead to go to the pictures on her night off. 'I think it could be a good thing. I've been wasting so much time running round after supplies, and at least this way we'll all get a fair share.'

Amy wanted to go to the Plaza to see Madeleine Carroll and Douglas Fairbanks Jr. in *Safari*. Once Paul had parked and switched off his half-dimmed headlights, it was pitch black and impossible to see anything. It was forbidden to shine a torch out of doors. He took Amy's arm.

'I hear there are more accidents and injuries due to the blackout than there are war casualties.'

'There's certainly more in our hospital. There were two last night, a man knocked off his bike by a car, and a pedestrian hit by a motorbike.'

'I saw your sister today. In the Bakehouse.'

'Katie? How is she? Haven't seen her for a couple of weeks.'

'Fine. Amy, are you sure she's having a baby?'

'Of course.' She saw Paul's face turn to her, a pale, pensive blur. 'What makes you ask?'

'There's absolutely no sign of it yet. She's reed-thin. A twenty-inch waist. And they're in no hurry to get married.'

'The twentieth of this month, the wedding's to be. I've already asked for a day off.' Amy sensed other people around her now, and she could just make out the white marble steps of the cinema.

'When is her baby due?'

'February, she said.'

'Doesn't seem likely to me.'

'What? She must be, Paul. She was dreading telling Mam. Hated doing it. Katie's quite shy really, doesn't like talking about herself at the best of times. Pa called her a slut and a stupid fool. She wouldn't have gone through that, unless . . .

Good God, what are you saying?'

'Just that she doesn't look as though she's having a baby at all, and certainly not next month.'

What Paul said struck a chord and made Amy feel uneasy. She sat in the unheated cinema with her coat wrapped tightly round her legs. The film unfolded before her but her mind was far away.

Months ago, before Nancy's wedding had been postponed, Mam had mentioned that against the odds it seemed Katie would be able to get into her bridesmaid's dress. What if she wasn't pregnant at all? What if she'd just imagined it?

It would be wonderful, of course, but Amy was feeling a niggle of guilt. Perhaps she hadn't given enough attention to Katie's problems. She hadn't helped her enough. She shouldn't have allowed her to go on thinking she was having a baby if she wasn't.

Amy had a morning off the following day, and went up to the Brents' house to see her sister.

She knocked and heard Daniel scurrying up the hall towards her. Katie opened the door wearing a loose printed pinafore that tied on her hips. It hung straight but was wide enough to hide a lot. Amy's first thought was that Paul was mistaken.

'I was just cleaning out the playroom,' Katie said. 'Come on in.'

She led the way to the kitchen, where she put the kettle on for tea. Then she took off her pinafore and hung it behind the kitchen door.

When she turned round, Amy was fighting for breath. Katie was wearing a slim red skirt. Her abdomen was as flat as a board. Paul was most certainly right.

She gasped: 'Katie! Where's it gone?'

Katie's midnight-blue eyes blinked. 'What?'

'The baby? You said you were having a baby. In February.'

'Yes.' Katie turned away, unable to look at her. She headed for the playroom.

Amy followed: 'Next month? You can't possibly be.'

'Amy, it was you that said it would be next month.' Katie's large innocent eyes met hers fleetingly.

'What do you mean?' Amy's head was swimming, she felt the most awful consternation. 'You haven't got rid of it? Katie, you haven't . . . ?'

'I haven't had it yet.' Katie's face had an unworldly quality. Amy knew then that she didn't understand.

'Katie, stop walking round. I've got to talk to you. This is important. Now, you are having a baby?'

'Yes, I told you.'

'That was at the beginning of July last year. You said you'd missed two monthlies?'

'Yes, I think I had then.'

'And since then?'

'Well, yes, they came back.'

Amy felt relief surging through her. She wanted to sing. 'Why didn't you say?'

Katie's blue eyes fastened on hers then. 'You know what this means?' Her sister continued to stare at her. 'You aren't having a baby at all.'

'But you said . . .'

'Good God, Katie! Did you see Dr Poole?'

'No.'

'You should have done! I thought you had. Why put yourself through all this – telling Mam – unless you were sure?'

'I was sure, Amy.' Katie looked so artless, so defenceless, Amy felt a stab of pity. Then she was guilt-stricken.

'You aren't having a baby. What made you think you were?'

'Jimmy . . . Well, you know . . .' She was having difficulty putting it into words. 'I let him make love to me. Like Mam said I shouldn't.'

Amy was suddenly rigid. The relief she'd felt creeping over her was cut short. 'You've not been doing it ever since?' She felt sick.

'Yes. I wanted to go on seeing him. Yes, I had to go on. Couldn't stop . . .'

'Jimmy wasn't willing to give it up?' Amy wanted to kick herself. She knew her own vehemence was frightening Katie.

'That's why we're going to get married.'

'Oh, Christ.' Amy couldn't believe it. She of all people should have realised. Katie didn't understand the basic facts of life.

'Are you sure you really want to marry Jimmy?' She was holding her breath, willing Katie to say: 'Of course I do. I love him.' Just as she had done last time. Instead there was a long pause.

'Paul doesn't like him much,' she said gently. 'He thinks Jimmy takes advantage. He's always late for work, and he's lazy, doesn't do much when he's there. Do you want to tie yourself to him for life?'

'But I've got to marry him, Amy, after all this. And what about the baby?'

'There is no baby. Don't you understand?' Amy wanted to shake her. The bright winter sun shone into the playroom, lighting up Katie's lovely face. Amy threw herself on to a chair.

It wasn't Katie's fault. It was her own. Hadn't she set herself up as Katie's guide? Hadn't she tried to make Mam's warnings clear? And yet when Katie really needed clarification, she'd let her down. How had she managed to forget when she herself had first learned the full facts of life? It was only after she started nursing. Only from the lectures. How could she have forgotten that?

Suddenly another thought crowded in. 'Did you say your monthlies had come back?'

'Yes, but I'm late now.'

Amy felt panic shooting through her.

'Get your coat. We're going round to Dr Poole. He won't have finished morning surgery yet. We've got to know one way or the other.'

'But I don't . . .'

'I don't care what you want, Katie. We can't go on like this. I only wish I'd had the sense to take you last July.'

'Well, I haven't been feeling too good lately,' Katie said slowly. 'I've felt quite sick in the mornings this last week.'

Amy felt rooted to the spot, numb with guilt and anguish. She couldn't believe what she was hearing. It was terrible news.

Amy felt she was having an awful day. It was her first on Weightman, the newly fitted-out women's surgical and gynae ward.

All student nurses were moved round every three months to widen their experience, and the first day on a ward was never easy. Amy felt too full of personal worries to concentrate on work.

When she'd first seen her name on the list for Weightman, she had been pleased because Fliss was there. She knew she'd see more of Paul and Auntie My when they came to visit. She'd even thought it might cheer Fliss up to be able to send and receive messages through her.

The layout of Weightman Ward was the first to be changed from the old Nightingale style. Instead of two long rows of beds, it was divided into bays, with six beds in each. Fliss had been given a bed by the window in the centre bay. Her pale listlessness upset Amy.

Fliss was the youngest on the ward by several decades; the other patients didn't have much in common with her. She seemed to spend most of her time looking out of the window. She had been in longer than anyone else, and didn't even have the luxury that the other patients had of being able to look forward to her return home.

'Paul's missing you at the café,' Amy told her. 'He's having to make a lot of changes with all the shortages. He's finding it hard going.' Fliss turned away, but not before Amy saw tears glisten in her pale eyes.

'I feel trapped in here,' she whispered. 'Away from everything. I'm not getting any better, even after all these weeks. I wish I was still working at the café. I wish I was back to normal.' Amy felt wrung out with pity.

Nurses were encouraged to read case notes, and Amy made a point of studying Fliss's very thoroughly. Her wound was still suppurating even after seventeen weeks. It seemed that no amount of re-dressings and treatment changes could make it heal.

The lines of Fliss's childlike face were drooping. Amy could see she was bored and depressed, and, of course, she couldn't feel well, not with the open wound she had. Doctors went out of their way to speak to her with the friendly familiarity they reserved for those incurring their pity, particularly those they were failing to cure.

Fliss was not the only patient on the ward Amy knew. Edna Ritchie had been friendly with Nancy when they were younger. Nancy had brought her home to play more than once. Amy had heard Katie talk of her since, as a nanny she'd made friends with in the park.

She'd come in with an incomplete abortion, and she wasn't married. Amy heard the other nurses talking about her. Admissions because of miscarriage were not infrequent, but in Edna's case there was some doubt as to whether it was the result of an illegal operation.

The gynaecologist had questioned her but she wasn't admitting anything. He'd decided to do nothing more. Sister thought he should have called in the police. If there was a local back-street abortionist, she was sure it would only lead to other girls being brought in, in a worst state.

Amy studied Edna's case notes with interest, as had every other nurse on the ward.

'Remember me?' she asked Edna, while she was doing the medicine round. She would not have recognised Edna had she seen her in the street. She thought her very attractive. 'I'm Amy Siddons. Aren't you friendly with my sisters?'

'Yes, Nancy,' Edna replied nervously.

'And Katie?'

Amy was surprised at her response. She seemed to draw herself up.

'For a time, yes, Katie too,' She was suddenly defensive, turning back to the book she'd been reading, thus ending the conversation abruptly. Amy could almost feel her antagonism for Katie. It made her wonder what her sister had done to cause it.

Amy was glad to get off duty at eight o'clock that evening. She went to see Paul instead of walking up to Ashville with the other nurses.

'I want to talk to you,' she whispered on the doorstep, when he answered her ring. She was too tired to spend the next two hours chatting to Auntie My.

'We'll go out,' Paul assured her, and while he got ready she went to the living room door.

'How's Fliss?' Auntie My wanted to know.

'I tried to cheer her up.'

'I'm sure you did, Amy.'

Amy knew she hadn't. 'She'd like another jigsaw puzzle,' she said. 'Anything to help pass the time. Have you got any more here? I'll have a look at home next time I go.'

Paul came thudding downstairs and Amy found herself outside on the pavement again.

'Sorry we can't take the car,' he said when they passed it at the kerb. 'Short of petrol.'

'Let's walk.'

'Come to the Bakehouse, it's too cold to stay outside tonight.'

'It's Katie. I haven't been able to think of anything else all day.'

'About the baby? Is she . . . ?'

'Probably.' Amy recounted what had happened. 'I made her see Dr Poole, but in the end it settled nothing. He told her it was possible she was a few weeks pregnant, but it was too

223

early to say for sure. He told her to come back in eight weeks.

'She asked me what she should say to Jimmy. I told her nothing. Absolutely nothing until she's certain.'

'Why didn't he twig?' Paul gripped her arm more tightly. 'He must know the score. He's a wide boy. Oh yes, he'll know. So why hasn't he explained things to Katie?'

'That's been bothering me all day,' Amy said. 'Going round and round in my head. He's deliberately let her go on thinking . . .'

Paul said grimly: 'It's easy to see why.'

When they reached the Bakehouse and had tucked the blackout curtain back in place round the door, she burst out: 'I feel terrible about it. It's my fault. I could have set her straight last July.'

'You couldn't . . .'

'Of course I could, Paul. I don't think she'd have kept on with him if I had. Anyway, I could have talked her out of seeing him, made sure she did what Pa ordered. At the very least I could have done that.'

He put his arms round her, hugged her to him.

'I got the wrong end of the stick. Now look what I've done to her.'

'It's not all your fault. Don't blame yourself, Amy.'

'She could have put Jimmy Shaw behind her long ago. She'd be perfectly all right now. I've let her down.'

'No, Amy, not you.'

'Who else has she got to rely on? Certainly not Jimmy. What else can she do now but marry him?'

Paul hugged her more tightly, then he kissed her. 'Your face is wet. Don't cry, Amy. I hate to see you upset like this.' He pushed his handkerchief into her hand.

'I can't help it.' She mopped at her eyes. 'Everybody says I busy myself nosing into things that don't concern me, yet I didn't for Katie. What was I thinking about?'

Paul kissed her again. 'You can't look after everything for her, love. Nobody can.'

'I don't know what I'd do if I didn't have you to turn to for comfort. Katie's only got me. Jimmy Shaw has used her for his own ends.'

BOOK FOUR
1940

BOOK FOUR

CHAPTER FOURTEEN

January 1940

Over the next few days, Amy got the distinct impression that Edna Ritchie didn't want to talk to her. It made her stop and ask herself why. She hadn't spoken to Edna since she was about twelve, so it certainly wasn't a grudge against her personally.

On the day Edna was to be discharged, Amy took her clothes to her and pulled screens round her bed so she could dress.

Sister had gone to lunch by the time Edna was ready to go. Amy was in her office when she came to collect her ration book.

Edna's parting shot was vicious: 'Your Katie's crowing, I suppose, that he's going to marry her. I wish her joy of him. I wouldn't touch him with a barge pole, not after the way he's treated me. He's a right bastard, that one.'

It left Amy gasping with horror. The implications didn't bear thinking about. Jimmy Shaw had got two girls pregnant at the same time! How could she tell Katie? But she couldn't let her marry Jimmy in ignorance of this.

It was Amy's afternoon off. After she'd been to the nurses' dining room to eat luncheon meat, cabbage and mashed potato followed by rice pudding and prunes, she walked up to the Brents' house in Park Road West.

She rang the bell and thumped on the knocker, but nobody answered. Impatiently, she strode off into the park to look for Katie.

She went round twice. It was a cold, blustery day and she didn't feel like a lot of outdoor exercise. She wanted to snuggle close to the fire in the nurses' sitting room at Ashville, gossiping and drinking tea.

She finally found Katie waiting outside the school for Bernard to come out. Amy was tired by this time and had decided there was no easy way to break the news to her.

'There's something you've got to know, Katie. You aren't going to like it. It's going to be very hurtful, but I can't let you marry him in ignorance.'

She saw Katie's face stiffen. 'It must be about Jimmy.'

Amy nodded. 'And Edna Ritchie. She's on the ward following a miscarriage. Or an illegal operation. She's saying Jimmy Shaw was the father. Sorry, Katie, but I couldn't let you marry him without knowing that. I mean, if he can't be faithful before he's married, what chance have you afterwards?'

She saw Katie sway. Her face went grey and pinched, but she was holding on to the pushchair and she stayed upright. Then, as she flushed with anger, children erupted into the school yard and Bernard came hurtling across to them.

He danced round like a dog newly released from its chain. Daniel kicked with delight to see him, jerking the pushchair, but Katie seemed to have turned to stone.

'Come on,' Bernard urged. 'I'm hungry. I want my tea.' After a long, shuddering sigh, Katie leaned on the handle and the wheels began to turn.

'He'll be in the Bakehouse now,' she said, her face stiff with determination. 'I'm going to see him. Have this out. Will you walk up and down with the children?' She was indicating Bernard. 'I'd rather they didn't come in.'

Amy would have liked to go in herself for a cup of tea and a warm-up, on this chilly January afternoon, but she said: 'Of course, if it'll help.'

Before the shop door closed behind her, she heard Katie ask Hazel: 'Is Jimmy in?'

Amy walked round the corner into Duke Street, pulling the reluctant Bernard by the hand. Moments later, she was surprised to hear Katie running after her.

'He's not there. Hazel doesn't know where he is. He went out this morning and promised to be back before lunch, but he didn't come.'

Amy was appalled. The pushchair had an irritating squeak as she continued to push it.

'Jimmy's never done this before. He always comes back for the busy period. Do you think he could have had an accident or something?'

'I don't know.'

'Come with me to his lodgings, Amy. He could be there.'

'He won't be. Not when he's supposed to be at work. He'll have gone out somewhere.'

'Where?'

'How do I know? To arrange something for your wedding?'

Katie shook her head.

Amy said: 'He could come back at any minute. I'd take the kids home and give them tea. You could try his lodgings tonight.'

'I hate going out alone in the blackout, but otherwise I won't see him until Thursday.'

'It'll keep.' When they reached Park Road North, Amy said awkwardly, 'It's hardly worth my walking up to Ashville now. Too late. I'll go back to the hospital. I'm sorry, Katie.'

Katie shot across the road when the lights changed, leaving Amy standing on the pavement.

She felt torn in two: hot with anger one minute and cold with fear the next. She strode up Ashville Road at such a pace that Bernard had to break into a run every so often to keep up.

It wasn't just anger and fear that made her burn. All the doubts she'd had about Jimmy were crowding back. There was jealousy that he'd been making love to Edna; regret and outright panic too, when she thought of the future.

She turned into Park Road West and hurried on. She heard a car coming up behind her but was too involved in her own worries to take much notice.

'Katie! For heaven's sake, Katie, stop a minute.'

It was only then that she realised the car was keeping pace with her along the pavement.

'Paul?' There was an intensity about him she hadn't seen before.

'Where's Jimmy?'

'I was about to ask you that. What's happened?'

'He's disappeared. So have the takings from the Bakehouse. The float, everything.' Paul was furious. 'I've got to find him.'

'I don't know where he is.'

'For heaven's sake, Katie! You know where he lives?'

She gave him the address of Jimmy's lodgings in Park Road South.

'He gave me that and I've been there. His landlady is raging mad. He's packed up and taken all his stuff. Skipped owing six weeks' rent. I need another address. What about his parents? Where do they live?'

'Liverpool. West Derby.'

'Do you know the address?' Katie shook her head.

'But you know where it is? He's taken you there?' Paul got out of his car and circled her angrily.

'No.'

'Come on, Katie, you must know something. You're going to marry him next week.'

'No, I can't help you.'

Paul's fury boiled over. 'Don't hold out on me. You're not playing fair.'

'I'm not holding out. I don't know.'

'I only took him on as a favour to you. Jimmy was never any good. Bone idle, and I reckon he's had his fingers in the till all along.'

'Who is this man?' Bernard pushed between them. He was being protective, standing with feet apart. 'He's not being very nice to you.'

Katie felt sick. She couldn't blame Paul. There seemed no end to the iniquities Jimmy had committed. Even now, she could hardly believe he was capable of all this.

'He's bound to be in touch with you,' Paul insisted. 'Well, isn't he?'

Katie went cold with horror. She was afraid that perhaps he would not.

'I don't know how you can marry a fellow like that. I'll have to go to the police. I'd have gone immediately if I hadn't been so concerned about you and Amy.'

'Oh no,' Katie protested. 'Don't do that. If Jimmy thinks the police are looking for him, he'll be afraid to come back.'

'He won't expect anything less,' Paul flared angrily. 'And he deserves all he gets. The last thing I need is to have cash stolen from the business. It could finish it. I'd screw Jimmy's neck if I could get my hands on him, and I blame you too. Don't ever ask any favours of me again.'

Katie felt desperate. Paul had been friendly and kind to her; she was horrified at his reaction now. Horrified, too, at all she had learned about Jimmy.

She turned and ran up the road to the Brents' house, towing Bernard behind her. As soon as she was safely inside she burst into tears.

There were times when Myra Laidlaw felt she was being sucked backwards towards a precipice, and at any moment she'd feel herself falling. She was finding it difficult to get back into the way of working.

'What you got that's hot, missus?' A new customer was leaning on the other side of the counter.

'Sausage and chips, pie and chips or hotpot.'

'Pie and chips, please.'

'With peas?'

'Yes please.'

Myra scribbled on the numbered pad and took the slip into the kitchen for Vera. Jack's way had been to shout the orders through, but when she'd tried it, she and Vera had got into a muddle when they had a rush on. Paul had been over the moon when she'd devised this system. It seemed to be working, up to now.

She found this the easier part of running the café, though nothing was really easy. She still felt rushed off her feet, and as though her brain had addled.

She was still struggling with the accounting system. It was exhausting, cashing up each night, with Paul explaining everything slowly over and over, and she'd been afraid at first that the books were quite beyond her. Really she was too tired to grasp anything new at the end of the day.

'On Sunday,' Paul told her. 'We'll go through it all again on Sunday morning when we're both fresh. The books are the important part, Mam.'

She couldn't come to terms with the speed with which things had changed since Jack had died. Anger rose in her throat. Why Jack? They'd both been so happy with things as they were. He'd left a great void in her life, and she'd so nearly lost Fliss too.

Seeing her lying inert on the hospital bed, fighting for her life, had been a second blow, catching her before she'd accepted the first. Now she had Fliss barely alive, reduced from a laughing, energetic girl to a thin, waif-like creature, caught in some no man's land between life and death. She shuddered every time she thought about her daughter. She was still afraid she might lose her.

She missed hearing her singing as she went about the house. It was too quiet without her. All Myra's energy had gone on pushing forward Fliss's career. Because she'd spent so much of her time at home training Fliss, she felt oddly out of kilter there too. It was impossible to feel optimistic after all these weeks. Fliss wasn't improving as she should be.

Then there was the bad news about the war, and the threat of Paul being sucked into it. Against his will, he had applied for and received a further deferment, he was pushing her harder than she could go. Making her learn every aspect of the business. Her head was stuffed full of facts that might or might not be useful.

'You're doing fine, Mam,' he kept telling her, but she didn't feel as though she was. There were often times when she had to turn to Vera for advice.

She didn't want Paul to be called up. She was dreading being left on her own to cope with everything. Dreading having Paul in a place where he could be killed or maimed like the rest of her family. Yet he couldn't wait to get away. Some stupid phobia he had about being called a draft-dodger.

There had been so many troubles, and now Jimmy Shaw fleecing them, taking money the business needed. It was one piece of bad news after another.

It seemed the happy family life she'd had was gone for good.

Alec had felt uneasy since he'd heard Bob Hood had been charged with theft. It niggled at the back of his mind all the time that Hood would try to do him down.

Peachey had been matter-of-fact. 'There's no evidence now. The woman should have complained about you immediately, had her bruises examined by a doctor.'

'Her neighbours have seen me,' Alec worried. 'Lots of times.'

'Accusations from Bob Hood can be made to sound like spiteful revenge. And he'll have to quote chapter and verse to get a police officer investigated.'

Even so, Alec dreaded having allegations made against him. It would make his position more precarious. For him, trouble could come from so many different sources.

One morning, as he went into the police station to start

his shift, Alec passed the postman, who was leaving. His footprints were still wet on the stone floor.

The reception desk was deserted. A small heap of mail had been tossed in the centre. Alec couldn't say why he paused there, but his eye was caught by the letter on top. It was addressed to Constable Alec Siddons.

He snatched it up. Cheap blue envelope and spidery writing he half recognised but couldn't put a name to. He tore open the envelope and his blood ran cold. It was from Bob Hood.

'If I go down, I'm taking you with me. I've let your boss know what you're up to. You're bent.'

Alec's throat tightened until he could hardly breathe. He could hear other people in the station, any minute they'd come in here. He fanned the mail out across the desk. There was another blue envelope with exactly the same spidery writing, addressed to Chief Inspector Courtauld.

'Christ,' he said aloud. His heart was pumping like an engine. He had that envelope in his pocket seconds before the duty sergeant came in. This morning it wasn't Peachey.

Alec was in a flat spin. He went straight to the cloakroom where other staff were getting ready to go on duty.

He shut himself into a stall to ensure privacy. Bob had printed the word PERSONAL on the chief inspector's envelope, to make sure nobody else opened it. Thank God he'd seen it in time. He tore it open with nerveless fingers.

Bob Hood wasn't much good at spelling but he'd got his facts right. He knew more than Alec had supposed.

'Alec Siddons is in cahoots with Sergeant Peachey,' he'd written. 'Both of them on the make. Diverting the course of justice to suit themselves. People like me don't get a fair trial.'

He'd gone on to list several instances. He even accused him of almost strangling Freda, when he'd hardly touched her.

Alec felt cold sweat breaking out on his forehead as he read. It seemed Bob was due to go to court for his theft of stamps and coins in two days' time. What if he said something then?

He tore the letters and envelopes into small pieces and dropped them in the pan. When he flushed it, they didn't all go. He stuffed toilet paper on top and pulled the chain again.

'Christ!' He kept having cold flushes. That had been a near thing, but he'd survived again, his luck was holding.

He'd type a reply to Bob Hood on official notepaper. Tell him his allegations were being taken very seriously and would be investigated. That should keep him quiet a bit longer. Given average luck he'd do a spell in jail.

After a few hours out on the beat, Alec began to feel better. He even felt little frissons of triumph that he'd got the better of the Hoods. He wasn't an easy man to topple. Some would say he was dicing with trouble, but he'd been getting away with it for twenty years or more. He'd survive a bit longer. His luck was definitely holding.

Katie set out milk and sandwiches on the playroom table, feeling that a trap was closing round her.

Amy had come in with her when she'd been to see the doctor. She'd done most of the talking for her. Katie had known Dr Poole since childhood but his change of attitude left her in no doubt that what she and Jimmy had done was very wrong. She'd felt ashamed and an outcast from society when she'd come out of his surgery.

Amy had been on her side and told her fiercely not to worry about what he thought. She'd already explained fully all Katie needed to know about how babies were made.

'I wish you'd told me before,' she'd said, and Amy had burst into tears.

'I wish I had too,' she'd sniffed. 'I let you down, Katie. I didn't stop to ask myself what you knew and what you didn't know.'

'Nobody ever talks about it. Even Jimmy didn't know.'

She saw immediately from Amy's eyes that she didn't believe that.

Katie shivered as she realised what that implied. She insisted: 'Jimmy thought as I did, that to make . . . to do what we did would always make a baby.'

'That's what he wanted you to believe.' She knew Amy was trying to be gentle, but there was no way she could soften that. 'So that you would go on. So that there would be no reason to deny him what he wanted. I feel awful every time I think that I could have told you and I didn't.'

Kate had never known her self-confident sister like this before, and had to reassure her that she didn't blame her.

The worst part, now, was not knowing whether she and Jimmy had made a baby or not.

If they had, it still seemed that the best way out of the mess would be for her to marry Jimmy. Except now she knew what he was really like, and she wasn't sure she wanted to marry him. Mam would still want it, though, and it might be better for the baby.

Paul had been certain Jimmy would be in touch with her again, though Amy said she didn't think so.

'Have nothing to do with him if he does show up,' she'd said. 'In the long run, you'll be better off without him.'

Katie was torn both ways. She'd still be tempted to marry Jimmy if he came back in time for their wedding.

Very slowly, the days began to pass. Each morning she told herself that Jimmy might be in the park today. She made countless journeys upstairs to look over the garden to the park beyond, expecting to see him waving and beckoning her to come out as he used to.

She looked at the red wedding suit in her wardrobe, and the new black high-heeled shoes that went with it. Remembered the joyous anticipation she'd felt the day she'd bought them.

She walked in the park and visited the lakes every day, but there was no sign of Jimmy. She had to assume he'd changed his mind about marrying her after all.

Katie felt she was dragging herself through her duties, setting out meals for the Brent children, taking them for walks, bathing them. When their parents were at home, she tried to pretend she hadn't a worry in the world. It wouldn't do to let them see. She was afraid they would ask what was troubling her.

She felt her sisters rallying round. Amy asked for an evening off on Thursday, so they could go to the pictures. Nancy took her for tea at the Ritz Cinema, and the following week to Henshaw House to have tea with Hilda in the kitchen while Mary Frampton was out.

Two days before the date set for her wedding, she asked Amy: 'I don't want to, but had I better go down to the Town Hall and let them know?'

'I'll go for you, if you like,' Amy volunteered. 'I'll tell them you're postponing the wedding. We don't have to give a reason or another date.'

'Thanks,' she'd said, and the next time she saw Amy, she knew immediately from her face that things hadn't gone as expected.

Amy hadn't been planning to tell her, but Katie had wormed it out of her.

Amy pulled her close. 'Jimmy hadn't arranged anything,' she said. 'There's no record that he ever went near the register office.'

It made Katie feel dead inside. Jimmy never had intended to marry her. All along, he'd meant to disappear like this. She'd loved Jimmy. She found it hard to believe. This was total rejection.

Even worse, she was increasingly sure she really was having a baby. There were changes in her body. At the end of February, Amy took her to see Dr Poole again.

This time he said: 'In this world, you can be sure your sins will find you out. You can expect your baby to be born at the end of September.'

Seeing Amy overwhelmed and tearful drove home to Katie even further the seriousness of her situation. The future now loomed horribly. She had bad dreams about the workhouse. She didn't know how she was going to cope.

For once even Amy didn't have the answer. 'Stay where you are, say nothing, and keep working as long as you can,' was the best advice she could give.

Two weeks later, on a Thursday afternoon, both her sisters took Kate to the Refreshment Room. They were having dried egg, bacon and chips before going to the pictures.

Amy said: 'We ought to tell Mam what's happened.'

Nancy added: 'And Pa.'

'He probably knows already.' Katie shivered. 'If Paul went to the police, Pa'll know Jimmy's disappeared.'

'He does,' Nancy said.

'I'm surprised he hasn't tracked Jimmy down single-handed,' Amy said. 'So he could personally wring his neck.'

Katie's seventeenth birthday fell that month.

'Mam's asking are you coming to tea,' Nancy told her. 'She says it'll have to be Sunday, because Pa's working on the day itself.'

Katie pulled a face. 'I don't want to. Pa will play hell with me.'

'Better if you do.' Amy was firm. 'Where else can you go when you can no longer work? Keep in touch with them, let them say what they want now. It'll be easier for you later on.'

'We'll all of us go next Sunday.' Nancy smiled reassuringly. 'I'll tell Mam to expect us.'

Amy took her into Robb's department store and picked out summer dresses for her to try on, buying one as a birthday gift. Nancy gave her two dress lengths so she could copy it.

At five o'clock, Amy called for her at the Brents'. Katie felt there was no escape. She hadn't been home since Christmas. She had to steel herself: she was dreading it.

Mam was fussing about in the kitchen when they arrived,

cutting bread and butter. Katie hung back behind her sister Amy. The atmosphere was terrible; Katie felt it close round her as soon as she crossed the step. She expected hostility from Pa but she'd been hoping Mam would be all right. Celia, however, whirled on her.

'So there's to be no wedding after all? You are in a mess. What chance will you have of a decent life now?'

'Mam, you promised you wouldn't say bad things.' Amy rushed to protect her sister. 'Do you like Katie's new dress? I got it for her birthday.'

'Many happy returns for Friday,' Mam said. 'Yes, but it's a summer dress. Not warm enough for February. I hope you aren't going to catch your death of cold.'

'I thought since it was my birthday, with a cardigan on top . . .' Kate began.

'It looks at least two sizes larger than you wore last summer.' Mam was spreading out the flowery material in the skirt.

Katie could feel the blush running up her face. It was.

'There weren't very many to choose from,' Amy said. 'The war is making a difference. That was the best fit we could get.'

'Still, Kate's going to need the extra width round her waist soon, and she can pull it in with the belt until she does. Very sensible of you, Amy.'

The kettle was singing on the stove. 'Do you want me to soak the tea?' Amy asked loudly.

Katie felt Nancy's hand on her arm. She was being led to the living room where she knew she'd find Pa. He was stretched out on one of the Rexine armchairs as usual. When he caught sight of her, he pulled himself upright.

'What a wicked girl you are! Doing this to us. No hope of a husband after all?' He leered at her. 'What a silly, stupid bitch you are. I could see that fellow was a con man as soon as he came through the door. Any fool could have seen it.'

Katie was left gasping. She felt the sting of tears behind

her eyes, and blinked angrily. She mustn't let them see how much she minded.

'Please go easy, Pa,' Nancy put in. 'We aren't all as clever as you.'

'A wicked girl is what you are, doing this to us. I'm so ashamed. I can hardly hold my head up in the road. What are the neighbours going to think?'

'Lay off it, Pa,' Amy said from the doorway. She was bringing in plates of cold meat. 'We're trying to celebrate Katie's birthday.'

'I wash my hands of the whole affair. Katie, I told you what to do, and you disobeyed. It's your lookout now, you'll have to get on with it. Why should I worry?'

'Because she's your daughter,' Amy said.

'Not any longer.' Pa pulled out a chair at the table and sat down. 'Not after what she's done.'

Katie could feel herself trembling. It seemed she had to face one humiliation after another, each worse than the one before. She was trying to shrink into her seat.

'Pa, when Katie can't work any more, she'll have to come home.' Amy's voice seemed to hold a warning. 'She's nowhere else to go.'

'She can go to the workhouse as far as I'm concerned. I'm not having her and her bastard here, living at my expense.' Pa was helping himself to most of the beetroot in vinegar.

'Don't say things you'll regret later.' Amy's lips were straightening with determination.

'Mam's made you a cake,' Nancy said brightly. It had the place of honour on the table. The meal was set out on the living room table because they were all family.

Mam came in with more plates. Her hands were shaking and Katie thought she looked a nervous wreck.

'You're lucky to get a sponge cake,' Mam said, handing the bread and butter plate to Alec. 'It's the best I can do. There's a war on.'

As she sat down, she knocked one of her Sunday teacups

off the table. It shattered with a crash that pulled Katie to the edge of her seat. Mam leapt to her feet in anguish. Nancy went to get the dustpan.

'He jilted you then, did he?' Pa asked. Katie couldn't answer. The truth was worse than that. He'd never had any intention of marrying her.

Duty dictated that they stay to clear away after the meal, but Katie couldn't get out of the house quickly enough. She set off down the road at a furious pace, with Nancy taking her arm on one side, Amy on the other.

'I can't go back home to live,' Katie burst out. 'Pa won't let me. You heard what he said. What am I going to do?'

Nancy squeezed her arm. 'Amy and I have put our heads together on this. The best thing we can come up with is a mother and baby home. They'll take you in a few weeks before the birth and keep you a few weeks afterwards. That will stretch to cover the three most difficult months.'

'It won't be any holiday,' Amy murmured. 'They make you work for your keep.'

'That'll be all right. I'd rather rely on strangers than hope Pa will relent.'

'We'll make enquiries for you,' Nancy said gently. 'Best thing is to stay working for the Brents as long as you can.'

'Until a few weeks before?'

'Say six weeks,' Amy said.

'Do you think I'll be able to?' To Katie it seemed impossible. 'Won't they notice?'

'Possibly,' Amy said. 'Being realistic, the answer is yes, they'll notice. I doubt if you'll get to the middle of August.'

'Arthur Brent has very strict ideas. If he finds out, he'll sack me. Where can I go then?'

'If only Nancy had a place of her own . . . I've got to live in at the hospital. I won't be qualified in time.'

'If Stan comes home, we'll get married,' Nancy said quickly. 'I might be able to get a flat then. You could come and keep me company.'

'Stan won't be able to stay with you,' Kate said.

'Not unless the war finishes quickly.'

Katie knew Nancy was always optimistic. It sounded like pie in the sky.

'You might have to go home,' Amy said slowly. 'For a few weeks. From when you can no longer work . . .'

Katie had already come to that conclusion. She shuddered. 'Could be months.'

'Anywhere else, you'd have to pay.'

'I've saved a bit. I'll be able to add to it.'

'If it was only for a few weeks, we could chip in to help,' Nancy said cheerfully. 'Couldn't we?'

'Katie will need money to buy things for the baby,' Amy said firmly. 'And she'll need somewhere to live when she comes out again, six weeks after.'

'With the baby.' Katie quailed at the thought.

'Yes, I'm afraid that's going to be an even bigger problem. Will you do that? Is that what you want?'

Katie didn't know what she wanted. She couldn't even think straight let alone imagine how she could ever support a baby of her own.

'I'll have another go at Pa, nearer the time,' Amy promised. 'To soften him up. I wish there was somewhere else you could go.'

Katie was worried stiff: the outlook was terrifying. The weeks began to pass too quickly. She wanted to stop time, keep things as they were. She could only just cope now.

Nancy applied for a place at the mother and baby home for her. Katie hated having to fill up the form they sent back, and go again to her doctor to get him to confirm the dates of her pregnancy. It seemed a further indignity.

The instructions were to return the form personally to the matron of the home, not post it, and to arrange a time to do this that was convenient for Matron.

Nancy arranged the appointment for her, because the post usually came before the Brents left for work in the mornings, and Katie didn't want any awkward questions.

She didn't want to take Daniel with her. He was growing more like Bernard, and picking up much more of what went on around him. She was afraid, too, that Matron might tell the Brents about her situation. On the afternoon Katie was to take her form in, Nancy came to take care of Daniel.

They walked to the bus stop together, then after making arrangements to meet again near the lake in a couple of hours, Nancy took Daniel into the park. Feeling very apprehensive, Katie got on the bus and went into town.

Bradshaw House was a depressing Victorian building of blackened brick. She found the massive front door intimidating.

A girl in a parlourmaid's uniform answered her knock and showed her to a chair outside the matron's office. She disappeared, having hardly said a word. Katie was kept waiting in the cold and cheerless corridor.

In the distance, she could hear the thin whimper of a newborn baby. It frightened her to think she would have to live in this dreary place.

Miss Cochran, the matron, looked formidable and unfriendly. Her office was warmed by a hissing gas fire.

'Katherine May Siddons, aged seventeen.' The woman gave her a sour look after reading from her form. 'You're very young to be in this situation.'

'Yes.'

'If your baby is normal, arrangements will be made for it to be adopted.'

Katie was struck by a new terror. 'Normal? Why shouldn't it be normal?'

The matron's lips pursed. Katie could feel her disapproval, she held it like a shield in front of her. 'Girls like you very often produce babies that are not. Almost always they are of lower than average intelligence. Your baby will have to be assessed when it's born. It's difficult to find adoptive parents for subnormal children.'

245

Katie suddenly felt protective of her coming child. 'I might decide to keep it.'

'Can you expect support from the father?'

'No.' She felt mortified.

'Then I don't think we could advise that. No, the best thing for both you and the child is adoption, if it's at all possible. We will arrange it for you.'

Katie had to struggle to say: 'Don't I have a choice?'

'Of course you do. When you've had time to think about it, you'll realise it's the best thing. You must learn to put the welfare of the baby before your own wishes, and not compound your mistakes. How can a young girl like you support a child?'

Katie stared at her shoes, polished up for the occasion. She'd already asked herself that, and had no answer.

'Very well then, Katherine. Come in on the twenty-fourth of August at two o'clock, and make sure you're punctual. This is a list of things to bring with you.'

Katie snatched up the list as it was pushed across the desk to her, and got out as quickly as she could.

CHAPTER FIFTEEN

May 1940

Alec had felt tension in the atmosphere first thing this morning, when with other officers working the seven until three shift he'd paraded to receive his orders for the day.

The parade was late starting and that was almost unheard of. They'd all noticed that Constable Dransfield was not with them. There were sniggers when somebody suggested he must have overslept, but then when Chief Inspector Courtauld came down they all knew something was terribly wrong.

He stood in front of them, looking stern and superior, letting his gaze linger on each in turn. That had been enough to make Alec feel uneasy, but when the chief inspector announced coldly: 'Constable Dransfield has been dismissed,' Alec felt his heart lurch in consternation.

Courtauld went on at some length about how Dransfield had also lost his good name and rights to a reference or a pension.

He had more to say about the distress this was causing his senior officers, and the smear on the honour of the force. Alec was hardly able to take it in. His mind was filled with one thought – why?

It took a long time for Chief Inspector Courtauld to come to the point. He was delivering a pep talk to them; gradually Alec became aware of what he was saying.

'Shameful behaviour . . . a most heinous crime for a police officer . . . accepting a bribe . . . disgraceful.'

Alec was listening avidly for the actual details, but none were forthcoming. So far as he had been aware, Constable Dransfield had been whiter than white.

He kept his eyes on the wall straight in front of him, afraid that his face would betray the panic he felt. It took all his self-control not to look at Sergeant Peachey. There must be no exchange of knowing glances. He'd put in twenty-three years with the force; to lose his pension rights would make a profound difference now.

When the chief inspector returned to his office, Alec's fellow officers were agog with the news.

There was a whisper that Dransfield had accepted a brace of pheasants from a licensed game dealer when he'd been inspecting his premises. If that was all there was to Dransfield's lapse, it seemed minor compared to some of the things Alec had done. And a huge price to pay.

As he went about his duties, Alec had been able to think of nothing else all day. He found himself looking anxiously behind him, expecting trouble from every quarter.

Now at the end of his shift, as he pushed his bike into his own yard, Alec was shaking. Anything like this seemed to take him to the brink. The Watch Committee would have him out too, if they got the merest inkling. This had really pointed out the risks he'd been taking.

He felt safer once he was home. Celia was grilling herrings and the kitchen was filled with their scent, but for once he wasn't hungry.

'Are you going out tonight, Alec?'

Across the table, her lined face was screwing up with anxiety. He wondered what could possibly worry Celia, who spent her days peacefully here in her home. She knew nothing of his problems; he never mentioned anything like that to her.

'Yes, you know I always do on Wednesdays.'

'Most days,' she sniffed.

'The one good thing about working seven to three is

there's enough of the day left to go out,' he said, to justify himself. He was beginning to feel a little calmer now.

'To the Legion, for a drink with the lads,' he added, in case she should ask.

He'd made arrangements to take Olive out, and that was something else he didn't talk to Celia about.

He took a bath. The water wasn't hot enough, Celia should have remembered to bank the fire up more. He put on the new suit he'd had tailored for him, and twisted in front of Celia's mirror to catch a view of his back. It was a fine wool worsted in silver grey with a faint stripe. He was pleased with it, he felt a different person out of uniform.

Celia's eyes raked him suspiciously when he went downstairs. 'Is that another new suit? You didn't say you'd ordered another.'

'Do I have to tell you everything?' He hadn't meant to snap, but today he couldn't stand suspicion of any sort. 'It makes sense to get it while there's still cloth available.'

'It looks very smart. Expensive.'

It had been. He had to be decently dressed to take Olive out. He didn't want her to be ashamed of him.

'You've got so many clothes. More than I have.'

'Get yourself something then,' he said to placate her. He knew she saved money from her housekeeping. 'I've told you to stock up on everything while you can.'

He put on his new white mackintosh and took the bus up to Oxton to Olive Driscoll's house.

He'd known Olive for the last seven years, ever since she'd come in to the station to report the loss of her pet poodle. She'd been upset, even a little tearful.

'I'm sorry to be like this.' She dabbed at her face with a lace handkerchief. She had magnificent green eyes that had the rare quality of looking their best when glistening with tears. He'd felt protective towards her, wanting to offer comfort.

'You must think I'm a sentimental fool to cry over a dog.

I lost my husband recently, it's left my emotions in tatters, and of course I shall miss Fido terribly. He's all I have now.'

Olive was a big woman, and beautifully dressed. Some would call her stout, but he was a big man and he didn't admire diminutive figures. Something about the way she looked at him made him want to be of service to her.

He'd made a special journey to the dogs' home the next morning and found that a white toy poodle had already been picked up. He was wearing a diamanté collar from which the name tag was missing, but he seemed to answer to the name of Fido.

Alec had called at her house, though she'd left a telephone number. It was a large villa on Budworth Road which took him miles out of his way. He was impressed with its opulence. There was a smart Lagonda sports car parked on the drive.

'Where is this dogs' home?' she asked, and all the time her green eyes implored him to help.

He started giving her directions, but she said: 'Will you come with me? I'm a fool at finding my way about.'

He'd left his bike leaning against a tree down near the front gate. Once he'd seen her house, he felt the bike might detract from his status. It was a problem for him now.

'We'll go in my car,' she said, waving towards the Lagonda. Alec was so tempted his mouth was watering. He'd craved a car like that for years. Even to ride in it would be a treat. He had to agree.

When she went to get her hat and coat, he pushed his bike round the back, out of sight. He felt bewitched by Olive and there was glamour about her car. He voiced his admiration of it.

'It was my husband's,' she said. 'I'm afraid it will have to go. I can't afford to run it.'

Alec wished he could buy it from her. He'd let her drive it sometimes so her loss would not feel so great. He wanted to ease the rough corners off her life for her.

At the dogs' home, the white poodle leapt into her arms

when his cage was opened. Her gratitude at being reunited with Fido was immense.

As she drove home again, Fido licked his face and left white hairs all over his uniform. She insisted on taking him into her sitting room for a drink.

She said she'd fallen on hard times, that her husband's death had left her with nothing, but Alec could see she lived in some style. Olive was middle class in a way Celia wasn't. He felt touched by her plight and wanted to help her in every way he could.

He discovered in the following months that she'd spoken the truth. Her husband's business had collapsed in the depression. Once his will was proved she had to leave her home.

He tried to help her find a suitable house to rent. She insisted on one in Beryl Road that was twice the size of his on Park Road North. Tearfully, she'd explained that she couldn't bear to live in anything smaller. He'd wanted to help her maintain as much of her previous lifestyle as he could. He'd even helped her pay the rent.

Alec felt that his life fell into separate compartments: the time he spent working; the time with Celia and Nancy; and the time he spent with Olive, which he enjoyed most.

Olive needed to be taken out, escorted to the best restaurants and theatres. She was used to enjoying life. She said that she felt they ought support local charities, and she'd bought tickets for a show at the Ritz tonight. Although it mostly functioned as a cinema, there was a stage show tonight to benefit the children's hospital.

Alec took the bus up Upton Road and walked round the corner to her house. He felt very much at home in her sitting room, with its big chairs upholstered in pale material and its fitted bronze carpet. It seemed a light and comfortable room.

She had coffee and ham sandwiches waiting for him. Then he was allowed to drive her into town in the Ford she'd bought to replace the Lagonda.

Usually he took Olive over to Liverpool where the chance of meeting people they knew was much less. But he had taken her out so often without mishap, he felt all should be well.

Still, the Ritz was a little close to home for comfort. His own girls frequented the place and he certainly didn't want to come face to face with them while he was with Olive. They would be unlikely to go to a charity show, though, and tickets tonight were expensive.

Olive had bought the best seats in the house and was wearing her fur coat and best blue hat. Once they were inside, they would be safe enough.

They were shown to their seats in the centre of the front row of the circle. One of the most charming facets of Olive's character was the pleasure she found in occasions like this. She was excited, and Alec felt his own anticipation being heightened by the atmosphere.

He bought two programmes and declined the change. It impressed Olive that he too gave to charity. He'd managed to buy her a box of chocolates: he wanted to do things properly when he was with her. He was biting into a cherry liqueur when he heard a laugh he thought he recognised. It was a moment or two before he could bring himself to risk a glance in the direction of the sound.

He felt physically sick. It had never even occurred to him that he might meet Chief Inspector Courtauld while he was out. Up until this morning, it wouldn't have bothered him much if he had.

Now it seemed that two compartments of his life had collided. The horror he'd felt this morning was rushing back, suffusing his body with heat. He felt sweat break out on his brow.

Suddenly he was afraid that by sitting here with Olive he would appear to be living above his income. She was dressed to the nines, with her fur coat thrown back against the seat. He did not want to attract attention from Chief Inspector Courtauld.

Alec pressed himself back into his seat, but there was no way he could reduce his bulk. He kept his face turned away, but he was more than conscious of danger lurking only a dozen seats away to his right.

There were to be two intervals, and Olive would expect to be escorted to the bar for a drink. No doubt Courtauld would be there in the crush. To stay here might be worse – he daren't risk it. He tried to see if Courtauld was nearer the aisle on the other side.

'Hello.' Olive was waving her programme to someone further up the row.

Alec felt paralysed. For one hellish moment he thought she must know the Courtaulds.

'Mary,' she said, 'I've been meaning to get in touch.'

Alec was able to look then. It almost knocked him cold to recognise Mary Frampton. She was with her husband Bill, only four seats away. Alec averted his head and held his breath.

'How about a drink together in the interval?' Olive mouthed along the row.

'Lovely.'

Alec felt his whole body crawl with fear. He'd met the Framptons once – or was it twice? – and there were two reasons why he didn't want them to recognise him tonight. Not only was Bill Frampton on the Watch Committee, but what if they mentioned this to Nancy?

He thanked God that at that moment, the lights began to dim. There was an expectant hush as everybody settled back in their seats and the curtains swished apart.

Alec felt a terrible urge to get to his feet and run. He had to fight it. Beside him, Olive was already beaming with pleasure at the children's choir. He couldn't think straight, could take in nothing from the stage. His head rang with the sound of shrill, childish voices.

He made himself sit still until he'd formulated a story to tell Olive. He didn't feel well. That was true enough now.

His head was thumping and his hands were clammy.

'Are you all right?' Olive whispered. 'You're very restless.'

'No, I feel dreadful. Quite sick.'

'You were all right a few minutes ago. Was it the ham sandwich?'

He passed her the car keys. 'I can't be sick here. I'll have to leave you.'

'Now?'

'I'm sorry. Terrible urgency.'

'Shall I come with you?'

'No, don't want to spoil things for you. Not more than I have to. I'll come and see you tomorrow.'

He pushed past her and went up the aisle. As he did so, he saw Courtauld climbing the carpeted steps in the far aisle, keeping abreast of him.

Alec expected to be challenged. He quickened his pace. The other man seemed to do likewise. It was only when he was coming towards him to leave by the same door that Alec realised it wasn't Courtauld at all, but a total stranger. The man went through the door, held it open for Alec to follow and then went into the Gents.

Alec could barely swallow. He could feel his heart pumping like an engine. Had he imagined the whole thing? What was the matter with him? When he got outside he was shivering and fear still knotted his intestines.

He was angry with Courtauld. He'd take a swipe at him if he were here now. Damn the pious Framptons too. Nancy was always singing their praises.

He was angry that his evening with Olive had been spoiled. There would have been supper with wine afterwards and even more to enjoy after that. He was angry with himself, too, for letting fear turn his mind like this.

It was Amy's afternoon off. She caught the bus to Woodside and called in to the Refreshment Room to see Paul.

She asked Vera for a cup of tea, then sat down at one of

254

the tables to wait. A moment later, Paul came bustling from the kitchen, smoothing his straight brown hair back from his forehead.

He asked: 'How's our Fliss?'

'Her consultant did a round this morning. Had another look at her wound. It's discharging the most awful stuff.'

'She's worse?'

'She's no better. Nothing seems to do her any good. He says he'll take her down to theatre again. Open up her wound and try cleaning up the infection surgically. Then he'll put new drains in.'

'Poor Fliss. So she'll have another operation? How awful for her.'

Amy tried to smile. 'Paul, she's quite pleased something more is being done for her. She's fed up just lying there waiting. She says she doesn't mind the operation if it will help heal her wound. She's desperate to be well again.'

'When will it be?'

'Next Wednesday.'

'It'll worry Mam,' Paul sighed.

Amy bit into one of the cakes Vera had brought over, and remembered what Fliss had said earlier that morning: 'It's terrible being cooped up in here in the summer. These rubber sheets are hot and they smell awful.' She'd pulled a wry face and sniffed. 'The stuff from my wound smells worse though. Even a proper bath would help.'

'How's the pain?'

'Better today.' She'd tried to smile but Amy thought she looked paler and thinner than ever.

Fliss had turned back to the window. 'All those lucky people riding on buses and walking in the park. Free to do what they want. It seems ages since I saw the inside of a theatre or even a shop.'

'Go out on the balcony and have a breath of fresh air,' Amy suggested.

'You're all getting on with your lives and I'm stuck here

255

in limbo.' Fliss sounded rebellious but she went out to lean against the rail, a forlorn and lonely figure.

Sister saw her from the office and ordered her back inside. She said it was too cold for patients to be out.

Auntie My was coming across from the kitchen to ask after Fliss. Amy decided she'd just tell her about the operation.

Since the middle of May, the news from France had been dire. The British Army was in retreat. Like everybody else, the Brents listened to every news bulletin. Katie had got into the habit of switching on the wireless to listen, even when she was alone with the children.

The Allied forces had left the line they'd been fortifying all winter to prevent the Germans over-running Belgium, and had fallen into a trap.

For the last day or so, the Germans had been saying they'd circled between the British and the Allied forces. That they'd formed a ring round the whole British Army, and were drawing it ever closer, cutting it off from the Channel.

This coincided with the first really hot spell of the summer. For over a week the sun had blazed down from a cloudless sky.

It was barely mid-morning, but already Katie felt exhausted. Daniel had reached the stage when he was up to all sorts of mischief and she needed eyes in the back of her head. It was even worse on the days Bernard was home from school. She was on the go from morning to night.

Now she was feeling a terrible need to sit down and put her feet up. Instead, she went to the back kitchen, where she'd put the children's bedding to soak overnight, and began to thump the posher up and down in the zinc tub. Usually this gave her satisfaction, but today she could feel the perspiration running down her face.

The months were passing. Amy had warned her she'd find she was more easily tired than she used to be, but she had to hide it from the Brents at all costs.

Rinsing the sheets in the sink and then turning the great wooden rollers of the mangle to wring them out was hard work, and Katie felt a little dizzy as she struggled to peg them out on the line in the garden. Bernard and Daniel were zooming round the washing pretending they were Spitfires, and firing make-believe guns at each other.

She felt blackness creeping over her, and the next thing she knew Daniel was crying in panic and Bernard pulling at her blouse. She was lying on the grass. Above her the sheets were ghostly grey outlines. Blood seemed to be pounding through her head.

'It's all right.' She put an arm round each child and pulled them close.

'What happened to you? What happened? You fell down dead.'

'No.' Katie knew she must have fainted. 'No, of course I'm not dead. I was pretending. Spitfires shoot to kill, don't they?'

Her head felt as though it was stuffed with cotton wool. Bernard pulled her up to a sitting position.

'I didn't think you were playing,' he said seriously. 'I thought it was for real.'

Katie knew she'd given the boys a fright, and she mustn't lie here in case the neighbours had heard Daniel and looked over the fence. Mrs Wooller next door had been in her garden cutting flowers when Katie had been at the back kitchen sink a few minutes ago.

She stood up and felt for Daniel's hand. The hollyhocks seemed a hazy blotch of pink. Amy had said she'd feel better once she was over the morning sickness, and on the whole she did. It was just that the future terrified her. Going to the mother and baby home seemed almost as bad as going home to live with Pa.

'It hardly shows,' Amy had assured her. 'You're holding on to your figure, but your face is pale. Blue shadows too, round your eyes.'

Katie didn't care how pale she was, but almost every day she appraised her changing shape in her wardrobe mirror. She'd made herself some summer dresses that were wider round the waist and had plenty of gathers in the skirt. She wanted to stretch this out another two months, six more weeks at the very least. She felt balanced on a knife edge.

Katie reached the kitchen and put the kettle on for elevenses. She allowed herself to sit down for a few minutes, though she was beginning to feel more normal.

Saturday was a bad day to have something like this happen. Mr Brent came home in time for lunch. Although it used to be the busiest day of the week for his wife, she said she was never busy now because she had little to sell. She had begun closing her shop early on a Saturday and coming home too.

Today, for lunch, Katie used dried egg to make scrambled eggs on toast, and added chopped fresh tomato to it to make it more interesting. She was feeling better, almost normal. Afterwards she took the boys out into the park, to get away from Arthur Brent's gaze.

She was finding it hard not to dwell on her problems. Edna Ritchie, she was beginning to think, had been lucky to get it over and done with quickly.

Jimmy had told her that Edna had thrown herself at his head, that she'd been jealous when he said he was in love with Katie. Now she wondered if he'd told Edna the same story about her, to prevent them comparing notes and realising he was two-timing them. It seemed likely.

Jimmy had thought of nobody but himself. Katie could face that now. He'd been seeking his own pleasure. Using her. Using Edna Ritchie too. He'd not cared about the problems he might be giving them. Not cared about the babies. He'd abandoned them all. Katie could understand the hate Edna must feel. Love could turn to hate when things like this happened.

'Forget him,' Amy had ordered. 'You must, it's better than hating him. Hate will hurt you too. Put him out of your mind.' But that was easier to say than do.

She felt torn in two every time she thought about her baby. She didn't want to part with it, but she knew she'd have little option when it was born in that mother and baby home.

She'd brought bread with her to the park, so the children could feed the ducks. It was still plentiful, but she felt guilty about doing it. There were posters everywhere imploring people not to waste food.

The boys kicked a ball about on the grass. Bernard set up two sticks to serve as goal posts and wanted Katie to stop the goals they were trying to shoot. Katie tried, but she wasn't putting her heart and soul into it. She felt too hot and sticky to move.

The sky was darkening, the atmosphere growing heavier. It felt as though a storm was coming. Even the little boys were running with perspiration by the time she took them home for tea.

'Is Mummy home yet?' Bernard asked his father, who was cutting the back lawn.

'Yes, but don't go near her, Bernard. She's lying down with a bad headache. It's the thundery weather, I think. She said would you mind seeing to supper tonight, Katie?' Usually, Mrs Brent cooked the main meal of the day.

Katie wasn't hungry. Her own head was thumping and she felt tired out. After fainting this morning she knew she should rest, but she was afraid to refuse. She didn't want to admit to any infirmity.

'Yes, of course,' she said, trying to sound brighter than she felt. 'What is it to be?'

She was relieved to hear it was cod in parsley sauce. Not too much work to that. She had a practice run for the children's high tea, and after that she bathed them and put them to bed.

Normally at this point she'd be able to take a bath herself, or have a rest until her own meal was ready. She felt exhausted as she went downstairs to cook again.

Mrs Brent had recovered sufficiently to come down to the sitting room and was sipping a glass of sherry. Katie wasn't offered any; she knew she was considered too young.

She peeled the potatoes and put them on to boil. Mr Brent had grown broad beans in his greenhouse and had taken them out of the pods to help her. Katie got everything simmering on the stove. The meal was almost ready, but she was so tired the kitchen was beginning to swing round her.

The cod was cooked. She'd chopped the parsley and had reached the last stage of making the sauce when she felt the same awful dizziness she'd experienced this morning. Suddenly she was afraid. She tried to grab the kitchen table, telling herself she must not faint under any circumstances. This time, she heard the crash as she went down. Blackness engulfed her.

'Look what you've done!'

Katie could see Mrs Brent's high-heeled shoes and silk stockings on a level with her face. She struggled to sit up. 'What a waste of good food.' Mrs Brent's voice was high-pitched with displeasure.

Katie had upset the skillet. The fish and the sauce she'd been thickening were all over the floor. Her hand hurt where the sauce had scalded it. She felt sick.

Mr Brent came to the kitchen door. 'What a mess! What are we going to eat now? Whatever came over you, Katie?'

'I queued for half an hour for that fish.' Mrs Brent was indignant.

Katie tried to get to her feet. The mess and the skillet were still eddying round her. She fell back; she couldn't yet find the strength.

'What is the matter with you?' Mrs Brent's voice was sharp with suspicion. Katie could see her bending closer. Peering at her. Lifting her clothes.

'Good God, you're not expecting . . . ? I do believe you are! All those times you went out at night? I knew no good would come of it. Arthur, she's expecting!' Katie wished the floor would open up and swallow her.

'Oh, you wicked girl! How could you? I thought you were looking heavier, and on the rations . . . Oh, I can't believe this.'

Mr Brent looked grim. 'Well, now we understand why you can't do your work properly. How can you when you're like this? You aren't capable any more.'

'I am,' Katie pleaded. 'It's been such a hot day. Please give me another chance.'

'You must expect hot days in summer.'

Mrs Brent said firmly: 'You aren't fit to take care of our boys in this condition. Get your things packed and get out of here tonight. We can't possibly keep you here like this. You'll bring disgrace on us too. You'd be a bad influence. No, you must go immediately.'

Her husband added: 'We'll pay you up to today.'

Katie felt tears scald her eyes and run down her cheeks. She couldn't stop them. She felt mortified. Slowly she got up, turned the gas off from under the pan of potatoes and dragged herself upstairs to her room.

The moment she'd dreaded had come suddenly, and much sooner than she'd hoped. She pulled her suitcase out from under her bed and started to put her belongings into it. She felt appalled at the prospect of going home. This time she wouldn't have Amy to hold her hand. She shivered at the thought of what Pa was going to say.

She left as soon as she could, without saying goodbye to the boys. Her case was heavy. She had a cardboard box too.

It was only just half past seven, but it was almost dark. Lightning flickered in the sky away to the west. She could hear the rumble of thunder coming closer.

On the way home, Katie had to pass the Victorian gothic pile that was Ashville House, where Amy lived. In the hope that she might have the evening off and still be there, she went up to the massive door and rang the bell. A girl answered, dressed in a taffeta party dress.

261

'Amy Siddons? She's not here. I think she's still on duty.'

Katie wondered whether it was worth waiting for Amy to come. She needed support. Amy had said she'd pave the way with Pa, but it had all come about so quickly. Katie was afraid she hadn't got round to it.

'Be about half an hour,' the girl told her. The rain was coming, huge drops like half-crowns were darkening the steps.

She ought to have asked the girl if she could wait in Amy's room, though she shared it with another, but now she couldn't hang about outside.

There was nothing else for it, she'd have to go home. As the rain grew heavier she quickened her pace. Only her mouth felt dry as she hurried up the back yard and let herself into the kitchen.

Her mother's startled face swung round from the sink to take in the suitcase, the cardboard box and the extra coat over her arm.

'What are you doing here?' she demanded sharply. 'What have you come home for?'

CHAPTER SIXTEEN

Celia Siddons could feel herself shaking. Katie didn't need to tell her what had happened, her drawn face said it all. Katie's crisis was on them. Celia's heart was pounding with shock.

'Who's that?' Alec called from the living room.

'It's me, Pa.' Katie walked up the hall as though going to her execution, and lowered her suitcase at the door.

Celia followed timidly. She was in time to intercept the long, hard look Alec gave her. She could see Katie trembling.

There was a small fire in the grate and the room was over-warm. Alec was lolling back in his armchair. He had hairs like black wire wool filling his nostrils and growing in his ears. The mat of black curly hair on his chest was visible at the neck of his shirt and as a grey shadow through the thin white cotton.

'Sent you packing, have they?' She knew he was jeering at their daughter. 'Sent you away in disgrace? Well, the time had to come, didn't it?'

'Yes, Pa.'

'I hope you're not expecting to stay here?'

'I'd like to. Please, Pa, if I may.' Celia could see Katie shrinking from him.

'After what I told you?'

'Just for a couple of months, Pa. I've made arrangements to go elsewhere to have the . . .'

'I hope you have. No, you needn't think you're bringing your trouble home. We can't have the stigma of an illegitimate

263

child here, can we, Mother? We'd be too ashamed. What will the neighbours think? I told you not to come.

'You wouldn't take my advice about that fancy fellow of yours. We've never caught him either. Hope the army's got him by now. No, Kate. I have to think of my position. There's the door. On your way.'

'What, now?'

'Of course, now.'

'It's pelting down and it's getting late.'

'It's barely eight o'clock.'

'Where can I go? I've nowhere else to go, Pa.'

Celia saw Katie's desperate gaze swing to her. The poor child looked defenceless, her chin resting on the big cardboard box she still held in front of her.

Celia knew she had to make some effort: 'Couldn't she stay tonight, Alec? The storm's broken . . .'

'If she stays one night, she'll want to stay another. Be on your way, Kate, before it gets any later.'

Celia gasped. Alec could treat them all as though they were criminals. He could be very cruel, very sure his behaviour was above reproach. She supposed being a policeman had made him like this. He never saw any point of view but his own.

She shivered. If he ever found out . . . But he wouldn't, there was no way. Now Nancy's wedding had been put off for the time being she felt better. The spectre of Victor Smith had retreated.

After all these years, even she could see it was unlikely Alec would ever find out. She ought to feel safer, more secure, but she didn't.

To see Alec's ire turned against Katie had reduced her to a jelly. She knew he'd turn against her too if he knew.

'Come on now, how many times do I have to tell you?' Alec got to his feet. Celia watched Katie retreat. Alec was picking up her case, taking it to the front door.

* * *

Katie heard the scrape as her suitcase was pushed out on the step behind her. The front door slammed with awful finality. Rain was sheeting along the road. A bus passed with all its lights on, spraying water from its tyres.

She was shaking with shock and fear. She had no idea where she could go at this time of night. Her mind was on fire with the awful things Pa had said. She'd heard of parents turning their daughters out but she'd never believed it would happen to her.

She yanked on her suitcase, leaning against its weight to lift it, and took three steps through the gate to reach the pavement. She was half blinded by rain and tears.

She thought she heard someone call her name but took no notice.

'Katie?' She felt a hand on her arm. It was Paul Laidlaw, his brown hair blowing in the storm. He'd run out in his slippers without a coat.

'I want a word with you.' He'd left his front door open. 'Come inside, we can't talk out here, it's tipping down.'

'No, Paul. I . . . I can't.' He'd been so angry last time they'd spoken. She couldn't stand any more anger tonight.

'Where are you going?'

'I don't know. Does it matter? I'll find somewhere.'

'In this?'

'I don't care.'

'I care, Katie.' His eyes blazed down at her. 'Come in, we're both getting soaked and Winnie Cottie will be making a huge drama out of this.'

He took her case and put an arm across her shoulders to draw her into the lobby. Already her face was running with rain. It was a relief to get under cover. He was helping her off with her coat, shaking the water off it.

'Come to the kitchen. I'll make a cup of tea.'

After the abuse from her father, Paul's unexpected kindness was making tears run down her face along with the rain.

'They've thrown me out,' she whispered. She'd been put

out by the Brents but she'd never expected Pa to do the same. He'd threatened, but she hadn't expected him to do it when it came to the point. She felt doubly rejected.

'I guessed. Amy's told me. You can stay here tonight. Have Fliss's room. I'll fill a couple of hot-water bottles to warm the bed. It's a long time since she slept in it.'

Katie's tongue was so dry and furred it felt too large for her mouth. 'What about your mother? She won't like it.'

'She's gone to spend a week with her sister in Southport. She needed a break. There's only me here.'

'Oh.' Katie sank down on a kitchen chair.

'Is that all right?' Paul was looking at her anxiously. 'I mean, you're not afraid? There's no one to chaperon you.'

'Under the circumstances, I don't think I shall worry about that.' She gave him a lopsided smile. 'Anyway, it's Amy you're fond of.'

'I'm fond of you both,' he said. 'It's Amy who says she isn't going to marry me till she's qualified and had a bit of fun.'

'Have you asked her?'

'Yes.'

'I didn't know. You're being very kind.'

'Amy would put a knife in my back if I let you go off on your own like that. I could hear your pa shouting from here.'

'Go to the workhouse,' he'd screamed at her on the doorstep.

'Does it still exist? The workhouse?'

'They've changed the name,' he told her. 'That's all. The function remains. I want to phone Amy and tell her what's happened. If she hasn't gone out she should be at Ashville by now. I'll see if I can get her.'

'What can Amy do?' Katie asked hopelessly.

'She'll need time to think. She's got to know. She'd want me to tell her.'

'I couldn't stay with her at Ashville. Well, I did one night. She took me to the hospital dance and it was too late to come home, but I had to get up at six thirty with the nurses and get out before the maid came.'

'You can stay here for a few nights. Mam won't be home till Wednesday.'

'She'll be furious if she finds out.'

'No. She's fond of Amy too, we both owe her a few favours.'

While Katie drank the tea Paul had put in front of her, she could hear the cadences of his voice as he spoke on the phone in the hall. She felt comforted by his care. She was incapable at the moment of looking after herself.

He came back and looked in the pantry. 'When did you last eat?'

She had to think. 'Lunchtime.' She wasn't really hungry, just empty.

'I've got some sausages. Those and fried bread? You'll feel better if you eat something.'

That brought scalding tears to her eyes again. 'You are kind, Paul.'

'Don't keep saying that. I haven't been kind about Jimmy. I went for you rather. I'm sorry.' He looked awkward now. 'We were both taken in by him.'

'I know, I feel very guilty about the trouble I caused you.'

'Jimmy caused the trouble, not you.'

'You needed the cash he took.'

'The business did. I've cooled down now, Katie. I know he conned us both. It isn't your fault, he's dropped you in worse trouble than he has me.'

The last forkful of sausage was halfway to her mouth when Katie heard somebody coming up the yard. The next moment Amy came into the kitchen, threw off her wet gabardine and was pulling her close. Drops fell from her little round hat as she hugged her. The tears that had threatened at Paul's kindness now overwhelmed Katie. Not everybody was rejecting her after all.

'What am I going to do now, Amy?' she wept.

'I'll fix Pa. You've got to have a roof over your head.'

Katie sniffed miserably. 'He's too hard a nut to crack.'

'No he isn't.' Amy frowned. 'We've got him stitched up, haven't we, Paul?'

The next day, being Sunday, Amy had a half-day and went straight up to the Laidlaws' house after lunch. Only Paul was in the kitchen.

'How is she?' The elastic band on Amy's plait had slipped. She could feel it coming loose. She brought it over her shoulder and her fingers began plaiting it back into place.

'Upset, poor kid. I've told her there's no need for her to go until Mam comes back. Mam might even be willing to let her stay here.'

'It's asking a lot,' Amy said. 'We won't be able to pay her.'

'I don't think Mam would mind.'

'We can't be sure.' Amy frowned. 'I'll get Pa on his own and have a go at him. Got to be ready in case . . . Better if Katie stays out of his way until I do. Then perhaps another day to let him soften up.'

'Kate will be on her own all day while I'm at work. Is that a good thing?'

'Have to be.'

'Give her plenty of time to rest.'

'I'll pop in when I'm off, to try and cheer her up. Nancy said she'd call round too.'

The war news seemed to go from bad to worse. All the following day, Amy waited, feeling tension mounting. The Germans were now rumoured to be only twenty-two miles away in northern France. They seemed to be gathering, poised to invade. All England was holding its breath, expecting to hear the worst.

When she dropped in again to see Katie that evening, she found Paul and Nancy already there with her.

'Have you heard from Stan?' she asked.

'I had a letter from him this morning.' Nancy's usually smiling face was drawn. 'But he wrote it over a month ago.'

'The post has gone haywire,' Amy said.

'Yes, I've already had letters he's written more recently. I wish I knew what was happening to him. The Germans are saying they've got the British in the bag. This is a disaster.'

'Some are getting out,' Paul said. 'Stan might do it.' It was only then Amy noticed Nancy had gone paper-white.

Katie seemed more self-possessed but was very quiet. She'd made a pot of tea and they were all sitting round the living room table drinking it. At nine o'clock Paul switched on the wireless for the news.

Amy listened to the calm voice of Alvar Liddell, the news reader, telling them that the little fishing boats were continuing to come back across the Channel from Dunkirk.

She shivered, feeling goosepimples lift on her arms. The news was terrifying. What was left of the British Expeditionary Force was coming home from France in dribs and drabs. All were dishevelled, with uniforms that were torn, dirty and sometimes blood-stained.

The official line was that it was a triumph for the fishermen and yachtsmen of England that they were able to bring so many soldiers home. For Nancy, it didn't hide the fact that the evacuation was a rout, a huge defeat.

Her face seemed to crumple before Amy's eyes. Nancy was crying. 'I wish I knew what was happening to Stan,' she sobbed. 'He could be dead!'

'On the other hand, he could be perfectly all right,' Amy said gently. She'd expected to be comforting Katie, not Nancy.

'I couldn't bear it if he's killed. I'm so frightened he will be.'

Paul got up to pour brandy into a sherry glass. 'Medicinal purposes,' he said. 'It's the war, Nancy. You're feeling the brunt of it just now. We can only hope Stan's all right.'

* * *

Nancy cycled up to Vyner Road at ten o'clock that night. The bus service had been drastically cut and those that still ran did not do so on time. In the blackness of winter Nancy hated being out in the blackout, but in the long blue twilight of summer evenings, she found cycling the easiest way to get about.

She stopped for a few moments at the Thermopylae Pass, remembering all the times she'd come here with Stan when they'd been able to look down on the lights of Upton stretching away into the distance below.

Tonight, there were no lights, just the thickening misty blue shadows of night. A pale star was just coming out, and a solitary vehicle was driving slowly up Upton Road on dipped headlights.

She knew Stan must be in grave danger. If the whole British Expeditionary Force was close to annihilation nothing could save him from trouble. She'd heard on the news of German Panzer divisions speeding across France in pursuit of the British. She wondered if she'd ever see him again. She regretted now that they hadn't rushed into marriage. They'd wasted years they might have had together. Her eyes felt hot and heavy with the tears she'd shed earlier.

The jitters she'd been having all week were hardening to dread. She was worried about Kate, but much more worried about Stan. He could be captured, injured, dead even.

She reached the drive of Henshaw House. The white gravel gave a bumpy ride but was easy to see. There was a shed behind the garage where she kept her bike, and just enough light for her to avoid the lawn mowers as she pushed it in.

She could see the merest chink of light where the blackout curtains in the kitchen hadn't been pulled close enough. She opened the back door and went into the scullery.

'Is that you, Nancy?' She heard Toby Frampton's voice from the kitchen.

'Yes.' She opened the door and went in.

The kitchen smelled of the toast Toby was making for himself. He turned round from the stove, smiling.

Ever since his call-up had been deferred at the beginning of the war, he'd begged his father to let him go. Now at last he was wearing the blue uniform of a RAF flying officer. He was stationed at Sealand just outside Chester, only twenty or so miles distant, and so was able to get home fairly often.

His grey eyes were shining with excitement. 'Good news for you, Nancy.'

'For me?'

Toby laughed. She could see he was revelling in the joy he was about to give.

'Your fiancé Stan Whittle is back in England safe and sound. What do you think of that, then?'

Nancy wanted to laugh with him, but found she was crying at the same time.

'Hey, I thought you'd be pleased.' He was offering her his handkerchief.

'I am, Toby. Delighted. How do you know?' She mopped at her eyes; they still felt heavy.

'He rang up here. You could have spoken to him yourself if you'd been home.'

'I can't believe it! Safe and sound?'

'Exhausted – he's had no sleep for nine days and nights – but sound of limb.'

'Wonderful! I'm so relieved! I've been imagining the most awful things. Did you speak to him, Toby?'

'No, Mother did. She's gone to bed, but she made me promise to wait up and tell you. He's in Dover, in a transit camp. He was about to go to bed and said he'll try ringing you again when he wakes up. Don't expect it early, he said, because he feels he could sleep for a week.'

'Just to know he's all right! I'm up on cloud nine.' Nancy felt exhilarated, exultant. 'I feel I could dance. It's the most wonderful news. The biggest worry off my mind.'

'Don't tell me you've got others?'

'Yes. What about your gran? Is she still awake?' Old Alice Peacock was not sleeping well. 'I'd better have a peep in her room.'

'She was awake five minutes ago and asking for her late night drink.' Toby nodded towards the Aga. 'I put some milk on to heat for her.'

'Good.' Nancy put out two dry water biscuits on a china plate. 'She tells me off every night when I take her these instead of the chocolate ones she loves so much.'

Alice needed constant watching to make sure she kept to her diet. 'I tell her we can't get chocolate biscuits any more because of the war.'

'True enough anyway. What other worries, Nancy? Aren't they totally eclipsed by the good news?'

'Not quite. It's my sister, Katie. The youngest.'

'Nothing serious, I hope?' Toby had the habit of lifting one eyebrow when he asked a question.

'Yes, it is serious.'

'Can I help?'

Nancy shook her head. 'I don't know how to help her myself. None of us do, we've been trying to think of a way. She's only seventeen and having a baby.' She hesitated, weighing Toby up. 'Not married.'

'But she's going to be? Married, I mean?' Toby's sympathetic eyes smiled at Nancy.

'We thought so. She thought so. Last January, it was to be. He disappeared, a couple of weeks beforehand.'

'Poor kid. That's a terrible thing to do to her.' Toby seemed shocked.

'You haven't heard the half of it yet.' Nancy couldn't stop talking about it now she'd started. She felt a twinge of guilt too, that she'd been so much more worried about Stan.

'His name was Jimmy. A handsome fellow he was too, but much older than her. He gave her a ring.' Nancy looked down at the small diamond on her own finger. 'Not an expensive ring, he didn't have a job.

'Then Paul, my other sister's boyfriend, gave him a job, so he could marry our Katie. Instead, Jimmy stole from him, then disappeared before Paul could do anything about it. Paul went to the police, but they've not been able to trace him.'

'Sounds as though Katie will be better off without him.'

'Mam thinks it's a terrible disgrace to have a baby without a husband, that any husband is better than none. It's never happened in our family before. Pa took an instant dislike to Jimmy, but was prepared to overlook that when Katie told them about the baby. They've thrown her out. Pa told poor Katie to go to the workhouse.'

Toby whistled slowly through his teeth.

'Mam's always been neurotic about us. Afraid men are going to take advantage. I suppose most mothers are?'

'I wouldn't know. Perhaps it's one of the penalties of having attractive daughters.'

Nancy groaned. 'Katie's the best-looking of us all. Lot of good it's done her.'

'Where is she now?'

'Amy's boyfriend has taken her in. His mother's away for a few days and doesn't know yet. Katie's a good girl. I can't imagine how she got herself into such a mess.'

'He must have been a real rotter.' Toby frowned.

'There's worse that I haven't told you yet. He got her friend pregnant too, at about the same time. Amy nursed her after she was admitted following an illegal abortion.'

Toby Frampton was like his father, serious and gentle. 'Good Lord! Poor Katie.'

'She's desperate for somewhere to live. She's nowhere she can go over the next few weeks.'

'There must be somewhere,' Toby said, thoughtfully.

She could see him frowning with concentration.

'You've thought of something?'

'Perhaps, perhaps, Nancy. I'll have to talk to Dad about it.'

* * *

The following afternoon, Amy stationed herself at the Laidlaw front window, waiting for Pa to cycle past as he came off shift.

She felt jumpy. The rest of her family said she was very daring in what she said to Pa. Mam said she went too far, that she'd try his patience and be sorry.

She was always short with him and quibbled a bit, but the truth was she'd never let the slightest hint of what she knew about him pass her lips.

Now she meant to confront him with his sins and it was making her nervous. She had to force him to do what she wanted, but what if she did it wrong? Pa could be an awful bully.

At that moment he came into view, pedalling his heavy black bike on the other side of the road. Amy took a deep breath and went quickly out through the Laidlaws' back yard to meet him turning into the entry.

He dwarfed her, in height and girth, and she thought his girth was still expanding. Close to, in his uniform, what she was about to do seemed very daring. Like finding fault with the laws of England.

He sounded grumpy: 'What do you want?'

'I want to explain something to you, Pa.' She'd followed him into their own yard. Pa pulled open the door of the shed and pushed his bike inside.

'For heaven's sake girl. Not out here. Can't you see I'm tired? I'm just coming home.'

'I thought you'd prefer it out here. I don't think you'll want Mam to hear this.'

He looked her squarely in the eye for the first time. His face changed. 'What do you mean?' He sounded suspicious.

Amy could feel her heart thumping. 'It's like this, Pa. Our Katie's at the Laidlaws'. I want you to go round there and say you're sorry for turning her out last night.'

'Eh? Don't be daft!'

'Then I want you to tell her you've had second thoughts. You want her to come home. That she's welcome to stay as long as she likes.'

'I'm not doing that.' He was indignant.

'Oh yes, you are. And while's she's living at home, you're going to be civil to her. No needling her, making her life a misery.'

He was snorting, red in the face with growing anger. 'And who's going to make me do all this?'

'You'll want to. Believe me, Pa, you'll want to.'

'What do you mean? Of course I don't want to. I won't.'

'I think you will. I know your secrets.'

'What secrets?' His eyes burned down at her threateningly. 'I haven't got any secrets.'

Amy felt a flutter in her stomach. 'Enough to upset Mam.'

'That's all you will do, you silly bitch,' he snarled. 'You tell her what you like. Chances are she won't believe you anyway.'

Amy stepped back. She hadn't thought of that. She wouldn't want to upset Mam and Pa knew it. It was a threat she couldn't keep.

He was glowering at her. 'You're trying to cause trouble for me, telling lies about what I do. That's what they'll be, lies.'

Amy swallowed hard. He was pushing past her, to put an end to this. She mustn't let him see her weakening.

'I can handle your mother,' he stormed at her. 'All you'll do is cause a row, but your mother will do what I want when it comes to the point.'

She took a deep breath. 'If you haven't done what I ask by tomorrow evening, I shall tell Mam all I know about you and Mrs Driscoll.'

'What?' His face went crimson and then white again. He was blustering. 'Who is this Mrs Driscoll you're on about? I know nobody of that name.'

Amy knew she'd got the upper hand now. She could see him sending furtive glances towards the living room window, but Mam would be in the kitchen now, preparing dinner for him, and the kitchen window looked across the yard, not down it.

'I expect you call her your fancy woman. Others might say mistress.'

'You bitch!' His great paw swung towards her face. Amy's heart was thumping but she stepped backwards in the nick of time. 'What are you trying to do to me?'

'I've taken a leaf out of your book, Pa. Blackmail, most people would call it. That is what you do, isn't it, when you want something?'

'How do you know? You're making it all up.'

'Been keeping tabs on you, Pa. Since I was a kid. It's been going on for years, hasn't it? I've followed you to her house in Beryl Road. Do you want me to describe her?'

Her father was staring at her aghast. She could see his hand shaking as he stepped backwards into the shed.

'I could mention Ethel Williams and Freda Hood too. We can all play at being detectives, you know. Couldn't believe it at first. Rest assured, I know it all.'

His whole attitude was changing; his voice dropped to a whisper. 'I'll half kill you if you say anything about this.'

'You do that and I'll write to the chief inspector. I'll make a formal complaint.' She was exultant with success. Pa was backing off.

'Katie needs help now. You're not to make things worse for her. You're the sinner in our family, Pa.'

She felt contempt for him because he'd folded up more easily than she'd expected. He was frightened. Pa was frightened of her! She couldn't believe it.

'I've got an evening off tomorrow, Pa. I'll be up to see Katie at five o'clock. If you haven't told her by then that she can come home, I'll be straight round to tell Mam.'

As Amy turned on her heel she felt a surge of power.

She'd never be scared of Pa again. She went briskly back to the Laidlaw house.

Just as she'd told Pa she would, Amy went to see Katie the next evening.

When she opened the front door to her, Kate's blue eyes were wide with wonder. 'What did you say to Pa? You did say something? You must have.'

'I told him he was uncivilised. That he was to treat you better.' Amy felt a delicious frisson of triumph every time she thought of Pa.

'He said I could come home if I wanted to. Such a turn-round. Would you believe?'

'I'd believe.' Amy smiled.

'Nancy's here,' Katie said, seconds before Amy saw her standing in the living room doorway. Nancy's face was wreathed with smiles. The colour was back in her cheeks.

'Everything's turning out wonderfully well,' she gurgled.

'You've had a change-round too,' Amy said, unable to believe her eyes. 'Last night . . .'

'Stan's back safe and sound. I'm so pleased. I spoke to him on the phone at lunchtime. He's had a bad time – it was a nightmare, he said – but he's all right. He expects to be home on leave in two or three days. I feel so lucky.' She laughed aloud.

'And the Framptons have found me a home,' Kate added. 'It seems I'm in luck too.'

Nancy said: 'I told Toby about Katie, and he suggested to his mother that it might be a good idea if she took care of his old nanny. Live with her. Mrs Frampton wants to see Katie and talk it over.'

'I'm thrilled to bits, Amy. I think I'd rather do that than go back home. I don't believe Pa can hold his tongue. You know what he's like.'

Nancy asked: 'What did you do to twist Pa's arm?'

'Quite a lot, and it seems I needn't have screwed myself up to do it,' Amy said. 'But you're right. Pa won't manage to control himself. Stay out of his way if you can.'

CHAPTER SEVENTEEN

June 1940

The next morning Katie felt on edge as she took the bus up to Henshaw House. So much depended on Mary Frampton taking to her.

It was Nancy who opened the door and led her into the sitting room to be introduced, but then she disappeared.

Mrs Frampton's kind grey eyes seemed to search her face. The large diamond rings she wore bit into Katie's hand as she shook it.

'Do sit down, Kate. Your sister has told us about you.' She felt that the older woman was trying to put her at her ease.

Mary Frampton carried her large rounded chest before her like a pouter pigeon. She was plainly dressed and had her short grey hair arranged in deep waves that clung to her head. Katie knew Nancy was fond of her.

'We're very fond of Nancy, she's been a great help to us all.' Mrs Frampton smiled. 'I'd like to help you if I can.'

Katie swallowed hard and fixed her gaze on the elegant velvet pelmets over the windows in the Frampton drawing room. 'Thank you. It's very kind of you.'

'Not that kind, my dear, because you'll be doing something for us too. Toby thought of it, and it's a good idea. I'm sure any sister of Nancy's can be trusted.'

'Oh, yes.'

'She tells me you are kind to people and very responsible.'

'I try to be,' Katie croaked. Was it responsible to be

having a baby without a husband?

'The position is that Nanny is getting very old now. She was my nanny first, so you'll not be surprised to hear she's eighty-nine. She's not really capable of living alone any longer.

'When Toby and then Louise, my niece, outgrew her services, we bought a little house in town for her to retire to. That was what she wanted, but I fear she can no longer look after herself properly. Every day, somebody has to go down to make sure she's all right. Hilda goes usually, or Nancy. They help her wash, light her fire, and take her food.'

Katie sat with her hands in her lap, thinking that the Framptons were generous to take such care of their retired nanny.

'We are all very fond of Nanny Drew. I did put it to her that she ought to go to a home, but she wouldn't hear of it. We'd almost accepted the idea that she'd have to come back here where your sister could keep an eye on her too.

'But she refused, and I fear my mother might be upset if she no longer has Nancy's full attention. She reads to her, you know, and is always on hand to help her out into the garden and indoors again when she's had enough. She needs a lot of help with dressing. Mother wouldn't want to share Nancy's attention, not even with Nanny.

'So Toby thought, if you went to live with her, you could see she was kept comfortable and had all she needed.'

'Live with her?' Katie's heart leapt with relief. It seemed like salvation.

'There are two bedrooms in her little house and they're both furnished. You'd be quite comfortable.'

'I'm sure I would.' Katie smiled tremulously. 'It sounds ideal for me. I'm very grateful. I don't know what to say . . .'

'Just be kind to Nanny Drew. Make her remaining days as happy as you can. She hardly knows what she does, poor dear. She's failing now, I'm afraid. If you could see she eats regular meals.'

'Of course. That's the least I can do. Perhaps I can read to her too?'

'I'm sure she'd like that. About wages . . .'

'I'll be happy to do it for nothing,' Katie blurted out. 'You know how I'm placed. I'm more than grateful to have a roof over my head and my keep.'

Mrs Frampton smiled. 'We must pay a little. You'll need pocket money and things for the baby.

'I'd like you to come here each day to the kitchen. Hilda, our housekeeper, will give you what you need for meals, and you can let us know how Nanny is. We'll want to know how you're both getting on, and one of us will pop in to see you from time to time. Will you be able to wash her and put her to bed?'

'Yes, I was planning to be a nurse like Nancy when I was old enough to start training.' Katie felt drawn to Mrs Frampton. She seemed genuinely sympathetic.

'It's a short-term arrangement, nothing permanent, you realise that?'

'Of course.' Katie made herself add: 'I've made arrangements to go to a mother and baby home a month before. At the end of August.'

'I suppose I'd better think about getting someone else to follow on after you. You'll be able to cope with Nanny until then?'

'Yes, I'm sure I will. I'm very grateful to have a roof over my head. I was afraid I'd have to go to the workhouse, but now . . .'

Mary Frampton said gently: 'The workhouse has been abolished, Katie. The old Poor Law . . . everything changed in 1929.'

Katie pushed her dark hair behind her ears. Paul had told her the name had been changed, but in every other way they continued to function as before. They were no more welcoming than they used to be. Just to think of it made her turn cold.

'Come with me to the kitchen and meet Hilda. I'll get her

281

to put a few things into a basket for your dinners, and then Toby can drive you down and introduce you.'

Kate rose to her feet, but Mrs Frampton didn't move. She was frowning and staring out of the window. 'There's no telephone – Nanny's a little deaf and couldn't use it – but there's a public phone box quite close. If you're worried, if there's anything wrong, I want you to ring me, we'd want to know quickly.'

'Yes, of course. I'd want to.'

'We don't know how much longer she's likely to last, you see.'

Toby Frampton was equally kind to her. He drove her back to the Laidlaw house to collect her things. Her suitcase was already packed in the hall. He wouldn't allow her to lift it. He carried it out and strapped it to the running board of his car.

It seemed a luxury to be sitting beside him. Katie had never been in a car like this before and couldn't believe she'd gone from being without a roof over her head to riding around like a lady. She felt as though she'd touched bottom and bounced back again.

She watched Toby Frampton, who seemed to be concentrating on the road ahead. She took in his straight streaky hair that varied from honey to gold, and the deep cleft in his chin. A devil's cleft, her father would call it. His eyes were sympathetic and kind, and grey like his mother's. They crinkled up when he smiled.

He felt her gaze now. 'You'll like Nanny,' he said, and for a moment his eyes met hers. She wondered what she'd seen in Jimmy's handsome looks. Toby had such a warmth and kindliness about him, it knocked her sideways. 'She'll be very grateful for anything you do.'

'I'm very grateful to have the chance to do it.' She knew she was not far from tears. Her voice broke.

'You'll be all right now.' She knew he understood. 'Don't worry.'

'Thank you for thinking of me.'

'This is it.' He was pulling into the kerb in front of a small house in the centre of town. 'Nanny grew up round here, she wanted to come back.'

The house was in the middle of a terrace, built of smoke-blackened brick. The front door opened straight off the pavement. Katie noticed that the step had been donkey-stoned to a lighter colour than the others in the row. The net curtains covering the windows were crisp and white.

'Better get the things from the back seat,' he said, starting to unfasten her case. Katie leaned over to get the basket.

'That's linen for your bed. I expect you'll find plenty here, but Mother thought it wouldn't be aired.

'We ring the bell three times, like this, to let her know it's one of the family.' Toby smiled at her. 'Then we let ourselves in with the key.' He turned it in the lock. 'We don't know how much she hears, but we don't want to frighten her.'

Katie nodded. The front door opened straight into the living room. She was surprised to find the little house beautifully furnished. An ornate gilt cage, covered with a cloth, hung in front of the window. Toby pulled the cloth off. A yellow budgerigar began to chirp.

'Nanny can't be up yet. She thinks a lot of the bird and usually sees to him first thing. His name's Mungo.'

The fire had burned away, leaving the grate half filled with cold ash, but the brasses shone from the mantelpiece. Even Celia would be satisfied that this house was clean and well cared for.

Nanny supported the monarchy. Katie could see mugs to commemorate the coronation of George VI and the silver jubilee of George V. There was a photograph of Queen Victoria, a commemorative plate and a tin tea caddy celebrating some other royal occasion.

'Nanny,' Toby called. 'Nanny, where are you?' A steep flight of stairs led upwards, barely a yard from the front door.

A light grunt behind her made Katie turn and look at the sofa. The tiny stick-like frame barely showed under the plaid car blanket.

'Nanny!' Toby said aghast. 'What are you doing here?'

Bleary eyes opened. Her skin was dark and wrinkled and shrunk back against the bones of her face. Her white hair was sparse and fine, and had mostly broken away from the tiny bun at the nape of her neck. She struggled to sit up. Toby went to help her.

She yawned, and Katie saw her tongue, pale and furred, and her gums, shrunken and bare. Her false teeth, the top set sitting neatly on top of the bottom, were on the small table beside her.

A claw-like hand shook slightly as it reached for them, then her sunken cheeks filled out and she smiled up at Toby.

'Nanny! You've been here all night. You didn't even get undressed.' She was wearing a brown cardigan over a thick navy jersey.

'I'm all right.' Her voice had the creak of age. 'Very comfortable. I'm not going into a home. This is where I want to stay.'

'You'll be able to, Nanny, don't fret yourself. This is Katie. Mother has sent her here to look after you.'

Katie put out her hand. 'Hello, Nanny.'

'I'm not your nanny.' Beady dark eyes surveyed Katie's face.

'No. What would you like me to call you?'

'Nanny, I suppose. Everybody else does.'

Katie smiled. 'Would you like a cup of tea?'

'Love one.' Two legs like stalks, in wrinkled wool stockings, came down to the carpet and felt round for slippers. Toby pulled them forward for her.

She asked him: 'Who is this Katie, then?'

'She's Nancy's sister.'

'Nancy who?'

'Gran's nurse. She comes here to see to you sometimes. You know Nancy? You must do.'

'Of course I do.'

'Katie is going to stay here and look after you. To see you get undressed and to bed in future.'

He began raking the ash out of the grate. Katie had put the kettle on the gas stove in the kitchen and had found sticks and coal outside.

'I'll do that,' she said. 'I'm supposed to be looking after her, not you.'

He laughed and went into the kitchen to wash his hands. 'Look after yourself too, Katie.'

'I will, don't worry. I'll be fine now. Thank you for suggesting me to your mother.'

'You can't say you aren't needed here.'

'Was she just waking up, do you think?' It was almost midday.

'Yes, goodness knows what time she lay down. It could have been quite late. I don't think time has much meaning for her any longer. I hope she isn't going to be too heavy a job for you?'

'She won't be. I'll get the fire going and make her some tea. Then wash her and see if she'll have some breakfast.'

Toby carried her suitcase up the steep stairs for her. 'Room could do with a bit of dusting, I'm afraid.'

Katie smiled at him. 'I'm perfectly capable of that. You don't know what it means to me to have a room I can call my own, and to know there is something I can do to earn my keep. I'll see to my things later.'

She unpacked the basket of food Hilda had sent with her. There was a small pan of stew that only needed heating, some rice pudding and two slices of apple pie. The little pantry was well stocked with vegetables to go with the stew. There were eggs too, and everything else they could possibly need. Outside in the yard, the coal box was almost full.

At the door, Toby lowered his voice. 'She's failing. We

didn't realise she wasn't going to bed. I don't think she's washing much either. Mum will be upset.'

'I'll see she goes to bed from now on.'

Toby was writing down phone numbers. 'Ring if you have any problems. The phone box is on the main road at the bottom. This is her doctor's number. He knows her well. He'll come round if you're worried. Or you can talk to your sister at our place, if you prefer. Get her advice first.'

He paused, and self-consciously dropped some coppers on to the paper. 'Best to have the change ready,' he said, and his smile crinkled his eyes.

Toby didn't want to offend her. There was a dignity about the girl. There seemed to be little family resemblance; she was not at all like Nancy to look at. She was much taller for one thing. Her hair was darker and curlier and longer, and she had an endearing habit of pushing it behind her ears, both sides at once.

Though she seemed mature and sensible for her years, he wondered if perhaps they were asking too much of such a young girl. He was afraid Nanny might die on her.

There was a sparkle about Nancy; she knew she was loved. Katie didn't have that. Quite the reverse. She seemed to be gritting her teeth and clinging on hard to survive.

Last month he'd been having dinner at his aunt's house. His cousin Louise was a year older than Katie and leaving school now, with nothing arranged to fill the long school holidays.

'Why don't you stay at Nanny's house and give her a hand?' he'd suggested. Louise was the last child Nanny had brought up. She had even professed to share their concern.

But, 'What if she dies on me?' she'd said indignantly. 'I'd be scared stiff all the time. Besides, she's so old and she's deaf. Slow to hear and slow to move. She'd drive me mad now.'

'You could get her meals for her.' Her mother had frowned.

'Save Aunt Mary having to send her housekeeper down all the time.'

'I couldn't, Mother.' Louise had wrinkled her nose.

'All right. Sleep at home, then. Just go daily and make sure she's all right.'

'No, I couldn't,' she'd wailed. 'Anyway, Angela's family have asked me to go to Cornwall with them.'

Nanny didn't seem to upset Katie, but Toby hoped she'd make out all right.

He thought Katie's face beautiful, but it was the face of a child. Her eyes were quite different. They were adult eyes, midnight blue, dark pools of suffering. He guessed Katie had grown up in a hurry, and wondered what had happened that she'd found herself in such dire circumstances.

'Was she raped?' he asked Nancy angrily, when he got back home.

'No.' Her voice was defensive. Everything about Nancy told him she didn't want to discuss Katie, so he didn't press her further. Now he wondered again what sort of man could be so heartless as to abandon a young girl like that.

He felt sorry for her.

Nancy felt euphoric. Nothing mattered any more because Stan was coming home.

She was sitting on the bed that had served her since childhood. Here in her own small room, a chest also had to serve as a dressing table. She had to crane her head to see herself in the mirror fastened to the wall.

Her brown eyes danced back at her. She'd washed her hair this morning and golden highlights glistened amongst the brown curls.

Nancy sighed with satisfaction. She was taking two weeks' holiday so she could spend every minute of Stan's leave with him.

In previous years, her holidays had been organised well in advance and the Framptons had engaged another nurse to take her place. She'd only found out Stan was coming home on leave yesterday and had had to ask for time off on the spur of the moment.

Because of the war, it had proved impossible to hire a private nurse, and the district nurse was run off her feet at the moment with war casualties who had been sent home.

Nancy knew she couldn't just go away without making some arrangement for the Framptons. She'd telephoned Amy.

'Would you do me a favour, Amy?' she'd wheedled.

'Depends on what,' Amy had said guardedly.

'A very great favour . . .'

'What?'

'Would you give the Framptons their insulin injections in my place?'

'Good Lord!'

'I've tried everybody else. It's such short notice and with the war . . . Look, you're on night duty, you can be sure of being off every morning. You could get up a bit earlier at night and go again before you have breakfast. Would it be too much to ask you to cycle up to Henshaw House for that?'

'Well . . .'

'Mrs Frampton is quite willing to do everything else for Alice. It's just the injections. Wouldn't take you ten minutes.'

'Twice a day. Plus cycling time.'

'Yes. So I can have a holiday with Stan. He wants us to go away somewhere.'

'I suppose I'll have to. All right. I'll need to borrow your bike.'

'Yes, of course.'

'When do I start?'

'Stan's coming home tomorrow. I begin my holiday then, but I'll go up myself and do it until we go away. Will you come with me tomorrow morning? So I can introduce you and show you where things are kept?'

She'd met Amy outside the hospital and fixed things up to everybody's satisfaction.

Nancy tingled with anticipation. This holiday was going to be special. Stan was coming up by train this morning and she was getting ready to go to Woodside to meet him. It was another lovely summer's day of rather hazy sunshine. Across the road, the trees in the park were in full leaf in the noon heat.

She'd regretted many times that she and Stan had waited so long to be married. During the last week or so she'd been afraid she'd lost the opportunity for good. This was her second chance.

She wanted to get married now, but she'd have to talk to Stan about it. Urge him to forget his careful ways. She wanted to be more like Amy, to grab at happiness while she could. With the war on, everybody was living for the moment. Attitudes had changed.

Nancy was taking a long time to get herself ready. She took the hanger out of her prettiest dress, a green and pink flower print from last summer. Stan had admired it then. She'd washed and starched it lightly for this very important meeting.

She hadn't been able to find anything she liked better in the shops. Like everything else, cloth was in short supply and that dictated skimpy cutting and practical, rather military styling.

She had re-trimmed her straw hat with pink flowers. Now she pinned it carefully on her head and slipped her feet into open-toed sandals. She was well pleased with her outfit.

She ran downstairs to find Mam still sitting in the living room where she'd left her, cradling a third cup of tea in her hands.

Nancy was worried about Mam. She seemed more anxious about everything. She said she was frightened of being on her own in an air raid. Not that they'd had a real raid yet, but Pa had to leave her when the siren sounded to go on duty. Mam went through agonies, expecting bombs to fall every time.

The meal they'd just shared had not been cleared from the top of the Morrison shelter which was now taking up the space where the old living room table used to be. Mam kept a mattress and some bedding inside for when the siren went. Nancy could see Mam's gas mask amongst the blankets there, ready and waiting.

'You'll be safe enough in the shelter. That's why I got it,' she'd heard Pa tell her. 'Safe against everything but a direct hit.'

'It's being by myself,' Celia faltered.

'I have to go.' Alec pulled himself up to his full height. 'Those are my orders, to go on duty as soon as the siren sounds. To help with civil defence. Very important now with the war on.' He'd been issued with a steel hat.

Mam's worried gaze met her daughter's, making Nancy glance uneasily away. Mam had pleaded with her to come back and live at home, so that she wouldn't be alone. But Nancy felt settled with the Framptons. Sometimes she got up in the night to Alice. She didn't feel inclined to agree when Mam had allowed Katie to be turned out on the street. Katie had been desperate for a roof over her head, and would have provided the company she wanted.

All the same, Celia was getting more gaunt, and the lines on her face seemed suddenly deeper. Nancy had never known Mam regret Pa's absence before. Rather she'd welcomed it because she could rest instead of preparing yet another meal.

And Pa was no longer pleased with the meals she did produce. Rations for two didn't stretch to many spreads of the sòrt he enjoyed. She'd heard him complaining bitterly about yesterday's Woolton pie, which had been vegetables in gravy under a pastry crust.

'You're going then? It's time?' Mam's eyes were lacklustre. 'I don't suppose we'll see much of you while Stan's here. You must bring him to see us.'

'Mam, he'll want to see you.'

She'd told her mother she'd be sleeping at home for the

next few nights because she was on holiday. Stan had said his parents would want him to spend a few days with them.

'After that, we could go away by ourselves for a real holiday,' she'd suggested on the telephone. 'I fancy North Wales. We need a bit of fun. What do you say?'

Nancy had only hinted at that to Mam. She desperately wanted Stan to herself. After all, she'd be a married woman by now if it hadn't been for the war.

'You'll be thinking of marrying while he's home?' Mam raised anxious eyes to her daughter's.

Nancy headed for the front door. 'I don't know, Mam.' She knew she sounded impatient. How could she know until she'd talked it over with Stan? Riding to Woodside on the bus, she could feel anticipation building up again.

The station platform was crowded. There were other soldiers travelling north who had been evacuated from Dunkirk. The train was late, but few ran on time these days. Nancy positioned herself near the ticket collector, afraid she'd miss Stan in the crush.

When at last the train shunted to a halt at the buffers, she could feel excitement filling her throat. She caught sight of him straight away. Alighting stiffly, thinner than he had been, coming towards her with the weary gait of an elderly man.

She knew he'd grown a moustache, he'd told her about it in his letters. A thin dark line, it gave his face character. But this Stan was unfamiliar. He was close enough now for her to see the dark shadows below his eyes, but he still hadn't seen her.

Nancy wasn't far from tears again. Ever since she'd allowed herself to weep when Dunkirk had fallen, she'd been unable to control them. She was living on a much less secure emotional plane now. The terrible events of war had brought it about.

Stan's dark eyes met hers in recognition at last. Moments later his arms were hugging her against a figure that seemed bonier than it used to be.

'Nancy, love,' he whispered. His moustache felt strange, rather tickly. It made her laugh.

They'd never been parted before in all the years they'd known each other. Meeting him again after such a long separation, she felt she couldn't quite bridge the gap. The easy familiarity had gone. The life she'd known and expected to last for ever had changed.

It would take time to feel as they had. She mustn't rush things. She didn't want to spoil what she and Stan had.

Visiting time on Thursday afternoons started at two o'clock. Amy was just making sure all the patients on Weightman Ward were ready, that all bedpans and washbowls had been cleared away.

A few visitors were already waiting in the corridor as she removed the screens and opened the doors so that they could come in.

A slim, dark youth asked: 'Am I in the right place? I'm looking for Felicity Lane.'

'Felicity Laidlaw, you mean.' Amy knew who he was. Dark and continental-looking, he had to be Fliss's singing partner. 'Isn't Lane her stage name? On your right, in the middle bay.'

'Slip of the tongue.' He smiled. 'Thanks.' He sounded like a native of Birkenhead, whatever his roots. Amy was pleased he'd come. Fliss needed cheering up.

When next she went up the ward, the visitors had gone and it was teatime. Fliss was lying curled up in a ball, with her face turned to the window.

'You want tea, don't you, Fliss?' She didn't answer. 'You're not asleep?'

'No,' she croaked. Amy heard the tears in her voice. She left the tea trolley to her colleague and pulled a screen round the bed.

'Fliss? Whatever's the matter?' She sat down. 'That was Yves who came to see you, wasn't it? Did he bring those two oranges? He must have queued for hours for them.'

'His mother did.'

'I thought you'd be glad to see him.'

'I am really,' she sobbed.

'Then what's the matter?'

'I want to get out of here. I want to get better. Do you think I ever will?'

Amy had already asked herself that. Fliss was no better after her second operation. The infection in her abdomen had not cleared up. Her face was paste-white from ill health and lack of fresh air and exercise.

'These things take time, Fliss,' Amy said as gently as she could. She knew she was offering platitudes.

'I've been patient, no one can say I haven't. Nine months I've been here now, and I'm no nearer getting out than I was after one.'

'I know, love, it's hard.' She remembered Fliss as she used to be, full of enthusiasm and life.

'Do you know what Yves told me? He's getting bookings. He's rehearsing a song and dance act for a variety show at the Empire in Liverpool. He thinks it's going to run for weeks and weeks, and the BBC want to book him to sing on air. In *Workers' Playtime*. I can't believe the luck he's having. It's fantastic.'

'He's jolly good. Got a good voice too.'

Fliss let out a long sigh. 'Yes. The worst part is, Amy, he's got himself another partner. He brought a photograph to show me. Her name is Mariella Tompkins and she's blonde and pretty.'

Amy knew how much effort Fliss had put into her singing, and how high her hopes had been. Paul had been so sure she'd make a success of it.

'He said he couldn't wait any longer for me,' Fliss sniffed. 'But he doesn't think Mariella sings as well as I did.'

Amy hugged her close. There was no comfort she could offer.

'If only I were well, all these wonderful things would be happening to me. I've lost my chance by being here, that's what's so dreadful. Wouldn't you be fed up?'

'Yes,' Amy had to agree.

CHAPTER EIGHTEEN

Nancy found the days of Stan's leave slipping away too quickly. He was very much changed. He'd lost all his energy. If she left him sitting in a chair for ten minutes he'd very likely nod off.

He didn't want to cycle or walk as he used to. The furthest they went was to sit in the park.

She held his hand and asked: 'Do you think we should get married right away? We could, if you want to.'

'It would be a rush,' he said. 'All those arrangements to make. I just can't think straight.'

She'd want to say: 'I'm still thinking straight. I think it's the best thing for us.' But Stan was exhausted physically and mentally. It seemed cruel to press him.

'I had to push myself to the limit, Nancy. To keep one step ahead of the Hun.'

Relatives on both sides wanted to know how he'd got home from France. Nancy shivered every time she heard him tell the tale.

'We set off in an orderly fashion in army vehicles with the rest of the platoon. When we ran out of petrol we set fire to the lorries so the Hun couldn't use them. Then it was everybody for himself.

'I didn't sleep for nine nights. Didn't take my clothes off in all that time. I had to keep moving. I was with two friends but one got killed. Strafed from the air. I don't know what happened to the other, we just got separated. I got a lift from an REME private on the back of a motorbike he'd found, but that broke down.

'I had nothing to eat except what I could scrounge or steal and no idea which way I should be heading. No maps and no ammunition. Just the terrible feeling of running for my life. I could hear gunfire and had to assume the Germans were coming from that direction.

'It seemed a miracle when I reached the coast but the beaches were being strafed and men were fighting each other to get on the boats. It was hell. I finally swam out to a Cornish sardine boat.'

Nancy thought fourteen days a pitifully short time to give him to recover. Too short a time for her to accept the change in him. Stan had never been able to do things quickly; he needed time to think and to put his experiences behind him. She felt like crying at the way things were turning out.

She came home late one night after leaving Stan at his home. Her parents were already in their room and their light was out. She tiptoed upstairs and went straight to bed. It was a warm night and the windows were all open behind the blackout curtains. Pa's voice was never soft; she could hear every word from the next bedroom.

'It's knocked Stan up. He's a different fellow. Don't know how much good he's going to be to our Nancy now.'

'What do you mean?' Her mother sounded drowsy.

'Well, look at him. Sitting about all listless like. You'd think he'd want a good time now he's home. Our Nancy had to press him to go to the pictures with her. Didn't you hear her at teatime? She's always run rings round him. I always reckoned she could do better than a Whittle. Now I'm sure.'

'They're still pretty close, Alec. I thought they might go off and get married while he was home.'

'No danger of that. He hasn't the energy.'

Nancy stifled a gasp at that. She still loved Stan. More than anything in the world, she wanted him to recover his strength. She wanted to feel as easy with him as she used to.

'Anyway, you wanted them to have a proper church

wedding, a big do, and it can't be done in the time.'

'By special licence,' Mam said. 'It could if they wanted it.'

'Nancy doesn't want to disappoint you. Not after all the work you put into those bridal gowns. They'd not be needed for the register office, not with a war on.'

Nancy strained her ears; she'd gone ahead with any sort of a wedding if Stan had not been against it.

'Wouldn't disappoint me,' Mam grunted. It made Nancy catch her breath in surprise. She'd expected Mam to be against a quiet wedding. 'Might be better if they got it over and done with. This wedding's been hanging over us too long.'

'Anyway, Stan'll have to go away again to fight. Goodness knows where they'll send him now. He can't go on being lucky. Not for ever.'

Nancy was biting her lip in horror.

'Better if they don't get married, I say,' Pa said. 'If he cops it, and he's quite likely to, she'll be a war widow, like you were. It wouldn't be much fun for her, would it? And with Kate the way she is, we don't want two of them, do we?'

That made Nancy catch her breath again, and the tears that had never been far away threatened to overwhelm her. But it made up her mind for her. Tomorrow, she'd insist on taking Stan away for a holiday somewhere. It would do him good. What they needed was time on their own. They mustn't waste any more of his precious leave.

The next morning, Nancy went round to Stan's home in Haldane Avenue with a copy of the *Liverpool Echo*. She was determined they'd pick out some holiday accommodation and go.

Stan's mother, who was plump and motherly, recommended a boarding house in Rhyl, where she'd spent a week with her sister earlier in the year. Stan seemed more cheerful and suggested they walk to the post office together to telephone to see if there were any vacancies.

When the answer was yes, Nancy immediately rang Amy, catching her just before she went to bed after her night shift. Then she went home to pack a suitcase, and she and Stan caught the afternoon train.

'Let's stay here in Rhyl for as long as we can,' Stan pleaded. 'I don't want to go home.'

He'd arrived at Woodside with a tan, but under it, his face had a greyish tinge. He'd looked drawn and unhealthy.

They walked along the beach and watched the tide race up the sand. They sat for whole afternoons in the sun. They didn't want the amusement arcades, the shops or the evening entertainment. Stan needed rest.

They had booked two single rooms, but when night came they huddled together in one bed, unable to face being parted again.

Nancy thought she'd heard all he'd endured in France, but now more was coming out. The horror he'd felt at seeing death all round him. There had been more blood and violence than he could stand. The carnage he'd seen had sickened him. It was all such a needless waste of life. She ached with compassion.

He told her he loved her, that his feelings had never wavered.

'When I ducked down in wet ditches to hide from passing vehicles on the road, or flung myself into waist-high nettles to take shelter from enemy Stukas overhead, my comfort was to think of you.

'When I felt exhausted and totally terrified, the need to get back to you gave me strength to go on.'

Nancy lay in his arms, trying to comfort him, until at last he fell asleep. She spent three nights with him like this before he even wanted to make love.

Once he started to stroke and kiss her, Nancy knew Stan was getting better.

'I'm a fool,' he murmured. 'You're what I want most in life. I've known that for years, and yet I did nothing about it. When I could have been making arrangements for our wedding, I felt numb and unable to push myself.'

Nancy sighed. She would willingly have made the arrangements if he'd told her how he felt. 'You've changed,' she said slowly. Of course he had. She should have expected it.

'I'm too slow. Too careful, always deliberating endlessly instead of getting on with it. I've wasted another opportunity to get married.'

Nancy said: 'You've always been a belt-and-braces man.'

'I'm a dull, staid stick for a girl like you.'

'Stanley Whittle,' she said. 'You are what I want.'

It had been Mam's idea, of course, carefully implanted, that she should remain a virgin until she was married. It was the virtuous thing to do. It would please Pa, too, and as a reward they would provide a big wedding. She would be able to wear a white wedding dress, the symbol of purity, with pride and honesty.

But Nancy had been wondering for some time if she and Stan had been too restrained. She knew they were missing out on what they really wanted. She was making up her mind now, as Stan's hand ran up her back, that she wouldn't miss out any longer.

After all, even little Katie had allowed a man to make love to her.

'Now we're here together we're going to make the most of it,' she whispered. 'It might be a long time before we get the chance again.'

The weather grew cooler and the wind blustery, but strolling along the promenade with Stan, with the taste of salt on her lips and the mournful call of seagulls in her ears, Nancy was finding contentment. With no family around, they thought only of each other.

Within two or three days, it was as though they'd never

been parted. Except that they were lovers now.

Stan said it was blessedly peaceful in Rhyl. They no longer listened to the news bulletins on the wireless, trying instead to forget the war. He said he felt well and very happy.

They had booked in for one week, then extended their stay to ten days. As the time passed, Nancy felt the first niggles of dread. She couldn't bear the thought of going home to be parted at night in their respective houses. Instead, they stayed where they were until the last day of Stan's leave.

That morning they took the train from Rhyl to Chester. They walked the ancient walls of that city until they could walk no more. They had lunch in a small café, and sat by the river for the last of the precious minutes they could spend together. Nancy saw Stan off on the last possible train that would get him to Aldershot before midnight.

Amy liked the night shift. The formalities were relaxed, and there was only one sister on duty. She had been put in charge of Ward 1, men's surgical, and usually the busiest in the hospital.

Where there were two nurses on the ward, they were each allowed an hour's rest in the small hours, while the patients slept. Officially, this was an hour for reading or study. On all wards, it was taken on two armchairs pushed together in a quiet spot, with a pillow and blankets. Cap and shoes were taken off. Amy always found sleep came instantly.

At the allotted time, the junior nurse would wake her so that she might take her place. Amy moved to the middle of the ward to keep an eye on things and write her report. After a tea break, in the dining room, the ward lights were switched on at five o'clock and the morning rush started.

Amy was usually wide awake when the day staff came on duty at seven thirty.

She went down to eat her dinner then with the rest of the night staff, but at eight o'clock had to return to the ward to read her night report to the ward sister. Since it was considered impolite to have Sister waiting for her, it usually meant hanging about the office first, and could take a long time if they'd had emergencies admitted overnight, or Sister was nit-picking. Then she was free until eight at night.

While Nancy was away, she'd promised to cycle up to Henshaw House to give the insulin injections in her place.

Bill Frampton opened the door to her the first morning. He smiled and pushed his heavy horn-rimmed spectacles further up his nose.

'Nancy said you wouldn't mind, but I do feel we're imposing on you. After all, you have been working all night, and you'll have to get up early to come back this evening before starting another night's work.'

'I don't mind coming, not for ten days or so. I've heard so much about you from Nancy.'

'All the same it's asking a lot.'

'Wednesday mornings could be a bit of a problem for me. I have to go to a lecture.'

'You mean you're expected to work a twelve-hour night, and then attend lectures?'

'Yes, but they're arranged between nine and ten so we can still get to bed early.'

He laughed. 'I wish I had your energy.'

'I could fit in coming here as well if you'd pick me up by car.'

'Of course, I'd be glad to. Very kind of you to offer, and I could run you back on my way to work.

'Come on upstairs. Alice, my mother-in-law, is still in bed.'

Amy took off her gabardine and left it over the banister. He led her into Alice's vast bedroom. The old lady was drinking tea, sitting up against a bank of pillows in her enormous bed. Mary Frampton got up from an armchair beside the bed where she'd been reading aloud from a newspaper.

'Hello, Amy, it's very good of you to come.'

Amy remembered the small dressing alcove off the room, with washbowl and cupboards. She already knew where to find the insulin and the glass dish of purple spirit that contained the syringes.

'I'll give you yours first, shall I, Mrs Frampton? While your mother finishes her tea.'

Amy studied the records Nancy had left of the doses she'd been giving.

'Have you ever thought of injecting yourself?' she asked as she drew insulin into the syringe.

'I've told her she ought to try,' Bill Frampton said from the doorway. 'Goodbye, Mary, I'll be off to work.'

'I couldn't.' Mary Frampton shuddered. 'Stick a needle in myself? It makes me feel wobbly just to think of it.'

'I could teach you,' Amy said gravely. 'Once you've done it, you'll find there's nothing to it.'

'I suppose having Nancy here has made me lazy. She's been wonderful. Neither Mother nor I have had to go back to hospital to be re-balanced in the three years she's been here.'

'I should hope not,' Amy said severely. 'It's her job to keep you out. Nancy's efficient that way, but she drifts a bit with the tide.'

'Not Nancy.' Her employer was indignant. 'We couldn't manage without her. She's been wonderful with Mother. She's eighty-nine next month and needs a lot of help now. She takes up most of Nancy's time.'

Amy smiled. 'You probably think I'm talking out of turn. Nancy certainly will. She won't want to leave this very comfortable sinecure you're providing. All the same, she should have taught you to do this.'

Mary Frampton pushed out her large rounded bosom and looked dubious.

'At the very least, she should have taught your husband. He could do it before going to work. It would only take him a moment. Less time than to fetch me here on Wednesday.'

'I expect he could manage it.'

302

'Let me teach you, Mrs Frampton. I'm sure you could. I taught a little girl of ten who lives near us. She manages fine now.'

Mary Frampton pulled a face. 'I suppose you think I'm an awful coward?'

Amy shook her thick black plait over her shoulder. 'No, I wouldn't like doing it to myself. If I had an indulgent husband who could provide me with Nancy, I'd probably let him. It's just that things are changing. There's a war on now.

'Look, you must know by now what you should eat and why, but I've brought you a book that sets it all out.' Amy drew it out of the pocket of her uniform dress. 'Read it, it'll refresh your mind. You'll see how you can manage.'

Amy watched the older woman purse her lips. 'Go on, say you'll try.'

'I suppose I've got to.' Mary was very reluctant. 'If you really think I could.'

'You'll feel so free if you do. I promise you, once you do it, you'll wonder why you stayed dependent on Nancy for so long. You'll never have to wait around for someone like me to come. This is the sensible way for you to cope.'

'Why are you going to all this trouble? Trying to persuade me?' Mary Frampton's grey eyes looked into hers. 'I thought you were just coming to stand in for Nancy.'

'Nancy will tell you I'm a busybody. Always giving people advice they don't want.' Amy smiled gently. 'But she could be called up if conscription comes for women, and everybody says it's going to. Her job here could hardly be classed as essential for the war effort. It's better for you to be prepared.'

Mrs Frampton sighed. 'Bill has been going on about that too. What a thoughtful girl you are.'

'Anyway, I think Nancy ought to do more for the war effort. Though she'd need to come back to the hospital to get her hand in again first.'

Amy began drawing up Alice's dose. 'How do you feel

303

about practising on your mother?'

'Not today,' Mary said in alarm.

'Perhaps tomorrow?' Amy suggested as they went back to Alice's bed.

Knowing that Alice's sight had gone, Amy took the empty teacup from her hand and put it on the bedside table.

'I've got your insulin here, Mrs Peacock. Which leg would you like it in today?'

'You're not Nancy.' Alice's voice was full of suspicion. 'Where is she?'

'I told you, Mother, she's gone for a well-deserved holiday. This is Amy, her sister. She's going to give us our injections for the next few days.'

'I'm not going to like this at all.' The old lady's voice wavered. 'It's the right leg's turn, I suppose. No, I'm not ready. I want to go to the lavatory first.'

'Mother! You could let Amy do it. Then she could go.'

'No. I want . . .'

'It's all right,' Amy said. 'Let me help you.' She slid the thin legs to the carpet and eased the bony feet into the slippers she found there. 'Where's your dressing gown?'

The old lady seemed more helpless than Nancy had led her to believe.

'I could do this, Mother.' Mary Frampton was holding out the dressing gown. Alice was standing stock still, not moving a muscle to help them. Her head was sagging lower as though she hadn't the strength to hold it up.

Amy guided one thin arm into a sleeve, and supported her upright while her daughter did the other.

'Come on then, Mother.'

Any felt herself tottering under the sudden weight she was holding up. Her first reaction was surprise that Mary Frampton could manage this on her own. Then she glanced at Alice's face and drew in a long, shuddering breath. Her head had flopped forward until her chin rested on her chest.

Amy knew immediately what had happened. She felt a

sudden surge of adrenaline. A patient on Ward 4 had died in this way on her.

'She's gone!' She'd meant to keep the urgency out of her voice, but she didn't quite manage it.

'Mother?' She could see Mary Frampton hadn't understood.

'She's had a heart attack. She's stopped breathing.'

'You mean she's died?'

'I'm afraid so.' Amy was trying to ease Alice back to the bed.

'But she can't have!'

Amy was feeling for her pulse. There was nothing there. 'I'm afraid she has. It's a shock for you, happening like this.'

'But she was talking to us.' Mary Frampton's eyes told Amy she couldn't believe it could happen so quickly.

Amy lifted the hand mirror from the dressing table and held it over Alice's nose and lips. There was no sign of any misting when she took it away.

'Better for her to go quickly like that. She didn't suffer at all. Harder for you, though.'

Amy could see that Mary Frampton was shaking with shock.

'Come on, let's go downstairs.' She put her arm round the older woman. 'We ought to ring for the doctor.'

Mrs Frampton couldn't turn away from the bed. Her grey eyes were glazed with disbelief. 'There's some hope then? Some doubt?'

Amy shook her head. She'd meant so that the necessary death certificate could be made out. 'No, he'll want to see her. It's the usual thing. I'll ring your husband at the same time, if you'll tell me the numbers.'

'Thank goodness you're here,' Mary Frampton sobbed. 'You know what to do.'

Hilda, the housekeeper, was coming out of the kitchen as they went down. Her face went paper-white when she understood what had happened.

305

'Could you make some tea for us?' Amy asked her. 'We could all do with a cup.'

It was a bittersweet homecoming for Nancy. She felt bereft without Stan and was hoping against hope that he'd get a posting close to home. With the war going badly, she was afraid he'd be sent off to fight somewhere else.

She'd had a wonderful holiday and felt more alive than she had for a long time. She even spared a thought as to how Mam was faring. She was looking forward to seeing the Framptons again. She'd bought two Penguin books to read aloud to Alice.

She could see a game of bowls being played in the park as she rode up on the bus. The grass was lush, the trees at their best in high summer. Everything shimmered in the heat of another sunny day.

She went round the back of the house and let herself into the kitchen. Mam came to the living room door as she took her suitcase into the hall.

'I was wondering when you'd get back.'

Nancy couldn't look her in the face as she explained about Stan catching his train from Chester. She knew she'd done what Mam feared most. With all the love she'd felt for Stan she was afraid it would show on her face, but her mother seemed wrapped up in her own thoughts.

'There's been big happenings while you've been away.'

Nancy was still glowing with Stan's love, only half concentrating. 'What's been going on?'

'Alice Peacock's died. The first day our Amy went up.'

'What!' Nancy had been expecting to resume her peaceful existence at Henshaw House. Suddenly the future seemed full of change, less secure.

'Heart attack. Came out of the blue.'

'Poor old Alice!' Nancy couldn't believe it. 'Mrs Frampton will be terribly upset. It's all been so sudden. I'll go up on my bike and see her.'

'Now? Don't be silly. You're still on holiday. They won't expect you until tomorrow morning. Surely that's soon enough?'

'It's never been that sort of a job. I think I should.'

'Yes, but will you have a job now?' Mam rounded on her. 'They aren't going to pay you to hang around all day with just one injection to give in the morning and another at night. I reckon you'll be looking for another job.'

That made Nancy think again. Later that evening, a few minutes before Amy would have to get up to go up to Henshaw House, she went to her sister's bedroom in the nurses' home. Amy was curled up asleep. She opened the curtains and let the evening sun in, then flung herself down on the foot of her bed. Amy's alarm clock went off; she reached out and silenced it.

'What's this I hear about Alice? I want to know what happened.'

Amy brushed the sleep from her eyes, pulled herself upright, and told her.

'It was a quiet funeral,' she yawned. 'I went, and so did Katie. She felt she should, since she's working for them.'

'You could have let me know.' Nancy felt indignant. 'I've looked after Alice for the last four years. I knew her better than either of you.'

'I was going to try phoning you, but Mr Frampton said no. He said you needed a holiday and it would be better to let you enjoy your fiancé's leave.'

'Even so . . .'

'You don't like missing anything, Nancy. Even a funeral.'

'It must have been a terrible shock for Mary. I wish I'd been there to help. How did she take it?'

Amy threw back her bedclothes. 'I've got to get dressed or I'll miss my breakfast. Both James and Toby came. They had compassionate leave. Cheered their mother up to see them. I've taught her to inject herself.'

'You've done what?' Nancy couldn't believe her ears.

307

'Taught Mary Frampton to inject herself,' Amy said, shedding her pyjamas. 'I've gone up on alternate mornings this week, just to make sure she's all right. Not worried, or anything. You should have taught her long ago. Sooner or later you'll be drafted. I've run through her diet with her, but she wants to talk it over with you.'

'Thank you very much!' Nancy gasped.

'More faith in you, you see. Can you make up a clean cap for me?'

'You have to poke your nose into everything. You're a meddlesome, interfering busybody.'

'But you asked me to . . .'

'Give the injections, that's all I asked. You've put me out of a job.'

Amy grabbed her towel and shot off to the bathroom. Nancy slumped back on the bed, fulminating at what her sister had done. She could hear voices and doors banging all down the corridor as the night staff prepared to go on duty.

Amy returned. 'It would have happened anyway. Without Alice you'd have nothing to do. Pass my dress over.'

Nancy obliged. 'I suppose so.'

'You've been saying you want to do something for the war effort for a long time. It was never right to stay there. You could do so much more.'

'I do fire-watching.'

'You might watch, but you haven't seen any,' Amy retorted. 'Now you needn't hang about.'

'I wish you'd stay away from my affairs.'

'Come on, Nancy, I'm going over for breakfast. You can't stay here.' Amy stood holding her bedroom door open.

Nancy got to her feet. 'I'm coming.'

She saw her sister smiling at her. 'Where's this sunshine you're supposed to shed on us lesser mortals?'

Nancy had to stifle her own smile at that, and prodded Amy in the ribs as she passed her.

Amy was always telling her how lucky she was too. The very next day, Nancy had proof that she could dismiss any worries about having made love with Stan. Her sins were not going to find her out. She was certainly luckier than Katie in that respect.

To Nancy, the whole atmosphere of the Frampton household seemed to have changed in her absence. Bill Frampton was working long hours, managing the office with fewer and fewer staff.

The house seemed quiet, and without Alice she felt at a loose end. There was absolutely nothing for her to do.

Her mother's death had been so sudden that Mary Frampton hadn't got over the shock. Nancy encouraged her to talk about it, thinking that might help. The only practical help she could offer was to help her sort through Alice's things.

After what Amy had said, it was on her conscience that she should have taught Mary to inject herself long ago. Already, she was managing very well, though she was not very confident.

'Check it for me, Nancy. Am I doing it right?'

'Exactly right.' Nancy talked about her diet until they were both sick of the subject.

'Your sister Amy is a very sensible girl.'

Nancy sighed. 'Amy always sees what other people should be doing. Puts herself out to tell them where they're going wrong. She's always making me do what's good for me.'

Nancy knew she'd imagined that her pleasant, comfortable routine here would go on for ever.

She had to broach the subject herself: 'Now that you're managing so well, you don't need me. I'm really in your way here all day. I think I should look for another job.'

'There's no hurry, Nancy. You're not in the way at all. I need you. I'm never sure . . . I don't want to end up in hospital again.'

'You won't,' Nancy assured her. 'You know what you can

309

eat and what you can't. You've been doing it for so long now, I'm sure you'll be fine.'

'What will you do?'

'Amy thinks I should go back to the hospital as a staff nurse.'

'Perhaps it would be for the best,' Mary Frampton said reluctantly.

Nancy went up to her room and wrote a letter of application to Matron. Two days later, Amy telephoned her at Henshaw House.

'Matron thinks you're back home now.'

'I put our address . . .'

'She told me to tell you to call in and see her this afternoon. About three would be convenient.'

'Right. I will.'

'Glad to see you've got moving.'

CHAPTER NINETEEN

Summer 1940

Nancy had to go shopping for black stockings before she could start work. She was glad they weren't fashionable, otherwise she would not have been able to get them at all. Mam was busy in the kitchen when she went home to see her. A pan was simmering on the stove.

'I'm making a savoury pudding from leeks and carrots. It's another of Lord Woolton's recipes. I heard it on the wireless this morning.'

'Will Pa like that?'

She thought Mam looked worried. 'I've got a few slices of corned beef to go with it. It's not easy to find anything, the shops seem empty. Will you stay and have some with us? Pa will be home any minute.'

Nancy said: 'If there's enough. How do you feel about having me home permanently?'

'Living here?' Celia looked up in surprise. She had a floury smudge on her chin.

'Yes. I'm going back as a staff nurse on Ward One. Matron asked whether I wanted to live in or out.'

'You can choose?'

'Yes, I'm not a student any more.'

'Live here, Nancy. You know there's nothing I'd like better.' Mam beamed at her. 'It's quite lonely, Pa's out a lot. I'd love to have you live at home again.'

They heard the yard door crash back.

'Here's Pa. Oh dear, he's early tonight. I'm not quite

ready.' Nancy saw how flurried it made her. The next moment Pa flung open the back door, and his huge bulk seemed to fill the small kitchen.

'Hello, Nancy. What are you doing here at this time?'

'She's coming back home to live,' Mam said. 'I'm so pleased.'

'I'm going back to work at the hospital, Pa.'

'So when do you start?' Mam asked.

'Tomorrow morning. They're short-staffed.'

'You should have taken a week or two off first. You deserve a rest.'

'It'll just be for a few months to get my hand in. Matron says she'll try and fit me in to have a few weeks in theatre too. Then I shall join up.'

'Join up? There's absolutely no need for that.' Mam was aghast. 'Nursing is classed as an essential occupation. You'd never get drafted, even if they call women up.'

'It's what I want,' Nancy said quietly. 'Stan is doing his bit for the war. I want to too.' He'd been posted to a camp near Salisbury. She would have liked him to be nearer, but at least he was safe for the time being.

He wrote to her almost every day. His letters were censored so he wasn't able to tell her much but she knew he was doing training exercises out on the plain. She was afraid he wouldn't stay there for long.

'I shall join Queen Alexandra's Imperial Military Nursing Service. I've sent for the application forms, I'll get a commission. Stan will be envious.'

'But you could be sent anywhere. Perhaps to the front line,' Celia protested.

'That's the whole idea,' she agreed. 'Amy thinks it's high time I did something useful.'

'Amy! What does she know?' Pa snorted, his face like thunder. 'There's no need for you to put yourself out. You stay here, you can help look after your mam. She needs you. Nobody will thank you for getting yourself killed.'

'I've just got to dish up, it won't take me a minute,' Mam said, unwrapping cloths from the steaming pudding. Nancy thought it smelled delicious.

'Leave it for a moment,' Pa said.

Celia looked up in surprise. 'You always want to eat as soon as you come in.'

'I've got something to show you first. Come outside.'

Nancy could see him rubbing his huge hands together in satisfaction, as he led them out to the side street. A black saloon was parked at the kerb.

'What do you think of this then?'

'You've got a car?' Nancy was amazed. 'My goodness Pa, it's wonderful. Where did you get it?'

'Bought it, of course. Been saving up for a long time. A 1937 Ford Ten. Smashing, isn't it?'

They sat inside. Walked all round it. Admired it. Nancy was shown the engine.

'I hope the pudding isn't going cold,' Mam said anxiously. That took them back indoors.

Nancy peeped into the living room. Knives and forks had been set out in readiness on the top of the Morrison shelter. She added another place setting for herself.

'Are you taking us out for a run in your car tonight?' Nancy asked, as she brought the plates to the table. Pa was given the lion's share. Nancy noticed that her mother's helping was very small.

'Not tonight,' he grunted.

'Go on, Pa,' she cajoled. In the past he'd always indulged her. 'I'd love a ride in it. So would you, wouldn't you, Mam?' Mam eyed her uneasily.

'Some other time. I've got to go out.' Pa had the most ferocious look on his face. He stabbed at the pudding with his fork.

'What on earth do you call this?' he asked.

'Leek and carrot pudding.' Mam sounded apologetic.

'Don't do this again for me.'

'I think it's nice, Mam,' Nancy said to support her. Actually, it wasn't all that good. She'd forgotten how Pa could carp. Or was he getting worse?

'I don't care what you think, Nancy,' he said roughly. 'I don't like it.'

'It's hard to know what to cook.' Celia was wringing her hands. 'The rations go nowhere.'

Nancy thought she didn't look well. Her face was putty-coloured, and there was something else. Mam had the look of an animal at bay. Pa stood over her, the all-powerful hunter. It made a shiver run down Nancy's spine.

'Go easy, Pa. Mam's doing her best.'

'I'm just telling her it isn't good enough,' he snarled.

Nancy found the following weeks harder than she'd expected. She'd grown soft at the Framptons. She'd not kept herself up to date with new medicines and treatments, so a normal day's work left her feeling over-tired and mentally stretched.

'You'll get over that.' Amy hadn't been sympathetic. 'You'll soon get back into the swim of things.' Nancy felt it was taking a long time.

Also, she'd been looking forward to living at home again. She'd left home when she was eighteen, and remembered only the warmth and affection that had surrounded her then.

The atmosphere at home seemed quite different now. Heavy, as though a storm were gathering. Just popping in for a cup of tea or a meal as she used to, she hadn't noticed it changing.

Mam was not the person she used to be. She'd always been fluttery and nervous but now she seemed a hundred times worse. The least thing would throw her into a panic.

Once she'd prided herself on the way she kept house. Everything had sparkled with cleanliness and the meals she'd produced had been good.

Nancy had looked round the living room the day she'd brought her suitcases back home. It was an untidy tip of old newspapers and clothes waiting to be ironed. The grate was full of cold ash, and the hearth too. Pa's ashtrays were overflowing, his slippers and a pair of shoes still lying where he'd kicked them off. Dust was thick on the mantelpiece.

She went to Amy's bedroom during her coffee break. 'Have you noticed?' she asked. 'What's been going on there since we left?'

'Of course I've noticed.' Amy's dark blue eyes met hers coolly over the book she'd been reading in bed.

Nancy went on quickly, 'I spend my time off trying to keep the place decent, with Mam following me round saying: "Don't do that now, dear. I'll do it. Leave it to me."'

'So why doesn't she?' Amy wanted to know. She had the air of one aiming to give nothing away.

'Goodness knows. She's on the go the whole time, duster in hand.'

'Not effective any more?' Amy suggested.

'Pa has changed too,' Nancy said. 'He's at her the whole time, she can't do anything right. Yet she waits on him hand and foot.'

'She always has.'

'Not like this. She's waiting for his orders, like a slave. Fawning on him. Almost wanting to be at his beck and call.'

'The best thing for Mam is to get out and about more. She's there on her own too much. Take her to the pictures.'

'And that's Amy's prescription?'

'Well, you did ask.'

'Mam doesn't want to go to the pictures, I've tried. She never goes out except to the shops on Duke Street to collect the rations. Why don't you try?'

'I have, Nancy. You've always been her favourite, I thought you might have more luck. I even asked Auntie My to call and invite her round for a cup of tea and a chat. She said Pa was due home soon, she hadn't time. She was cooking his dinner.'

'She's lost interest.'

'Lost interest in her appearance too. She looks so much older.'

'Don't I know,' Nancy retorted. 'Her hair was hanging in lank strings. I insisted on cutting it for her. Then I washed it and curled it up.'

'Insist on taking her out too,' Amy persisted. 'It's the only thing.'

Nancy took a deep breath and let the air escape slowly. 'And I thought it would be pleasant to live at home again.'

Nancy felt she could cope with Mam on her own. The trouble came when Pa was home too. On her day off she prepared a salad and left it between two plates on the kitchen table for him.

Mam had looked shocked. 'He hates salad. He won't eat it.'

'Then I'll eat it later,' Nancy said.

Then she'd taken Celia down to the Refreshment Room for a meal. The midday rush was over. Auntie My had sat down with them and they'd had a laugh. She said she was using carrots in everything, even puddings. Vera was even grating beetroot into apple pie, to make the apples go further. They were calling them blackberry and apple. Nancy tried one and found it quite good.

'The things we have to do.' Myra had laughed. 'Customers expect food substitutes these days. They understand about shortages. As long as the stuff tastes all right, they don't mind.'

Afterwards she'd taken Mam to New Brighton on the

ferry. She seemed better for the blow. There was a little colour in her cheeks.

As they rode home on the bus she could feel Mam stiffening with tension. 'Pa will have come home.' His shift finished at three.

'Probably gone out again,' Nancy said. He usually did. When they got off the bus, they could see his car parked in the side road alongside the house.

'He's still here.' Mam grabbed her arm. Her fingers bit in hard enough to hurt.

'He hasn't taken us for that run he promised us,' Nancy said.

Celia's steps had slowed.

'He'll be going out soon,' Nancy comforted, but she wished Amy were here too. The smell of frying hung heavy as a haze in the kitchen. The two plates with the salad between were still on the table.

Pa's face was black with rage when they went into the living room. There was a greasy plate in front of him. A knife and fork lay on top of it.

'Where do you think you've been?' he thundered at Celia. The house seemed taut with tension.

Nancy tried not to shiver. 'To New Brighton on the ferry,' she answered. 'We had a walk along the prom. A good blow. I thought it would do Mam good.'

'I don't want you to take her out jaunting. It's her job to get me something to eat when I come in from work.'

'I made a sardine salad for you, Pa.'

'I don't eat sardines or salad,' he ground out. 'She knows I need something hot. A man can't survive with an empty stomach.'

'I'm sorry,' Celia whispered. 'I'm sorry, Alec.'

Nancy moistened her lips and turned on him for the first time in her life. 'Listen, Pa. Don't you think you're a bit hard on Mam? You're turning her into a nervous wreck. What's the matter with you?'

That made matters worse. Nancy could feel his aggression billowing up. His face turned puce.

'There's nothing the matter with me. You keep out of this. Keep your mouth shut.' Nancy heard her mother gasp with horror.

'Celia, I'm still hungry. Is there any cake? And you can make me a cup of tea now you've bothered to come home.'

'Yes, Alec,' she said, though she didn't move. Her faded eyes were transfixed on him. Nancy could see her fingers shaking.

Pa lowered his head. 'Go on, woman. Get on with it.'

The atmosphere was suddenly explosive. Nancy felt her scalp crawl with horror. She could feel hate and fear and power sparking between her parents, and one stray spark could blow them all sky high. She gave Mam a gentle push towards the kitchen. She couldn't breathe properly.

Pa never used to be like this. He used to bounce her up and down on his knee as a child. She'd put her arms round his neck and her face up to be kissed.

Now he was like a tiger stalking his prey. She could feel the killing instinct. He wanted to tear the timid deer limb from limb.

'What did you find to cook for yourself?' she asked. 'I didn't know we had any eggs left.'

Suddenly his burning eyes were glowering at her. She couldn't have said anything worse.

'You're putting your mother up to this. She wouldn't do it if you weren't here. I shouldn't have let you come back. You're as bad as the other two, and after all I've done for you.'

Nancy was shaking at the ferocity of the attack.

'I used to like you. I never thought you'd turn against me like this.'

Behind her in the kitchen she heard the crash of shattering pottery. She went quickly to see what had happened. Her mother was in tears.

318

'I've broken two cups,' she choked.

'We've got more, Mam. It doesn't matter.' She put an arm round her shoulders.

'Of course it does.' Pa had followed her out. 'There's a war on, you silly bitch. It's not easy to get more.'

'Mam's upset . . .'

'So she should be. I'm not having you here, Nancy, if you don't behave yourself. Encouraging her like this.'

Nancy knew she couldn't possibly leave her mother alone with him. Not now.

She opened the cake tin and cut him a slice of Madeira cake. Pushed the plate at him. She saw her mother hadn't yet got round to filling the kettle. Nancy did it for her and put it on the gas before that caused another outburst.

'I'll bring your tea in when it's ready, Pa,' she said as calmly as she could. She was hoping he'd go back to the living room and leave them alone. After a moment he did.

Mam continued to sob. Nancy closed the kitchen door quietly.

'He's a bully,' Nancy fumed.

'He's a good man, really.' Celia's faded blue eyes were stark with terror.

A shiver ran down Nancy's back. She felt as though curtains had been dragged from her eyes.

'No, Mam. Look how he treated Katie. He's a selfish bully.'

That seemed to pull Mam up short. 'I wish I could help her . . . I can't cope with Katie. Do what you can for her, Nancy.'

'Of course. But it's you I'm worried about. You mustn't let him walk all over you.'

'How can I change anything now?' Celia asked, warming the teapot.

Two days later, Nancy came home for her afternoon off to find Mam quite agitated.

319

'There's a telegram for you. I hope it isn't bad news.'

Nancy ripped open the orange envelope. She laughed aloud, her first feeling was of joy. 'Stan's got leave! A forty-eight-hour pass. He'll be home tonight.'

Celia was stony faced as she asked: 'Embarkation leave?'

That made Nancy catch her breath. The telegram didn't tell her, but she was afraid Mam might be right. She went straight back to the hospital and asked Sister if she could change her day off. She didn't want to work while Stan was home.

She was thrilled and walking on air at one moment, terrified that he would be sent away to fight again the next.

They had such a brief time together. His train was late and travelling time cut into it. Stan looked well but was resigned.

'We've all been issued with new kit,' he told her. 'We're being sent somewhere hot.'

Although they'd firmly decided to get married on Stan's next leave, it was impossible at such short notice. They spent most of the time sitting in the park with their arms round each other. It was the only place they could go to get away from their families.

Nancy wouldn't have missed it for anything. It was wonderful to see him again, but it was all over much too quickly.

It was some time before she heard from him after that. She knew he was in North Africa, but not where, and he was not allowed to tell her. The address he sent her was an Army postcode.

He sent clues that he hoped the censor would not blank out, but she couldn't always work them out. The secrecy added to her fear. She didn't dare think about what might happen to him.

Katie liked Nanny's small house. She could relax and feel at home in it. She had nothing to hide, everybody knew about the baby. The days were passing and building up into weeks. Far too quickly for her, because the mother and baby home loomed ahead. She would much prefer to stay where she was.

The Framptons were treating her with such kindness that she felt she had to repay them by taking the best possible care of Nanny.

Bill Frampton regularly looked in for ten minutes on his way home from work. He was so tall he had to stoop under the low ceiling of the living room. Kate thought he looked out of place there, in his immaculate business suit.

He came one evening to find her cooking a meal in the kitchen, with Nanny calling urgently for her to come and find her glasses. Two minutes after those had been restored to her, Nanny wanted her cardigan on because she was feeling chilly.

'You're not finding this too much for you, Kate?'

'No, easier than looking after small children. Nanny keeps dozing off, so I get a chance to rest.'

Katie was determined to manage anything required of her. She knew why he asked. She could no longer hide the fact that she was having a baby. It was plain to see.

'I expect she wants you to make her a cup of tea every hour.' His grey eyes smiled. 'And we all know she takes eternity to eat her meals.'

Katie nodded. Nanny seemed to masticate each mouthful for what seemed hours, but swallowed very little. Then she'd say she was hungry again when the meal was cleared away.

'She can't be hurried in any way or she becomes flustered.' Katie didn't mind that it all took up a lot of time. 'I might be the same myself one day.'

Bill Frampton smiled. 'We all might.'

She said: 'The stairs are the worst part. They're so steep, Nanny finds them almost beyond her strength, and they're narrow too, so I can't stand abreast to help her. I have to stay on the step below where it's both harder for me and I can help her less.'

Every bedtime, Nanny jutted her chin towards the stairs. 'Don't want to go up there. It's too cold,' she'd grumble. It was summer and to Katie, the unheated bedrooms felt pleasant, but she knew Nanny felt the cold.

'So far, I've insisted she goes up every night.' Toby had wanted it. 'She can't get a good night's sleep down here on the sofa.' But it was hard work getting her up and even harder getting her down again in the morning.

'We'd better do something about it.' Mr Frampton was frowning.

Katie pushed her heavy dark curls behind her ears. 'When the sirens go at night, I ought to get her down to the cellar, but that's another flight of stairs and they're even steeper.'

Bill Frampton opened the door and looked down. 'I'm glad you've got a light here.'

'I've cleaned the place out and taken down a couple of deck chairs and some blankets, just in case,' Katie said anxiously. 'But Nanny refused point blank to get out of bed last night. I don't think she hears the sirens wail and therefore she isn't frightened to stay upstairs.'

'How about you, Katie? You're frightened?' He seemed to be studying her face.

Katie shivered; the very sound instilled terror in her. It was like a wailing banshee. 'Yes, I'm frightened.'

'So am I,' he said. 'It's quite a responsibility for you, looking after the old lady on your own. Did you hear on the news that the Luftwaffe bombed London last night?'

Katie shuddered. It had terrified her to think of London being bombed. It was too close. She'd heard about it on Nanny's wireless. She was listening to all BBC bulletins in awful fascination, though Nanny had lost interest in most things, including the war.

'Do you think the planes can get this far north?'

'I don't know, Katie,' he said. But she could see from his

face that he thought it more than possible.

'Shall I arrange to have her bed brought down? There's room here by the cellar door. Would that be easier for you?'

'Oh yes, and Nanny will be pleased. She's nice and warm in here.'

'Leave her in bed, Katie, if the siren goes. They've all been false alarms so far. She's too old and frail to be woken and taken down to the cellar. You go, but leave her in bed.'

Later the same day, Hilda came from Henshaw House and brought the gardener with her. Together they collapsed Nanny's bed and carried it down to the living room.

'Safest place is against the fireplace wall,' the gardener said, as he re-assembled the bedspring and the flock mattress. Hilda helped Katie make it up again with clean sheets and then spread the gold taffeta eiderdown on top.

Left alone with Nanny, Kate listened to reports of heavy attacks on British shipping, and frightening accounts of German planes regularly coming to bomb British cities. It was said that people in the south could see air battles going on over their heads. It was the end of July and the Battle of Britain had begun.

Up on Merseyside, Katie still felt distanced from it, even though the sirens sounded from time to time. What really brought the war close for her was hearing that bombs had been dropped in Neston, Irby and Thurstaston, though they had fallen harmlessly in fields. August came and she was beginning to feel heavy and ungainly.

A few nights later, the wail of sirens jolted her awake only half an hour after she'd climbed into bed. She lay there for a few moments clutching the bedclothes round her head in panic, but she knew bedclothes wouldn't save her.

She shot out of bed and pulled some clothes on over her nightdress, then grabbed the pillow and eiderdown off her bed and rushed downstairs. The wailing rose and fell, piercing the night.

In the glow from the dying fire, she could see that Nanny's

eyes were still closed. Katie left her where she was, glad that Bill Frampton had told her to do so.

In might be better for Nanny but Katie felt very much alone. She left the cellar door open as she went down. Wrapping herself in blankets, she pulled the eiderdown over her head and tried to sleep on a deck chair. All the time, she was straining her ears, listening for the throb of aero engines or the crump of exploding bombs, though she didn't know what to expect. The only sound was of Nanny snoring, but her heart thumped with dread for a long time.

Katie woke up in the morning, stiff from her cramped position, but relieved to find no bombs had been dropped. Nanny's bleary eyes were open when she went up.

'What you doing down there?' she demanded.

'The sirens went. I thought there was going to be an air raid.'

'I didn't hear anything.'

'No, it was a false alarm.'

'Glad you didn't get me out of my warm bed for nothing. Silly, I call it, going down there. How about a cup of tea?'

Mary Frampton called in to see them two or three times each week, usually in the afternoons, but she came that morning to see if they were all right.

Katie prided herself on always having Nanny ready to receive visitors. She liked to have the living room neat and tidy and the fire built up.

This morning, she'd given Nanny breakfast in bed and lit the fire.

'You've forgotten to get Mungo up,' Nanny complained. 'Poor bird, he'd be under his cloth all day if I didn't remind you.'

'I haven't forgotten him,' Katie returned. 'I was seeing to you first.' She whipped the cloth away, and Mungo began to sing.

'He's good company. Open his cage, let him out.'

Katie did so. To start with, she'd been a bit nervous about

letting him fly round the room, expecting difficulties in getting him back, or at the very least splodges on the carpet. Once a yellow feather drifted down, but never anything else.

Nanny loved having him out. She'd talk to him, and he'd perch on her bed rail and sing.

'You don't like Mungo,' Nanny said often in an accusing voice.

'I do,' Katie protested. 'I like to hear him chirping.' But she felt an urge to duck every time he flew over her head, and preferred him in his cage.

Katie had decided that Nanny's hair needed washing this morning. To avoid using the stairs, she was doing this in front of the fire with jugs and bowls.

She had reached the stage of rubbing Nanny's hair dry with towels when Mary Frampton banged on the knocker and let herself in.

'Oh!' Katie said, conscious of the bowls of dirty water on the table and the mess of clothes and tea cups about the room. 'I like everything to be nice when you come.'

Mary Frampton laughed. 'You mustn't worry about that. You've got a good fire going and I'm delighted to see Nanny being so well cared for. Nobody could do more for her.'

Katie was combing Nanny's thin white hair up in to a bun. 'I'm not very good at this. Will it do, Nanny?' She gave the old lady a hand mirror to see the effect.

'Doesn't feel right,' Nanny grumbled. 'Here, let me do it.'

'You look very nice this morning,' Mary Frampton told Nanny. 'A clean blouse too.'

Katie saw her duck as Mungo flew over her head, and hid her smile.

'You'll lose this bird one day,' Mary said, 'letting him loose like this. He'll be out of a window before you know it.'

'Mungo would never leave me.' Nanny frowned.

Katie got out his packet of seed. She shook a little into his bowl, left the cage door open and stood back. Mungo flew inside and started to eat. Katie fastened him in.

'That's better.' Mary Frampton smiled at her.

Nanny lowered her arms with a sigh and flung down the comb before she'd managed to secure her bun. Her wispy hair was all round her shoulders again. 'I could do with a cup of tea,' she complained.

'I've got the kettle on.' Katie picked up her hairpins and re-did the bun for her. Then as she ran round emptying bowls of water and tidying up, Mary Frampton chatted to them.

'Toby has a forty-eight-hour pass. We are so looking forward to seeing him again. I've come in to town early to see if I can get something extra for dinner. Only four ounces of bacon each a week. It's all right for the ladies, but for the men it's very meagre.

'I queued and got some cod. Fish isn't on ration yet. I'll leave it here for your dinners, Katie.'

'Won't you need it for Toby?'

'No, I got some liver too. He likes that.'

When she'd gone, Katie was left thinking about Toby Frampton.

That night, Katie again heard the air-raid siren piercing her sleep. She lay snug and warm in bed, listening to the eerie rise and fall of sound filling the night. Moaning Minnie, the neighbours called it. She told herself she must be braver than she'd been last night. She'd been quaking with fear for hours, yet no bombs had fallen.

Because Mr Frampton had told her not to get Nanny out of bed, and Nanny had told her she was silly to go down to the cellar, her fears were soothed. She could feel herself drifting off again.

She was jolted awake by the most phenomenal volume of sound outside. The anti-aircraft guns at Bidston were firing, interspersed with an ominous *crump crump*, followed by a rushing sound.

Another *crump*, and the disorientating feeling that the house had moved on its foundations. Katie was gripped by paralysing terror. She felt she was about to be blasted to bits, burned to death or buried alive.

She could feel the perspiration on her forehead as she slid heavily out of bed to twitch the blackout curtains aside. It was a clear, moonlit night. She could see searchlights sending further shafts of light up into the sky, illuminating the fat shapes of the barrage balloons.

She heard a thin scream from the living room below, and knew Nanny was as terrified as she was. She was already turning away to go downstairs when the window shattered and broken glass burst into her room. Mrs Frampton had brought her tape to crisscross the windows, but not enough to do them all.

The blast flung her back on to her bed. Her wardrobe door had been ajar; it crashed it back so hard that the mirror shattered.

Katie's heart was in her throat and thumping so hard she thought it would burst. The blackout curtain was blowing into her room. Every time it lifted she could see moonlight glinting on the broken glass on the floor. She wanted to run but dared not put her bare feet on so much glass. Feeling awkward and ungainly, she edged along her bed and snatched her best shoes from the wardrobe, forcing her feet into them. Then she grabbed her best coat and pushed her arms into that. She was shivering with cold and terror now.

She gathered up her eiderdown and leapt for the landing. She needed the safety of the cellar tonight. The light worked when she switched it on, and she saw the stairs descending steeply in front of her. She was barely halfway down when she felt the house shake again and the light went out.

Somehow, in the sudden dark, she missed her step and fell. She knew she screamed, it came curling out of her before she could stop it. She landed with a crash at the bottom, the wind knocked out of her. She had to lie still for a few moments as pain jabbed in her abdomen.

All the time she could hear Nanny screaming, 'What's

happening? Are you there, Kate? What's the matter?'

Katie had meant to be braver than this. It would only make Nanny worse if she panicked. 'I'm coming,' she called, as the pain receded.

'What is it? What are you doing?' Age made Nanny's voice crack.

'I'm here. It's all right, Nanny.'

There was no glow from the grate tonight, the fire had gone out. The living room was pitch black. Mrs Frampton had brought candles for just this emergency. Where had she put them?

'What's happening to me?' Nanny's voice came again, querulous and frightened.

'It's a raid.' As Katie felt her way across the room to the bed, there seemed to be a volcanic rumbling. Then, with an almighty roar, every remaining window in the house was sucked out. All the doors burst open and were blasted back on their hinges, crashing against the walls.

She was propelled forward, banging her head against the brass bedhead. She couldn't stop herself.

She was screaming now, her terror totally out of control. She was in a maelstrom of crashing masonry, splintering wood and whirling dust. She was terrified that the ceiling was about to come down and crush her. Some last vestige of self-preservation made her roll under the bed.

She was choking in the dust and had a horrible acrid taste of soot in her mouth. Masonry continued falling in a crumbling rush like a waterfall. She felt the foundations shaking. The noise was hurting her ears.

Katie felt something heavy land on the bed above her, and with an almighty jolt the foot collapsed. She snatched her feet up, but one caught, wedged tight to the floor by the bedspring.

She thought the end was coming, that she would be crushed to death. She wrapped her arms round her head to protect it and lay very still, gripped by searing panic.

328

She didn't know how long she lay there expecting the worst. Long, sick minutes dragged past, and gradually the noise died down. She realised now that the top of the bedspring had held in its notch on the bedhead. She had space but was coughing and choking because of the dust. She could see nothing, everywhere was pitch black.

'Nanny?' she called cautiously. There was no answer. 'Nanny!' All the time she was tugging at her trapped foot, trying to free it. It didn't hurt; the pain she had was in her abdomen. Her foot jerked free at last, leaving her shoe behind.

Katie stifled her sobs and began to feel round. She had to get out from under the bed. Her fingers encountered what seemed like a wall of loose rubble and soot wherever she pushed them. Her fingernails were full of it. She tried to feel upwards over the mattress; she thought she could feel sheet, but she couldn't get her hand far enough up to touch Nanny. She was worried about her.

Katie was panting in desperation. She was trapped. Buried alive. Not knowing whether the house still stood above her. All she could be sure of was that the floor had held.

'Nanny? Can you hear me? Are you all right?' There was no reply and no movement on the mattress above her.

She had never felt so alone in her life. She seemed to have been here for ages.

All was quiet now. She screamed again, hoping that somebody might hear her and come, but when she listened again, the drip, drip of water was the only sound she could hear.

She shivered, she felt frozen stiff. She no longer had the eiderdown she'd started to bring down with her. She tried to edge off the cold lino on to the carpet square, and wished she'd gone down to the cellar when she'd had the chance.

She'd be comfortably wrapped in blankets and eiderdown if she had, instead of shivering in this tiny space.

Katie felt another pain coming. It gripped her with terrifying ferocity, holding her rigid for three minutes.

Gradually it faded, leaving her sweating and in a state of heightening panic about her predicament. The pains were getting stronger and more frequent. The baby must be coming. Somebody had to come and help her.

CHAPTER TWENTY

At Ashville House, the ancient central heating boiler was housed in one of the cellars where it put out more heat than ever reached upstairs. That room in the cellars was always cosy. The next had large brownstone sinks where nurses could wash personal clothing, and washing lines crisscrossed both.

There was a whole series of cellar rooms, stoutly constructed by Victorian builders, high, vast and dark, with ghostly shadows cast by the inadequate electric light. Long ago, they'd been used for storing wine, food and fuels. Now they were put into use as an air-raid shelter.

Amy didn't dislike going down there. The Ashville cellars had a homely, lived-in air, and she felt safer there than upstairs in her bed. There was competition for space in the room that housed the boiler, because the flagstoned floor soaked up the warmth.

Every nurse provided herself with something to lie on, which had to be stored on top of or behind her wardrobe upstairs. Garden deck chairs were the most common, being light and generally available from home. There were several camp beds, a hammock hung from hooks across a corner, and a few old army-style bedrolls.

Like the others, Amy had thought it a bit of a lark at first, but after a few false alarms she was getting tired of broken nights in less comfortable surroundings. It made it harder than ever to get dressed and down to the hospital in time for breakfast at seven o'clock the next morning.

When the siren sounded its warning, Amy knew she had no choice but to hurry down to the cellar. Home Sister took a roll call to make sure everybody was there.

Tonight, Amy couldn't settle to sleep. There was too much noise outside. She was listening, like all the other girls, to the throb of engines, the sound of anti-aircraft guns and the blast of exploding bombs.

She could hear a whispered debate across the cellar, as to whether it made Ashville House safer to be surrounded by almost two hundred acres of park. Somebody pointed out that the Birkenhead docks were less than a mile away as the crow flies. Another that Cammell Laird, the ship builders, were not too far away in the other direction.

Amy huddled under her blankets, comforted by the occasional creak of a deck chair or a light snore from a colleague. She knew she dozed off and on and that outside the night was quiet again.

She was blinking then in the sudden light. The single bulb swung on a long flex from the middle of the ceiling. Amy assumed it was time to get up until she saw Home Sister, stout and middle-aged, standing in the doorway in a girlish pink dressing gown.

'I want volunteers,' she said. 'To get up and go on duty now.'

'What's the time, Sister?'

'It's four thirty. Air-raid casualties are being brought in and the night staff can't cope. They want nurses with casualty and theatre experience.'

Amy sat up. Around her everybody else was throwing off their blankets.

'Not everybody,' Sister told them. 'We'll still have to staff the wards for the rest of the day.'

Amy found she was one of those whose services were required. She ran upstairs to her room to throw on her uniform and the group hurried through light early morning drizzle to the hospital. The blackout was absolute; not a chink of light showed except in the half-covered headlights of an ambulance drawing up to the doors of the casualty department.

Every bed and most of the chairs were filled with waiting patients. All were wet, bedraggled and filthy. The rain had turned the heavy dust from bricks and soot and plaster to a mud-like paste that stuck to everything. They had to wash patients to find the wounds.

For them all, it was a new and frightening experience. When she first went on duty, Amy thought it chaotic, but with the extra staff, grazes and contusions were soon dressed, cuts sutured and broken bones set. Both theatres were working flat out to deal with more serious injuries, and there were terrible tales of friends and relatives who had been killed.

Amy noticed that some of the patients were giving addresses close to where Katie was living with Nanny. She asked about that street but none of them seemed to know. Although very concerned, she was kept so busy she could do nothing more about it.

It was mid-morning and order had gradually been restored when Amy was told she could return to her normal duties on Weightman Ward. On the way upstairs, she had to pass the telephone kiosk next to the switchboard. She shot inside.

There'd been talk of putting a phone into Nanny's house, but due to the war it hadn't happened yet. She asked the telephone operator to put her through to the Framptons' house.

Hilda answered.

'It's Amy Siddons. I'm a bit worried about my sister Kate. Do you know if she and Nanny are all right?'

She heard the gasp at the other end. It frightened her.

Hilda said cautiously: 'Haven't you heard?'

Amy's heart turned over with dread. 'No, what's happened?'

'The house . . . It was bombed . . . Nanny was . . .'

Amy felt a surge of impatience. 'Katie? What's happened to Katie?'

'She's in hospital . . .'

'No,' Amy cried, suddenly terrified for her. 'No, she isn't here. I'd have seen her if she'd been brought here. I'm at the hospital now.'

'The maternity hospital in Grange Mount. The baby was coming early.'

'Yes, of course.' Amy felt weak at the knees. 'Of course. They'd take her there.'

'Mr Frampton went down to see your parents. To let them know. He said Nancy was at home too.'

'I think it's her day off. Is Kate hurt, otherwise?'

'Shocked, I believe. They had to dig her out of the rubble.'

'A direct hit? The house, I mean?'

'No, bomb blast, but it's badly damaged.'

'And Nanny?'

Hilda's tone was more guarded. 'I'm afraid she was killed. Isn't it terrible?'

When Amy put the phone back on the hook, her hand was trembling. She took a deep breath and immediately lifted it again, asking for the maternity hospital.

When Amy explained who she was to the midwifery sister who answered, she found she knew her slightly. She'd done her general training with Nancy.

The sister said: 'Nancy's here with me now. I'll let her tell you what's happened.'

Nancy's voice sounded strained. 'Katie's just had her baby. A stillbirth. From the time she was brought in, nobody had heard its heart. It's all been very traumatic here.'

'How is she?'

'Very tearful. She was buried under all that rubble for six or seven hours. She's still shaking and very upset. Whether about losing the baby or the aftermath of being incarcerated, I don't know. Bit of both, I suppose. She's in a state. So is Mam.'

'She's there with you?'

'Yes, she's with Katie now.'

'I'm glad you took Mam to see her.'

'Don't think it's the best thing for Katie.'

'Why not? Is Mam very upset?'

'Mam's over the moon. Almost singing with joy. She says she feels let off the hook. Keeps telling Katie that losing the baby is the best thing that could happen to her. She'll not lose face. She'll not have that millstone round her neck for the rest of her life. That we can all get back to normal and forget it ever happened now. Mam's going completely over the top. It's a bit soon for that.'

'Poor Katie. She's not hurt anywhere else?'

'Her foot is sore. It's been crushed, but not badly, and she's bruised from a fall on the stairs.'

'Tell her I'll come and see her this afternoon.' Amy put the phone down slowly. Mam might be right, but Kate wouldn't be seeing it that way just yet.

As soon as she'd eaten lunch at the hospital, Amy caught a bus to Charing Cross and then walked up to Grange Mount. By the time she reached the hospital, visitors were being allowed inside.

She'd had no reason before to come to this part of town and the Palladian façade of the maternity hospital surprised her. So did the marble-floored entrance hall. Although built on a smaller scale, the style was far grander than that of the General.

The wards seemed small and old-fashioned after Weightman. Katie was in a corner bed. A wire cradle hung at the foot. The sheets on the cot mattress were neatly turned down. It was empty.

Katie had mauve shadows under her dark blue eyes. Her face was paper-white. Amy thought she'd never seen her look more beautiful.

'How are you, Katie?'

'All right. It's all behind me, isn't it?'

'I'm glad to see you're looking on the bright side,' Amy

335

said, pulling out the chair to sit down.

The ward was filled with the sounds of babies. One cried, others snuffled and grunted softly. All the other cradles were occupied; some swung with the kicking of the babies.

Visitors were peering into them, smiling and cooing with admiration. Amy watched Katie looking round and knew she mourned the loss of her child. There were one or two proud fathers here, although it was afternoon and many would be working. Katie wasn't able to look at them. She wanted to be part of a family, in the way the other women were.

'Perhaps it's for the best, Katie.' She saw the tears well into Katie's eyes.

'It was a girl,' she choked. 'They think it was the fall. I fell down five or six stairs in the dark.'

'Nobody's fault,' Amy tried to placate. 'The baby couldn't have known anything.'

'If only I'd got up when I first heard the siren. There'd have been plenty of time . . .'

'You didn't, Katie, and this is how things have turned out. No good worrying about it now.'

'But if . . .'

Amy suddenly realised that a man in airforce blue was approaching Katie's bed behind a large bunch of roses. Tall and ruggedly built, his straight hair was streaked with different shades from corn to gold. He stood awkwardly at the foot.

'Hello, Katie. Mother sent the flowers to cheer you. And here's your ration book. Sister says you must have it with you.'

Amy had been trying to place his square jaw and friendly eyes; she realised now he was Toby Frampton.

'Thank you, the flowers are lovely.' Katie was burying her face in the petals but not before Amy had seen her eyes filling with tears again. Katie was very weepy.

'Just from the garden. Good thing it's summer. The florists don't seem to open for business any more.'

She could see Katie was trying to compose herself: 'It's kind of you to think of me.'

'Can't stop thinking about you.'

Suddenly he was choking with emotion too. He seemed very concerned. 'Terrible things happen to you, Katie. This time it's my fault.'

'Yours?' Amy couldn't stop herself. 'How can it be your fault?'

He was offering Katie a clean handkerchief from his pocket. 'Katie wouldn't have been in Nanny's house if I hadn't organised it.'

'You weren't to know it would be bombed.' Katie was dabbing her eyes, trying to smile up at him.

'We were all very grateful for what you did.' Amy got up to fetch a chair for him. 'It seemed the best thing for Katie at the time.'

'It was my own fault,' Katie said softly. 'I should have got out of bed when the siren sounded, I'd have been all right if I had. And if I'd got Nanny down to the cellar she would have been all right too. That's the awful part, thinking of Nanny being killed. I shouldn't have let her stay in bed.'

'Dad says he told you to leave her there. Nobody's blaming you, so you mustn't blame yourself.'

'I was supposed to be taking care of her. It was my job. She was terrified, I could hear her screaming. I couldn't get to her quickly enough.'

'You know what else Dad's saying? That Nanny was so frail she couldn't have lasted much longer. She couldn't do anything for herself and she hated being dependent on others. It made her crotchety and she never used to be.'

'You're just trying to be kind,' Katie sniffed.

'No, I'm not. Dad says he thinks she'd see it as a blessing. To go quickly like that.'

Amy could see Katie staring up at him, wanting to believe what he said. She put out her hand to him. 'I'm the other sister, I'm Amy.'

His grasp was warm and firm. 'I guessed. You're like Katie to look at.'

'I'd like to look more like her,' Amy pushed her thick dark plait over her shoulder. 'Katie's turning out to be the beauty of the family.'

Toby was looking at Katie again. 'You must have had an awful time,' he said.

'I was frightened. I really thought I was going to die. There was so much dust, I was fighting for breath. And I was pinned there and couldn't get out to help Nanny. I was almost certain she was dead on the bed above me.' Amy watched Toby feel for Katie's hand.

'The ceiling came down on top of her,' he whispered. 'There were two huge chunks of plaster and brickwork on her bed.'

'Were you there?' Katie asked.

'Yes, don't you remember me talking to you?'

Katie shook her head numbly.

'Dad thought a bomb might have fallen close to Nanny's house. We went down as soon as the all clear sounded. It was such a shock to find the roof gone. We had to dig you out.

'When we didn't find you in the cellar we didn't know where to look. We knew you'd be somewhere there under the rubble. We knew where Nanny's bed was, and started shifting stuff to get to her, but when we found her, we were afraid you'd been killed too. Then I heard such a strange whimper. In all, it took us a couple of hours to get you out from under the bed. You were only half conscious by then.'

'I remember a nurse washing me.'

'You were as black as a sweep. Covered in dust.'

'I don't remember much else. Pain, of course, and I've never been so terrified.'

Toby smiled. 'It's shaken us all up, Katie, I can tell you.'

Amy swallowed hard and saw Katie's watery smile falter.

'I must tell you about Nanny's budgie,' Toby said briskly.

Amy knew he was trying to steer them to less emotional subjects.

'Mungo? Is he all right?'

'Right as rain. I'd seen what was left of his cage when I was digging for you, Katie. Just a few strands of twisted wire on the floor. I didn't think he could possibly have survived, but when daylight came, a neighbour pointed him out to us. He was sitting on the windowsill, singing away. There was no glass left in the window.'

'Were you able to catch him?' Katie asked.

'Not then. We went home and Mother produced a cage from the attic. I didn't expect to find him still there when I went back, but he was. I let him see me put a bit of birdseed inside and he flew in. Mother's going to keep him.'

The bell was being rung to indicate that visiting time was over and they must all leave. Amy stood up and tucked her chair under the bed.

She kissed Katie's cheek. 'You'll feel better in a day or two,' she assured her. 'I'll come again.'

Toby had retreated stiffly to the foot of the bed.

'Goodbye, Katie,' he said. 'I won't be able to come again. I've got a forty-eight-hour pass, it's up at midnight. I hope all goes well for you from now on. It's high time your luck changed.'

Amy was conscious of his heavy footfall on the ward floor as he accompanied her to the door. He was opening it for her. She waved goodbye to Kate.

'Poor kid,' he said. 'But she's looking so much better. I'm pleased to see her sitting up and talking. She was in a bad way last night. Crying out for help. Screaming when I touched her.' His troubled eyes met hers.

Amy shivered. Kate had been in labour last night, giving birth alone and buried beneath rubble. She could envisage nothing worse.

Outside in the street, Toby Frampton stopped by a car. 'Can I offer you a lift?'

'Thank you, I'd be grateful. It looks very sporty. What is it?' The only car Amy had ever ridden in was Paul's.

'A Riley Merlin. Do you want to be dropped at the General?'

Amy looked at her watch. 'I'm not on until five. The bottom of Ashville Road will be fine. I'll go up to the home for an hour.'

'An hour? But then you'd have to walk down again. Would you like to see Nanny's house? The damage?'

She hesitated. 'I don't want to take up your precious leave if you've anyone else you'd prefer to spend it with.'

'It's not always possible. To spend one's time with . . .' Amy wondered whether he was trying to say he'd have preferred to stay with Katie. 'It's difficult to fit leave in with that of friends.'

The journey took only minutes. Amy felt sick when she saw that the roofs had been ripped off half a street of houses.

'This one was Nanny's.'

The walls of the terrace were standing, but there were no front doors or glass in any of the windows. She could see the stairs in Nanny's house, bare of carpet now. Everything was covered with a thick, mud-like substance still sticky after the rain.

Pathetic little heaps of belongings had been collected in piles on the pavement and a large notice read:

LOOTING

Looting from premises that have been damaged by or vacated by reason of war operations is punishable by death or penal servitude for life.

'Seems a bit drastic,' Amy said with a shiver.

'Dad and I salvaged what we could. Mother took everything that seemed to belong to Katie to your home. Nancy said she'd wash her things for her.'

'Katie's lucky to have got out alive,' Amy breathed,

covering her face. She dared not look at the damage, nor think of the people who had died here.

Toby put his car into gear and moved off immediately. 'Not a very good idea after all. I'd like to take you for a spin but petrol's so scarce now. How about tea and cakes at the Ritz instead?'

'That would be very nice.' Amy liked him. There was a friendly warmth about all the Framptons.

'On second thoughts, I'm not sure about the cakes either. Mother was complaining they didn't have any last time she went.'

'Blame the war,' Amy said. 'A cup of tea would be fine.'

She was weighing up whether she should suggest going to the Refreshment Room. She could guarantee that if they had cakes there, they'd get them. But Paul would hate to see her with a man in uniform. Especially an RAF officer. He was getting paranoid about still being in civvies, afraid of being called a draft-dodger. And Auntie My might get the wrong end of the stick. Amy said nothing and let him take her to the Ritz.

'Are you a pilot?' she asked him.

'I'm training to be a navigator.' He was frowning over his cup. After a pause he said: 'Kate was very upset. It must have been a terrible experience for her.'

Amy had been trying to get away from discussing Kate. Now she said briskly: 'So she's lost the baby. Do you see that as a bad thing?'

He stared at her with troubled eyes, but said nothing.

'I see it as a blessing. Our Kate can turn over a new leaf now and put Jimmy Shaw and his baby behind her.' Since she'd had time to think it over, Amy had been feeling relief. Mam was right but too ready to push her opinion on Katie.

'It's hard for her at the moment.'

'But in the long run, easier. She'll come to accept it.'

Amy put her elbows on the table and rested her chin on her hands. 'The best thing for Katie is to start nursing, and the sooner the better. She must, before her eighteenth birthday. Women could be getting their call-up papers by then. It would be just like our Kate to get herself drafted into a munitions factory for the duration.'

He smiled: 'Nancy said you were good at organising others. Pushing them in the direction you think is best for them.'

'With sisters like mine, I have to be,' she retorted.

Because Amy was on night duty, the easiest time for her to visit Katie was in the mornings. She asked Sister if she might do so regularly, and was given permission, although visitors weren't generally allowed then.

'How is she?' she'd ask each morning as she went in.

'Getting on all right, but feeling a bit down,' Sister would say. Some days she said 'despondent' or 'listless'. Amy would recount what had happened during the night and give Katie snippets of family news. She found cheering her wasn't easy.

'Put it behind you,' she advised. 'Try to forget about the baby. You'd have found it very difficult to . . .'

'It's not just that.' Katie's eyes swam with anguish. 'They'll want to send me out in a few days. Where can I go?'

'Home,' Amy said. 'Pa told you you could, didn't he?'

'That was months ago, and I turned his offer down. I went somewhere else.'

'His offer is still open,' Amy said decisively.

'Isn't there somewhere else I could go?' Katie pleaded.

Amy paused. 'Auntie My would have you like a shot, but I don't like to ask. We don't know how long you'll need to stay and we can't offer to pay her. She's got her own money worries.'

'After what Jimmy did,' Katie said through tight lips.

Amy said briskly: 'It'll be better for you at home now Nancy's there. She's bringing Mam to see you, isn't she? Ask Mam, next time she comes.'

'I already have.'

Amy stared at her. 'What did she say?'

'That she'd ask Pa.'

'Well then, what are you worried about?'

'She didn't do it. Said she'd forgotten.'

Amy could see Katie blinking hard. 'I'll have a word with Pa on my nights off. I'll get everything straightened out in good time, I promise.'

Amy went back to the General. Instead of going to bed, she went to the dining room to see if Nancy was there on her mid-morning break.

She was turning away, disappointed at being unable to spot her sister in the crush of nurses round the tables, when Nancy appeared in the doorway behind her.

'I want a quick word,' Amy said, and led her out into the courtyard garden between the hospital buildings. 'About Katie . . .'

'I know what you're going to say,' Nancy said. 'She's worried whether Pa will let her come home again.'

'Have you had a word with him?'

'No. Amy, he doesn't even like me being there. I told him he ought to go to the doctor, that I thought he was overwrought with the war and everything. He nearly burst a blood vessel. Mam's scared stiff of him and I don't blame her. He's giving me the willies.'

'It's as well you're there then. Katie's nowhere else to go.'

'You tell him, Amy. He'll take it from you.'

'I will. How did you get on in that bad raid?'

'It was awful. I was terrified, and Mam was worse. I couldn't quieten her. She was screaming. Not a wink of sleep all night.'

'Where was Pa?'

'Tucked up in bed. Said he had to get his sleep, and he might as well die there as anywhere else.'

Amy was exasperated. 'He's been trained to help the

343

general public. You'd think at home he'd want to help Mam.'

'Help? It would be no help at all to have him in the shelter, believe you me. He's at Mam the whole time. They're better apart.'

'Leave him to me,' Amy said grimly.

She was due for four nights off duty. She knew Paul found the ten nights she worked a long dull stretch.

'We're going out on your first night off,' he told her. 'I've bought tickets for the Empire. George Formby's on.'

'Lovely. Shall I come down to the café to pick you up?'

'Yes, any time after five. We'll have something to eat before going.'

Amy decided she must deal with Pa first. When she came off duty that morning, she set her alarm clock and went straight to bed. At four o'clock, she got up and took a bath to wake herself up. It was no good being half comatosed when she went to see him.

She thought he'd have had time to get home and eat, but not long enough to go out again.

Amy hadn't been home for some time, and she'd thought Nancy had been exaggerating, until she caught Mam alone in the kitchen and said: 'Go and see Katie tonight, Mam. Tell her you want her to come home.'

'It's not up to me,' Mam said fearfully. 'You'd better clear it with Pa.' Amy left her mother washing up and went to the living room door.

The Morrison shelter took up more space than the table had. Pa was semi-prone in his Rexine armchair but there was less room for him to stretch his legs. The room was cramped now.

Amy saw him looking at her warily over the top of his newspaper.

'I don't want her here,' he said.

'Where else can she go?'

'I don't care where she goes. She'll only make trouble here. I don't want any of you here.'

'You've forgotten, Pa, the little chat we had in the shed that time.'

He was on his feet in an instant, coming closer. There was menace in his eyes, colour running up his cheeks. 'Don't you come here threatening me, Amy. I won't have it.'

A trickle of fear ran down her back but she stood her ground. It seemed Pa's antagonism had hardened to hate. Amy was tall for a girl but Pa was six foot two and built like an ox. He could make anybody feel threatened.

She said as calmly as she could: 'As far as I'm concerned, nothing has changed. What I said then still stands. I'll open my mouth to Mam and Nancy. Tell everybody what you've been up to.'

She saw him raise his arm. She held her breath, staring back at him and trying not to flinch. After long-drawn-out seconds, it fell back harmlessly.

'Which way do you want to play it?' She could put more confidence in her voice now. 'Come on, I want an answer now. You haven't got all day to make up your mind.'

He lowered his face close to hers. She could see loathing for her in every line of it. Loathing, but fury too. And fear. Pa was afraid of what she could do. She turned her back on him.

'I'll tell Katie she can come then.' She knew that at last she had the upper hand. Celia came in, wiping her hands on her apron.

'Nancy can't always be here, she has to go to work. Mam would like to have Katie at home. Wouldn't you, Mam?'

'I wouldn't mind,' Celia said timidly. Her hands fluttered up to cover her face for a moment.

Three days later, Amy got a taxi to fetch Kate from hospital. Mam hadn't been to see her again, and she was understandably nervous about coming home.

As Amy carried Katie's suitcase into the hall, Pa was coming downstairs in his moleskin trousers and Harris tweed jacket.

'Here's Katie,' she announced. 'You said she could come home.'

'You're the one saying she's got to come,' he said, glaring belligerently at Amy. She clenched her teeth, and Katie hung back looking scared.

'You agreed, Pa.'

He turned on Kate then, full of aggression. 'You behave yourself. No mischief, and don't worry your mother. Do you hear?'

Katie took a step backwards in alarm.

'Pa,' Amy protested. 'This isn't part of the bargain we made. I've told you what I'll do if . . .' She half expected him to come at her like a tornado; instead he backed down.

'All right, I've said it's all right, haven't I?'

Amy smiled and smoothed her wiry dark hair back from her forehead. 'Are you going out now?'

'It's my day off. Any objections?' His eyes burned into hers, projecting hate at her. 'Don't you ever come home again, Amy. I'll put up with the other two, but I'm not having you. I don't want to see you hanging round your mother, bothering her. Stay away from now on.'

'Pa!' Katie protested. 'You can't say that to Amy.'

'You shut up, or I'll be saying it to you too.'

Amy lifted Kate's suitcase, trying not to show how ruffled she was. 'I'm not staying, Pa. Just want to give Katie something. Come on, Katie.' She almost ran upstairs.

In the bedroom they used to share, she brought out an application form from her pocket.

'Fill this in, Kate, and post it.' It was an application form for nurse training. 'It'll be a few months before it's all organised, but I can't think of another way to get you away from here.'

Kate turned it over with a sigh.

'What's the matter? You've always said you wanted to do it.'

'I do, Amy.'

'You'll feel better in a day or two. This is the only way you'll be able to get away from here. The sooner you do it the better.'

CHAPTER TWENTY-ONE

Autumn 1940

'Thank God that baby of yours died,' Pa sneered, as soon as Amy was no longer there to hear. 'A blessing I'd call it. A great blessing, eh, Celia? I wouldn't have let you bring your bastard here. Think of the disgrace.'

Katie knew she couldn't look to Mam for support. Mam had said much the same to her.

'You're a lucky girl, Kate. It would have been round your neck for the rest of your life. Without it, there's nothing to stop you looking for another job straight away.'

Kate swallowed hard; she'd been worried about having no job.

Amy had said: 'Don't look for work just yet. Better if you have a rest first and get your strength back, try to forget all you've been through.'

'I've said you can stay here,' Pa grunted, 'but there's no reason why you can't pay your own way. I don't want you sponging on me for long. I hear the munition factories pay best.'

Katie shivered. Amy had also promised to ask Auntie My if she could stay with her if Pa got her down too much, but she didn't want to be a burden on Auntie My either.

When Pa went out on that first day, she'd collapsed on his chair in the living room, and the Morrison shelter had caught her eye. She couldn't see how there could be room for all of them in that. Pa would need at least half the space himself and would probably take more. She was afraid he would not allow her inside it. Her mouth felt suddenly dry.

'Does Nancy go in there when there's a raid?' she asked Mam.

'Yes, of course.'

'What about me? Is there somewhere else?'

'No, you can come in too.'

Katie measured the distance across it with her eyes. Perhaps if they all sat cross-legged, instead of lying down, there would be room.

'But Pa . . . ?'

'Pa believes in staying in bed. Whether there's a raid or not.'

Kate was filled with relief. She was still having terrible dreams about being buried alive. That was something she couldn't get out of her mind, and the mournful wail of the air-raid siren sent shivers down her spine.

When it went, she was always down in the Morrison shelter before Mam and Nancy. Making space for herself, pushing aside all the things Mam thought essential to keep there, such as gas masks, indigestion tablets and important papers. Katie had leafed through them: insurance policies, certificates of birth and marriage and Nancy's state registration papers.

Sometimes, now, the siren went in the daytime. If Mam happened to be preparing a meal for Pa, she'd carry on, though a warning meant Pa's homecoming would be delayed.

Katie stayed in the shelter whether she could hear bombs dropping or not. She was afraid the same thing would happen to her a second time.

Mam didn't seem to resent her presence at home; rather she seemed to cling to her in a way Katie hadn't expected. The sight of Mam's fear made Katie feel worse. Mam shook like a leaf both when there was an air raid and when Pa was in a bad mood. Katie was afraid she was growing more like Mam.

'We don't see much of our Nancy,' Mam complained,

'you'd think she'd spend more time at home now.'

'She'll be here all afternoon, Mam, and she sleeps here every night.' Katie was always glad to see Nancy come home. Amy came too, when she knew the coast was clear. Katie looked forward to having their company.

Nancy was still Pa's favourite; he was gentler with her, whatever she thought. Katie knew that Nancy's presence stopped Pa hectoring her about her mistakes, bad judgement and wanton behaviour.

Both Nancy and Amy gave her pocket money and took her and Mam on outings. They encouraged them to go to the pictures on their own and have tea at the Ritz.

'Better for both of you not to be stuck at home all the time,' Amy had said.

Katie was glad to find Pa wasn't home all that much. He'd always gone out a lot in his off-duty time, and now he was working long hours as well, it seemed he was rarely with them.

The next course in the nursing school started in October and Katie was hoping to get a place. She'd sat the entrance exam; it was just a question of waiting to hear the result. She wished the letter would come. She needed to know.

'I'm not sure whether I've done well enough,' she'd worried to Amy. That was something else that was keeping her awake at night.

'I felt just the same,' Amy assured her briskly. 'And Nancy was a nervous wreck while she was waiting to hear.'

'Yes, but if not . . .'

Amy grinned and wrinkled her nose. 'With me and Nancy making such a success of it, it won't matter if you've written a load of nonsense. They'll be bound to jump at having you.'

Katie threw a cushion at her.

Every time mail dropped through the letter box, she ran to the front door to see if it was for her. At the beginning of October, the letter she'd been waiting for came. She opened it with nervous fingers. When she found she'd been given a place, she wanted to shout for joy.

She began to feel better after that. She hadn't been capable of thinking for herself when she'd first come out of hospital. She'd needed Amy to push her in the right direction.

All her life it had been like this. Mam had been around but her sisters had provided more practical help. Amy had always been the most opinionated about what she should do and had helped her most. She felt a bond with Amy, she was both her sister and her best friend.

Katie was told to report to the hospital at five o'clock one Sunday afternoon. Amy walked down with her and left her in front of the right door.

She'd already been measured for her uniform, and now it was issued to her, and a bedroom allotted in the nurses' home. Everybody said how like Amy she was. Katie liked the feeling of being the third Siddons sister to train here.

She knew something of what to expect. The uniform was familiar. She grasped at the first demonstration how to turn what looked like a muslin tray cloth into a cap. She'd heard so much about the place she felt more at home than the rest of her fellow students.

Perhaps she was not so confident the next morning when she reported to Weightman Ward at seven thirty, and patients started calling her 'Nurse'.

The first hour and a half of the day was spent getting a taste of working on the ward. After that, for the first eight weeks, she would be spending the rest of the day in school.

Fliss was the one patient who knew it was her first day, and she greeted Katie like an old friend. Katie had been in to see her during visiting hours once or twice, but now she was seeing her regularly and getting to know her. Because Paul had been so kind to her when she was in trouble, she wanted to do her best for Fliss.

She asked Sister about Fliss's medical history, and Sister explained it all to her and put Fliss's file in her hand. Katie felt sick as she read the notes and was full of sympathy. For the first time she realised the extent of Fliss's problem.

Fliss's wound was continuing to suppurate although every known treatment had been tried. She'd been down to theatre twice after the original operation to have the wound explored and washed out with antiseptics. New drains had been inserted but they had failed to clear up the focus of infection.

'She looks ill,' Katie said.

'Not surprising,' Sister Wade sympathised. 'Poor girl, she's been here such a long time. She's in some pain but that's not her main problem. She's been taking up an acute surgical bed here for over a year and we haven't cured her. There's talk of transferring her to a less acute hospital.'

Katie stared at her in dismay. 'The doctors aren't giving up on her?'

'It's not possible to cure everybody.'

'Where will she go?'

'St Cath's, I expect. On a ward amongst the chronically sick and elderly. Her prognosis is poor after all this time.'

Katie was appalled. 'Does she know?'

'Not yet, so see you don't let anything slip. She'll be staying until after the royal visit.'

This was meant to be a surprise, a spur-of-the-moment visit, but everybody had been given a few days' notice. The royal couple wanted to see the dreadful bomb damage for themselves and sympathise with the people who had been injured and made homeless.

'It seems too cruel to send her away before that.'

'It won't make up for . . .' Katie choked.

It seemed to Katie that all she could do about it was to tell Amy. She always knew what to do for the best. Amy was back on day duty and due to sit her final exams in a few months. Katie had to walk up to Ashville to see her because it was Amy's day off. She found her sitting on her bed surrounded by notebooks.

'Poor Fliss. It's been at the back of my mind that it might

come to this,' was all she said. Then she lapsed into silence for five full minutes, frowning at her bedside rug.

'Auntie My will be very upset,' she said at last. 'I suppose I should prepare her. Look, I've got a hospital exam this afternoon and I've got to get on. I've got to have Hodgkin's disease at my fingertips, and I know nothing at all about it.'

As autumn turned into winter, the air raids became more frequent and the bombing heavier. Like everybody else Paul hoped for dark, overcast nights, with heavy cloud, or better still, nights that were too stormy for aircraft to fly.

By late October, the moon was waxing larger and larger.

'I dread fine moonlit nights,' his mother said, looking up at the sky before they went under the stairs. They were all getting used to sleeping in places other than their beds.

That night the bombers came early, wave after wave.

For Paul, the night was horrendous. He'd been awake for hours, crouching under the stairs with his mother. He'd found it impossible to calm her fears when he was shaking himself.

They'd felt the house rock on its foundations when the explosions came. It seemed incredible that it didn't crumble about their heads. The bombs seemed to be falling very close. The noise hurt his ears and Mam said she could smell burning.

For months they'd been told to expect this, but now it was happening it didn't make it any less shocking.

'I do hope Fliss is all right,' his mother worried over and over. 'Surely they'll see the hospital? They wouldn't bomb that?'

Paul was worried too. The Bakehouse was only two streets away from Vittoria Dock, and the docks were a prime target.

He'd come back up to bed when the all clear had sounded at four o'clock and had fallen into a heavy sleep. His alarm clock had only half woken him and he'd felt himself drifting off again. Now at last he was fully awake and knew he was late.

He slid swiftly out of bed and went out on the landing to listen. There was no sound from Mam. She must still be asleep.

The acrid smell of smoke and burning was in his nostrils. He opened the door of Fliss's small bedroom. Broad daylight was coming through the window. Miraculously Park Road North seemed no different. The leaves were falling now from the trees in the park and had blown against the railings. A bus drove past on its way to Woodside.

He went back to his own room at the rear of the house and opened his curtains. Smoke was drifting upwards in dark spirals from several different parts of the docks. Great clouds of it hung over the river.

Paul threw on his clothes and went straight out to the car. He drove down Park Road North to the hospital. Its familiar outline was reassuring. It didn't seem to be damaged at all. He turned into Livingstone Street and circled back to Duke Street to check on his café.

When he turned the corner and it came into view, the shock made him almost mount the pavement. Tired workmen were trying to clear debris off the street. The sight of the Bakehouse sickened him.

The door had blown off and all the windows had gone. Inside it was a shambles of broken crockery and cake crumbs. The glass display shelves were now bare, twisted metal. Tables and chairs were blown over and damaged. Everything was covered with soot and dust.

He went through to the kitchen, crunching glass beneath his shoes. The door had blown off one of the ovens. His big wooden trays were splintered and broken.

'It's not safe in there,' an air-raid warden shouted to him. 'The ceilings could come down at any moment. Come out now, while you can.'

Paul thought of all the time and effort he and his father

had put into making it an attractive place; the anguish he'd felt because he couldn't make it pay; what Fliss had suffered because she wouldn't walk away and close it. He was filled with despair.

In one short night it had all gone. There was little worth saving. He picked up a few pieces of cutlery and, fearful now, went back to his car.

He raced down to Woodside. All was normal here, all the buildings seemed undamaged, including the Refreshment Room. Vera had opened up and was filling the kitchen with the scent of crisping bacon. He wanted to cry with relief.

Myra Laidlaw looked round the Refreshment Room feeling for the first time a tingle of satisfaction. She understood at last the attraction it had had for Jack.

It was too late for her to share the running of it with him. She saw now that it would have added another dimension to their life if she had gone on working in the business. But nothing could change that now, and she realised that life had to go on and she must make the best of it.

Jack's death had turned her in on herself, she'd been spending too much time alone. Working in the café brought her closer to other people.

It also kept her on her feet all day, gave her less time to feel sorry for herself, and because she was working hard, she was sleeping better.

Not that everything in the garden was lovely. She couldn't bear to think of Fliss still incarcerated in that hospital when she could have been launched on her career by now. And she was worried about Paul.

He kept telling her how pleased he was that she was taking some of the burden of running the business off his shoulders. It was easier to manage now the Bakehouse was closed.

To see it devastated by bombs had come as a shock for Paul, but later in the day he'd said to her: 'Perhaps it isn't a

355

bad thing. It gets us out of that lease.'

Because the building had been damaged by enemy action, both the owner and Paul would be compensated by the Government for their losses.

Paul was pushing more and more on to her shoulders. She knew why he did it, and was grateful to be able to ease herself into the job this way. Myra knew she should never have been out of it.

The door pinged. Amy Siddons came to the counter, smiling at her as she opened her camel coat. Paul had told her to expect Amy; he was taking her to the first house at the Ritz and she was coming in for something to eat first.

'Paul's got something special for you,' Myra said. 'Some fish. I'll tell Vera you're here so she can start cooking it.'

Amy reminded her so much of Alec Siddons. Myra found it strange that she was fond of one yet loathed the other. They had the same strong, straight nose and dark, tightly curling hair. Amy's thick plait was crinkly rather than smooth. Tiny droplets of moisture stood out on it and the café lights made them sparkle as she moved.

Paul came out of the kitchen in a blast of hot air, and at a pace that said he didn't want to waste a moment of her company. Myra watched him land a chaste kiss on her cheek and usher her to a table. Every movement he made told her clearly that he loved Amy Siddons. Even as he wiped down the red gingham oilcloth, he was bending towards her to catch every word she said.

He was back behind the counter switching on the tea urn to fill a cup for Amy. 'I'll have one too,' she told him and took both to Amy's table and sat down with her.

'You were right,' Myra told her.

'About what?' Amy's dark blue eyes fastened on hers.

'You told me I'd feel better if I came back to work. Well, I do. I should thank you for nagging at me.'

'Paul was desperate for a hand. It's good for you both.'

'It's taken me a long time to realise you were right.'

356

Amy leaned over and kissed her cheek. 'Auntie My, you look so much better. I'm so glad.'

'It's good to feel useful instead of being a drag on Paul. How do you know these things when you're so young?'

'I know how I'd feel in your place.' Amy smiled. 'You were too close. Nancy says I overdo it. That I put my oar in too often.'

Myra laughed.

'Paul could see it too. It was what he wanted.'

'He wants to go away to fight, Amy.'

'I know.'

Paul brought two plates piled high with fish, chips and peas and sat down at the table.

'If you'd like to spend your nights off with us sometimes, and sleep in Fliss's room, you'd be very welcome,' Myra said. 'Paul tells me you don't go home any more.'

'Pa told me to keep away. I caught him on the raw one day.'

Myra smiled. 'I did too. Anyway, if you feel like a few nights away from the nurses' home, both Paul and I would like you to come.'

'My nights off next week are Sunday and Monday. Is that too soon?'

'Of course it isn't. You're good for Paul. Good for me too.'

Amy woke from a deep sleep. The room seemed tiny but smart with its kidney-shaped dressing table flounced and frilled in mauve to match the curtains. It took her a moment to remember she was sleeping in Fliss's bedroom.

From below she heard the piano bounce into a jaunty introduction, then Auntie My's voice, strong and throaty, took up the words of 'Lilli Marlene', the tune the British troops had stolen from the Germans and made their own.

Paul's head came round the door. His straight brown hair was an untidy ruffle which had not yet been combed.

'Auntie My seems more cheerful,' Amy said without lifting her head from the pillow.

'It's a long time since I heard her sing,' Paul whispered, and his smile lit his face with vivid charm. 'Now I know she's better. It's a weight off my mind.'

At breakfast, Auntie My said she'd go down to the café to check what supplies needed to be ordered for the coming week.

'She's better at that than I am,' Paul told Amy. 'Very much better at deciding what can be made from the rations we're allowed.'

This morning Auntie My's halo of reddish hair was standing out more – Amy thought she must be going to the hairdresser again – and she was wearing lipstick. She was looking more like she used to.

'All we need is good news about Fliss and we'll really be back to normal,' Paul said.

The following morning being Monday, the Laidlaws got up early. Amy went down in her dressing gown to have a cup of tea with them.

'What are you going to do this morning?' Auntie My asked her.

'Get out my books. It's time I started revising. I'll be sitting my finals in February. Can't believe the time has gone so fast.'

'You'll pass, Amy.'

'I mean to, but I need to study.'

'What will you do then?'

'Join up.'

'They could send you anywhere,' Paul said, his face suddenly horrified. 'They have field hospitals in the front line.'

'I know. That's where I want to go.'

'Nursing's a reserved occupation. You could stay on at the hospital here.'

'Paul, you're desperate to join up and help the war effort.

Surely you can understand that I want to too?'

Amy heard the post slither through the letterbox on to the front door mat. Auntie My got slowly to her feet to fetch it.

Paul was frowning: 'I'd prefer to think you were here. Near Mam and Fliss. It would be safer for you.'

His mother's footsteps came back more quickly. 'Letter for you Paul. Looks official.'

Amy heard the chill of anxiety in her voice. She straightened up in her chair and read the words On His Majesty's Service on the envelope as Paul took it. Her stomach seemed to turn over.

'My call-up papers,' Paul said, tugging them out on to his plate. 'It's no surprise, is it, Mam? We knew they were coming.'

'I wish you'd applied for another deferment.' The colour had gone from her face. 'You would have got it.'

Paul sighed. 'Couldn't go on dodging the war. I shall try for the RAF. Perhaps I can still be a pilot.'

'What will I do without you?' Myra asked, her eyes wide with anxiety.

The words echoed in Amy's mind. She'd blithely talked of going away to do her own thing, but now Paul's departure was imminent she hated the idea of being parted from him.

'Mam, you'll cope. You know you're competent. You can run the business yourself now. You don't need me.'

But *I* do, Amy wanted to tell him. How would she fill her days without Paul?

On the morning of 6 November, Katie found the early bed-making round more frantic than usual, with many more sheets and pillow-cases being changed. The cleaners swung their polishers over the parquet floor with more energy than usual. Everything on the ward had to be spick and span in time for the royal visit.

The windows had already been thoroughly cleaned, and everybody was hoping there would be no air raid to spoil the

359

effect of their labour. Weightman Ward was bright and light, with its green counterpanes and silvered metal bedsteads and lockers.

Fliss whispered that the royal visitors would definitely be coming to Weightman because it was in the new wing and the showpiece of the hospital, and wasn't she lucky?

There was to be no school that day. It was deemed that the new students wouldn't want to be excluded from the occasion.

Katie was given the job of making sure every patient had a neat and tidy locker, and she went round collecting up every scrap of rubbish. She was tidying away a copy of last night's *Liverpool Echo* when a review caught her eye. It gave fulsome praise to the show at the Liverpool Empire. There was a photograph of Yves Fellipi. He and his partner were being tipped as stars of the future.

Katie tore out the page, folded it, and slid it under her apron into the pocket in her dress. She knew Fliss would be interested in what was happening to Yves and meant to give it to her.

Every patient sat up against a bank of pillows with covers that looked freshly ironed. Even very sick patients were combing their hair and trying to look their best.

Fliss's auburn hair had grown halfway down her back during the time she'd been in hospital. Today she'd tied it back with a peach ribbon. Her cheeks looked unusually flushed with excitement.

She was wearing a new peach nightdress with a lace collar. Her mother had knitted her a fluffy bed jacket in the same shade to go over it, specially for the royal visit.

From the windows at the end of Weightman, it was possible to see up Park Road North. A crowd was gathering. Already it stretched halfway down Conway Street. Outside the hospital itself, children were ranged along the front of the pavement waving little Union Jacks.

'They're coming!' the cry went up.

The morning dressing round came to an abrupt halt. The

staff nurse rushed her trolley back to the clinic room until after the visit. It wouldn't be fair to any patient to be screened off with their wound bare when royalty came round. With nothing to do, the senior nurses were craning out of the windows too.

Katie stationed herself near Fliss's bed. Her window looked out on to the forecourt below. Doctors had been asked to park their cars elsewhere today so it was empty. Matron and members of the board of governors were coming out in readiness to greet the visitors. A wave of anticipation swept through the ward.

At last, Katie saw the royal car drive slowly on to the forecourt. She watched the introductions being made and Matron escorting the King and Queen up the front steps into the hospital. The King was wearing the uniform of a field marshal.

The waiting time became more nail-biting. Around her, patients were discussing how beautiful Queen Elizabeth looked in her misty blue two-piece, topped with an Arctic fox-fur. How kind she was to make this journey in wartime to cheer them up.

At last, the double glass doors to the ward were propped open. Sister was being introduced and then the party was escorted round the beds.

Close to, the Queen looked even more beautiful, in her matching blue halo hat and with a diamond maple leaf brooch in her lapel. She shook Fliss's hand and asked her how she was. Katie heard her say: 'Very well, thank you, ma'am.' Though it wasn't the truth. Sister seemed to be telling her about Fliss's illness.

'I do hope you'll be better soon,' the Queen said, turning back to her with a gracious smile. 'Sister tells me you've been very brave.'

There was more. Katie thought Fliss did very well. She would have been tongue-tied in her place. Every woman was taking in details of the royal outfit, admiring her complexion and her poise. When the visiting party went on its way, all the patients seemed brighter. A holiday aura permeated the hospital for the rest of the day. There were special celebratory meals.

'This is more like it,' Fliss giggled to Katie. 'I can't complain things are dull here today, can I?'

Katie felt her heart sink. Poor Fliss, little did she know what was in store for her when this was over.

She felt the newspaper crackle in her pocket as she moved. What had she been thinking of? To let her see that would only make matters worse. It would show with awful clarity what she was missing. Katie went briskly to the sluice and slung the page into a sack of rubbish.

Katie had completed her preliminary training in the school and had started working full-time on Weightman Ward. She was on duty when Fliss's consultant came to do a round, accompanied by his registrar with his houseman trailing behind. Sister escorted them.

Kate was one step ahead, pulling screens round the next patient. Another nurse loosened bandages and dressings so as not to delay progress for a second longer than was necessary.

She thought the screens were round Fliss's bed for a very long time. The round almost seemed to have stopped there. Kate was heavy with foreboding.

'Just chatting to her, perhaps,' the second-year nurse whispered. 'Everybody's sorry for her; she's been here such a long time.'

When Katie went to pull the screens to another bed it took only one glance at Fliss's face to know she'd been told the bad news.

'My wound won't heal,' she choked. 'The doctors say they've tried everything they know. They can't cure me.' She burst into tears. Katie put her arms round her and decided to leave the screens where they were.

'You mustn't give up hope,' she whispered.

'The doctors have. How can I hope if they say it's impossible?'

'There must be something . . .' Katie felt helpless.

'I want to stay here,' Fliss sobbed. 'I know everybody and it's near home. Easy for Mam and Paul to visit. I want them to try something else. There must be something that will cure me in this day and age.'

'St Cath's isn't far. Auntie My will still visit you.'

'It's not on the way home from the café, though, is it?'

'No, but we'll all come.'

'Why me? I was going to do so much. Mam thought I could be a star. Everybody did. I haven't sung for over a year and not even seen a show.'

Katie shared her anguish.

'I'm frightened that I'll have to spend the rest of my life in bed. Be a chronic invalid. I'll never get better now the doctors have given up on me.'

There seemed little comfort Katie could offer.

'Never give up, Fliss. There has to be something . . .'

BOOK FIVE
1941

CHAPTER TWENTY-TWO

February 1941

Alec had been on duty for fourteen hours. The police were an important part of the civil defence service. Now that air raids were a common occurrence, his orders were to stay on duty if there was a warning during his shift. He must not leave until the all clear had sounded.

If there was a warning a few hours prior to his shift, as had happened last night, he was to go on early. They were all working a prodigious amount of overtime.

Bombs had been falling all night. He'd spent the first four hours pulling the dead and injured from houses in Henry Street. When he went back to the central police station for a break, he found more bombs had fallen in the streets behind it that stretched down to the river. He'd not been keen to go when ordered down there, but as he got nearer he could feel hope beginning to flutter in his stomach.

Hope turned to certainty. He felt triumphant. Four houses in a terrace had been devastated, and one of them was the home of Freda and Bob Hood. He was glad they'd copped it. Nobody was more deserving of being bombed out of house and home.

What he didn't know was whether they'd been inside at the time, or whether they'd been sheltering elsewhere. He hoped they'd been here. He hoped they were dead.

Their surviving neighbours were crowding round, some helping. It was his job to question them to find out where they should search for the dead and injured. Alec felt his heart turn over with satisfaction when he heard someone saying they had seen the Hoods at home.

He set to work digging into the remains of their house with tremendous energy, spurring the rest of the team to greater efforts. They found no survivors – no bodies either, but human remains. Very definitely human remains.

Alec felt he could be reasonably sure they'd both perished. He was exultant.

Bob Hood had been released from prison only a week ago. Alec had been worried in case he tried to follow up the complaint he'd made. Now he could forget all that. Luck was firmly on his side.

It had taken many hours to sort out the mess there. They found three bodies and sent seventeen injured to hospital. Alec had not felt tired at all. He'd gone on working like an engine.

After that he'd been directed to a parade of shops close to Market Street that had been damaged by blast. He was exhausted, but felt keyed up with euphoria. His uniform was white and stiff with dust from plaster and bricks, his hands were scratched and smudged with soot and blood.

The all clear didn't sound until he was due to go home. All he wanted to do by then was to put his head down and sleep.

He thanked God he had a car, even if it wasn't the SS Jaguar he'd dreamed of. He wouldn't have had the strength this morning to pedal home.

He drove slowly, his eyes prickling with fatigue and dust. He could feel grit round his collar, under his nails and even in his hair.

'I'll have a bath, Celia,' he shouted as soon as he opened the back door.

'The fire's only just been lit.' She turned anxiously from the sink. 'Let me feel the tank, see if it's warm enough.'

'I've got to have one,' he said. 'I feel filthy. And you'll have to do something with my uniform before tonight. Get all this dust out.'

'I'll put it on the line and beat it. Then give it a good brush. Your breakfast – do you want your egg boiled or poached?'

'Poached.' He felt hungry. He'd had nothing since midnight, when he'd eaten the sandwich Celia had cut for him. 'Have you got anything to go with the eggs?'

'Bread and marge.' Her tired blue eyes met his apologetically. 'There's only one egg left.'

Alec grunted with annoyance, picked up a carving knife and went out to his car. He'd managed to pick up some stuff from a little general shop that had been bombed. Its owner had been sheltering in the cellar and had had to take his wife to the hospital when they'd been dug out.

They'd had eggs, but none had survived the raid, they'd splattered everywhere. Alec thought of the half-side of bacon he'd managed to find.

He looked round before opening the car boot, but there was nobody about. Though he'd brought his carving knife out, he couldn't cut through the flitch of bacon here. He'd have to wait until he got it to Olive's kitchen. She had decent knifes and cleavers. He'd bring half home for himself. He didn't want Celia to know he took food to someone else.

He'd also picked up a few sausages and a great slab of butter, which must weigh at least three pounds. He tore the paper in which the stuff was wrapped and divided it up, carefully tearing the butter paper again to remove the name of the shop he'd taken it from. He had to eat to keep his strength up.

'We haven't had so much butter for ages,' Celia said when he put it on the draining board. 'And pork sausages? Where did you get them?'

'Nobody else wanted them so they were given to me.'

'Why didn't anybody want them?'

'From a bombed shop. They were covered with dust and rubble.'

'They look clean enough to me,' she said suspiciously. 'Are they black market?'

Celia was making him nervous. 'Course not,' he said. 'I told you, they were given to me. The owner was grateful, I dug him out of the rubble.'

He felt better after his bath and a decent breakfast. It gave him his second wind. He might as well go up to Olive's straight away.

'I've put a hot bottle in the bed for you,' Celia said.

'I think I'll go out for a bit first,' he grunted. He'd meant to get his head down and go this afternoon, but it made sense to get the stuff out of his car as soon as possible.

Since the bombing had started, the only thing that kept him sane were his visits to Olive Driscoll. Her house seemed a haven. She kept her garden neat, and even in winter it was bright with flowering shrubs. She'd had a trellis put up to keep her vegetable patch and Anderson shelter out of sight from the house. Olive didn't want anything to spoil the comfort of her home.

He did his best to keep it well supplied. Shops, off-licences and pubs were continually being bombed. It was one of his duties to stop looting, but it was almost impossible. He'd managed to get several bottles of good brandy for Olive last week, and today he had some tinned food for her as well as the bacon.

He opened Olive's front gate and backed the car into the short drive. She saw him from the window and came out, looking neat in a plain green skirt and jumper.

'Lovely,' she said, when he showed her what was in his boot. 'You are kind to me, thank you very much.'

She kissed him. She smelled of lavender water. Usually, her green eyes sparkled when he brought her goodies, but today they did not. There was something constrained about her manner. He followed her inside with the large cardboard box containing tins of fruit.

'Burn this carton as soon as I've gone,' he advised. 'And

all the wrappings.' He busied himself getting out her chopping board to deal with the bacon.

'Mustn't get fat on your nice trousers.' She took a manly striped apron from a drawer. Usually, she fastened him into it with a provocative flourish. Today, she left him to tie it on himself.

'It's smoked back. Shall I cut you a few slices while I'm at it, or can you manage?'

'Cut me a few, please. Can I get you some breakfast?'

'Just had it,' he said. 'And I'm on my way to bed.'

'Some coffee?'

'A drop of that brandy, perhaps. When I've finished here.'

Alec found himself on her comfortable settee with a glass in his hand. She'd given him a treble measure. Often she'd say as a reward for his generosity: 'Upstairs afterwards?' This morning, he was too tired even to be interested in that. He stifled a yawn.

She'd been hovering uneasily by the window. Now she came to sit opposite him.

'There's something I want to tell you, Alec.' Her voice sounded different.

That stopped his attention drifting. 'Is something the matter?'

'No. It's just that somebody has asked me to marry him.' Her green eyes looked into his. 'I've accepted.'

His sleepiness was banished. He jerked upright.

'Who?' He was indignant. Olive had another man? After ten years, he felt settled with her. He hated the idea. 'Who?'

'I don't want him to know about you, Alec.'

'Of course you don't!' He slapped his glass down. The brandy came over the lip in a tidal wave. 'You're ashamed of me. Of what we've had together.' He knew she'd never thought him quite good enough for her.

'No, Alec. The offer is too good to turn down. I have to think of what I'm getting out of life.'

371

For all her ladylike ways, Olive was a woman on the make. She had to get money and the trappings of middle-class comfort from somebody.

He was furious. She'd found a better provider. She didn't want him any more! And she was sitting there with her long legs neatly crossed telling him this in cold blood. He couldn't believe it.

He was fond of Olive. He liked to have her clinging to his arm when they went over to Liverpool. He'd even wished he'd married her instead of Celia. Would have done, if he'd seen her first.

'Who is he?' he choked.

'His name's Charles Hollingsworth.'

It hurt that she wanted to throw him over like this.

'Charles Hollingsworth?' His mouth felt dry. 'Not the schoolmaster?'

'Headmaster, yes.'

Alec was fluttering with sudden panic. 'He's also a councillor?'

'Yes, I believe so.'

'And a member of the Watch Committee,' he added faintly. The Watch Committee dealt with police discipline. Fear was prickling his scalp. 'Has he been here?'

'Yes, of course.'

'You haven't mentioned my name?'

'No.'

'But you talk to him about your friends?'

'You are in a class apart, Alec. I don't want him to know about you.'

'My God, he could have me dismissed. Just like that.' There was a cold feeling in his belly.

'I've never mentioned your existence.' She looked frightened now.

'How long have you known him?' He couldn't keep the bitter note out of his voice.

'About eighteen months.'

He'd been in danger all that time. She'd been two-timing him. 'Where did you meet him?'

'At a charity do, to raise funds for something.'

Anger and frustration were furring his throat. 'I love you, Olive. You said you loved me.'

'I am fond of you. Really I am.' Her green eyes wouldn't meet his. She got up again, paced to the window.

'But you love him more? Is that it?'

'You can't marry me, Alec. What sort of a life do you think I have, here on my own? Waiting for you to come. Being kept a secret.'

'I thought you were happy.'

'I want a husband. Someone here all the time. Someone I can talk about. He's offered.'

'What about me?'

'You've got your wife and family. What have I ever had but their leftovers?'

'It's not like that, Olive. You mean a lot to me. I bring you all sorts of presents. I take you out when I can.'

'I know, and I'm very grateful, don't think I'm not. But I don't want you to come again. I think it would be better if we had a clean break.'

Alec shivered. He felt his world collapsing around him. It kept happening. Sooner or later all his women threw him over. And this time for a member of the Watch Committee. He couldn't get over that.

'Don't ever mention my name to him. If he knew I brought you stuff like this, we'd both be in bother.'

'Of course I won't.'

He'd trusted her and she'd betrayed him. She'd only have to whisper his name to Hollingsworth and he'd have so many questions to answer. His palms felt clammy. He was frightened. What he'd done, he'd done for her.

'You're booting me out . . .'

'It's not like that.'

Olive knew where the brandy had come from. She knew

he couldn't afford to give her what he had from his wages. She knew too much. He'd never kept secrets from her.

He'd always been nervous of what she'd say to others. She was outgoing, said things without thinking first. He wanted to believe she wouldn't tell Charles Hollingsworth.

But she'd been a widow for ten years. She could say she'd taken up with him without realising he was married. That he'd misled her. That she hadn't known he was doing things he should not. If she opened her mouth, just let a little hint slip, he'd be broken. And she could do it at any time. Even months from now. Alec felt himself break out in a sweat.

Her voice kept coming at him, justifying what she was doing. 'He's a widower. Very respectable . . .'

'And I'm not?' His temper suddenly exploded. He was standing over her, his hands on her shoulders. They slid up her smooth neck.

'Don't do that, Alec.' Her voice was cold. 'You don't know your own strength.'

She tried to shake him off but he tightened his grip. He wanted to hurt her as she had hurt him. He wasn't going to let her get off so lightly. She didn't realise what she was doing to him.

His fingers bit into the soft flesh of her neck. He heard her gasp. He didn't want to lose her. He loved her. She was struggling and he had to tighten his grip.

It shocked him when the strength went out of her body and she collapsed. He was holding her up by the neck. When he let go, she was a bundle of green wool at his feet. Her face was blue.

'Olive? I'm sorry . . . I didn't mean . . . Olive?' He tried to shake her.

Suddenly Alec was choking. He felt dazed, punch-drunk. This time he'd really done it. He could feel panic crawling up his throat.

He hadn't meant to hurt her. She'd driven him to it. It wasn't murder, more an accident.

He bent closer, willing her to come round and sit up. She wasn't breathing. He couldn't believe it was that easy to kill a woman. There were dark bruises on her neck where his fingers had squeezed the breath out of her.

Olive was dead and he was in terrible trouble. How was he going to survive this? He looked round her sitting room. His fingerprints were everywhere in this house. The glass he'd drunk from still had brandy in it. He tossed it back and took the glass to the kitchen. He filled the sink with hot water and washed it thoroughly.

Stay calm, he told himself. Nobody knew better than he did how exhausted the police were. The extra civil defence duties were crucifying them all. With carnage all round them from the bombing, would they be likely to work their guts out to discover who had strangled Olive?

Alec fastened the apron round his waist again. Forced his huge hands into her rubber gloves. Found a soft yellow duster and some furniture polish.

Stay calm. He must think carefully. An hour spent here now might help him avoid disaster. He knew what they'd be looking for.

What had he touched here? Door knobs. For good measure he polished the fingerplates on the doors as well, both sides. The coffee table, the wooden arms of the settee. A good thing Olive was house-proud. She'd have dusted and polished since his last visit, wouldn't she? He went round all the furniture in case she had not. He did all the doors.

The carton he'd brought was still on the kitchen table. He flung the tins back into it, in case they were traceable. The bacon too. No point in wasting it. He'd take it away with him. He carried it out to the boot of his car.

He scrubbed the cleavers and knives he'd used and put them away. Carefully dabbed round the kitchen. He rushed to polish the phone, because he remembered using it last time he was here.

Footprints? The carpets would tell them nothing. He looked

375

at the quarry tiles in the kitchen. They looked all right, but he polished them over just to be on the safe side, sliding with a duster under each foot. He took the dusters away with him, and the apron and rubber gloves, so that everything would look normal.

Her driveway was short of gravel and it had rained recently. He could see a clear imprint of his tyre marks on the impacted earth beneath the stones. His heart was in his throat again. Keep calm.

He drove his car into the road, and went back to the garage, where she kept her gardening tools. Carefully he raked the imprints away and then covered the marks of the rake with what gravel remained. He flung the rake into the back of his car and drove off. He'd done all he could.

The neighbours would be questioned, no doubt about that. His car could well have been seen here regularly. Usually he parked it in her drive, but it was still visible from the road. Would any of them remember the number? They'd had no reason to note it down. Alec knew how rarely people did. All the same, the thought made him shudder. He'd sell it and buy another, that was what he'd do.

Nobody knew about him and Olive. They'd both kept it quiet, hadn't they? But Amy knew, and that brought another niggle of fear.

When Alec got home, he found that Celia had gone out again. The girls were really encouraging her to neglect her duties, but for once he was glad. Better if no one saw him like this.

His face looked back at him from the glass in the hall stand. Guilty. A man frightened for his own life now.

Stay calm, he told himself. He went out to his car and sorted through the carton of food. He would sell most of this on. No need to give anything away in future.

The fire in the living room was dying back but there was still a red glow from the coals. He tore the carton into pieces and threw them on, until the flames roared up the chimney. The name and address of the shop from which he'd taken it was printed on it twice.

Then he pushed the apron and rubber gloves into the middle and poked them down. The stench of burning rubber filled the room but at least he'd got rid of them. When it had died back enough, he banked the fire up with coal.

Then he poured himself a stiff brandy and took it up to bed. His head was beginning to spin. He felt utterly exhausted. He was still shaking. He knew that what he'd done was horrific.

It was no longer a question of keeping his good character so that he could keep his job. Stealing now seemed a minor transgression. He stood to lose everything, even his life, if he was brought to book for this. He would have to be very careful.

He craved sleep but he couldn't get off. His mind was on a treadmill which kept coming back to Olive's body slumped at his feet, her face tinged with blue.

He knew he dozed. He heard Celia and Nancy come in. He heard the buses passing in the road outside. When evening came and it was time to get up and go to work, every muscle in his body ached with fatigue.

He could say he was sick and stay where he was, but that would only draw attention to him. Better if he reported for duty and appeared to be normal in every respect.

He felt sick by the time he was dressed, and for once refused the breakfast Celia was cooking for him. The *Echo* had been delivered earlier in the evening. Olive's photograph was on the front page. The column of print told him nothing he didn't already know, but just to see it scared him to death.

The siren went before he set out, and the bombs were falling before he reached the station. Other officers were interested in the murder enquiry and asked questions. Alec felt a little better once he knew they had no firm lead.

He was sent to Chester Street where a terrace of houses

had received a direct hit. He drove down to have a look. The fire service were there, wardens were digging for survivors. There was terrible devastation. But he was so tired he could barely put one foot in front of the other. He could have fallen asleep here behind the wheel of his car.

Instead, Alec drove home and was back in bed before midnight. He had it to himself because Celia was in the shelter. He set the alarm, and slept like the dead but Celia came up at five thirty and woke him.

He got dressed, feeling refreshed, and went back to Chester Street. The last victim was just being loaded into an ambulance. He knew he'd timed things well. The crew told him there had been four killed and nineteen ferried to hospital. He had no trouble imagining what to put in his report. He said he'd had a busy night.

He went home again feeling he'd cleared the first hurdle. He was due for a day off now and then a change of shift. He could rest.

The car worried him most. That could give detectives a clear lead. It would tie him to the murder. He told himself the houses were wide apart, he didn't think Olive had had much to do with her neighbours. They would have no reason to take an interest in her visitors. Just as long as there wasn't a twelve-year-old boy living next door with a passion for cars.

Later that morning he drove it over to Liverpool and sold it. He knew it would solve nothing if his number had ben noted, but he didn't want the sight of it to jog somebody's memory. The car was giving him the willies.

He was tempted to indulge himself with an SS Jaguar. He could afford it, but that would draw attention to the fact he was living above his means. Not many constables owned a car at all.

He bought another black Ford Ten that looked very similar but was two years younger. He'd not mention that he had a new car, perhaps nobody would notice.

He shivered. Fear trickled down his spine. He didn't feel

378

safe anywhere, at home or at work. He had nowhere to turn. He was living on a knife edge. At his time of life he should be able to take it easy, instead of being kept on his toes, expecting trouble to erupt at any moment.

CHAPTER TWENTY-THREE

March 1941

Amy felt exhausted as she came out of the Liverpool Royal Infirmary after her written examination. Around her, her fellow finalists from hospitals all over Merseyside were chattering like birds, comparing answers and lamenting loudly that they were having second thoughts.

The group swept her down the hill to Central Station. She was not displeased with what she had written, but she felt drained. It was too soon to celebrate – the practical exam still hung over them all – but Paul had suggested they go out somewhere. Most of all, she needed a cup of tea.

Instead of going over on the underground with the other nurses from Birkenhead, she jumped on a tram going to the Pierhead. She felt she needed a breath of air, and the ferry would take her to Woodside close to the Refreshment Room.

It was a damp, dark afternoon and from the boat the Birkenhead bank was already lost in the gathering dusk. No light showed anywhere. It was so cold she left the rail and went to sit in the saloon after all.

The café would soon be closing, Auntie My and Paul would be clearing up for the night. She expected to find them relaxed and ready to hear her news. She let herself into the warm, smoky atmosphere and pulled the blackout curtain back across the door. There were only two customers left.

Auntie My's cheeks were scarlet. Her hair always seemed to fluff out in a huge halo round her head when she was distraught.

'He's heard.' She pounced on Amy the moment she caught sight of her. 'He's got into the RAF.'

Paul bustled out from the kitchen looking somewhat heady too. 'I'm to report to RAF Sealand in five days' time. I'm in.'

It brought Amy up sharply, made her take a deep breath. She hadn't thought what it would mean not to have his constant company. Ever since they'd been children they'd seen each other almost every day. Perhaps not that often recently, because she'd been studying, but she'd known he wasn't far if she wanted him. Now . . . It made her realise just how much she loved him.

'Mam, you knew I'd have to go somewhere sooner or later.'

'I was hoping it would be later, but I'm glad you've got what you want.'

Paul sighed. 'I don't know yet whether I'll get pilot training. I've still to be selected for that.'

'You stand a good chance,' Amy said. 'Go for it.'

He smiled. 'How did you get on?' He was gentle, full of care for her.

'All right. Quite well.'

'That's all you've got to say about it?' His eyes twinkled at her.

'Until I know the result.'

'I thought we'd have something to eat here with Mam first, she's saved us ham and mushrooms. Then what about the pictures? There's a double feature at the Plaza. The Saint in *Double Trouble*, followed by Doris Day in *The Village Barn Dance*.'

'Lovely,' she said.

For Amy, it was like coming home to sit down at a table covered with gingham oilcloth. She got herself a cup of tea while Auntie My dodged in and out of the kitchen.

Since she'd been working at the café, Myra had decided it was easier if they all ate before going home. It saved the rations and it saved work at home. Tonight, Vera wasn't staying, she was on her way to see a friend.

Auntie My was on edge. 'What will I do without Paul? I don't know how I'll manage. And with the bad news about poor Fliss being moved. Have you heard when she's going?'

'No, they'll keep her as long as they can.'

Paul brought three steaming plates to the table and sat down. Amy sniffed appreciatively. It was a long time since she'd eaten. Auntie My came to join them, bringing a plate of toast.

'There's nothing but bad news all round.' She sounded almost in tears. 'Our Fliss is going to be a chronic invalid for the rest of her life.'

'You mustn't think that,' Amy told her gently. 'Medical knowledge is increasing all the time. One thing the war is doing is speeding things up. There are all sorts of new treatments, and new drugs.'

'That's all in the future,' Paul said sadly. 'Fliss needs something now. Something to make her well and get her home.'

'Penicillin is here now.'

'Would it cure her?'

'They say it cures almost every infection. It's the genuine miracle cure.'

'Then why don't they give it to her?' Auntie My demanded.

'Because we don't have any yet.'

'I thought you said it was here?'

'I meant that it has been discovered.'

'I remember reading about penicillin a long time ago,' Paul said slowly.

'It was discovered in 1928, but nothing was done to develop it, not for ages. It is being made in this country now, though only in small amounts. It has to be grown like a plant and that takes time.'

'I read that it was being used in field hospitals.' Paul bit into a slice of toast.

'What there is is going to the armed forces. They have to keep the men fighting fit.'

'Are you sure it would cure Fliss?'

'I've talked to her consultant about it. We know the germ that's causing Fliss's problem, and penicillin is known to be effective against it. But it's like gold dust.'

'Can't it be bought? I'd pay almost anything,' Auntie My said.

Amy shook her head.

'But soon?' Paul asked. 'They'll get some soon?'

'Hopefully.'

'It's the war!' Auntie My exploded. 'Everything is for the war. What about our Fliss? That surgeon is sending her to St Cath's anyway, so he isn't planning to do anything more for her.'

'He says it's common knowledge that penicillin could cure her. Getting it is the only problem. He's promised to write that on her notes. You can talk to her new doctor about it when she's there. Ask him to try and get some. It is a glimmer of hope, Auntie My. The best I can do.'

'Amy, love, you do wonders for us. I don't know what we'd do without you. At least you'll still be here to help me when Paul's gone.'

'For a little while,' she said.

An hour or so later, Amy was sitting in the darkness of the stalls at the Plaza. Paul was holding her hand tightly as he watched the film. Amy couldn't lose herself in George Sanders' exploits as the Saint. The fact that Paul was going away shut out everything else.

The Doris Day film was almost over when there was an air-raid warning. A few months ago, that would have brought the show to an abrupt end and emptied the cinema. But the public was getting blasé.

'Shall we stay?' Paul whispered. Amy agreed, but kept an ear tuned for sounds of explosions outside. A few people edged up the row and went out, but most stayed to see the end.

Ten minutes later, when the film finished, the cinema was emptied as quickly as possible. Amy stumbled out into the night to find wardens waiting outside to direct them to the nearest shelter. She hung back, letting the rest of the audience stream past her.

'I don't want to spend hours sitting in a shelter and then have to walk up to Ashville in the middle of the night,' she whispered. 'Better if I can get home now and get my head down for the night in the cellar.'

'Better for me too. Mam will worry if I'm not back. Terrible nuisance, not having enough petrol.'

Paul was teaching his mother to drive the car, but was only able to use it for that and fetching goods from wholesalers.

'Nothing much seems to be happening yet.' Amy was looking up at the sky. Searchlights crisscrossed it, flickering back and forth, picking out the silver mass of an occasional barrage balloon, but all was quiet.

'I wonder if we'll be able to get a bus back,' Paul said, pausing at a bus stop. In a raid, buses were ordered to head straight back to their depots, then the service was suspended. Because the Laird Street depot was close to where they lived, there were always buses heading in the direction they wanted to go.

'Here's one coming.'

It went past them without stopping. Bus crews were ordered only to drop passengers, not pick up more, but sometimes it was possible to get on. Another bus following behind did the same.

'Come on, we might as well walk.' Paul took her arm. 'It isn't all that far.' There was still no sound of planes or gunfire.

If it hadn't been that they were expecting bombs to start falling, it would have been a pleasant night for a walk. It was

384

clearer now and there was enough light from the moon to see where they were going. They kept close in against the buildings. If they were seen by a warden, they would be directed to a shelter.

The all clear went.

'Thank goodness for that,' Paul said. 'A false alarm. Now we can take it easy.' He slowed his step, put an arm round Amy's waist.

'I can't believe I'll be going into the RAF,' he said seriously. 'I thought I'd lost my chance.'

'Five more days.' Amy shivered and felt Paul pull her closer.

'I'd have joined up at the beginning of the war if Dad hadn't died.'

'You're getting paranoid,' Amy told him. 'About being in civvies after all this time. You want to go more than ever.'

'Of course I do. Everybody else is doing their bit for the war effort. I feel I'm shirking . . .'

'Sometimes things turn out for the best,' Amy said. 'Think of the dreadful losses they've suffered. At the height of the Battle of Britain, new pilots were only surviving for an average of three weeks. I'm glad you weren't a pilot then.'

They came to the main entrance to the park and Paul led her inside. Now that some of the railings had been taken down to be used as war materials, the gates were no longer locked at night.

'It's kept you here with me. I'm grateful for that.'

'You and me, we've always been close, Amy. Leaving you is going to be the hardest part.'

'I'll go myself, if I pass my finals.'

'You'll pass. I'm going to miss you.' He pulled her closer, kissed her cheek. Then let his lips slide to hers. 'I love you.'

Amy felt her heart turn over. Paul had first told her that when he was sixteen. He'd been doing it regularly ever since.

'We'll be married, Amy, one day.'

'You've been saying that for years.'

'I mean it.'

'I know you do, Paul. It's always been a comfort to think that one day it will happen.'

She half turned to look at his face; she was almost as tall as he. His dark eyes met hers, full of tenderness and love. He was all she'd ever wanted.

'Let's do it now,' she said. 'Before you go.'

He stopped walking and pulled her tight against him. He was silent for what seemed a long time. 'Just like that?'

'If you're sure?'

'Of course I'm sure. There's never been anyone but you.'

'We're both twenty-one now, we can please ourselves.'

'Inspired thinking.' She saw him smile delightedly. 'Let's do it!'

Amy felt a frisson of excitement. 'I feel positively intoxicated.'

It seemed they had the park to themselves. The pale road wound ahead, the trees leafless now, stark black branches against the sky. The night was cold, and above them an occasional searchlight still probed the sky. She wished she could hold this moment in time for ever, with Paul's cheek warm against her own.

'What will our families say?' he asked.

'Does it matter? Look at Nancy. Going through all the hoops. Going to tea with Stan's family, bringing him back to tea at our house. Getting engaged, saving up. Drawing up lists of guests and getting Mam to make wedding cakes and bridal gowns. What does all that matter anyway? Who wants the frills?'

'Impossible anyway, in wartime.'

'What I want is to be your wife. I want to feel closer to you. Be with you every moment I can. That's what counts, not the wedding itself.'

'There's nothing to wait for. You're right, Amy. Why didn't I see that?'

'I feel sorry for Nancy, she's left with nothing after having her hopes built up. We don't want that. I bet she wishes now she'd gone right ahead.'

'When I can't be with you, Amy, knowing we are married, that we're totally committed to each other, will bring comfort.'

His lips came down on hers again. Harder, and with more passion.

The feeling of exhilaration didn't leave Amy. It built up overnight, until sparkling effervescence seemed to touch everything. Even getting up in the cold before a winter's dawn the next morning. Even the routine of making beds.

Amy had a morning off. When she was free at nine thirty she went down to the café to collect Paul. She knew he felt the same happiness. He couldn't stop smiling, his brown eyes sparkling. Without saying anything to Auntie My they went to the register office.

'You'll have to apply for a special licence,' the registrar told them, but yes, with that they could be married on Saturday morning. That was Amy's day off for the week.

When they returned to tell Auntie My, she let out a whoop of surprise and threw her arms round Amy in joyous abandon.

'I'm delighted. Thrilled. No, not surprised at all. I knew how he felt about you. I hear nothing else but Amy this, and Amy that.' Her laugh came rumbling out in glorious anticipation. 'I knew you wouldn't waste time. You're not the sort.'

'I'm glad,' Paul said, 'that you haven't said I'm rushing things.'

'With this war, you've got to grab at happiness when you can. You must all come back here after the ceremony. I've got a couple of bottles of wine put away at home and I'll find us something to eat.'

'Lovely.' Amy kissed her. 'Better than going to a restaurant. More homely.'

'Saturday's our easy day,' Myra told her. 'It'll all fit in well.'

'I'm going to use some of our precious petrol ration to drive Amy home, Mam. So she can invite her mum and dad. She's got to be back at the hospital in less than an hour for lunch. Let's go, Amy.'

She felt on top of the world as they went up the yard. She found Mam at the sink, peeling a mound of pickling onions. Tears were streaming down her face.

'We're getting married, Mam. Paul and me. At eleven o'clock on Saturday morning.' Excitedly, Amy kissed Celia's damp cheek. 'Say you're pleased for us.'

'Has Pa said you can?' Celia fumbled in her apron pocket for her handkerchief. She blew her nose, mopped at her eyes.

'I haven't asked him. You're all invited. The whole family.'

'Pa won't like it,' she sniffed. 'He'll want to give his permission.'

'Mam, I'm twenty-one. I don't need it.'

'I think you should have asked.' She was looking at Paul, her voice accusing in tone.

'I'm sorry,' he said.

'Pa won't expect any such thing from me,' Amy said firmly. Even this didn't dampen her excitement. Paul was holding her hand, she felt him squeeze it.

'Saturday, you said?' Mam's worried face turned to Amy again. 'I can't possibly arrange anything by then. It'll be too much of a rush.'

'There's nothing for you to arrange, Mam. It's to be a quiet wedding, not a jamboree. All you have to do is come to the register office.'

'Your Dad's on mornings. Eleven o'clock won't be convenient.' She was dabbing her red eyes again.

'If he doesn't want to come, that's all right. If he does, he'll have to swap his duties.'

'He's not going to like this.' Celia's eyes were fixed on Paul. Amy guessed that her choice of groom was the first thing Pa would object to.

'Mam, he doesn't like anything I do. I don't expect him

to. But I thought you'd be pleased to get one of your daughters to the altar. You've been trying very hard with the other two.'

Amy woke up in Fliss's bedroom on her wedding morning. Paul brought her a cup of tea and drew back the pretty mauve curtains.

'Blustery but bright,' he said, bending to kiss her. 'Weather fit for a bride.'

Amy's dark, crinkly hair was loose from its plait and spread all over her pillow.

'Has Auntie My gone yet?'

Myra had said she'd open up the café without Paul's help this morning: 'It's your wedding day. I can't expect you to work. Anyway, I've got to get used to running the place on my own.'

'Yes, we're alone.' He kissed her again. 'Do you think it would be jumping the gun if I . . . ?'

Amy smiled and pulled the bedclothes over him. 'Ours isn't going to be a traditional wedding. No point in wasting precious time.'

Amy could hear Paul singing in his bath. She knew love had brought the same fizz to him.

She'd got up and had her bath in plenty of time. She'd never felt happier nor more certain that she was doing the right thing.

She put on the new red wool suit she'd managed to buy in Bunnies in Liverpool. It showed off her slim waist. She was so used to seeing herself in uniform she'd hardly realised she had a figure.

She'd failed to find herself a hat, but she didn't suit hats anyway, her plait seemed to get in the way. Auntie My had found a bit of velvet that matched the velvet collar on her suit. She'd suggested she ask Winnie Cottie to make her a headband.

She put it on now to hold back her dark hair. Today, she meant to leave it loose; it hung in ripples almost to her waist. She looked different, exotic almost. She was pleased with the result.

A couple of days ago, Amy had slid into a chair beside Nancy in the nurses' dining room to tell her she was getting married. Nancy had looked a little miffed at first. Then she'd smiled and wished her all the best in the world.

'I should have had the guts to do what you're doing,' she'd said. And when Amy asked her to work in her place on Sunday morning she'd agreed readily, and had gone with her to Matron to clear the arrangement. It meant Amy could have a one-night honeymoon.

The next day, Nancy had insisted on taking her home. She'd made Mam open up the cake tins to find the second tier of her wedding cake.

'Will it be fit to eat after all this time?' she asked.

'The icing is still perfect,' Mam said with satisfaction. 'It'll be better than ever because it's had time to mature.'

Nancy opened the little box of ornaments she'd bought all that time ago and set out the silver horseshoes and wedding bells on top.

'I want you to have it, Amy,' she'd said. 'No good keeping it for next Christmas. I'll take it down to the Refreshment Room and give it to Auntie My.'

From the window, Amy watched Nancy and Katie escorting Mam to the bus stop. She knew they were on their way to the Town Hall.

Mam was wearing the outfit she'd organised for Nancy's wedding. A tan felt hat and a wool suit in the same colour, that she'd made herself. Amy had seen her try it on.

'Might as well give it an airing,' she'd said, tugging endlessly at the jacket. Now she was wearing her fox fur round her shoulders to finish the outfit off.

Paul came from his bedroom looking unfamiliar in his best suit, with his straight brown hair still damp and slicked down. On his thin, good-looking face was the look of a cat who's been given a saucer of cream. Amy kissed him again, and told him he looked exactly right. The short journey down to Hamilton Square in the car seemed almost unreal.

The wedding party had gathered before they arrived at the register office. There was Auntie My, Mam, Nancy, Katie and Winnie Cottie, who also looked unfamiliar in a smart coat with a big fur collar.

Amy thought the ceremony exactly right. There was no fuss. The room was small and smelled of furniture polish. When it was over, everybody seemed to be kissing her.

Paul filled the car to capacity for the short drive to the café. Even so, Nancy and Katie were left to run down behind them.

They went in to find that Auntie My had pushed three tables together under the window, and covered the gingham oilcloth with a white damask cloth from home. The wine and the wedding cake were set out at one end. Paul opened a bottle and handed brimming glasses round.

Other customers were being served by Vera just as usual, but there weren't many of them. Vera came bustling out of the kitchen to kiss Amy and congratulate Paul.

Her sisters came in with faces flushed with exercise and fresh air. Amy had been a little worried about both of them. She was afraid they might feel she was upstaging them. They had both wanted this for themselves.

Nancy was her usual sunny self. Katie had them in tucks of laughter recounting how ladders had run in all directions as she'd tried to put on the only pair of flesh-coloured stockings she had. Neither Nancy nor Mam had a spare pair to lend her. Stockings had been unobtainable for months.

'I helped her paint her legs,' Nancy said. 'Show them, Katie. Don't they look smart?'

Katie held out a shapely leg for them all to admire.

'I didn't know you'd come out without stockings,' Mam said aghast.

'Such a cold day too,' Winnie Cottie said. 'You could have worn your black ones.'

'Not exactly fashionable.' Katie pulled a face. 'Wouldn't go with my green dress.'

'We all did it in the summer,' Amy said. 'You could buy special tanning cream.'

'This is gravy browning,' Katie giggled. 'It was all we had. And eyebrow pencil to draw the seams. It looks great, doesn't it?'

Nancy laughed. 'It looks good until it starts raining.'

Auntie My and Vera had managed to conjure up a good meal of steak, chips and peas, with tinned plums baked in a pie.

To Amy, it seemed a friendly family party. After everybody had drunk the health of the bride and groom, she suggested they drink a toast to Fliss too. All glasses were recharged and raised.

'We thought,' Paul said, 'we'd go up to St Cath's now and take her some wedding cake. She's bound to feel a bit left out.'

'Take my camera,' Auntie My insisted. 'Get somebody to take her picture with you. There's two left on the roll.'

'Come with us,' Amy urged. 'We won't be staying very long and Fliss will want to see your wedding outfit.'

'Then we'll bring you and the car back here and take the train,' Paul said. 'We're going to have a one-night honeymoon. The destination is secret.'

'Very romantic, I'm sure.' Auntie My smiled.

'Chester,' Paul had already told Amy. 'No point spending a lot of time travelling. I've booked a room at the Grosvenor Hotel. As it's only one night, we can afford to splash out.'

It was over all too soon. It left Amy more restless than she'd ever been before, and with her studying behind her as well, everything felt flat.

She twisted her wedding ring on her finger and thought of Paul. She was missing him terribly. It felt as though he'd been wrenched from her.

After six weeks, he came home for two days' leave. He was ecstatic.

'I've got what I've always wanted,' he told her. 'I'm being sent to Canada for pilot training.' Amy was thrilled that he looked so well and seemed to be enjoying his new life. Though it niggled that he seemed to be coping better without her than she was without him.

Amy sighed to Nancy: 'Canada seems a long way away.'

'No further than North Africa and a whole lot safer,' she'd retorted.

Myra said: 'Come and see me as often as you can. I miss him too, but at least I've got you here. You must still come for your days off.'

The blitz went on, everybody was going short of sleep. The hospital was full of the injured, and the news was bad from every front.

At last came the day Amy had been waiting for, and she heard she'd passed her finals. Nancy gave her a congratulatory hug at morning break.

Amy laughed. She was pleased, of course she was. This was something she'd set her mind on when she was at school. She'd done it at last.

'What are you going to do now?' Nancy asked.

'I want to join the QAs. The army.'

'Queen Alexandra's Imperial Military Nursing Service.' The wordy title rolled off Nancy's tongue.

'Yes. Why don't we both join together?'

'Me too?' Nancy's eyes clouded.

'You said you were going to, that you wanted to do your bit. Come on,' Amy urged.

'We're doing useful work here. The only difference is we'd be looking after army personnel instead of civilians.'

'I'm going,' Amy said quietly, 'even if you aren't.'

'They won't have you yet. You need post-qualification experience.'

'Then I'll go as soon as they'll have me. How long are you going to drag your feet?'

'I'm not dragging my feet. If Stan gets leave, I want to be here. I'm going to marry him next time.'

'You've got a long wait now. Stan could do two years in North Africa before he gets leave.'

'I know and I'm not going to miss my chance again,' Nancy said with dogged determination. 'I'll join up when I'm married.'

'Kate will be ready to do it by then,' Amy said, running short of patience. 'You're a drifter, Nancy. The time is never right for you. You always want to put everything off. Now there's a war on, everybody else is living for the moment.'

'Live now, pay later,' Nancy said.

'I'll go without you then,' Amy retorted.

CHAPTER TWENTY-FOUR

On her day off, Nancy cycled up to see how the Framptons were getting on. It seemed strange now to be crunching up the gravel drive of Henshaw House. The garden was not as spick and span as it used to be. She knew they no longer kept a gardener.

Mary Frampton encouraged her to call round from time to time, for a cup of tea and a chat. She liked to talk over her diet and said rationing was making both that and dinner parties more difficult.

Nancy had noticed the gradual changes. Mrs Frampton now managed the house without any help. She seemed to have more energy. She even looked younger. Yet the house seemed unchanged, as gracious and comfortable as ever.

'Bridge? Yes, I still play a little.' She laughed. 'But I don't have much time for that now. I'm doing WRVS work, you know. Making tea and helping to find accommodation for those bombed out. Finding them clothes and all that sort of thing.'

It amazed Nancy that she was now working for others, when before the war she'd had people working for her.

'I need things to do, to keep myself busy. I don't see much of Bill. He works all day at the office and then does air-raid warden duty three nights a week.'

'He must be worn out, with all these raids.'

'I do wish they'd stop. When Bill is home, he's usually too tired to do anything.'

'How's Toby?'

She saw the older woman wince. 'He's completed his training, soon he'll be flying on raids over Germany. He's got a posting to Duxford.' She sighed again. 'That will give me something else to worry about.'

'He'll be having leave first?'

'Yes, just forty-eight hours, but it's something. We're looking forward to that. I do hope we'll be spared a raid, or we won't be able to stay home to see him.'

Nancy thought of the comfortable, easy life she had led in this house. It was gone for ever for all of them now.

Officially, Toby Frampton's forty-eight-hour pass didn't start until midnight, but he was free to go at five o'clock. He got in his car and left as soon as he could. It gave him another evening at home.

It was only twenty or so miles, but driving in the blackout, straining to see the white line on the road in the puny beam of his dipped headlights, wasn't easy.

Not even a chink of light was showing from Henshaw House when he reached it. His mother had redoubled her efforts when she'd heard a neighbour had been fined twenty shillings for allowing light to leak out round the blackout curtains.

Inside, all was warm and bright. His mother wrapped her arms round him in greeting. She told him again just how anxious she was going to be for his safety when he started flying on missions to Germany.

His brother James was in the RAF too, but he seemed to have been given a desk job in Scotland. James wasn't too pleased about it, but his parents certainly were.

His father was yawning and looked just about all in when he arrived, but he made an effort to be welcoming, and poured some beer for him to have before supper.

'Your father's had to go out the last three nights,' his mother said, coming into the sitting room to have a glass of sherry. 'He's an ARP warden now. I do hope he won't have to go again tonight.'

'We all hope that, Mary.' Bill yawned again.

Toby couldn't get used to seeing her going backwards and forwards to the kitchen to deal with the supper. Eventually, he said: 'Why don't we come and sit in the kitchen while you cook?'

He and Dad sat at the table and opened more bottles of beer. They ate in the kitchen too.

'Less trouble for your mother,' his father said. They'd sat over the meal, talking for a long time. Toby had just made a second pot of coffee when the sirens began to wail.

'They get earlier and earlier,' his mother complained.

'I'll have to go.' His father took his steel hat from the hall stand. 'It mightn't be much tonight, just a few bombs on the docks. Take your mother to the shelter, Toby.'

'Might as well take the coffee too,' she said, picking up the pot and two cups.

Toby followed her out to the Anderson shelter in the garden. It surprised him to find how sure-footed she was in the dark.

'I get plenty of practice,' she laughed. 'Running up and down this path.'

It was a bitterly cold night. Toby huddled in a blanket, and thought longingly of his warm bed. He could see moisture glistening on the inside of the shelter.

'It sounds like more than just a few bombs on the docks,' he said, but his mother seemed to have dozed off.

He wondered how she could when the night was full of engine noises and the crump of high explosives and the guns at Bidston banging away.

He went outside, still draped in his blanket. Over the town and the river, the sky was crisscrossed with searchlights. Mary was awake when he went back.

'They're getting it down in town tonight. I hope your father's all right.'

'I could see several big fires. I'd just as soon be up in the sky delivering the bombs than on the receiving end on the ground.'

He dozed off himself. The all clear woke them both. Toby was surprised to find they'd been in the shelter for over four hours.

'I'm going to bed,' his mother said, as she went wearily back indoors. They'd reached the landing when the phone rang. Toby ran back downstairs to answer it.

'Toby?' It was his father. 'Are you all right? And your mother?'

'We're both fine. Nothing's dropped near us.'

'It's been terrible down here. A direct hit on a pub. Three killed and ten injured.'

'Can I come and help, Dad? I feel awful sitting here and doing nothing.'

'I think we've got them all out now. Happened hours ago, right at the beginning of the raid. We're just damping down a fire, just about got things under control, but you could do something for me. Will you come and pick me up? I'm all in, and my car's got a flat tyre.'

'Of course I'll come. Can't I change the wheel?'

'You won't be able to see, not in the blackout.'

'There's moonlight. It's quite bright.'

'I've left it in a narrow alleyway. It was pitch black then.'

'The moon's higher now. I'll change it, if I can.'

'Get the spare keys from your mother, and see what you can do. You know St Anne's church? First right after that, then first right again.'

'I'll find it.'

'Don't show any light,' his father warned. 'I'll see you there. In about half an hour.'

Toby had never seen the town like this at two in the morning. Civil defence forces were still out in strength. He passed several newly bombed buildings where clearing up was still going on. Fire engines were damping down incendiaries and there was an acrid smell of smoke everywhere.

He found his father's Rover in a dark and quiet alley. He pulled in behind it. There seemed to be one other car up ahead.

Toby decided he could manage to change the wheel as long as he put all the nuts into his pocket as he took them off. He might as well get on with the job now as come back in the morning.

He'd brought a torch with half the glass blacked off. He shone it momentarily into the boot. By the time his father turned up, he'd already got the new wheel in place and was just tightening things up. He was fastening the damaged wheel on to the back of the boot when a large figure in police uniform walked quietly past them.

Something about him attracted Toby's attention. He was carrying something heavy. His father was staring at the policeman, rigid with tension.

Toby saw him open the back door of the car parked ahead of his father's. Heard the chink of bottles as the burden was placed carefully on the rear seat.

When the man went to get behind the steering wheel, Toby thought he glanced towards them in a somewhat furtive fashion. Toby peered more closely. Was it Constable Siddons? He made a move to go to speak to him and felt his father's hand on his arm. Together, they watched him drive slowly off.

'Was that . . . ?' Toby shivered.

'I saw him earlier this evening,' his father murmured. 'He was arresting a man for looting. Now . . .'

'He wouldn't!' Toby said. 'It wasn't him. We're mistaken.'

'You saw his uniform.'

His father was pushing him towards his own car. 'You've as good as finished here. See if he goes home.'

Park Road North was a long, straight road bright with moonlight. Toby was in time to see the car ahead turn into the side road next to the Siddonses' house. He pulled into the kerb opposite, and saw the burly figure carrying the heavy load towards the Siddonses' back yard.

Filled with dismay, he put his car in gear and drove home. His father arrived moments behind him. Once in the kitchen Toby put the kettle on to make tea. His father was hollow-eyed with exhaustion and with his face black with smoke, but it was easy to see he was more concerned about other things.

'Was it Siddons?'

'Yes. What are you going to do?'

'My duty is clear. As a member of the Watch Committee, I should make my suspicions known to the superintendent.'

'He's Nancy's father! Surely . . .'

'That makes it harder, but I have to do it.'

Katie went shopping down Grange Road on her next day off. She had plenty of clothing coupons and now that she had a job, she felt she should get herself the warm winter coat she needed.

She found few to choose from and none that she liked, and decided she might as well go over to Liverpool and see if the big shops there had anything better to offer. On her way, she would stop in at the Refreshment Room at Woodside and have a cup of tea.

She was crossing Hamilton Square when she saw Toby Frampton walking towards her in his uniform.

'Katie? It is Kate Siddons? Yes, of course it is. You look so different, I nearly didn't recognise you.' She could see his brown eyes assessing her, crinkling as he smiled. It was his warmth and kindness she remembered most.

'I've had my hair cut.' Her eyes met his. She was surprised at the depth of interest she found there.

'But you had such pretty hair.'

'Too much hair,' she laughed. 'I'm a nurse now and I had to do something to get it off my collar. It was hard to get it into a bun and not long enough to make decent plaits.' She put up her hand to feel the short bubbly curls all over her head. 'Less trouble this way.'

'It's still pretty, but . . . Makes you look older.'

'I am older.' He laughed then. 'Are you on leave again?'

'Yes, forty-eight hours. I've got my wings, I'm a fully fledged navigator now, and I've got a posting to RAF Duxford. Going on Monday.'

'Where's that?' Katie broke off as the siren started its mournful wail.

'We'd better get under cover somewhere.' He took her arm. 'Come on. The underground station's just round the corner.' Hamilton Square Station was on the low-level railway line going under the Mersey to Liverpool.

Katie froze. That awful siren had brought terror thudding back. Everybody else told her they were frightened of air raids. But she knew that what she felt was far, far worse. Her legs were too stiff to move. She couldn't hurry. Toby said again: 'Come on.'

She hated going down in the lift. It was like going into a tomb. She worried that the crowd descending with them would not get out again.

At the far ends of the platforms, deep below ground, rows of bunks had been fitted against the wall because people spent the night here.

Toby led her towards them. The place was filling up as trains disgorged passengers who decided to stay where they were until the all clear sounded. Some of the upper bunks were still unoccupied.

'We can sit up there,' he said. 'Can you climb up?'

Katie was shaking like a leaf and felt incapable of doing anything. She could feel her heart pounding and her legs felt as though they were made of elastic.

'Come on, Katie.' Toby guided her foot to the lower bunk and half lifted her up to the top one. 'We'll be all right here.'

They were sitting on wire springs. The public was expected

401

to bring its own mattresses and bedding. Toby pushed himself back against the wall and pulled her back beside him. The wall felt wonderfully solid but cold.

She couldn't banish from her mind the awful feeling of being buried alive, half suffocating with soot and dust and racked with pain. She'd called out to Nanny again and again. Just to know she wasn't alone would have been the greatest comfort.

She knew she was shaking. 'I feel such a coward. Just the thought of another raid and I'm gripped by the most awful panic. Convinced the same thing will happen to me again.'

She felt an arm go round her shoulders and pull her against him. The warmth of his personality was like a blanket round her shoulders. She'd never known anyone so comforting.

'It can't be exactly as it was last time.'

'I keep telling myself that,' she choked.

'You mustn't be frightened,' he said gently. 'I know that's easy for me to say. I haven't been buried alive.'

Katie looked up at the great blackened curve of the roof and down to the shiny rails snaking into the black tunnel. She didn't like it here, but the rest of the crowd didn't seem to mind. They were shouting to each other and even laughing.

'We're too far below ground for a bomb to bother us,' Toby murmured. 'This is considered the safest place to shelter. We can't even hear what is going on up top.'

Katie felt her trembling beginning to subside. 'Will we know when the raid is over?'

'Yes, the sirens have to be audible everywhere. The all clear will sound, and we'll all go about our business, you'll see.'

Below them somebody started to sing 'Roll out the Barrel'. Everybody was joining in, the chorus was taken up on the platform on the other side of the lines. It echoed cheerfully round the tunnels.

'It wasn't like this last time.' Katie whispered. The dim

light caught his hair, lighting up the gold streaks. She saw him smile.

'That's better,' he said, and his lips came down on hers, warm and gentle. A feathery kiss.

It made her catch her breath. Nothing had been further from her mind. In the maternity hospital when he'd come to visit, and before that at his grandmother's funeral, she'd met his gaze and felt a stirring of interest, but she hadn't expected him to feel it too.

She wondered again what she'd ever seen in Jimmy. Toby's warm manliness was far more attractive. She told herself she was a fool even to think of it. She had to forget men, all of them. She couldn't go through what she had with Jimmy, ever again.

Besides, Toby knew of her past and was unlikely to take her seriously. He wouldn't want Jimmy Shaw's cast-offs. If Jimmy had thought she wasn't good enough for him, Toby was unlikely to feel any different. After all, he knew exactly what had happened.

Toby Frampton could feel Katie quaking against him like a captured bird fluttering with fright. Her eyes were bigger than usual and so dark a blue they seemed almost navy. He pulled her against him in a gesture of comfort but the next minute he could feel her body go rigid with tension.

At the time, he'd been conscious that his father would disapprove of him stopping to talk to her in Hamilton Square. If the warning hadn't come at that moment he'd have gone on his way, before she'd been able to make him feel like this.

He'd thought of Katie as little more than a child, because that was how Nancy had presented her. Capable Nancy was almost part of his family. He'd first taken an interest in Katie because Nancy wanted him to. Now he knew there was a magical quality about her.

They'd all seen her as a wronged child, needing help and deserving pity, but he'd been surprised when he'd taken her down to Nanny's house. She'd shown plenty of spirit. In her own way she was as capable as Nancy.

When he'd helped dig her out of the bomb-blasted house, her pitiable state had made him ache with compassion. He'd seen it as his fault that she was there at all, while Dad blamed himself for implying it was safe to be anywhere but in the cellar.

Toby had thought of her often since he'd seen her sitting up in bed with violet shadows under her beautiful eyes. He'd felt drawn to her, but he hadn't intended to kiss her. Hadn't meant to show his interest. She was far too young for him, though her eyes had never been those of a child. Too much had already happened to Katie.

The crowd sang 'Run Rabbit Run', then someone started on 'The White Cliffs of Dover', and soon the tunnels were ringing with song. The atmosphere was jolly, almost like a party. There was no room for fear here. He could feel her body gradually relaxing against him.

'You're going away?' she asked. 'You started to tell me.'

'I've been posted to Duxford. I shall be flying bombers. Operational at last.'

Kate began to talk about her first days at the hospital and he told her about life in the RAF.

When the all clear sounded, the change in her was miraculous. She was laughing as though she hadn't a care in the world.

The crowd began to surge towards the exits. Toby caught her as she pushed herself off the top bunk. The hug he gave her was spontaneous, he hadn't intended to do that either. He wished now he wasn't going so far away. He wanted to stay with Katie.

They went up in the crowded lift and out into the dusk of early evening. He held on to her arm, keeping her close. No bombs had fallen as far as they could see.

'All those hours down there and nothing happening,' he heard a man grumble. Toby felt the all clear had gone before he was ready for it. He was reluctant to let Kate go now.

'Would you have a meal with me?' he heard himself asking before he'd given it any thought. 'I'm hungry after that.'

There was a glow about her as she smiled agreement. She had more poise now. He wasn't sure about the new hairstyle though. He'd liked the big cloud of curls and her endearing habit of pushing it behind her ears.

'Shall we try the Woodside Hotel? Though I'll have to ring my mother first. She's expecting me home for supper.'

He could see Kate waiting outside the phone box, watching every movement he made. His father answered the phone.

'Toby, you can't possibly absent yourself. Your mother's going to a lot of trouble over this meal.'

'I've invited a girl to have dinner with me, Dad.'

'Your mother's got something special. It'll be your last meal with us for a long time, and she's cooking it herself. She'll be disappointed if you don't come and eat it.'

Toby could hear the irritation in his voice. 'Sorry, Dad.'

'Bring the girl with you, if you must. There should be enough. That would be better than not coming at all.'

'I'll do that. You know the girl already. It's Katie Siddons.' He put the phone down quickly. He knew his father wouldn't want any closer ties with the Siddons girls, not after what he'd seen.

He went out, pulling a wry face, to tell Katie what she was in for. He hadn't intended introducing her to the family table so quickly either. How he wished he hadn't seen her father the other night.

He watched the colour run up her cheeks and fade again.

'Toby, you don't have to worry about me. I can go back to the hospital for supper.'

'They've invited you, Katie.'

'Your parents will want you to themselves. They won't be seeing so much of you now you're going far from home.'

He'd forgotten she was shy. That she was already known

405

to his parents might make it easier for them, but he guessed Katie would feel less at ease because she'd been employed to look after Nanny.

'Come on,' he said: 'It'll be a help to have you there. Last suppers can be hard going.'

'I don't want to push myself in. It's a family occasion.' Her reluctance was like a wall he had to break down.

'The family have already said all they can about my going away. If you come, it will prevent Mother saying it all over again. Do come and cheer us all up.'

They reached his parked car. He opened the passenger door for her. After a moment's hesitation, Kate got in. She was reminded of the last time she'd been in his car, when he'd taken her to Nanny's house. She watched his hands on the steering wheel, and worried about what she'd let herself in for.

For several months, she'd gone to his home almost daily. Mostly, she'd got no further than the kitchen. She'd talked to Hilda, the housekeeper, and collected supplies.

Sometimes, Mary Frampton had come down to ask her how Nanny was. Several times she'd taken her into the drawing room to give her magazines and newspapers that the family had finished with. Once she'd taken her into the garden and told her to cut some flowers to take back. She had always been unfailingly kind.

'Mother's household is shrinking fast,' Toby said. 'I don't think she likes it. She's missing Gran, and my brother and I are away most of the time.'

'Nancy's left them too.'

'And Hilda has joined the Wrens. They couldn't expect her to go on looking after them with a war on. It's changed their life. Home isn't the same any more.'

Katie felt that his home had changed less than hers. The drawing room was as elegant as the day she'd first seen it.

She got the distinct impression that his parents were not pleased to see her. She thought Mary Frampton a little withdrawn, and very much stiffer in manner than she had been on previous occasions. Katie felt it was because she'd intruded on a family occasion. They wanted Toby to themselves.

She was aware that Toby was drawing her out, so that she gave them news of Nancy and Stan Whittle, and then of Amy, but his parents didn't loosen up.

Although there was no help in the house, Katie thought the dining table was set out with enough style to suit a banquet.

They ate roast chicken while she tried to think of things to tell them about Nanny's last hours that they might not know. She thought they did unbend a little then.

Afterwards, when she'd helped Toby clear away and wash up, she said, trying to smile: 'I want to leave early. Your parents will want you to themselves for the last hour or so.'

'They're tired,' he said, and she knew he was making excuses. That he thought they should have been more welcoming.

'I'll drive you back to the hospital,' he insisted, though she tried to dissuade him.

As he pulled up in front of Ashville, he said: 'If I write to you, Katie, will you write back?'

She felt herself flush with pleasure. 'Of course.' He leaned over and kissed her, pulling her close.

'I'll have to go.' She could feel his reluctance. 'It'll be a long time before I can see you again. Just when I was getting to know you.'

Katie was feeling for the door handle.

'Wish me luck,' he said.

She leaned in to kiss him. 'All the luck in the world, Toby.'

Toby went back home to say goodbye to his parents. He was afraid they were not going to part on the best of terms. Somehow, with the best intentions, he always seemed to get on the wrong side of his father.

The signs had been there all through supper. He'd known before taking Katie home that it was the wrong thing to do. He'd opened his mouth without thinking, and then he'd been reluctant to tell her that the meal he'd offered her was off. Anyway, he'd enjoyed her company and wanted more of it.

Still, he'd been a fool to take her home when his father had been up in arms about Alec Siddons the other night. He doubted anyone had enjoyed the meal.

His father had not been rude to Katie, rather he'd gone through the motions of hospitality as though to show that the situation had been forced on him against his will. The atmosphere had been stilted. His mother had been rather starchy.

He let himself into the house. 'Toby?' his father's voice called from the drawing room. He had to force himself to the door.

'Did you have to embarrass me like that, Toby?' Bill demanded. 'You were there with me the other night. You saw her father with your own eyes, and yet . . .'

'I like Katie.'

His mother said: 'She had a baby, Toby. We offered help, of course, but I'm not sure . . . that you should go out of your way to be friendly now.'

'I met her by accident. We sheltered from the raid together and got talking. I've said nothing to her about her father.'

'I should hope not,' his father exploded. 'She'll hear soon enough.'

'We all found Katie honest when she looked after Nanny, didn't we? I thought you liked her.'

'I did. I'm fond of Amy too, and Nancy's a lovely girl. But it's hard enough to do my duty without you creating new liaisons with Kate. We don't need that.'

'Have you said anything yet, about Siddons?'

'The superintendent is a client of mine. He'll be coming to see me next week. I thought it would be a good opportunity.'

408

'I'm sorry, but this is to do with Alec Siddons, not his daughters.'

'I'd rather not have my family associating with them. With all the girls in this world, why did you have to pick on her?'

'Katie has done nothing wrong, Dad.'

'You've put me in an impossible position. I'm a member of the Watch Committee, and I believe I've seen with my own eyes evidence that Alec Siddons is looting. Enough evidence to have him investigated. What am I supposed to do, Toby?'

'Can't you forget what you saw?'

'Don't be ridiculous. If the man's looting, he's got to be stopped. He's supposed to be above suspicion.'

Toby was feeling warm under the collar.

'He'll be in big trouble if this is proved. He'll be sacked.'

'How can they prove it now?' Toby asked.

'How should I know? Search his house, I suppose. It'll take him time to empty all those bottles. He must have taken them from that pub that was bombed. The landlord was killed and his wife taken to hospital. Would you believe he could think of looting under those circumstances?'

'Perhaps they didn't come from there. Wouldn't the bottles have been broken?'

'There was a cellar. The rest of us were trying to dig out the casualties but I saw him there shifting cartons like the one we saw him carrying. I thought it odd at the time.'

'It will upset the girls, be terrible for their mother.'

'He's the one who should be bearing that in mind, not me. I repeat, I don't want you involved with the Siddons girls.'

'You forget I'm going to Duxford on Monday. I won't have much opportunity to get involved with them.'

'It's for the best Toby,' his mother said as he kissed her goodbye. 'I don't think Katie is a suitable girl for you. Not knowing her history.'

He slammed out to his car in a foul mood.

Everybody agreed that the air raids were getting worse. They were more frequent, lasted longer and were heavier. There had been a bit of a lull over Christmas, but the New Year saw the bombers back. They'd come for three of four nights on the run, then give Merseyside a break.

When Katie went off duty at eight o'clock, she went down to the cellar at Ashville as soon as she could. She was amazed to see other nurses sleeping through heavy raids. For her, such a thing was impossible. She lay awake, in a state of mortal terror.

There had been a heavy raid the previous night, bombs had dropped closer than ever before. Park Station, only a few hundred yards from her home on one side and the hospital on the other, was damaged so badly that trains wouldn't be running through it for some time.

Casualties had poured into the hospital. The staff were more organised to cope now. Nurses took it in turns to be on call, and slept in the home behind the hospital. Only very rarely were extra nurses called on during the night, but that was one occasion when they had been.

Katie heard Home Sister come round the cellar in the middle of the night, shaking nurses awake. She pulled her blanket over her head, dreading the time when it would be her turn.

'You're safe enough for a while,' Amy told her. 'You're still first year, and mostly they need nurses who have done their stint on casualty.'

Katie hoped she was right; she was afraid she'd be no use at all.

By evening, everybody was yawning and hoping for a quiet night so they'd be able to catch up on their sleep. The cellar filled up early. Katie was fast asleep before the warning sounded. It half woke her; she groaned, turned over and slid back into a light doze.

She was jolted back to full consciousness by a most

410

ferocious explosion that seemed to be only a few yards from her head. She sat up on her deck chair, her heart pounding with terror.

There were more explosions, some close, some more distant. Katie felt the foundations of the old house shaking. Around her, everyone else was awake. She heard a scream, quickly stifled.

'Try and get back to sleep again, girls,' the home sister advised. Katie lay back, but she couldn't possibly sleep. This raid sounded far worse than the one that had buried her.

Ten minutes later, they heard a police siren, and a banging on the front door. Home Sister went upstairs to see what they wanted. Another explosion shook the house while they waited.

She came back and told them all to dress as quickly as they could. A police car had come to let them know that every nurse was needed. This time the hospital had been damaged, the phones were dead.

With her heart in her mouth, Katie threw her uniform on. It was one in the morning. In a silent group they half walked and half ran down the road. Usually, the hospital waited for the all clear before calling the nurses down from Ashville and Beechwood.

The sky was alive with searchlights and throbbing engines. As she reached Park Road North, Amy came alongside her and looked to her left.

'Our house is still standing,' she panted. 'So is Auntie My's.'

Kate couldn't speak; she was gripped with panic. She could see that windows had been blown out of some of the nearby houses. She didn't want to go any further and her step slowed. Amy took her arm. She was swept along with the others.

Katie could smell the smoke before she could see the hospital. The glow in the sky above it was unmistakable. It was on fire. It looked much the same from the road except that the front forecourt was full of fire engines and water ran in torrents everywhere.

Ambulances were being turned away while others were trying to get through the fire engines to evacuate patients to other hospitals.

Katie took one horrified glance inside. A solitary lamp half lit the scene. Doctors were trying to work by torchlight.

In the front hall, she heard that the twin operating theatres had been put out of action by bomb blast and that incendiaries had started a fire which was being brought under control.

She wanted to turn and run, but dared not. She was sent to help on Weightman Ward. It was in chaos. The lighting had failed throughout the hospital. The emergency generators had been damaged and wouldn't work either, and it was very cold.

Katie looked round, shivering, inert with shock and horror. She could taste again the soot in her mouth, and feel the pain ripping her in half. She felt a scream flutter in her throat.

A woman moaned. Every patient was awake and needed reassurance. The windows had gone. There was glass crunching underfoot and on beds. Many patients had received cuts from it that needed attention.

'Wake up, Siddons.' The staff nurse gave her a push. 'Stop gawping round and do something useful. Get this glass swept up before it causes more trouble.'

Katie gulped, realising she'd been sent here to help and that the other nurses were already at work. There were people who needed help just as she had that night.

She started sweeping up glass she could hardly see, then gave out extra blankets. The nurses were telling patients that the worst was over. Katie repeated the words so many times that she came to believe it herself.

The lifts wouldn't work without power, so there was no way of evacuating the very ill. Patients from Ward 4, which had sustained more damage in the blast, were being pushed on to Weightman on their beds. There were so many patients

412

on stretchers in between the beds that the nurses could hardly move around.

At last the emergency generators were made to work and permission was received from the gas board to use the gas. Katie started making cups of tea for all those who could take fluids by mouth.

In the daylight the damage looked worse, but at least most of the building still stood.

At breakfast, the nurses were saying it was the worst night they'd ever lived through, but Katie felt it had done one good thing for her. By having to help others, she'd got over the terrifying panic that used to grip her at the first wail of the sirens. Like everybody else, she was still frightened of air raids, but she'd found she could still function. She was able to put behind her for good the horror of being buried alive.

BOOK SIX
1942-1946

CHAPTER TWENTY-FIVE

Summer 1942

Myra drove as fast as she dared up to St Cath's. She knew just how much Fliss looked forward to visiting hours and she didn't want to be late.

Without Paul, she was kept busy at the café and had begun to feel she'd got a grip on life instead of being pulled along by it.

She parked the car and felt in the passenger's footwell for the two eggs she'd brought to supplement the hospital diet. Fliss liked an egg for her tea. Only bread, scraped with a little margarine and jam, was provided, and the bread never seemed fresh. She'd brought her a piece of cake too.

It tugged at Myra's heart to see the old withered faces as she walked past them up the long Nightingale ward. It was bright with sunshine this afternoon, though some of the windows at the far end had been boarded up after a recent raid. Most of the patients had their eyes shut as they dozed away the afternoon. They were mainly in their seventies or older.

Not all, though. Myra nodded and smiled at a woman of no more than middle age, who was lying flat without pillows. And here was another, fifty at the most, both her hands and arms bandaged. They were new in.

Every bed was full. In fact it looked as though there were more beds than there used to be; they were pushed closer together now.

Her poor Fliss still looked a child amongst them. Seventeen

years old, and incarcerated in hospitals for nearly three years. What could she possibly have in common with these old ladies?

For once, Fliss was sitting straight up in her bed and smiling. Her mass of auburn curls had been freshly combed. As she approached, Myra thought she looked more cheerful than usual. She put up her face to be kissed.

'Mam, Sister says I can come home.' Her eyes danced with excitement.

Myra laughed outright with pleasure. There was nothing she wanted more and it was so unexpected.

'That's wonderful. When?'

'She said soon. She wants to talk to you about it.'

Myra was overjoyed. She'd been told Fliss would have to stay where she was until her wound stopped discharging.

'You're better then? I'll go and see her now.' Myra laughed again. Fliss's excitement was infectious. 'That's great. I can't wait.'

She hurried back up the ward. Sister was in her office with the door ajar. She looked up when Myra knocked.

'Mrs Laidlaw. Do come in, I want a word.' Myra was waved to a chair at the side of her desk.

'Fliss says she's better and she can come home. I'm so pleased.' She felt another surge of pleasure, but she noticed the sister was tightening her lips. She looked serious.

'It's not quite like that,' she said gently.

'Fliss says . . .'

'Yes, we want you to take her home, if you can manage. I'm afraid there's no change in her condition really. Her wound is still discharging, that's no better.'

Myra had a sinking feeling in her stomach.

'We're desperately short of beds. We have to take bomb victims, you see, and we never know how many . . . We're sending home all our chronic patients . . . Every one we can.'

Myra felt cold inside. 'I'll be glad to have her back home, anyway. She wants to come.'

'There's someone to look after her?'

Myra froze for a moment. 'Well, I work. I have my own business.'

'Fliss won't be able to do much for herself, I'm afraid. She's been in bed for a long time, and an infection like hers saps the strength.'

'I'll get somebody to come in.' Myra thought of Winnie Cottie. She'd be glad to go in at dinnertime. Perhaps Celia would help too.

'We'll arrange for the district nurse to come in and dress her wound. Your own doctor will take over, though we'll see her back in clinic from time to time. It's really a question of whether you can manage.'

'I'll manage somehow. She'll be better in her own home. How soon can I take her?'

'Tomorrow?'

Myra smiled. 'That'll give me time to get her room ready. Tomorrow morning?'

'After eleven,' Sister confirmed. 'Better say half past, to allow me time to fix things up.'

Myra was pulled up short. She couldn't be away from the café over the dinner hour. It was their busiest time. Vera wouldn't like it and she'd be hard pressed to cope.

She swallowed. 'Can we make it afternoon? Say three o'clock?'

'That will be fine.' Sister smiled.

Myra made sure she was on time the following day when she went up to the ward with Fliss's clothes. She'd been unsure what to bring for her. Fliss had worn nothing but nightdresses for so long. She chose a full dirndl skirt to go over the pad of cotton wool on her dressing and the many-tailed bandage.

Fliss's cheeks were pink with excitement. 'I can't wait to get dressed. To have real shoes on my feet again.'

Sister pulled screens round Fliss's bed. 'She'll probably need a bit of help from you,' she said.

419

Myra was shocked to find how much help she did need. Fliss was exhausted and breathless by the time she had her dressed. She'd shot up while she'd been in hospital, and her skirt was too short. It was also very loose at the waist. Myra had to help her button her coat and tie up her shoes. A nurse appeared with a wheelchair to take her out to the car.

Fliss was over the moon on the journey home. Exclaiming at every turn in the road. Horrified at the bomb damage.

Myra parked right outside the front door and had to help Fliss inside. She went straight in to the front room and tried a few notes on the piano.

'You'll be able to practise again,' Myra told her. 'You'll soon get back to the standard you were.' She hugged her. 'It's lovely to have you back here.'

But she couldn't help but notice that Fliss's face was white with exhaustion. Her skin was transparent and there were deep blue shadows below her eyes.

It almost broke her heart to see Fliss trying to climb upstairs. She had to keep resting and it took her a long time to reach the top. When Myra remembered how she used to fly up and down so effortlessly, she felt like crying.

Winnie was only too pleased to help. She invited Fliss round to her house for her lunch.

'She'll be glad of a change of scene,' she'd said. But Fliss wasn't strong enough to get next door. Not yet. Winnie brought her food round and kept her company while she ate it.

The district nurse began to come late in the evening, because of the number of patients she had to see, so Nancy offered to change Fliss's dressing every day for her.

'How is it?' Myra wanted to know, the first time she came.

'Much the same.'

'Still discharging?'

'Yes.'

'But compared with when you first saw it?'

420

'Much the same, Auntie My.' Nancy couldn't look at her.

Myra knew she hadn't realised just how ill Fliss was, until she got her home and could see for herself.

Fliss came downstairs to spend every evening with her when she returned from work. Then she went to bed in the Morrison shelter.

She started to play the piano a little. She even started to sing. Her voice lacked the power it had once had; like her muscles, her vocal cords hadn't been used for a long time.

Myra had a good cry about it, round at Winnie's where Fliss couldn't see her do it.

Amy was desperate to do all she could to help the war effort. Paul had gone to Canada to be trained as a pilot. He seemed a very long way away, though both she and Auntie My were delighted it was a safe place. Now she wanted to have the war won and Paul home again.

After three and a half years at the General, she felt she needed a change. As soon as they'd take her, she went with another girl from the hospital, Jean Meredith, to join the QAs.

They found themselves part of a new intake, being issued with their uniforms, and were amazed to find that this time they were provided with every item of underwear as well. Amy giggled, holding up a pair of the huge khaki knickers she'd been given, elasticated at knee and waist.

'Not wearing those,' Jean Meredith snorted. 'My gran wears that sort. I prefer camiknickers.' The whole intake collapsed laughing at them.

Amy, along with everybody else, neatly folded the offending garments into her chests of drawers and continued to wear her own.

They were given the rank of second lieutenant and taught the ways of the army. They learned to salute and march. They laughed at that, too; they didn't think they marched very well. After basic training Amy was posted to the Royal

Herbert Military Hospital at Woolwich.

On her first morning, she found the differences between there and the General far greater than she'd supposed, and admitted to herself that they were going to take a bit of getting used to. For a start, apart from a few doctors and porters, she'd been used to working with women. Suddenly she found herself addressed as Sister and the only woman on the ward.

All the other nurses and orderlies were male and members of the Royal Army Medical Corps. They were all privates, corporals and sergeants who wore white gowns over their uniforms.

The patients wore uniform pyjamas, green army issue. They were also given white towelling dressing gowns. They were all young. Flowers were unknown, visitors rare, because the patients came from all over the country. Every evening, they would each be issued with one bottle of beer. She was to ensure it was drunk immediately and the empty bottles collected.

Amy was surprised to find that her patients were not all battle casualties. These were treated in field hospitals nearer the front, and only the most severely injured came back to Woolwich.

Servicemen got sick like civilians, and they had road accidents and training accidents. She was surprised too to find that her ward was not over-busy. She'd been run off her feet many times at the General after a raid. Here, there seemed enough staff to keep everything orderly and calm.

The other difference was that some cases on her ward were being treated with penicillin. Amy felt herself tingling with hope.

It was the first time she'd seen it. She took the sealed rubber-topped phials from the fridge and looked with awe at the clear orangey-brown liquid. The patient was injected with it every four hours, night and day.

That first week, she saw a man very ill with pneumonia

recover as though by magic. He was sitting up drinking his beer, saying he felt reasonably well, within two days. Amy was so sure it would cure Fliss too.

However, it wasn't a stock item on her ward that she could order as much of as she wanted. It was considered a scarce and valuable tool here, used only to treat the very ill and those who could almost be guaranteed to benefit from it.

Each patient had his supply prescribed specially for him, and every unit prescribed had to be given to complete the course, so there was never any left over. Amy pondered on how she could get a course for Fliss.

Her ward was provided with a pharmacy basket and order book. When the supply of a stock item was used up, the bottle was tossed in the basket and a new one ordered. The basket, together with any special prescriptions, was taken down to the pharmacy daily by an orderly.

One day, when another of her patients had been prescribed penicillin, Amy picked up the basket and went down to find out what the set-up was.

The pharmacy had a hatch where baskets and prescriptions were handed in. As she'd expected, it was staffed entirely by men. The door was kept locked, the window barred. The Dangerous Drugs Act required drugs to be kept safely.

Amy stood at the hatch and made a point of making herself known to the pharmacist. She could see the electric light glinting on the bottles of medicines. It seemed like an Aladdin's cave for the sick.

She handed in the prescription for penicillin. 'The miracle cure,' she said. 'I've never seen it in use until now.'

'Yes, it's saving thousands in front-line field hospitals,' the pharmacist told her. He was an unbending, middle-aged warrant officer with a moustache.

She saw him go to the refrigerator and take out a small box. There were lots more like it stacked inside. When he opened the box, she saw the little bottles inside, each with a rubber seal, each containing the precious fluid. He selected three for her to take back to the ward, and noted the batch numbers in his register before handing them over.

'Can you get all you need of it?'

'No, it's like gold dust,' he told her. 'We've got to be very careful and account for every unit.'

Amy felt he was treating her overtures of friendship with suspicion. As well he might, she thought grimly.

'Laboratories are working flat out to make more, but it's a slow process,' he told her.

'How soon will it be available for civilians?'

'One day,' he said, making it sound an impossible hope.

Amy wanted to ask him to give her some, but couldn't bring herself to do it. Discipline was strict. She'd learned enough to know he'd be on a charge if stock was found to be missing and he couldn't account for it. He had no reason to risk that for her.

She didn't think she could ever persuade him to do it because she had no other way of making contact. The warrant officers lived in their own mess. The sisters were kept very separate from them. She knew she'd have to find some other way to get it.

Some of the doctors who came to her ward were young. Like her, they were a long way from their homes and families. She had some social contact with them.

One in particular was friendly. She provided him with cups of coffee in her office. Jack Dailey came from Aberdeen and was married with two boys. He talked of his family a good deal, for which she was grateful.

She told him about her sister-in-law, making Fliss's story as tear-jerking as she could. He agreed with her that penicillin could solve her problem.

When some social event was being held in his mess, he invited her over. She made an effort to entertain him with bright chatter. She told him all about Paul.

When Amy was given weekend leave, she went home to Birkenhead. It was eight in the evening when her train got in, and Myra came down to Woodside to meet her in the car.

'Fliss is waiting up to see you,' she told her. 'She's had rather a bad day.'

Fliss seemed less well than Amy had expected. She played the piano and sang for her, but nothing went with the verve it used to. She gave up after quite a short time and lay down on the sofa.

All weekend, she was listless and ate very little. She ran a slight temperature in the evenings, and said she didn't feel well. The wound was no better. It served to harden Amy's resolve. Penicillin was being used to treat men who had not been ill as long as Fliss. It didn't seem fair. She had to get some for her as soon as she could.

Amy had been in Woolwich for six months when she was given fourteen days' leave. In the week before she went, she made up her mind to ask Jack Dailey if he'd write a prescription for a patient who didn't need it and allow her to take the penicillin home with her for Fliss.

He'd invited her to dinner at his mess on the night she asked him, and he'd had rather a lot to drink. But not enough to do what she wanted.

'No, Amy. I can't do that,' he said, sober as a judge the moment the words were out of her mouth. Nothing she could say would persuade him.

There was one last thing she could do, and she made up her mind she would have to try it. Here, there was a colonel, not a matron, in charge of the hospital. He made twice-daily inspection rounds of her ward, usually accompanied by other officers.

A couple of days after her dinner with Jack, the colonel came without his retinue. He was tall, severe, and old enough to be her father. She accompanied him round the ward, updating him on the progress of each patient, and answering his queries about diagnosis and treatment. Two had been treated with penicillin. Both had made spectacular recoveries. He stopped to have a word with them.

When they reached the ward door, she said, 'May I have a word with you?' She led him into her office, her heart thumping as she steeled herself to ask.

She told him about Fliss, ill for nearly three years, and the impossibility of getting penicillin in civilian hospitals.

He straightened his lips, and stared out of the window, considering it.

'It must seem hard,' he said, 'seeing it used here, and yet being unable to get any for your sister-in-law.'

'If it wasn't for the war,' Amy replied, 'she'd have had it by now and be able to get on with her life.'

'There's a growing black market in penicillin.' His austere face was stern.

'But I don't know how to make contact with that. I don't know any black-market dealers.'

'I'm not advising you to go through that channel,' he thundered.

Amy took a deep breath. 'I don't mind paying for it. I don't care what it costs. Not if it will put Fliss back on her feet.'

'It might not. Nobody knows what the black marketeers do to it. They want to make as much profit as they can.'

'You mean they dilute it to make it go further?' Amy was aghast.

'Buying from that source, the customer should expect that.'

'Oh, I see.'

'Once water has been added, the penicillin goes out of date within a month.' Amy knew that. Penicillin was dated when it was issued from the pharmacy.

'The black-market customer has no way of knowing when water was added, or how much, or whether it was sterile. A black marketeer isn't likely to know anything about sterility. Is he likely even to care?' Amy was horrified at the thought.

'He is concerned only with profit. To increase that he could be diluting it and putting some into used bottles. That

426

way, you could end up injecting your sister-in-law with contaminated fluid.'

He was glowering at her fiercely. 'Don't touch it from that source. It won't do her any good, and might do her harm. At the very least, you'll raise hopes that will be dashed.'

Amy stared silently at the wall in front of her, considering herself reprimanded.

He said softly, 'I don't suppose one course will make that much difference here.'

Through a haze of tears, Amy could see him writing.

'They're trying to improve the supply. Growing it in milk bottles in laboratories all over the country. It must get easier soon.'

He pushed something across the desk to her. She saw it was a prescription for penicillin made out in her own name. Tears were running down her face but they were tears of gratitude. All she had to do was to take it to the pharmacy. The colonel was gone before she could thank him.

Until the day came for her to go on leave Amy kept taking the prescription out of her drawer and gloating.

At last Fliss would get her chance.

Amy arrived back at Woodside early in the afternoon, and walked straight across to the Refreshment Rooms. Auntie My was behind the counter and came round to throw her arms about her.

'I've got it,' she whispered. 'I've got some penicillin for Fliss.'

She saw Myra's big eyes glaze over. She was half laughing, half crying. 'I can't believe . . . Will it really cure her?'

'I think so. I'll start her on it straight away.'

'Aren't you hungry? You must eat first.'

'I've been on the train for five hours. There's never a restaurant car these days. I'm starving.'

Within minutes she was sitting down to a large plate of sausage, egg and chips.

'It's all we've got left, I'm afraid,' Myra mourned.

'This is great,' Amy assured her.

Afterwards, leaving her big suitcase for Myra to bring up in the car, she took her hand luggage and went up to Park Road North on the bus.

Myra had given her a key. She let herself in quietly and found Fliss asleep on the sofa in the living room. Amy stood at the door looking at her for a moment; her face was as white as paper against her dark red hair.

Then Fliss's big eyes opened, and the next moment Amy was hugging her. 'I've got some penicillin for you,' she told her.

'Penicillin? I've heard about it, and what it could do for me.' In her excitement her cheeks glowed with colour. 'You've brought enough? All I'll need?'

'Yes, a full course. Pukka stuff. Meant for the armed forces, but no one deserves it more than you. You've been very patient.'

'I'm so pleased. Thank you, Amy.'

Amy went into Auntie My's kitchen and set about sterilising the syringes she'd brought with her.

'I can't believe you've got it,' Fliss chortled, turning over the little bottles.

'It'll mean a lot of injections.'

'I'm not bothered about having injections. I don't care what you do to me if it makes me better.'

Later that evening, they were still sitting round the supper table when Amy heard a knock on the front door. Myra's eyes met hers.

'That's probably Nancy, she usually looks in about this time when she's coming off duty. To change Fliss's dressing.'

Amy went to the door. Nancy looked tired, and the glow she'd always had was gone.

'Hello, Amy.' Her smile brightened as soon as she saw her sister.

Amy leaned against the sitting room door, watching Nancy renew the dressing. She'd forgotten how quick and neat her movements were, and how dainty Nancy was.

The wound looked putrid and inflamed. Fliss was bubbling with excitement as she told Nancy about the penicillin she'd started on.

Amy went to help fasten Fliss's bandage back in position.

'You did the right thing by going away, but then you always do,' Nancy told her.

'She wouldn't have been able to get penicillin for me if she hadn't,' Fliss laughed.

'No. I should have gone with you. Would have done if I'd known how things were going to turn out here.'

'What's the matter? How's Mam?'

'Not good. Falling apart at the seams. Come home with me, Amy, and see for yourself. Tell me what I can do for her, because I've tried everything I can think of. She hardly knows what she's doing. Pa's destroying her.'

'He's not there that much . . .' Amy started.

'Oh, things have changed since you left. He doesn't go out any more, except to work.'

'But with the car . . . ?'

'To work and back, that's just about it. He brings whisky home, in fact he brings quite a lot of things home. He's driving Mam up the wall. Me too. He's terrible. I can't even speak to him.'

'But you're his favourite.'

'He doesn't have favourites any more. He's sort of turned in on himself. You know how he took a dislike to you?'

'Yes,' Amy said cautiously.

'He's taken one to Mam now. Sometimes I get the feeling it's hardly safe to leave her alone with him. I worry about her when I'm working.'

Amy got to her feet. 'Come on. I'd better see her.'

She was filled with dread as Nancy led her through the kitchen and into the living room. Mam was sitting in an armchair listening to music on the wireless. Nancy turned it down.

'Hello, Mam.' Amy kissed her. Celia's skin felt cold. She was hollow-eyed and gaunt. She seemed to have aged years in the six months Amy had been away. 'How are you?'

'Fine,' she said, though clearly she wasn't.

'Nancy says you haven't been too well.'

'I'm as well as anybody. It's just the war. I'll make you a cup of tea.' She made a move to get up.

'I'll do it, Mam,' Nancy said. 'You stay there and talk to Amy.'

Amy watched Celia settle back in the chair and close her eyes, and knew her mother had nothing more to say to her.

'Almost as though she doesn't know who I am,' she said to Nancy.

'She does. She's like this with me sometimes, as though she's too tired to care. She potters round in the mornings. Sometimes gets Fliss something to eat at lunchtime. We've got to do something,' Nancy hissed at her with the kitchen door closed. 'But what?'

Amy shook her head. She didn't know. There was an air of hopelessness about Mam. About the house, too.

That night, when Amy went to bed in Paul's room, she set his alarm clock to wake her up in four hours to give Fliss her next injection. The penicillin had brought so much hope, she didn't mind how much trouble it gave her.

'She seems brighter from the first dose,' Auntie My said.

'That's the hope it gives her.' Amy was trying to be logical, but Fliss was certainly better than she had been on Amy's last visit.

Then, within forty-eight hours, the improvement in Fliss was so great nobody needed to look for it. When Amy dressed her wound, it had stopped discharging, and looked less inflamed.

'It will heal now,' she was able to tell Fliss.

Fliss's temperature no longer went up in the evenings,

and her appetite was picking up. Amy started taking her out to the park, where they could sit for an hour.

Fliss was so thrilled to be in the open air, it more than repaid Amy for the trouble she was taking. She had been out so rarely over the last three years that everything seemed new and exciting.

Amy made her take it gently. Her wound was going to take a few weeks to heal completely, but already it looked so much better. Every day she walked a few yards further, trying to get her strength back.

She grew a little stronger every day. She could get up and down stairs without stopping halfway to rest. She was singing much more. There seemed to be renewed joy in her voice.

'I need lots of practice to get back where I was,' she said. And set about getting it. Soon they could all hear the giggle in her voice. Just as it used to be.

Yves came round to see her, and they sang a duet. He talked of getting a gig for her.

'It's just like old times to hear you,' Winnie Cottie said, and brought Celia round to hear her the following day.

Celia listened and then clapped her hands. 'Very nice,' she said politely.

When it was time for Amy to return to London, Myra shed tears of gratitude.

'I think the bad times are behind us at last,' she said.

Nancy returned home for her morning off. She meant to tidy her bedroom and do some washing. She came in the back way, and was taking off her uniform gabardine in the hall when she saw Stan's letter on the mat by the front door.

Stan's letters were a comfort, a reassurance that he survived and still loved her. She snatched it up, ran to the living room and threw herself on a chair to read it. His letters always brought pleasure but this morning she felt such a surge of joy she leapt to her feet again.

'Mam? Stan's hopeful he'll be given leave soon.'

'When?' Her mother came to the living room door with a duster in her hand.

'He doesn't know yet. He says he'll be coming home, and listen to this . . . "I expect to get a posting in England after that. It's the usual thing after two years out here." He won't be going back! Isn't that wonderful?'

'He's not been there two years yet.'

'Not far off. It's a month since he wrote this. He could be on his way any time now.'

Stan had gone to Egypt in 1940. Since then, the war had raged back and forth along the North African coastline, taking him with it. He'd fought in a series of campaigns for control of the chain of small ports. Cut off from these, with nothing but desert to the south, an army was quickly deprived of water, fuel, ammunition, food and reinforcements, and had to retreat. Nancy had followed his progress with the help of an old atlas.

Stan had helped capture Tobruk from the Italians at the beginning of last year.

That same night, Nancy was drinking cocoa and listening to the nine o'clock news with her mother, when her hopes received a setback.

She'd heard already that Rommel had launched a new summer offensive. The bad news tonight was that it was proving successful and the Afrika Korps had recaptured Tobruk. The fighting had been heavy and the Eighth Army were said to be retreating further along the coast under the onslaught.

'Doesn't sound as though Stan's likely to get leave. Not just now.' Mam's eyes were studying her.

Nancy was shivering, fearful for Stan's safety again. 'It looks as though it will be later rather than sooner.' She was blinking hard with disappointment. Wait, wait, wait, that seemed to be her lot.

'I expect he'll get here eventually.' Mam was trying to comfort her.

'Yes.' Providing he's spared. Nancy couldn't say the words but she thought them. Stan had had wonderful luck not to be injured in all the years of fighting he'd gone through. She wondered how much longer it could hold.

She daren't think like this. She must dwell instead on good things.

'I'm just going to Auntie My's for half an hour,' she said to her mother, and flung her coat round her shoulders.

The Laidlaw house drew her like a magnet these days. It was bright and jolly and full of hope. Her own home seemed a place of discord and tension by comparison.

With the front room window open, she could often hear the foot-tapping beat of music from next-door-but-one. Sometimes it was the piano, tonight it was the accordion. Fliss's voice soared effortlessly above it, crystal clear and strong, in 'Roll out the Barrel'.

She sang fast, with the old lilting giggle back in her voice. She sounded as though she was enjoying herself. Nancy listened on the step outside, feeling cheered in spite of everything.

Fliss had recovered her strength and had started to go to the café with her mother in the mornings.

Myra sent her home on the bus as soon as the lunchtime rush was over. She wanted her to have time and energy to practise again. She'd arranged more piano and accordion lessons for her.

Nancy knew how Auntie My had had to back-pedal on her wish to see Fliss sing professionally. Her illness had made it a hopeless dream. But now both Myra and Fliss were burning with ambition again and full of confidence. When Myra came home in the evenings, they practised together. A professional career seemed a distinct possibility again.

Myra opened the door seconds after Nancy knocked. Since Nancy had gone in every day to change Fliss's dressing, she'd always been made very welcome.

She hadn't realised the Laidlaws already had a guest until she was inside.

'This is Yves,' Myra said. 'Yves Fellipi. Fliss met him at dancing school. You've heard us talk of him?'

Nancy thought he looked theatrical with his black hair and dark skin. Beside him, Fliss was radiating excitement.

'Guess what, Nancy? Yves has got me a slot on *Workers' Playtime*. It'll be broadcast. I can't believe it.'

Fliss was making tremendous progress. Her cheeks were apple pink again and though still slender, she'd put weight on in all the right places.

'It'll be from a munition works canteen, Fliss. The acoustics will be terrible, and the show will be padded out with amateurs from the shop floor.'

'I don't care, just so long as they'll let me sing,' she laughed.

Nancy thought how very like her mother she was with her big, shining eyes.

'We were just trying to decide on the numbers I should sing.'

'Big advantage you playing the accordion,' Yves said. 'Helps a lot in places like that when there's only a piano.'

'We're on at the Empire next week. Marietta and me. Come and see us.'

'I'd love to,' Fliss breathed.

'I'll get tickets,' Myra promised. 'Nancy, would you like to come with us?'

'If I'm off. Thursday I could.'

'We'll sing our final number as a trio,' Yves enthused. 'You play your accordion, and Marietta and I our banjos. We'll have a practice . . . And I'll put a word in for you with the manager, he's always looking for new acts. I'd forgotten just how good you were, Fliss.'

Nancy was smiling as she let herself out of Auntie My's front door and turned to run the few yards home. Then she saw the car drawing up outside her front door. Stan's father was getting out. She knew by the way his whole figure drooped that he was bringing bad news. His face was haggard, his eyes heavy. Nancy froze. He came up to her and put his arms round her.

'We've had a telegram,' he choked. 'Stan was captured at Tobruk. He's in Italy. A prisoner of war.'

Nancy felt icy fingers clawing in her stomach. 'He wasn't injured? He's all right?'

'They didn't say he'd been injured.'

Nancy groaned. She'd thought the waiting was nearly over; now it stretched ahead of her once more. It would be the end of the war before she saw Stan again and she couldn't even hope for an earlier date.

Nancy put her head on Jim Whittle's shoulder and wept. He was patting her back awkwardly. She knew he didn't know how to deal with her grief, that he was barely in control of his own.

'His mother's right upset,' he choked.

'At least we know he's alive,' she said. 'It could be worse.'

'And he isn't alone,' his father added. 'They took a lot of prisoners at Tobruk.'

CHAPTER TWENTY-SIX

Spring 1943

Alec had spent Sunday walking his beat feeling thoroughly fed up. It was a day of stiff breezes and fitful sunshine, and people were out and about enjoying themselves while he'd had to work.

It had just gone three when he came off shift, climbed in his car and set off for home. All day he'd been asking himself what he was getting out of life. Damn little, and what he had, he had to struggle for.

The car, of course, he had that. Not exactly posh, but it was a decent car, and he had his own ways of getting all the petrol he needed. If nothing else, war was opening up new ways of making money.

Olive Driscoll's murder remained unsolved. At that time, too many were being slaughtered by German bombs for one more death to cause much concern. The police had been overworked and exhausted.

He missed Olive, though she'd been nothing but a money-grabber. She'd been out for all she could get from him. Get me this, she'd pleaded, and I want that, and like a fool he'd done his best for her.

And what had he got out of it? Another huge headache that had kept him on a knife edge for months. It wasn't easy to live like this, always expecting trouble. Never feeling safe about anything.

He blamed Olive for turning against him, yet he was bored without her. There was no fun.

What he needed was another woman to put a fillip into his life. He knew that as soon as he'd eaten and settled back in his chair, Celia would come into the living room and say: 'Aren't you going out?' From the look on her face, he knew she wanted him to go.

Even Nancy kept saying: 'Not going out, Pa? Isn't it your day off?'

He felt unwanted. They resented him staying at home, and now he had nowhere else to go. His family huddled in the kitchen, leaving him alone in the living room. He could hear them chattering like magpies.

Celia was colder than ever. Not that she'd ever been generous with her affection. Her attitude had always been to lie back and think of England, and she had many different ways of letting him know he was asking too often.

'What's got into you, Alec?' She'd struggled out of his arms last night. He had seen her in the lamplight, wrinkling her nose in distaste. 'You never used to be like this.'

It was too close to the truth. As though she suspected he had nobody else to fall back on now. He wished he had, somebody he could have a laugh with. Celia was always so miserable.

He told himself another woman was another danger, but luck had always been on his side. He'd survived many near disasters, and he would again. He had to do something. He felt like a monk.

Alec drove wearily up Park Road North. From a hundred yards away, he saw Nancy in her red coat come out on the pavement. He had to get closer before he recognised her companion. It was Myra's girl, and they were setting off somewhere.

Only yesterday, on his way to work, he'd seen Myra Laidlaw parking her car behind his in the side street.

'Hello, Alec,' she'd said as she'd hurried past. She was holding her head up. There was bounce in her step again.

His eyes had followed her up the entry. Myra had a bit of

437

go about her. She'd learned to drive Jack's car and run his café. It was nearly four years since he'd died, and she looked as though she was over him now.

Alec had always been fond of Myra. He drove into the side street and pulled up. Her car was ahead of his now.

It had shaken them all, Jack dying like that. He'd been a young man still. But Jack had been doing Alec down all his life. Letting him know he'd done better out of that business than the force had done for him.

He thought of Myra, and all the times he'd heard her and her daughter singing in their front room. He'd hated it. They always sounded as if they were having a better time than he was.

'Reaching for the moon, aren't they?' he'd sneered to Celia often enough. It was some comfort that Myra had failed to carve out a career for herself on the stage, but she'd always thought that girl of hers was going to do better.

He'd thought Fliss was going to be another non-starter when she'd been taken ill, but she'd been caterwauling again since she came out of hospital. He'd been home one dinnertime and heard her sing on the wireless. Nancy had raved about her success after that.

What really rankled was that Myra had been his girlfriend to start with. He'd seen her first, working at the Connaught Hotel when he'd been inspecting licensed premises. He'd stopped to talk to her, asked her out a few times. She'd been a handsome woman, big and busty. Damn it, she still was. There was a bit of life about Myra, she seemed to enjoy everything.

He should never have let Jack set eyes on her. He might have known he'd want her too. Jack had elbowed his way into her life, lured her away. The next thing Alec knew she was working down at the Refreshment Room and walking out with Jack.

He let himself think of Myra. He needed someone he could get his arms round. Someone with flesh on their bones to give him a bit of pleasure. Holding Celia was like holding a skeleton. Myra was a widow now. Things had changed for her. With Jack gone, perhaps she'd like a bit of comfort?

It was half past three. A good time to call on her and find out.

Alec got out of his car and went up the back entry, working out what he should say. Celia would have his dinner ready, but there was more than one sort of appetite to satisfy.

Myra's yard door opened easily to his touch. He had to bang twice on her back door before her face appeared round her living room curtains. He smiled at her and heard her footsteps coming through the kitchen.

'Hello, Alec.' She sounded surprised. She was wearing a bright blue dress that strained slightly across her chest, pushing her breasts up into soft curves. He couldn't take his eyes off them.

'I thought I should come and see how you are, Myra.'

'That's kind of you.' Her big eyes were blinking at him uncertainly, but she stood back for him to come in.

He eased his helmet off, placed it in the crook of his arm in the prescribed manner. It seemed too officious a stance. He put it down on her table. 'How are you managing?'

'As well as can be expected.'

She looked uneasy. He was afraid she'd take a lot of softening up before he was going to get anywhere. If only she'd offer him a cup of tea now. The kettle was on the stove, a teapot beside it under a cosy.

'Is there any way I can help? I should have done more for you.'

She was shaking her head. Her ginger hair stood up in a glorious halo round her face. 'I'm all right now, thanks.'

'Perhaps if Jack hadn't fallen out with me, had this silly feud . . .'

'It was your idea, Alec.'

'Jack thought . . .'

'Your idea, not Jack's. Anyway, that's long since over

and done. Amy and Paul are married,' Her breasts were rising and falling as she breathed. Magnificent breasts.

'I just wanted to say, I think we should forget it. Put it all behind us and be friends.'

'Good. Yes, agreed.'

He had the feeling she wanted him to go. He wasn't making himself clear at all.

She said: 'Nancy's been very kind. She's been round often since Fliss came home, and I can't tell you how grateful I am to Amy.'

Alec stepped forward and kissed her cheek.

'What's that for?' Her tone was sharper, suspicious. Her cheeks were suddenly running with colour.

'Just trying to be friendly, Myra. You need all the friends you can get now. I could make things easier for you. Take you out a bit. Cheer you up. You don't want to sit around on your own all day.'

He felt her recoil. 'You can cut that out, Alec Siddons. I can do without help of that sort, thank you.'

'Don't be hasty, Myra.'

'What makes you think I'd want anything to do with you?'

Alec smiled slowly. 'You've always had a soft spot for me. Why else would you have persuaded Jack to buy this house all those years ago?'

She laughed and it grated on his nerves. 'Jack bought it to please me, he thought it was what I wanted. But he was wrong, the last thing I wanted was to be close to you.'

Alec took a deep breath. 'You know how I've always felt about you. I've put you on a pedestal.'

'Stay away from me. Friendly is one thing, this is another. I'm not going to be your bit on the side.'

'I'll be patient.'

'I won't ever be ready, Alec. Not for you.'

Alec felt nonplussed. This wasn't going as he'd hoped. 'Think it over. You'll see the advantages. Give yourself time.'

'If you lay a finger on me, I'll go straight round to Celia.' There was a suspicious glitter about Myra's big eyes. Tearful rather than jolly.

Alec knew now he'd misjudged things. He told himself to keep calm and get out without losing face.

'Perhaps I am rushing things a bit,' he began.

Her temper snapped and she blazed out: 'I wouldn't let you near me if you were the last person in the world. You're off your head. Amy said you'd gone queer, and goodness knows what you're doing to poor Celia. Driving her into an early grave by the look of her.'

He was already backing off when he saw Winnie Cottie's wrinkled face come round the hall door. Suddenly, the blood was pounding in his head.

Her laugh cackled out. 'You at it again, Alec Siddons? You'll have poor Jack turning in his grave.'

'It was nothing like that.' He knew he was blustering. He grabbed his helmet and stepped back towards the door. Damn Winnie Cottie! Always where she wasn't wanted.

Rage caught in his throat, engulfing him. He burst out: 'That café was once my father's, it should have been mine by rights. But Jack took it as he took everything else. He ousted me from my rightful place. He owed me and he knew it.'

Myra's eyes were glittering with anger now.

'Jack gave in to you too easily. Gave you everything you asked for. He was always a soft touch, and don't think we didn't all know it. But that's over now. You should have known I'd want nothing to do with you.'

'You're a bitter man, Alec Siddons.' Winnie Cottie was edging closer, her hairnet pulled down across her forehead. 'I'm glad I was here to witness this. What an act you put on.'

Alec went out, slamming the door. He heard her shout: 'I'll get you for what you did to Randall. One day, I'll see you get your comeuppance. You're a rotter, and we all know it.'

He was almost running down the yard. His head was thumping as he let himself into his own kitchen. Celia had been sitting at the table staring into space.

'You're late today.' She jumped to her feet and rushed to the stove to dish up roast beef. Alec slumped on to a chair in the living room, the sweat heavy on his brow.

Alec had been sitting by the living room fire for the last two hours. He was still feeling shaky inside. He was worried. He knew now it had been a big mistake to approach Myra. He should have known he couldn't put the clock back. Now he was afraid she'd say something to Celia to make more trouble for him.

He should never have let that feud end. It would have kept the Laidlaws away from his family. But now Amy was married to one of them, and Celia and Nancy always round there. There was nothing he could do to keep them apart.

And as for Winnie Cottie, she'd hounded him for years. The woman was round the bend. She couldn't forget Randall. Over twenty years and it might have been yesterday.

It would only take a few words from Amy or Winnie Cottie. Or Myra for that matter. Myra's mouth was big enough. She had problems keeping it closed.

Suddenly, Alec pulled himself up on his chair. He told himself he was a fool to worry like this. Nobody would tell Celia anything. They knew it would upset her more than it would him. Even if they did, he'd be able to handle her.

He had to get his priorities right. Celia might not like him having other women but she'd get over it. It needn't make too much difference.

He could forget Winnie Cottie too. She was just a vindictive old woman. There was nothing she could do to harm him now.

His biggest danger could have come from Olive's death, but clearly detectives had turned up nothing useful from the neighbours. If they were not on his track now, they never would be. He'd been too clever for them. Surely he could feel safe from that now?

His main trouble once again was likely to come from being found out in some petty crime and being dismissed from the force.

Alec tried to make himself more comfortable on his chair, and the newspaper he'd brought home fell to the rug. There was nothing of interest in it. The news was all depressing: shortages of this and that, so many aircraft missing, or so many ships. The only good thing about the war was that the air raids had finished.

No, that wasn't quite true. War had opened up new ways of earning. He took his bank book out of his pocket. He kept it on him at all times. Didn't trust Celia not to go poking about for it if he left it in his drawer.

The pages were filling up, and he gloated for a moment on the total. If he'd had to rely on his wages, he'd never have saved money like this. He studied the figures carefully.

Over the last few months, he'd made more on the side than his police wage, and he had to work all the hours God sent for that. He was sick to death of it.

Hadn't he always promised himself he'd get out after twenty-five years? He'd been toying with the idea recently.

He felt his pulse quicken. He'd have his time in at the end of the month. Here was a way to end his worries about being dismissed. He could retire on pension. Not that it would be enough to live on, but it was too much to have snatched from him if he was dismissed for misbehaviour.

He'd not give them the chance to dismiss him. It was the obvious thing to do. After all, he wasn't going to get promotion. All the force gave him was work and worry.

He could start afresh. Branch out on his own. Be his own boss. If he couldn't make a go of it, he could get a job in security of some sort.

He'd already got his contacts. Police work had given him those. He was on good terms with lots of publicans, and they

443

were all doing good business. What other way was there to forget the purgatory of war? Impossible to buy booze in off-licences now, it all went to the pubs.

Publicans all had money. They wanted to buy decent food, petrol, luxuries of any sort, and they couldn't. But he could provide them in exchange for alcohol.

He knew all the market traders and several butchers. They wanted booze and would trade food for it. Alec felt he knew the black market inside out. He knew when and where to increase his own mark-up.

This way he'd have more time to do it. It wouldn't pin him down like police work. Wear him out so he had no energy for anything else. In future, he wouldn't just dabble. He could make a lot more money than he was doing now. When the war ended, he'd be rich.

It wasn't exactly legal, of course. But his customers wouldn't drop him in it, because they'd implicate themselves and their supply would dry up. It would be in their interests to keep their mouths shut about what he did for them.

Another thing, he ought to have some immunity from the police. They wouldn't immediately think of him as a black marketeer. He'd been one of them.

'Celia,' he called, 'the fire's going out. Fetch some more coal.'

She came in to get the scuttle, wiping red hands on her dirty apron. 'Aren't you going out today, Alec?'

'No.' Surely she could see he wasn't?

'We've got to go easy on the coal. There's not much left.' She was shabby, her carpet slippers were worn and spotted with grease.

'Celia,' he announced, 'I've decided to retire.' He could feel the adrenalin rushing through him.

'What do you mean?'

'What I say. Retire. Leave the force.'

She was screwing up her face. 'But what will we live on?'

'Don't you worry about that. Leave it to me.'

If it went well, he might be able to get her away from here before she heard more than she should. That would end all his worries.

'We might move house. Get something bigger.'

'What for, now the girls have grown up?'

'Something more comfortable.'

'Yes, Alec,' she said, going back to the kitchen.

He'd never need to work again. It would be like winning the pools. The more he pondered, the more he realised he'd been a fool not to think of it before.

He got up and took a bottle of whisky from his supply in the sideboard. Poured himself a stiff one. He drank it and poured another.

He'd do it. He was going to live without worry from now on. He got up and yanked the sideboard drawer open to find a writing pad. Then, he carefully wrote out his notice of retirement.

Tomorrow morning, he'd go up to Courtauld's office and hand it to him. Nothing would give him more pleasure.

CHAPTER TWENTY-SEVEN

Summer 1944

During her afternoon off, Nancy cycled up to see Mary Frampton. It was a long time since she'd been. Nancy knew she was the favourite Siddons sister there, as well as at home, but recently she hadn't been made quite so welcome.

Nancy thought she knew why. She'd seen letters for Katie pushed into the rack in the nurses' dining room. The Framptons did not like Katie attaching herself to Toby. They could be kind to her, even generous, but they did not want her in the family. Not after she'd had an illegitimate baby.

It had taken Katie some time to admit that Toby was writing to her. Only when she'd opened a letter in the coffee break and several snaps had fallen out. The girls on that table had passed them round and murmured their approval.

After that, Nancy heard about the day Katie had sheltered from a raid with him. She was still very guarded about what she did say.

'I am fond of him,' was as far as she would go.

'Fond of him, Katie?' Nancy had laughed, lifting her eyebrows. 'I'm fond of Toby, and I've known him longer than you have.'

Katie's face had lit up then. 'But not so well,' she'd grinned. 'You don't know him so well.'

'You know him well enough to know if it's serious. He came on leave last year and you spent every minute with him that you could.'

'How can I be sure?' Katie's smile had faded. Nancy

knew the affair with Jimmy had made her very cautious.

'If only I could see more of him. First, he was at Duxford, then near Glasgow, and now he's back near Cambridge and on daylight raids.' Nancy saw the longing in Katie's blue eyes, and had to shrug off her impatience.

'We're all in the same boat, Katie. I'd like to see more of Stan.'

She'd tried to tell Katie that Toby wouldn't give her a raw deal. But like anybody else, Toby could change his mind. Perhaps he hadn't even made it up yet.

Mary Frampton always asked her how Katie was when she visited, but Nancy sensed strain.

When she rang the bell, Mary Frampton took a long time to come to the door. As soon as she saw her face, Nancy knew something was terribly wrong.

'Oh Nancy! I'm glad you've come.' Mary Frampton's eyes were red. She was clinging to her as soon as she'd closed the door, desperate for comfort. 'It's Toby.'

'What's happened?'

'We've had a telegram. It came yesterday. Missing. Presumed killed.'

Nancy felt the blood drain from her. There was ice in her stomach. She couldn't bear to think of Toby being dead. She took the older woman into the sitting room and collapsed beside her on to a sofa.

'Poor Toby! Such a terrible waste of life.'

She was biting her lips, struggling to control her tears. Mary was mopping her eyes again.

They'd all known this could happen, but it didn't make it any easier to bear now it had. Nancy was filled with anguish. She saw Toby's face before her; sensitive grey eyes, the deep cleft in his chin, his hair streaked with gold. He was too young to die.

'Only presumed killed?' her voice croaked.

'His plane was shot down over Germany. Dusseldorf.' Mary Frampton's voice was little more than a whisper.

'When?'

'Last week, Tuesday. We got a letter this morning from a friend of his who was on the same raid. He saw smoke coming from Toby's plane after it was hit. Then he saw the tail burst into flames and some of the crew bale out. He said at least three parachutes.'

'Then there's still hope,' Nancy insisted. She shivered as she realised she'd have to tell Katie, and what this would mean for her.

'He'd flown twenty-six daylight ops. This was his twenty-seventh.' His mother let out a long-drawn-out sigh. 'I've been so afraid it would happen. He was looking forward to doing his thirty and getting leave again.

'I know he managed to get his thirty in last time, but to do it the second time round . . . We all know hardly any of them manage it. I knew the odds were he'd get shot down first.'

'That was in the early months of the war,' Nancy said. 'The odds are better now.'

'What do the odds matter?' Mary Frampton sounded irritated. 'It's happened to Toby now.'

Nancy knew the odds still mattered to Amy, and to Auntie My and Fliss.

'I told you about Paul, Amy's husband? He got his wings in Canada. He's come back as a sergeant pilot. He's been posted to Mildenhall, not far from where Toby was. He's in bombers too.

'I had a letter from Amy the other day. She managed to get a weekend to coincide with his. They spent it together in London, and according to Amy had a whale of a time. Paul had flown six missions then.'

It was a long time before the older woman spoke.

'How is Amy?' She sighed. 'Such a strong-minded girl.'

'Enjoying herself, I think.' Nancy had to stamp down on the twinge of envy she felt. 'She says everything is going well for her and Paul.'

Nancy sighed. Things were not going well for her. How

many times had she wished she'd married Stan when she had the chance? She wished she'd joined the army with Amy when she'd had the chance. Now she was stuck at home because she was afraid to leave Mam there alone.

She was worried about Pa. His police helmet no longer dominated their hall. She daren't talk about it. The back bedroom Amy and Kate had once shared was now stacked high with cartons and boxes, and Pa had put a lock on the door.

It was only too obvious what he was doing. Mam said she'd seen him taking fur coats up there. Pa was dealing in black-market goods.

When she was leaving, Mrs Frampton said: 'You'll let Katie know?'

Nancy nodded, feeling quite sick at the prospect. She cycled home through drizzle, trying to decide how best to do it.

Katie hardly ever came home now. She wouldn't come over the step if she knew Pa was home. Today, she'd had an afternoon off, and had taken Mam into town.

She would see her as they were both going on duty at five, but she couldn't tell her then. Better if she waited until eight o'clock, so Katie would have a little time to herself.

She walked up to Ashville with her, heavy with the awful news. Though she'd meant to wait until they'd reached the privacy of Katie's room, she couldn't keep it to herself any longer.

Kate stared ahead, her face desolate, her pace never faltering. Her anguish was only too obvious.

'I should have had more sense than to fall in love with him.'

'He might still be alive. One of those parachutes might have been his.' Nancy knew the best Katie could hope for was that Toby would be a prisoner of war too.

Nancy didn't linger over her hospital supper. She ran down

to the cloakroom to get the *Picture Post* magazines that Mary Frampton always saved for her.

She meant to give them to Jim Whittle, who she knew would have been admitted to Ward 5 this afternoon. She wanted to pop in to say hello to him.

She was seeing more of Stan's parents. Going round to their house seemed one way of keeping in touch with Stan. Mostly they talked about him, but nobody had had news of him for a long time.

She'd had two letters from him after he'd been captured, through the Red Cross. So at least she knew for certain that he was a prisoner.

She wrote to him almost as often as she used to, and sent him parcels, but there was no way of knowing whether he received them.

As she hurried down the ward she could see Jim Whittle at the far end, sitting up in bed wearing new striped flannelette pyjamas. He looked unfamiliar and ill at ease.

Everybody told her Stan was like him, but she couldn't see it, not with Jim's grey hair and thin lined face. She bent to kiss his cheek.

'Good news from North Africa,' she said, letting her pleasure in that bubble out. The tide of war had changed again. The Afrika Korps was now in full retreat after being defeated at El Alamein, and the Allies were getting the upper hand.

'I don't suppose you've heard anything more from Stan?'

They always asked each other that. Nancy shook her head.

'He wouldn't be able to tell you much if you did get a letter. Everything's heavily censored. They wouldn't let him tell you what a rotten place he's in.'

'Or even where it is exactly,' Nancy said.

'I wondered if you'd come up to see me tonight.'

'You should have known I'd want to wish you well for tomorrow, though I'm sure you'll be all right. It isn't a big job.'

Jim Whittle was having an operation on his foot. A wall had collapsed on it while he'd been on warden duty, some time ago, and it hadn't been right since.

'Not for that, Nancy,' he said. 'It's your birthday tomorrow. Ethel's got a little gift for you. She was afraid I'd forget it if I left it till tomorrow.'

He rummaged in his locker and brought out a small parcel. 'Happy birthday. How old will you be?'

'Twenty-nine,' she laughed. 'Getting on a bit now, aren't I? I'll be an old maid if Stan doesn't get home soon. Lovely, can I open it now?'

'Not until tomorrow,' he said, pretending to be severe.

'It's very sweet of you both. To think of me at a time like this. It's hard to find presents of any sort.'

'Nancy, we're very fond of you. While Stan isn't here to do it, we think we should.'

Nancy tried to smile her thanks. The Whittle family had always been kind to her. She noticed then that the first visitors were coming into the ward.

'Goodness, is it that time? I must go back on duty. Is Ethel coming to see you tonight?'

'No, she's afraid to be out in the blackout, she's leaving it until tomorrow. But a cousin of hers is down from Glasgow and said he'd come in. I haven't seen him for years, so we'll have plenty of catching up to do.'

'I'll have to run. See you again soon.' She kissed his cheek. 'Don't worry about a thing.'

A moment later, his visitor was pulling out the chair to sit by his bed. 'You're on very friendly terms with the nurses, Jim.'

'Not all of them. That was Nancy, our Stan's fiancée.'

'A pretty girl.' Victor Smith was watching her walk rapidly down the ward.

A few moments earlier, he'd paused in the ward doorway, and let his gaze go from bed to bed as he sought Jim. The staff nurse laughing with him had caught his eye.

451

'It's her birthday tomorrow,' Jim said. 'She'll be twenty-nine. Ethel has saved some chocolate for her.'

That made Vic sit straighter in his chair. The name Nancy had struck a chord. Celia had taken out an affiliation order on him and he'd had to pay it all through the last war. He'd evaded it as soon as he could because he couldn't afford it, but he wasn't proud of doing that. What was the date tomorrow? It couldn't be just a coincidence . . . or could it?

'Your Stan will do well for himself there.'

'Nancy's a lovely girl. Always happy.'

His curiosity was suddenly raging. He had to know. 'She's got a bit of style. From a decent family by the look of her. From around here, is she?'

'Yes. Her father was a policeman. No, wait a minute, he's her stepfather. Celia was married before.'

Victor felt fire run through him.

Nancy was following the progress of the war closely.

The Axis was defeated in North Africa, and the invasion of Italy had begun, though progress there was painfully slow. At first, Nancy had been hopeful that camps of British prisoners would be overrun and Stan would be freed.

Six months later, she had another letter from him via the Red Cross. She was thrilled to have proof that he was still alive and well, but she learned he'd been sent with other prisoners of war to Germany.

He told her he was receiving some of her letters, and how much they meant to him. It made her write more often. She became resigned to the waiting and the monotony of life at home.

Everybody seemed to be suffering from war-weariness now. People were having to cope with ever-reducing rations and shortages of every sort.

She felt guilty when anybody complained of shortages. Pa was producing plenty of everything for the larder. She knew he feasted on the fat of the land and went short of nothing.

Mam seemed to eat little and was growing more strange.

Nancy continued to eat most of her meals at the hospital, but it didn't stop her feeling deep shame that Pa was cheating. That he was growing rich on the black market while others had to make do and mend. She was terrified he'd be caught. Then her shame would become public knowledge. She tried to keep her mind on more cheerful things, and even now there were plenty of those.

After four months of uncertainty, she received a note from Mary Frampton saying they'd heard that Toby had parachuted to safety and was also a prisoner of war. It wasn't lost upon her that she'd written to her and not to Katie.

Nancy had come home at five for her evening off. Before taking off her coat, she ran down to the box near the station to telephone.

'Such wonderful news, Mrs Frampton. I'm so glad.'

Mary Frampton sounded over the moon. 'A letter from the Red Cross. Just that he's alive and well.'

'Do you have an address where we can write to him?' Nancy asked. She knew Katie would want that.

Katie hadn't mentioned Toby through all the months of uncertainty. Nancy thought she was bottling things up, showing too little emotion.

She went down to the hospital at eight o'clock to meet Katie as she came off duty, pleased to have such good news for her.

Katie couldn't stop smiling. 'It's such a relief knowing for certain he's alive,' she exulted. 'You don't know the joy that brings. At least now I can hope he'll come back one day.'

She was so transparently delighted at the news, it made Nancy feel she was moaning too much about Stan's lot.

Katie had completed her three years' training and was now state registered and working as a staff nurse.

Nancy could also rejoice with Auntie My about Fliss. She'd been taken on by Yves' agent and was getting regular work. She was nineteen now and looking the picture of health, dancing on stage with tremendous vim and vigour. Success was making her more confident, and putting a polish on her act. Fliss was good news all the way. Nancy made a point of seeing every show she was in.

Auntie My also revelled in Paul's success. He'd flown his thirty raids on Germany. Amy had written that he'd been given fourteen days' leave after that, and she'd managed to get time off too.

'It was one big celebration. Paul's got a commission now, and been posted to a training base. It's near enough for us to meet from time to time.'

But the next time Amy wrote she told Nancy she was now serving with a mobile field hospital somewhere in southern England. She said they had their own transport, tents, electricity generators, operating theatre and X-ray equipment.

D-Day came, and brought Nancy a tremendous lift. It made victory seem closer. At the time she hadn't realised that Amy had gone over to Normandy a few days later, and was right behind the front line.

Gradually the Allied armies advanced across northern France and into Germany. Nancy felt that soon, with just a little more waiting, Stan and Toby would be liberated and able to return home.

CHAPTER TWENTY-EIGHT

Summer 1945

For Nancy, the end for which she'd waited so long came suddenly. A week before peace was actually signed, she had a telegram from Stan announcing that he was back in England.

At the station, he'd thrown his arms round her, as full of excitement at their reunion as she was. Nancy was overjoyed. This time, Stan was not exhausted as he had been after Dunkirk.

He'd been kept waiting too, deprived of his freedom and the good things in life. He meant to enjoy himself now, and he wanted to be married as soon as possible. Nancy thought he looked a little older, more mature, and as brown as a berry.

'I've had nothing else to do but sit in the sun,' he told her. 'It was hot there.'

When he smiled, which was often, his teeth seemed whiter and stronger by comparison. His brown hair was several shades lighter, his moustache almost sandy and his eyebrows, lashes and the hairs on his arms were bleached to gold.

'Wonderful to have you home so quickly.' Nancy hugged him.

'We were liberated by the Red Army. Took us all by surprise, I can tell you. They told us to make our way to Odessa, where we'd be able to catch a boat to England. We walked, it took us three days. The boat was an old tramp steamer, but none of us cared about that.'

Nancy was determined to forget her worries about Mam. Her turn for happiness had come at last and this time she was going to grab at it.

Victory in Europe was declared. Church bells rang out and everybody pulled down their blackout curtains. The celebrations started, flags and streamers appeared everywhere. Decorations were improvised from anything red, white and blue that could be put together. Welcome home notices appeared in windows.

Street parties were arranged for the official day. Not in Park Road North, but all the side streets were having them. Nancy was told she'd be welcome at four of them. There were huge celebrations in the hospital.

Nancy gloried in the fact that Stan was here to enjoy it all with her. It really seemed her bad times were over.

Paul came home on leave, looking fit and well, but Amy was still in Germany with her mobile field hospital, and couldn't make it.

Nancy persuaded Mam to make a sponge cake and some jellies for the Morely Avenue party, and then took her there. Fliss played her accordion and sang. She told Nancy she'd sung at every party from Bray Street to Asquith Avenue.

It was late when people started going indoors to their beds. Stan kissed Nancy goodbye before walking up to Haldane Avenue on his own. Nancy took her mother indoors and made a cup of tea in the kitchen.

'I suppose you'll be wanting to get married now?' Mam asked her, wiping down the draining board while she waited for the tea to brew.

'Golly, yes. We won't let the chance slip through our fingers again. We were fools not to do it before the war. We'd have been married for nearly six years by now.' Nancy knew that would have brought her comfort in the dark days. 'Think of the time we've wasted.'

'Stan would still have been captured.'

'Yes. But now you can put on the wedding at last.

Everything you planned for me all those years ago.'

Nancy saw her mother staring at her, moistening her lips. The party spirit hadn't touched her all day, and now she looked haunted. 'You still want that?'

'Why not? We've got the dresses and wedding cake ready and waiting. Might as well use them. It's not that easy to get anything else right now.' Nancy felt on cloud nine. She wasn't going to let anything spoil this for her.

'I'm so happy, Mam, things are going my way at last. I'll have to let everybody know. It mightn't be easy for them to get leave on the spur of the moment.'

'You'll be asking the same people?'

Nancy laughed outright, as joy bubbled through her. 'Everything comes to she who waits. I do hope Amy will be able to get leave.'

'That list of guests you had . . . You won't want all of them, not now?'

'Mam, they won't all be alive now, will they? Not after six years of war.'

'But if they are?'

'I expect so. Who do you want to ask?'

Her mother shook her head numbly. 'I don't know.'

The following day, Nancy and Stan fixed the date of their wedding by finding out when the vicar could manage it and the church hall would be free. June the first was the day they decided on. Nancy was laughing with excitement at the prospect.

She was caught up then in a flurry of outings with Stan and last-minute preparations for their wedding. She continued to go to work. Stan didn't know yet when he'd be demobbed. It might take several months.

Pa seemed to be spending more time in the living room drinking whisky than he used to. Nancy didn't want to have black-market food at her wedding, so she made no move to involve him in the preparations.

She considered Auntie My to be the catering expert and

went to her for advice. As the reception was to be held in the church hall where there were few facilities, Myra had advised finger food. She'd suggested it would be easier to make at home or in the Refreshment Room kitchen, leaving only the setting out on the table to be done there.

Nancy had an afternoon off duty. She walked home quickly, in order to change and meet Stan. Matron had agreed to give her two weeks' holiday, and she was still feeling little shivers of excitement every time she thought of her wedding.

She noticed the car standing outside her home as she walked up. As she drew closer, she recognised it as Bill Frampton's and quickened her step. He wouldn't call there unless he had very good reason. She wondered if it could be that Toby had come home.

Fifty yards nearer, and she could see that it was actually Toby on the doorstep. That gave her another burst of excitement and she broke into a run. Her father's voice carried down the road.

'She doesn't live here any more. Don't come bothering me. Kate doesn't come near us. Haven't seen her in years and don't want to.'

'Toby?' Nancy called. He turned and swept her into a bear hug. 'I'm so thrilled to see you back home.'

'I thought it was Kate you were asking for,' Pa said irritably and slammed the door.

'It was.' Toby laughed.

'Pa gets more like Hitler every day.' She laughed with him.

'Thank goodness you came home then. How do I get in touch with Katie? I didn't feel I could march into the hospital and demand her whereabouts from the first person I met.'

'She's just come off duty with me. She'll probably be walking up to Ashville now.' Nancy waved towards the car. 'We could catch her up.'

'Wonderful.' He added diffidently: 'By the way, there isn't . . . ? I mean, Katie hasn't . . . ?'

'She hasn't got another boyfriend, if that's what you're asking. There hasn't been anyone else.'

His grin broadened. 'How is she?'

'Fine, apart from being envious. Stan's been home a week. What kept you? She's been wondering.'

'Had to wait longer to be liberated. Some folks are luckier than others.'

They turned right into the road through the park and passed the group of nurses halfway up. Toby jerked the car to a stop and leapt out on the pavement in front of them. By the time Nancy got out, he was swinging Katie off her feet in another bear hug.

Nancy hadn't seen her look so happy for a long time.

Toby was waiting in the car outside the gates of Ashville. Katie had asked for five minutes to get out of her uniform. He'd driven Nancy back home, because she too was in a hurry to change and meet Stan.

He pushed his hair back from his forehead. Coming home had been a more emotional experience than he'd expected. From Germany, England had looked like the promised land. His mother had wept.

'Tears of joy,' she'd choked, but they were no less heart-wringing for that.

Last night, his father had said to him: 'What will you do now?'

'Try to pick up where I left off. Can I come back to the office?'

'You know I'll be more than glad, Toby. What I've always wanted is to see you and James running the firm. I'm past retirement age, I'll be happy to hand over to you two as soon as you're ready.'

His father was looking older, his face more drawn. The war years had not been kind to him. His hair was snowy-white now, though no less thick.

Toby couldn't bring himself to ask about Katie, but he

459

wanted news of her. He made it sound a more general enquiry. 'How are the Siddons girls?'

'Nancy keeps in touch. Did you know Amy went over to France just after D-Day with a mobile field hospital? She followed the troops right into Germany.'

He had to ask directly after all. 'And Katie?'

'She's qualified now, like her sisters.'

Bill was obviously uneasy. The light glinted on his horn-rimmed spectacles. He said: 'About that argument we had. The night you were leaving for Duxford.'

Toby remembered it well, he'd had plenty of time to ponder on it.

'You were going to report Constable Siddons? What happened?' There had been no mention of any resulting scandal in the letters he'd received from Katie.

His father looked embarrassed. 'I never did tell any-body . . . about what we saw him doing. Couldn't bring myself . . . It was your last night at home and you'd asked me not to.'

'Nancy wouldn't have been pleased if you had, nor Amy. You'd have felt bad about that.'

'I felt bad because I failed to do what I saw as my clear duty,' he retorted. 'It helped when Alec Siddons retired from the force.'

'He retired? With character intact?'

'Yes. A year or so later.'

'He was lucky you kept quiet.'

'Once he'd left the police I felt better about it.'

'What is he doing now?'

'According to Nancy, he's living on his pension.'

Toby had pondered this. 'You said you didn't want to be associated with the family, but you've kept in touch with Nancy.'

'Your mother . . .'

'The Siddons girls have done their bit for their country. You can't say they haven't. You're fond of Nancy, and you

460

said you were grateful for what Amy did for Mum.'

Toby wanted to say that they'd learn to love Katie too, but he couldn't talk about that until he'd seen her again. What he hoped for might not be what she wanted. Three years was a long time to keep a girl waiting, particularly when they'd had so little contact.

Toby drove into the park, but it was too sunny a day to sit in a car. Now he looked at the girl walking beside him. She was almost as tall as he was, reed-slender and wearing a pretty summer print dress. Her face was even more beautiful than he remembered.

In his German prison, he'd imagined this moment a thousand times. Thinking about Katie had been his main source of pleasure, and he'd had plenty of time for thinking over the last years.

He'd been excited about meeting her again but a little nervous too, only half trusting his own memory. Now he saw the sun lightening her dark curly hair with bronze, he was quite sure she was the right girl for him. He knew he'd be happy with her for the rest of his life.

What he didn't know was how she felt about him. He was still uneasy about that. She wasn't quite as he remembered.

'You've changed, Katie.' She was more in command of herself. More confident.

'It's over three years since you last saw me. Of course I've changed, we both have. A lot has happened to us.'

'Things were slow where I've been.' He smiled. 'Tell me what's happened to you.'

It took her a long time to reply. 'I needed those years. To get over what happened. To put it all behind me.'

He felt for her hand. 'You've not put everything behind you?'

The midnight blue eyes fastened on his, as though understanding his need for reassurance that she hadn't grown away from him.

461

'Only the bad things. I've learned to forget them. I've been growing up, Toby.'

'Thank you for writing. Your letters meant everything to me. I lived for them. I had nothing else.'

'I wanted to.' They'd reached the lake in the upper park. The sun was glinting on the water, the covered Chinese bridge looked romantic. Toby made a move to sit on the bench overlooking the lake.

He saw her hesitate. 'Would you rather sit on the grass?'

'No.' She smiled, throwing herself down on the bench. 'Just scotching another ghost from my past.'

Toby bent across to kiss her. 'We need to get to know each other again,' he said, but he knew the old magic was there for him. He was almost certain from the way she returned his kiss that it was for Katie too.

For Nancy, everything seemed to be happening at once.

The day before the wedding, she and Stan went down to the café to make last-minute arrangements with Auntie My. While they were there, Amy came across from the train.

Nancy looked up to see Amy pause at the door in her khaki battledress. She seemed to have a new confidence. She caught sight of them and her dark blue eyes sparkled with excitement. Then, with a whoop, she came charging across to hug her sister.

'We're all proud of you, Amy, going to France.'

'Auntie My?' Amy was hugging her. 'Paul isn't home yet?'

'You've beaten him to it. His train's due in at eleven tonight.'

'Stan, lovely to see you so fit and well. At one time, I thought I might get close enough to see you liberated.'

'I was much further east.'

'Weren't you frightened, Amy?'

'Terrified at times.'

'You went over on D-Day?' Vera wanted to know.

'A few days later, there were other nurses there before me.'

'But on landing craft?'

'Yes, over the side down a scrambling net to a launch. Didn't like that much. The sea was pretty rough.'

'Oh Amy, you are brave. Then what happened?'

'We set off inland in the back of an open lorry. There were thousands of troops, tanks, vehicles of all sorts, the hardware of war. The skies were filled with Allied planes taking off in clouds of dust from makeshift runways.'

'And I missed all that,' Stan mourned. 'Cooped up, doing nothing all day.'

'But a hospital of tents?' Nancy couldn't envisage such a thing.

'We lived in tents too, and it took a bit of getting used to.' Amy laughed. 'We took the worst cases from army casualty clearing stations prior to sending them home.

'Complicated operations were carried out in the most primitive conditions. Dreadful burns. I'm surprised so many survived.'

'What did you do for them?'

'Gave them injections of morphine, intravenous drips, penicillin. Then they were flown home from improvised airstrips. We looked after wounded Germans too. Sometimes the Tommies grew agitated at finding Germans next to them.

'We used primus stoves for sterilising dressing bowls and heating drinks, positively archaic. We had no running water, hygiene was almost a luxury.'

They were all staring at Amy in wonder. She had been in the thick of the fighting.

'I'm thrilled for you, Nancy,' she said. 'Your turn at last. You've got everything organised?'

Nancy smiled. 'There's still lots to do.'

'Nancy's beginning to feel overwhelmed,' Stan told her.

'Can I help?' Amy asked.

'Come and help Stan and me sort out the church hall. There's lots to do there.'

While Amy dropped her bag off at Auntie My's, Nancy popped in to see how Katie and Mam were getting on.

She'd taken Katie aside last week and said: 'I'd like you to go home a bit more. Mam sees nothing of you.'

Katie had looked troubled. 'Pa sent me packing last time I put my head round the door.'

'Yes, but someone needs to keep an eye on Mam while I'm away. She's not managing very well, and she'd welcome a hand from time to time. Pa's horrible to her too.'

Nancy found Katie helping Mam with her baking. They had several sorts of cake cooling on racks.

'Are these for the reception?' Nancy asked doubtfully. Her mother had not offered to help.

'For the party here,' she said. 'Afterwards.'

'Are you still having that?' It surprised Nancy. 'You didn't say.'

'Pa said.' Her mother was looking at her with clouded eyes.

She'd known Pa had been thinking of it all those years ago, but he and Mam had become almost recluses since then. They never invited people in and rarely went out. With rationing getting stricter, weddings had become simpler and parties fewer.

'Pa's brought a nice ham,' Mam said. 'I'm boiling it now to make sandwiches, and he's got two firkins of beer, one for the church hall and one to stay here.'

'I thought he'd dropped the idea.' Nancy was afraid Mam would be exhausted by the ceremony and the party in the church hall. She couldn't see Pa welcoming anybody here.

'He's doing it for you, Nancy.'

She frowned. 'I'll be gone, Mam. We want to catch the five o'clock train.'

Katie looked surprised too. 'I thought these cakes were for the church hall,' she whispered.

'Come up there with us now,' Nancy urged. She walked up arm in arm with Stan, listening to Amy and Katie talking behind her. The door of the church hall was already open when they arrived. Winnie Cottie was there, sweeping it through.

'I know you want it to be nice, Nancy,' she said. 'And the youth club never clean up after themselves.'

Nancy knew Winnie had appointed herself in charge of the hall. She spent her Thursday afternoons here helping with the pensioners; making and serving them tea, though many were younger than she.

It took them more than an hour to put up trestle tables and spread sheets on them because Mam didn't have large enough tablecloths. They set out glasses and cups and saucers and made sure the urn in the kitchen was working.

That night, though Celia's head was swimming, she went on rolling pastry at the kitchen table. She needed to get the steak and mushroom pies made tonight.

The kitchen was hot and fragrant with the scent of newly baked sausage rolls. The last batch was in the oven now. It was late and Nancy had gone to bed. She'd been so excited, so full of high spirits that Celia felt she could take no more of her, not when she felt so frightened herself.

She could feel her gut twisting now. She'd asked Nancy half a dozen times exactly who was being invited to her wedding. She'd asked Stan the last three times he'd come over the threshold.

'We haven't had time to send out formal invitations,' he'd grinned. 'It's by word of mouth this time. We aren't going to worry too much about who comes.'

'Stan hasn't seen his relatives for years.' Nancy had smiled up at him. 'They're all inviting us round now he's back, and we're just asking them to come.'

'And my mother's seeing to the rest,' Stan had added.

'But we need to know,' Celia had insisted, pushing her

thinning hair from her forehead. She needed to know most desperately. 'The numbers . . . How much food . . . ?'

She wanted Victor Smith to be dead. More than anything in the world she wanted that. Since she'd seen his name on the first guest list all those years ago, she'd been praying he'd been killed in the blitz, anything. The dread that he had not was growing.

'We have made a list of those we've asked,' Stan had said easily, earlier this evening. He'd taken it from his pocket to study it. 'Can you think of anybody we've forgotten?'

The blood had been pounding in her head, and she'd wanted to snatch it from him. 'Is it the same as that first one?' she'd demanded.

'More or less. My grandmother's no longer with us, and you remember my Auntie Sis was killed in a raid? Then two of my cousins were killed in France.'

'The rest?' she'd asked breathlessly.

'A few changes. Nancy's asked a lot of nurses from the hospital. I've lost touch with some of the friends I had before the war. Bert was killed in the Atlantic. Do you remember Bert Hansell?'

He was offering the list to her. Celia clawed for it, looking for the name she dreaded. It was there, leaping off the page at her. Victor Smith.

Celia felt the room spin round her. She'd told herself time and time again that there must be hundreds of Victor Smiths about. Thousands. That it probably wasn't him at all. Even if it was, he'd never recognise her after all this time, of course he wouldn't. And he'd never seen Nancy. What was she worrying about? She had to calm down.

She was going to make four big steak and mushroom pies and then go to bed. She was spooning the meat mixture on to the pastry when she heard Alec's footsteps coming up the yard.

It made her drop the pan on the table and bend over it in consternation. Her hands were shaking again. She put them

466

behind her. Alec mustn't see them.

He stood at the door surveying her preparations for the wedding feast. She saw the tide of red seep up his neck and flood his face.

'Where's my supper?' he thundered. 'For God's sake, Celia, what's the matter with you?'

'I forgot!'

'Bloody hell. How can you forget that?'

She was panting. 'I never know what time you'll be home now . . .'

'I told you I'd be home about midnight,' Alec retorted. 'I don't work set hours any more. I always tell you. You remembered last night.'

It always churned her up to see him lose his temper.

'You can have sausage rolls . . .'

'I need a decent meal. I've been out working since lunchtime.'

'The steak and mushroom pie won't be long.'

Suddenly Alec was sniffing: 'Can I smell something burning?'

'Oh!' she gasped and rushed round him to the oven. 'Just in time.' She pulled out the last of the sausage rolls. They were almost black.

'You've burnt them. Nobody can eat those.' There was disgust in his voice.

Celia had burned her finger. 'They'll be all right,' she said, sucking it.

'For heaven's sake! I brought home a T-bone steak for my dinner. And some mushrooms to go with it.'

Celia felt herself sway again. She'd put all the mushrooms he'd brought into the pie mixture.

'It won't take me a minute,' she said, trying to keep the sound of tears out of her voice. She rushed to the living room, but couldn't think why she'd gone there. The fire had gone out. She went back.

'Steak with mushrooms and chips. Damn it, it isn't asking

467

much that you cook the odd meal for me.'

She found the steak in the larder and put it out on the grill pan.

'Good God, haven't you done the first thing towards it?' Alec exploded. 'What have you been doing all day?'

She'd fallen asleep earlier in the evening, but she couldn't tell him that. Nancy had woken her when she'd come in.

'The wedding . . .'

'You can leave all that to Nancy.'

'But you told me you wanted a spread put on here.' Celia couldn't cope with Alec when he was like this. She couldn't even think straight.

'Just a few sandwiches, but they can wait till tomorrow.' He was biting into one of her better sausage rolls. 'You need to keep your mind on what you're doing, Celia.'

'There's been so many people here. Coming and going, about the wedding.'

'Who?' he was asking suspiciously.

'Katie came.' She remembered that Katie had come to help. 'Amy's home for the wedding too.'

'You shouldn't let them worry you. Show them the door if they're getting you down. Was there someone else?'

'Myra came round this morning . . .'

'What the hell did she want?'

'She asked if I'd like to work a few hours at the Refreshment Room.'

'Bloody hell, woman, you can't cope here. How would you manage to go out to work as well?'

The steak was cooked. She had nothing to go with it but bread. She slid it on a plate.

'This is it then?' Alec sat down in front of it. 'I was looking forward to a decent meal.' He started to eat.

'I'm sorry, I'm tired . . .'

'I'm not surprised. It's nearly one. Put those blasted pies away until tomorrow.'

'I can't now. They have to cook.'

'Get yourself up to bed, woman. I'll be up myself soon and I want to sleep. I won't be able to if you're down here banging away.'

Celia turned off her oven and felt the tears roll down her face. She cried for herself and for what she'd done all those years ago. There seemed no end to her troubles. She was afraid there never would be.

CHAPTER TWENTY-NINE

Nancy was up early on her wedding morning. She'd only been in the kitchen a few minutes when Katie knocked on the kitchen window to be let in. Amy and Paul came across from Auntie My's a few minutes later. Mam got up to help as soon as she heard them. There was hardly room for them all in the narrow kitchen.

'It's a long time since I've seen so much food,' Nancy said as they all set to, cutting bread and making ham sandwiches.

'Where's Pa?' Katie wanted to know.

'Hopefully he'll stay in bed a bit longer,' Nancy said, knowing they'd all be relieved if he did. But he came down half an hour later.

'I'll have some breakfast,' he announced from the kitchen door. 'Egg and bacon.'

'Not now,' Amy said, as Mam made a move towards the frying pan. 'We're busy, Pa.'

'It had better be soon,' he grunted. They saw him go into the living room, heard the chink of glass from the sideboard.

Nancy was filling the kettle. 'I'll make tea and toast for him. He's getting out his whisky and I want him sober at twelve o'clock.'

Mam lit the living room fire for him. He stayed by it, complaining that he hadn't had a decent breakfast. By the time Auntie My came round with her car to help them transport the food to the hall, Pa was calling for more toast.

Nancy thought Mam seemed all of a dither, confused

between which plates of food were to stay at home and which were to go to the church hall.

'We'll have to leave you and Pa to get organised here,' she told her. 'We need to go up to the hall with Auntie My and get the food set out. Come on,' she said to her sisters.

Auntie My's contribution of canapés, pork pies, and Scotch eggs was spread on great wooden trays. She'd brought Winnie Cottie with her, and together they carried the food in. Auntie My had to go back to the café, but Winnie stayed to help them set it out.

Nancy had to leave before they'd finished. She was going to the hairdresser's. She went home to fetch Mam to go with her.

Pa was in the front room opening up the wind-up gramophone and stacking the records alongside. He lowered the needle and a rather scratchy record of 'Lily of Laguna' began to play.

'Get this carpet rolled up, Nancy,' he said to her.

She surveyed the carpet square with its bright geometric pattern. Heavy furniture was anchoring it to the floor. 'What for?'

'So you can dance.'

'Pa, I don't think anybody will want to dance here. Who have you asked?'

'Open house, anyone who wants to come. Except those Laidlaws, I don't want them here.' He hiccupped. 'Nor Winnie Cottie.'

'I think you should leave the carpet down.'

'That means you don't want to help,' he said, turning to glower at her.

'I'm due at the hairdresser's, Pa. And so is Mam.'

The Morrison shelter from the living room had been dismantled, and was stacked in the back yard. The old table had been brought back and was covered with their best white cloth. Mam was setting out plates of food.

Nancy put two ham rolls on a plate and offered them to

471

her father. 'You'll feel better if you eat something,' she said. Then she grabbed Mam's hat and coat from the hall stand, helped her into them, and hustled her out into the yard.

The last hours seemed to be passing too quickly. By the time they got home again, it was time to start dressing.

She'd left her wedding finery hanging on the wardrobe door in her bedroom. Her suitcases were packed ready to go on honeymoon. They'd decided on Llandudno and Stan had booked a room in a small hotel.

Amy and Kate were waiting for her, already changed.

'How do we look?' Amy asked, twirling in the gloom of the landing.

Nancy smiled. They both looked slender in their peach taffeta bridesmaid's dresses. She wasn't sure she'd have chosen the sweetheart necklines and puffed sleeves this year; her taste had changed. The style suited Katie better than it did Amy.

'The artificial flowers have survived their years in the box well.' Amy was beaming at her. They wore them on hair bands. Amy's hair rippled dark and loose down her back, Katie's curled up round her head.

They both tried to help her dress, but there wasn't room for three in her tiny room, so Amy left to make sure Mam was getting ready.

Nancy took a look in her mirror. The ivory satin felt cool and luxurious. The style she'd chosen years before was still right for her. A cap of pearls kept her veil in place. She had no bouquet – flowers were difficult to buy. Instead, Auntie My had loaned her a little case of ivory leather holding hymn and prayer books.

Katie had made small posies for the bridesmaids from paper doilies and a bunch of roses and sweet peas Toby had brought from the Frampton garden.

Nancy lifted her skirts and went downstairs. Pa was still in the front room, playing his gramophone. She'd heard it scratching out tunes popular more than twenty years ago.

Songs from the First World War. Nancy remembered them all from her childhood.

Amy was pinning Pa's buttonhole into the lapel of his best grey suit. They were all ready when the doorbell rang.

'Are you going to drive us to the church, Pa?' Nancy had asked him a couple of days ago.

'Drive you? It isn't far. Hardly worth getting the car out. There's no disgrace in walking to your wedding. Not now there's such a shortage of petrol. Lots of brides do it.'

So Stan had put it to his father, who had offered to run Mam and her sisters to the church to protect their hair and wedding finery from the weather. Then he was going to return for her and Pa.

'You're getting a good do, like we promised,' Pa said, his aggression forgotten. 'Your mam sets great store by weddings. Amy did her out of all this by getting married on the spur of the moment. And marrying one of *them*.'

'I hope everything will be all right.'

'Of course it will. Aren't I doing my best for you?'

'Yes, Pa.' She thought his grin seemed a little foolish and wondered how much whisky he'd had.

'I'd have driven you to the church. You know that. You didn't have to ask the Whittles. You were always my favourite, Nancy.' He straightened up. 'I always wanted to do my bit for a hero's daughter.'

Nancy hoped he wasn't going to get maudlin.

'It'll be a wedding such as an officer and a gentleman would have given you. I've been very pleased to bring you up in his stead. Felt I was doing my bit, taking over his responsibilities. Sometimes it's better to choose than accept those nature sends.'

Nancy stifled a groan. She was afraid he'd drunk too much.

It was a cool and cloudy summer's morning but the rain was holding off. By the time Nancy got out of the Whittles' car at the church door, trying to cope with her unaccustomed

473

long skirts, she was feeling frissons of nervous excitement.

Amy and Kate were waiting in the porch, the organ was playing softly. Jim Whittle kissed her veil where it touched her cheek and went quickly into the church. Pa's lips hovered the other side of her veil too. She could smell whisky on his breath but he seemed all right.

'The very best to you, Nancy,' he said, pushing open the door from the porch. 'You've waited long enough for this.' The music stopped and Nancy felt a ripple of expectancy from the congregation.

The organ began to play again. A long way in front of her, she could see Stan standing to attention at the altar. He turned and smiled as the music swelled. This is it, she told herself, urging Pa forward.

As she went up the aisle on her father's arm, Nancy couldn't help but notice the man. He was at the end of a pew on Stan's side of the church and had turned right round to face her.

He kept his hazel eyes full on her face. His gaze seemed to engulf her, taking in every movement she made. He was so intense she could almost feel his curiosity, and something else she couldn't define. She felt a niggle of unease.

Everybody else in the congregation gave her friendly and admiring glances as she passed them. She found that reassuring, it was what she'd expected. There were a lot of nurses in church, all those who could get time off. They were part of her old life.

Her mother was easy to pick out, in her large tan felt hat and her fox fur. She was in a pew almost opposite the staring man, on the other side of the aisle. Nancy expected some sign of recognition from her as she passed, but Mam seemed oblivious. Instead her gaze was transfixed by the same man. Every line of her tan wool suit was stiff with tension. There was torment in her eyes. Nancy felt a cold shiver run down her spine.

Mam had kissed her before leaving for the church and had

seemed in more of a dither than she'd expected, but she'd not been like this. Now she looked wretched, in the depths of despair.

Even when she'd swept past the man, her full skirts swishing, Nancy could feel his eyes fasten on her back. She could feel the burning fever she'd generated in him and she couldn't understand why.

She reached Stan's side at last. He was wearing his staff sergeant's uniform. His gaze was reassuring, full of love. His deep suntan made him look wonderfully handsome. She stood close enough to feel him against her arm. He towered over her, lanky as ever.

'Dearly beloved, we are gathered together here in the sight of God . . .'

As the marriage service began she was shivering with foreboding. She told herself she was being silly, she must concentrate on the service. Behind her, Mam coughed nervously, her distress obvious.

If the man had stood between her and Stan throughout the ceremony, he couldn't have intruded more. He was unsettling her, upsetting her, spoiling the most important day of her life. The day for which she'd waited so long.

Stan noticed her restlessness and turned with a nervous half-smile to reassure her.

After signing the register, she came out of the vestry on her new husband's arm and met the man's full gaze again. She was unable to look elsewhere. He had a tight, sardonic smile as though he fully intended to make such an impression on her.

She glanced fearfully at Mam. She seemed agonised. She was clinging to the back of the pew in front with white knuckles and didn't look up as she passed.

As they posed at the church door for a photograph she whispered to Stan: 'Who is that man? He keeps looking at me.'

'Everybody's looking at you. You're the bride, love.'

'Not staring, like he is.'

Stan turned to look in the direction she was indicating. Nancy met the man's knowing gaze again. She couldn't avoid making eye contact.

'That's Uncle Vic. He can't take his eyes off you. Nobody can. You're a beautiful bride. People haven't seen a show like this since before the war. Relax and enjoy it.'

Nancy couldn't relax. She'd been building up to this for six years. It was the beginning of her new life, she was going to live happily ever after. It was meant to be a dream wedding and it was turning into a nightmare.

'He gives me the creeps,' she whispered to Stan.

He laughed. 'Not poor old Vic? He wouldn't hurt a fly.'

'Keep him away from Mam, she's terrified of him.'

'She can't be,' Stan said. 'There's nothing to be afraid of.'

But her mother had moved as far away from him as she could get and looked sick with worry. Her face was the colour of paste. That man had certainly spoiled the day for her.

They walked round to the church hall. The sun had come out and the wind had dropped. Even so, she was shivering as she joined the receiving line just inside the door.

Mam looked totally wretched. Nancy felt for her hand to comfort her. She was shaking. Nancy could see her looking along the line of people waiting to congratulate her and Stan. She knew what Mam was dreading. It was imprinted on her face.

'Congratulations. I do wish you every happiness.' It was said to them time and time again. Usually with a glance at Stan's uniform. 'Thank goodness the war's over and you won't have to go away again.'

'You look lovely, Nancy.'

The hall was draughty and she was cold. Every hand that shook hers seemed to give her warmth but she couldn't keep it. Nancy thought she was turning to ice. The man came at last.

His eyes were dark and knowing and made her shiver.

Grey hair, parted in the middle. It waved across his head like her own. Gaunt and angular, in shiny brown shoes and a formal charcoal pinstriped suit cut in a style popular a decade ago. He looked old-fashioned.

His hands were workman's hands. A lifetime of manual labour had broken his nails and provided rough skin and calluses.

Nancy was searching her memory for any connection he might have with Mam. She'd never heard her mention anyone. She never went out alone. How could she be interested in a man like this? Perhaps in his youth he'd been handsome. He was tall, as tall as her father but slim. Time had put deep furrows on his face.

'Mr Victor Smith, my mother's cousin,' Stan said. The man's eyes told her he had a secret he wanted to share with her. Something of vital importance.

'Congratulations,' he said to Stan. Nancy saw him bend towards her, felt his lips against her cheek. She recoiled in horror.

Winnie liked weddings. She particularly liked being in charge of the refreshments in the church hall. As soon as Nancy and her groom went into the vestry to sign the register, Winnie slipped back to the hall. She had last-minute preparations to see to.

There was a lovely smell of food as soon as she unlocked the door. It looked a delicious spread. Myra produced food that was as good as any you could get these days.

Winnie took off her best coat and went to hang it behind the kitchen door. A man's rather crumpled mackintosh occupied the peg she considered hers.

Winnie snatched it off and marched with it across the hall. Something heavy in the pocket banged against her knee as she did so. She felt round it, recognising a full bottle. Snorting with disgust, she hooked it on to the row of coat pegs just inside the door.

'Give me one guess,' she said aloud. Only Alec Siddons would bring a bottle to his daughter's wedding and keep control of it himself.

In the tiny kitchen, Winnie switched on the urn to boil the water for tea. Then the electric oven, that had been donated to the church by Mrs Catchpole and was such a boon for heating sausage rolls and meat pies.

She sighed with satisfaction when she felt the warmth coming through. Twice last month there had been a power cut on the day of the pensioners' tea, and she'd had to use the Primus. The other women were scared it was going to blow up in their faces, and told her she was a wizard at managing it, but it had taken some getting used to. Winnie had been dreading a power cut today.

Last night, Alec Siddons had set up his firkin of beer on a low table just outside the kitchen door.

'You don't intend going thirsty tomorrow,' she'd heard Amy say to him.

'For the men. Got to give our Nancy a decent send-off.'

Then he'd growled at her. 'Winnie? The youth club won't be in tonight? Don't want to broach this if they are. Can't have them helping themselves.'

'They were in last night.' She could hardly bring herself to be civil to him. 'We wouldn't be able to set the tables up if anyone was coming tonight, would we?'

'Good, then I'll do it now and give it time to settle.' She watched him trying to knock the tap in.

'You're not very clever at that,' she said, standing arms akimbo. 'You're making a mess.'

'Don't get enough practice,' he grunted, ignoring the pool he was allowing to dribble on the floor.

'You'll have this place smelling like a bar,' she scolded. 'Aren't you going to clear up that mess?'

'I can safely leave that to you,' he'd said, taking one of the tea cups she'd set out in readiness, twiddling with his tap until the cup was half full of cloudy beer, then drinking it back.

478

Nancy had rushed to get the mop and bucket out. 'It's all right for the men,' she said. 'But there's little enough for those who don't like beer.'

'There's nothing to be had anywhere.' Myra sounded worried. 'It was all drunk to celebrate victory in Europe last month. All I could get was half a bottle of brandy. It won't go anywhere amongst a crowd of this size.'

'I've got a bottle at home,' Winnie had volunteered. 'It was given to me before the war. Some liqueur. It's still half full. Will it be any good?'

'Yes,' Myra smiled. 'Punch, that's what we'll make. We can use any odd bits of spirit. I've got a punch bowl at home, and I'll bring up Jack's soda fountain. I know where I can get plenty of squash and lemonade.'

'Just the thing,' Stan agreed. 'My dad's got two or three half-empty bottles in the sideboard. I'll see if he'll let us have them.'

Winnie put the sausage rolls in to warm, and squirted soda water into the punch. It looked pretty with the precious orange floating on top. Myra certainly knew what was what when it came to catering.

People were starting to come in. She picked up the tray of sherry glasses she'd filled and began offering them round.

Winnie had only to look at Alec Siddons to feel her resentment building up. He was on her territory here, and encouraging a crowd of men to gather round the beer keg.

The punch was proving popular too. She tipped in a bottle of fizzy lemonade.

'It'll need a bit more than that, Winnie,' somebody laughed. She tipped in a tin of real orange juice and the last of Myra's brandy.

Toby Frampton brought several glasses to be refilled while she was stirring it.

'How is it?' she asked, tipping a little into his glass. He let it roll round his mouth.

'Could do with strengthening up a bit.'

Winnie tipped in the last few ounces from a bottle of gin and went back to the kitchen to turn off the urn, which was boiling. More tea was needed too.

She saw Alec Siddons follow her in. And insult upon injury, his scruffy old mac was hanging behind the door again. On top of her best coat now.

She saw him take out his whisky, refill his own glass, and put the bottle back. What a mean streak Alec Siddons had. They were all his guests but he was keeping the best for himself.

Fliss was helping a group of ladies to the punch. 'It's almost finished, Winnie,' she called. 'Is there anything left to make more?'

'Yes, plenty,' Winnie said. She'd see the ladies got their share of what was available. She tipped in another bottle of lemonade and added some orange squash. Then, when Fliss had gone, she took the bottle of whisky from Alec's mac pocket. It was quite safe to do so. She could hear him making his speech. She couldn't help but notice he was slurring his words and swaying a little.

Nobody was watching her, all eyes were on Alec. Winnie tipped a good portion of what remained into the punch bowl, making it good and strong. It shocked her a little to see how much she'd used. Less than a quarter left. Alec would certainly notice that.

Winnie had another idea. Alec Siddons deserved all he got. She went to the cupboard where the Primus stove was kept. Behind it, she kept the bottle of methylated spirit.

Well, methylated spirit was what she usually used. But last month, when she'd gone to the chemist she knew on Duke Street to get some more, it looked different.

'It isn't purple,' she said, when he brought her bottle back. 'Looks like something to drink.'

'I don't advise that. Give you a bit of a hangover,' he'd grinned. 'It's industrial spirit.'

'Probably run out of purple dye,' Winnie had said. 'Everything's in short supply.'

'It'll work fine in a Primus.' He'd been right, it did.

Alec Siddons looked as though he'd have a hangover tomorrow in any case. She'd give him a better one.

Winnie felt for the bottle of industrial spirit and carefully poured a good amount into Alec's bottle. He deserved to have his head blown off. It wasn't the revenge she'd craved all these years, but it was something. It gave her pleasure to think of Alec with a splitting head.

He was drinking whisky chasers. When he moved from the firkin to fumble in his coat pocket she pretended not to notice. He raised his small glass to his lips.

Winnie held her breath, waiting for an exclamation of disgust. It didn't come. She watched him weave his way back into the crowd and hid her smile behind her hand.

Celia gulped at the glass of sherry that was put in her hand once the introductions were over. Her mouth was dry and furred with nerves.

She had to lose herself in the crowd, stay away from Victor Smith. Since the day she'd first seen his name on that guest list, this had been hanging over her. He was a ghost from her past, beckoning her back. Making her relive those awful times. She'd never had any reason to think kindly of Victor Smith. He'd treated her badly, been a rotter of the first order. And now, after all these years, he'd come back to spoil what she'd salvaged for Nancy.

She'd wanted to see her daughters safely married. Especially Nancy. Getting them married seemed the only guarantee that they wouldn't end up as she had.

The food looked more attractive than she'd expected. Katie had told her that Fliss had brightened up the tables by laying squares of red crepe paper over the sheets.

Nancy had been sure everybody would be hungry because it was lunchtime. Myra and Amy were trying to usher people towards the buffet.

Amy was offering her two plates of food; she wondered where they'd found the parsley to decorate them. She took a sausage roll.

'Auntie My made these,' Amy whispered.

It was an effort to get it down. She didn't want to eat, though the other guests were tucking in.

'Wonderful spread,' they were saying. 'Pre-war standard here. How did you manage all this?'

Celia had heard that nowadays brides often had to make do with a cardboard cake. Amy had told her she'd seen one triple-tiered edifice, made pretty with silver spangles and imitation icing that glistened, but once the photographs had been taken, the dome had been lifted away to reveal a small plain cake on a plate beneath.

There was no pretence like that for Nancy. Her cake was real, though it was almost six years old. It was a pity that oil from the almond paste had soaked into the icing and given it yellow patches.

'If only I had some more icing sugar,' Celia had said, 'I could cover those marks and make it look fresh.' But there had been no icing sugar in the shops for years.

Nancy had been afraid it wouldn't be fit to eat after all this time, but she had pooh-poohed that. Nancy wouldn't be able to get another cake at such short notice, not these days.

The crowd parted and she caught sight of Nancy in her bridal gown, hanging on to Stan's arm and smiling up at him.

Nancy was happy, quite sure she was marrying the right person. Celia ought to feel happy too. Instead, Victor Smith was making her scalp crawl with dread.

She'd thought she'd shaken him off. That she'd managed to survive the disgrace he'd brought her. She'd thought all that was behind her and could be forgotten.

All these years she'd kept it from Alec. It would take only

a few words from Victor Smith to bring the edifice of lies crashing down about her ears.

Alec must never know, he'd feel deceived. He'd be furious with her. And what would Nancy think?

Celia thought she'd forgotten what Victor looked like, but she'd recognised him the minute he came into church.

When she realised he'd recognised her too, the shock was worse than a bomb going off under her. She couldn't breathe. The strength had ebbed from her knees. She'd been catapulted into this crisis.

Perhaps if she went home now? But he might say something to Nancy. He'd been eyeing her. He knew only too well that Nancy was his daughter. Celia ached with indecision.

A woman she didn't recognise was refilling glasses.

'Nancy makes a lovely bride,' she said. 'You must be very proud, Celia.'

'I am,' she assured her. She'd had her empty glass in her hand. When she looked down it was full of cloudy orange-tinted fluid. Her mouth was dry with fear. She sipped it, it tasted very alcoholic.

'Tea? Is there any tea?'

'Of course, in the kitchen.' She headed off in that direction. There were guffaws of raucous laughter from that end of the hall. Alec was holding court round his firkin of beer. She saw him lift a small glass to his lips. So he'd brought whisky too.

Winnie Cottie was filling cups at the tea urn. 'You all right, Celia? You look a bit pale.'

'I'm fine.'

Balancing a cup and saucer in one hand and her glass in the other she went back to the hall. There was nowhere for her to sit, but she found a place in the corner where she could put her glass on the windowsill and lean against the wall. Around her the noise level was increasing. Voices were lifting with greater animation. Everybody seemed to be enjoying themselves.

Then she saw Myra opening the piano and her daughter putting the strap of her accordion over her shoulder. She'd heard there would be a bit of a concert. The lad, Yves, was getting out their music. Then Myra was banging on the table for silence.

Fliss started with 'The White Cliffs of Dover'. Her clear voice filled the hall.

'Almost as good as Vera Lynn,' Celia heard someone say. Fliss was wonderfully good, but of course she was a professional now. She'd heard Yves had helped her a lot. He was getting out his banjo.

Fliss and Yves sang more Vera Lynn songs. Myra was good on the piano. They played faster, the merriment increased, making Celia feel more miserable.

The girls kept coming round with plates of food. She took a ham sandwich she didn't want.

Soon Myra had the guests joining in the choruses. 'Hang Out the Washing On the Siegfried Line', 'Lilli Marlene', and 'The Lambeth Walk'. Everyone was singing at the tops of their voices and swaying to the music. All except Celia; the last thing she felt like was singing.

At last everybody was clapping. The concert was over, even the encores they'd been persuaded to do.

The crowd parted again and she saw Victor Smith coming towards her. She knew he was going to speak to her.

'Celia? You remember me? Such a long time, but I've spent most of my life in Glasgow. Funny how we were thrown together and then apart.'

She was sweating, couldn't take in what he was saying. She eased her fox fur back a little from her neck.

'It's all in the past now. A long way in the past. My wife died before the war. Willie was lost at sea and Jock killed in France. Nothing to show for that side of my life.'

His face came nearer, intent on saying more that she didn't want to hear. 'Except Nancy. What a lovely girl she is.'

Nancy stole another look in the man's direction. His eyes were still following every move she made. He was ruining her day. Ruining it for her mother too.

An hour ago, she'd taken hold of Mam's arm. 'What is he to you?' she hissed, nodding in his direction, but her mother had shaken her head in agony.

Nancy was sure Mam shared his secret. She could see that Mam was frightened of him; she'd hardly spoken to anybody or eaten anything.

There was only one way she would find out and that was to ask the man himself. All through the speeches – and her father's was quite long – the man's gaze had never left her face.

Now she watched him go over to speak to her mother. Nancy could feel the electricity spark between them, could sense Mam's tension from the other side of the hall. From the look on her face she might have been expecting the end of the world. Mam was turning her face from him. Nancy could see terror on it. She pushed through the guests, towards her.

'Mam, what's the matter?' Her panic was plain for all to see.

'Who are you?' Nancy turned on the man. 'What do you want? Coming here and spoiling the day for us all.'

She felt her mother slump against her and realised she was fainting. The man caught hold of her too and helped lower her gently to the floor. Her large felt hat was pushed over her face. Other guests were moving back in alarm.

Stan was at Mam's side in an instant, wanting to help. Pa pushed closer, elbowing Nancy out of the way.

Nancy was choking with rage and fear. She gathered up her long skirts and whirled on the man. She caught at his arm and pulled him round to face her.

'Just who are you? What are you trying to do to us?'

'I'm a sort of cousin of Stan's mother.'

'I know all that,' Nancy rounded on him impatiently.

'Why are you staring at me? What am I to you?'

'My daughter,' he said.

Nancy felt she'd been stabbed. Every muscle in her abdomen contracted painfully.

'Better take her home.'

Celia knew it was Stan Whittle's voice. She could see other people round her as though through a fog. Her gut was full of foreboding.

'Too much excitement for her.' She was aware of Victor Smith craning towards her.

'She's been working too hard getting it all ready.'

That was Alec's voice, and it sent new waves of fear washing over her. The last thing she wanted was for Alec to talk to Victor Smith, but now it seemed she couldn't prevent it.

Celia hardly knew what she said: 'I had to do it. You do understand? I had to cover it all up.'

'Don't worry, we'll have you home in no time,' Stan assured her. 'Half an hour on the bed and you'll be as right as rain. Dad's going to run you home, he's gone to fetch the car to the door.'

'We'll come with you, Mam.' Nancy's face was serious and unsmiling. She seemed to hold herself aloof. Celia knew then that Victor Smith had told her he was her father.

'It's time I went home to change. The party's almost over here anyway.'

The noise was so loud it was hurting Celia's ears. She covered them with her hands. This wasn't social chit chat, it was a blazing row. Alec was shouting at the top of his voice. This was what she'd dreaded all along. Her disgrace was going to be a public humiliation.

She heard the thwack. The sound of bone hitting bone. Followed by an instant's silence as everybody turned to look. Then noise broke out again.

'What's happening?' she croaked.

'Good God,' Stan said. 'It's a fight. Let's get her out of here.'

Celia felt herself being bundled outside and pushed into the front seat of a car. It moved off. She could hear Nancy and Stan behind her.

'Are you feeling better now, Mam?'

She turned round in the seat. 'Don't tell him. Don't say anything, not to Pa. He doesn't know. He mustn't know.'

'Mam, I think he already does. Is it true then? That man, that awful man . . . ?'

'Don't say anything.' She was very conscious of Stan's father hearing all this. He couldn't miss it, not when he was beside her, driving the car. 'Not here. Nobody must know.'

Stan's voice came softly from behind her. 'Uncle Vic's all right. Really he is. Just a lonely old man.'

Jim Whittle said: Vic? What's he done? What's all the fuss about?'

CHAPTER THIRTY

Amy knew that most of her attention was on Paul. She'd not seen him over the last year and it was wonderful to be with him again.

It was only when they paused for a photograph at the church door that she'd realised that Mam was acting strangely and Nancy was concerned. In the excitement of the moment, she'd brushed that aside as being nothing out of the ordinary.

She'd enjoyed the reception. There were a lot of girls there she'd known well, nurses she hadn't seen since she'd left the hospital. She'd wanted to introduce Paul to them all. The time had flown. She'd been pleased everything was going well for Nancy.

She'd done her share of duties, handing round plates of Scotch eggs and meat pies cut into quarters.

She thought Pa's speech a little long-winded. There had been words, too, he hadn't quite got his tongue round. The guests had cheered mightily when he sat down. They'd seemed unaccountably boisterous.

Nancy had been worried that the drinks she'd been able to get would not go round.

'Just about enough for one glass of sherry each to start,' she'd said. 'Auntie My says we'd better be careful with the punch or there won't be enough for the toasts.'

'There'll be plenty of tea,' Amy had consoled. 'Lots of people prefer it.'

Instead, alcohol had flowed like water. She'd seen lots of punch going round; her own glass had been refilled several times. Pa must have brought more than that firkin of beer.

She'd been thrilled to hear Fliss sing. Even more thrilled with her glow of health and display of energy. The concert had gone down marvellously well. They'd all really enjoyed it.

It was only then that she'd realised things were going wrong, that Mam was in a real tizz.

Myra had started collecting the empty plates from the table. Almost all the food had gone now. The crowd was thinning out.

Then suddenly, Mam was on the floor, with Nancy calling out for help. Amy had rushed over. Mam looked terrible, grey-faced and ill.

'She's only fainted,' Amy said, trying to reassure all those nearby. She was relieved to see Mam starting to come round. 'She's all right. Lie back for a minute, Mam. Could you all move back a bit to give her more air?'

Amy was only half aware of the noise. She didn't see the fight break out. It was Pa shouting his head off at some man that first drew her attention. Then the crunch as his fist crashed against the man's jaw.

Nancy was clutching her arm in a panic. 'See that dreadful man? He says he's my father!'

Amy's eyes shot across the hall again. The man was on the floor, a limp bundle of pinstriped charcoal suiting. Paul was trying to stop Pa kicking him. Others were shouting. Bill Frampton, his face white with shock and outrage, was hurrying his wife to the door. Many others were following.

'What do you mean? How can he be your father?' She could see Nancy was really upset.

'Of course he isn't! He's some relative of Stan's.'

'Then why . . . ?'

'Stan says he doesn't know what's got into him. He thinks he's had too much to drink.'

'I don't think Mam would have anything to do with him.'

'Nor do I. He's just causing trouble.'

Amy caught sight of Winnie Cottie's face. She looked appalled. They were all shocked by the sudden change of atmosphere. There was a crush round the door.

Auntie My was saying: 'Go home, Amy. Take care of your mother. Nancy will have to leave if she wants to catch her train.'

'I think we should all get out of here,' Amy gasped. 'Let Pa fight his own battles. Other people are going to get hurt.'

'Yes, come on, this is nothing to do with us. We can come back later to get our things.'

'Let me tell Paul,' Amy said.

'He's seen you, he's coming.'

'Get your coat, Winnie. We're going.'

'I only meant to give him a hangover,' Winnie was moaning. 'I must have overdone it.'

When Amy looked round, her mother and Nancy had gone, and Myra was pushing everybody out in front of her. The church hall door slammed shut behind them.

Amy was being swept down the road home in a tight group. Fliss was holding on to her arm on one side, Winnie Cottie on the other. Kate was on the end of the line with Toby Frampton. She could see the peach taffeta of her long skirt flapping uncomfortably round her legs as her own dress was doing.

Amy took a deep, shuddering breath. All these years she'd been priding herself that she knew everything. She'd nosed into Pa's under-life. Prised out all his secrets. It had never occurred to her that Mam might have something she wanted to hide. She'd seen her as the innocent party.

Even now, she couldn't believe it. But who else could that man be? She couldn't talk about what she'd heard. None of them could. They walked quickly in silence. It was too awful.

The front door of the house was wide open. It seemed that already people were gathering inside.

'Everybody's moved down here,' Toby said. 'I can't believe the party's going to start up again.'

'Not safe to stay at the hall, not if they're going to fight,' Myra said.

'What can I do to help?' Paul was asking.

'Make some more tea,' Amy said. 'Would you mind handing round the food, Katie?' Amy pushed past the Whittles to get upstairs, and ran up to her mother's room.

Celia, whey-faced, was lying on her bed, her arm across her eyes. Nancy was striding up and down in a state of agitation.

'It's true, then? He is my father! I can't believe it.'

Amy tried to calm her. 'What does it matter now? You've got a husband. Go and get changed, Nancy.'

'Mam, you said my father was a hero, killed in the Great War . . .'

Amy said firmly: 'It's time you left for your honeymoon. Stan's waiting downstairs.'

'How can I go now?' Nancy's pretty face screwed up with anguish.

'Go,' Amy implored. 'What good do you think you can do by staying here?'

She pushed Nancy into her own small room. 'Get this gown off and your going-away suit on.'

Amy was undoing the tiny buttons down the back of the bridal gown as she spoke. 'The less notice we take of all this, the sooner Mam will get over it.'

'Mam'll never get over it, being humiliated like that, in public too. Neither will I. That man was hateful. I don't want him for a father.'

'You haven't had him,' Amy pointed out. 'You've had Pa. Do you think he's been any better?'

'Poor Pa. You can't blame him for this.' The scratchy strains of 'Lily of Laguna' began to float up from the front room.

'I blame him for the trouble in the church hall. He made

sure your reception ended in a shambles.'

'He's not been such a bad father to me.'

'You don't need a father any more. Nancy, you're grown up and a married woman. You can cope without.'

Nancy was shedding her long skirts and Amy was pulling the hanger out of her new royal blue suit when they heard Pa's voice in the road outside.

Seconds later, they heard him shouting in the hall below. 'Where's Celia? Where's she gone?'

'I'd let her be, Alec.' Myra's voice sounded calm.

Footsteps were storming upstairs. Amy tossed the suit to Nancy and rushed out on the landing. The sight of Pa's raging face made her catch her breath. Myra was trying to restrain him.

Nerves jangling, Amy tried to bar the way to the front bedroom. 'Mam's resting, Pa,' she said as calmly as she could. 'She fainted.'

One swipe from his mighty arm sent her reeling. Winnie Cottie had been following him; her arms kept Amy upright.

'I've turned him into a savage,' she moaned. 'I never meant to cause you trouble.'

Pa slammed back the bedroom door so it rebounded against the wall. Amy had a glimpse of Mam's terrified face lifting from the pillow.

'You had a fancy man,' Alec roared at her in a voice that could be heard all over the house. 'He says he's Nancy's father. I got him by the throat and he admitted it.'

Amy heard her mother moan.

'Calm down, Alec.' Myra closed the bedroom door quietly.

'A hero, you told me. An officer and a gentleman? He's nothing but a labourer. A weak little runt.'

Amy swallowed hard. 'You haven't hurt him, Pa?'

'I've taught him a lesson, I can tell you. He won't forget it in a hurry.'

'Don't let him near me,' Mam moaned. Her fear was making Amy's scalp crawl. She'd never realised until now just how frightened Celia was of Pa.

'He was trying to get off with you again. You told me you were married, and you never were. Lies, nothing but lies, and I believed you.'

Amy could feel the blood pounding in her head. Pa had gone berserk, his face was puce. She mustn't let him see she was frightened. That would make him feel stronger, give him the upper hand.

'What's good for the gander can be good for the goose,' she said coldly. 'Mam's done nothing that you haven't been doing over and over, Pa. Calm down.'

'She's a slut and you're meddling in things that don't concern you. Interfering in my business. You can get out of here and stay out. I don't want you in this house. I've told you before.'

The alcohol fumes were strong on Pa. There was no arguing with him in this mood.

Myra said: 'Celia's been a good wife to you, Alec. She's washed and scrubbed and cooked for you, and never looked at another man since you were married.'

'You've got nothing to complain about, Pa,' Amy breathed. 'Not after all you've done.'

'I should never have done it.' Winnie Cottie was wringing her hands. 'But you're a wicked man, Alec.'

'Out of my way, woman.'

Myra was given a push that sent her hurtling across the room. She fell against the dressing table, sweeping lace mats, scent bottles and combs on to the floor.

'You're going to get what you deserve,' he spat at Celia. 'I'll screw your bloody neck for you.' She rolled off the bed and flung herself into Amy's arms.

Amy could feel her cringing, and they both saw Pa's great arm rise to strike. She pushed Mam behind her into the corner and heard her taffeta skirt rip as Celia trod on the hem.

'Don't you dare hurt her,' she spat back at him. 'Can't

493

you see what you've been doing to her all these years? You've been systematically destroying her. She's terrified of you.'

Alec lunged at Amy instead. She screamed as his arm whacked about her head, but she kicked back at him.

'You little bitch! You spitfire. You've always been a thorn in my side.'

She saw him coming for her again. She was choking with fear. Amy knew she was no match for a man of Pa's size.

Out of the corner of her eye, Amy saw Winnie coming up behind him. She swung her heavy crocodile handbag at him like one possessed. It caught him off balance. The gilt catch burst open, scattering oddments across the room.

'You're a wicked man, Alec Siddons,' she shouted. 'You'll come to a bad end.'

Pa keeled over like a great oak being felled. They heard his head crack against the brass bedstead. Felt the house shake as he crashed to the floor.

Amy was transfixed by Winnie's elated face. Alec groaned but didn't move.

'That's cut him down to size,' Myra giggled nervously.

'Oh my God,' Celia breathed.

Amy could hear footsteps pounding upstairs. Paul's anxious face came round the door. 'Are you all right? What's happened?'

A Strauss waltz was playing downstairs, but its first vigour was fading. The gramophone needed rewinding. The music slowed and distorted as it ground to a standstill.

Amy came to life again.

'We're all fine – except Pa. Bit of a fracas. Please Paul, don't let anybody else come up. Come on, Mam, let's get you out of here while we can.'

Nancy was just opening her bedroom door. 'What was that noise?'

'Pa fell, he was like a raging bull.'

'Are you all right, Mam?'

494

'It was me he hit,' Amy complained. Her face was sore down one side and so was her shoulder. She felt light-headed.

'Are you ready to go, Nancy? It's time, isn't it?'

'Yes.' Nancy looked very smart in her going-away suit and little blue hat. She was trying to peer into the front bedroom, but Auntie My and Winnie were crowding out.

Stan was waiting at the bottom of the stairs. As soon as he saw Amy bring Nancy's cases out, he ran up to carry them down. They all followed him out to the Whittles' car.

Somebody had chalked 'Just Married' on the back, and tied tin cans and old boots to the bumper. Jim was going to run them down to the train at Woodside.

Everybody went out on the pavement to see them off, even Mam. Nancy kissed them all. There was no confetti and no rice to be spared for throwing.

Jim Whittle pulled away from the kerb to a small cheer. Amy waved with the others and saw Nancy and Stan waving through the back window all the way down to the lights at Duke Street.

Myra went indoors and ran upstairs. Amy followed slowly with Celia.

'He's going to kill me,' Celia whispered. 'I'm frightened.' She had to rest halfway up, her face grey and sweating.

'Not if I have anything to do with it,' Amy retorted.

'You'll go away again,' Mam said fearfully.

'He'll calm down. He'll be all right by then. Come and lie down on Nancy's bed, and I'll see how he is.'

Myra came to the front room door. Her eyes seemed enormous. 'Amy, he hasn't moved!'

Amy's throat tightened. Mam gave a little cry and reached him before she did. Pa lay still. He wasn't breathing. Amy felt for his pulse but she knew she'd feel nothing.

'Is he dead?' Myra breathed.

Amy nodded, shocked that the possibility hadn't occurred to her until now.

'He can't be.' Mam was crying. 'What have we done?'

Myra's face was ashen. 'What are we going to do now?'

'I've done it, at last.' Winnie was euphoric. Her lined face was wreathed with smiles. She laughed hysterically. 'I told him I'd get even with him. He did Randall down. I've done it at last.'

'No, no.' Amy was agitated. 'It was an accident.'

'I hit him with my handbag. You saw me do it. He's got what he deserves.'

'No! You did nothing. Do you hear? Nothing.'

'But it's my revenge. I told him . . .'

'No,' Amy insisted.

'You don't understand.' Winnie's face was creasing up in laughter. 'I didn't want him to fight and cause you trouble. Of course I didn't, but I slipped him a Mickey Finn. It was all my fault.'

'Nonsense, Winnie,' Myra said, giving her a hug. 'I feel a bit hysterical myself.'

Amy was trying to think. 'Pa's caused enough trouble for all of us in his life. Now he's dead, nobody is going to be blamed for it.'

'We've got to do something,' Myra worried. 'We can't just . . .'

Downstairs, the 'Skaters' Waltz' started up with fresh momentum.

Amy said firmly: 'Everybody at the wedding saw him beat and kick Vic Smith. They'll all know why. He was shouting at the top of his voice. Lots of people saw him in a fine old rage.'

'You're right.' Myra was holding her hand. 'All we have to do is say he came here and we saw him try to attack Celia. That is what happened.'

'We can swear he tripped and hit his head,' Amy said. 'Too drunk to know what he was doing. Winnie didn't touch him. Who would think it likely,' she looked at Winnie, 'a frail seventy-year-old widow and him a huge hulk of a man.

'Mam? You agree? That's what we'll say?'

'I thought he was going to kill me. I didn't see anything else.'

'You didn't touch him, Winnie. Don't you dare say you did.' Amy could feel the perspiration on her forehead. 'Pa came up. He was furious with Mam. He lunged at her, fell and hit his head. End of story. We'll all say the same. We're all eye witnesses. It was an accident.'

'Are you sure he's dead?' Mam asked in a hoarse voice. 'Really dead?'

'I'm afraid so,' Amy told her.

'Thank God. Thank God for that,' Mam said, and burst into tears.

Myra was staring at her aghast. 'Hadn't we better phone for an ambulance?' she croaked. 'We've got to be practical.'

'Yes,' Amy agreed. 'We'll say he died while we were waiting for it to come.'

'We'd better go and break the news downstairs. Mam, come and lie down in Nancy's room, where you can't see him.'

'No, I'm not staying up here by myself.' Amy saw her moisten her lips. 'I'm coming down for another cup of tea.'

It was a long time before Amy could think of Nancy's wedding without coming out in a cold sweat.

'Poor Nancy,' Auntie My had shivered. But at least Nancy hadn't known about Pa dying at the time. She'd gone away on her honeymoon.

But it was all in the past, and now, a year on, she'd had time to settle down. Nancy was very happy; Stan was all she'd ever wanted. They had their own house, as well as a baby daughter. The whole family loved little Lorna.

There had been no fuss about Pa's death. It had been accepted as an accident.

Amy remembered how they had huddled together for support on that awful day. Mam and Auntie My, Winnie,

Katie and herself, all in their wedding finery but with dread on their faces. Amy felt closer to them all as a result.

They all agreed that Mam had been much better since Pa's death. She was working part-time with Auntie My down at the café and quite enjoying it. Joining in more, and making a new life for herself.

Everybody was talking about making a new start now the war was over, but Auntie My said precious little had changed. Rationing was tighter than ever, and austerity was the order of the day.

They all felt tremendous relief that there would be no more killing and no more maiming. Amy felt sweet satisfaction that Paul had survived without mishap.

War had brought suffering and horror to many. Amy thought sadly of Katie's terror in the air raids, and of Nancy having to wait and wait, with her patience stretched to the limit, but they had both been able to put all that behind them.

Amy didn't dare talk to anyone but Paul about what war had brought her.

'It was the experience of a lifetime. I wouldn't have missed it for anything,' she'd told him. 'It made me see things clearly, what's important and what isn't.'

Paul's brown eyes smiled into hers. 'I felt exhilarated many times, once I got over my terror.'

'You enjoyed it? Go on, admit it.'

'Some of it. Yes, at times it was very exciting, a real challenge. And we won.'

'But I'm glad it's over,' Amy said. She was glad that her life and those of her sisters would not be like Mam's had been. The postwar world was going to be very different.

Katie had told herself many times that she'd got over Jimmy Shaw, but the truth was he was still a grey spectre hovering behind her.

'Marry me, Katie?' Toby had asked her, soon after he arrived home.

Katie had felt her heart turn over. There was nothing she wanted more, but she felt unaccountably wary.

She knew she had complete freedom of choice this time, circumstances were not pushing her into it. She was being coaxed by Toby, and that was very different.

'I'll wait if you don't feel ready,' he'd said. 'Now the war's over and I'm home for good, you can take your time. I just want you to know I'm not going to change my mind. I love you and I always will.'

Katie thought about it. There was such a warmth about Toby, such a lack of subterfuge, she knew she could trust him.

'I know.'

'What is it then?'

How could she explain about the shadow Jimmy still cast on her? She had desperately wanted to marry him, and she'd pushed him as hard as she'd dared to make him do it. It was a comfort to feel Toby pushing her instead. But there was something she could never get away from: the baby she'd almost had.

'Your parents . . . I can feel them drawing away from me. Holding back. They don't think I'm right for you.'

It worried her, because they'd gone out of their way to help her when she'd been in real trouble, and Nancy was very fond of them.

'I know you're right for me,' he'd told her. 'It's me you're marrying, not them.'

'Yes, but . . .'

'They're getting used to the idea. They know how I feel about you. Don't we spend every moment we can together?'

'I do love you, Toby.'

'That's all that matters.'

She shook her head. 'They think you can do better for yourself. They don't approve of me because I had a baby. Out of wedlock.'

He lifted her chin and kissed it. 'I thought you told me you

499

were over all that? That you'd pushed it behind you?'

'I have. They haven't.'

'Katie, that's not true. I think they accept that the blame wasn't all yours. It might not be that at all. I think they disapproved of your father more than of you.'

Choosing his words carefully, Toby told her how his father believed he'd seen Alec Siddons looting. 'But Dad did nothing about it. He didn't want to upset Nancy.'

'Pa's been dead for a whole year,' she breathed.

'Exactly. And they can't visit the sins of the father on his children. That sort of thing has no place in the postwar world. They know you're the only girl I ever wanted. Come on, Katie, say you'll marry me. I'll not stop asking you until you do.'

'I do want to be your wife, of course I do. I just want everybody to like the idea.'

He kissed her again. 'I love the idea. If they don't, they'll soon come round.'

'I do hope so.'

'We'll go and buy the engagement ring, then go home and show it to them. You'll see.'

Toby helped her choose a traditional three-stone diamond ring. Katie couldn't stop looking at it winking on her finger. She thought it magnificent. He led the way into the sitting room at Henshaw House.

'We're engaged,' he announced. Toby had never been one to beat about the bush. 'On the fourth time of asking, Katie has agreed to marry me.'

Katie went forward to show them her ring. Bill Frampton kissed her cheek.

'We've been expecting it for some time,' he said.

'I've been trying to persuade her for some time,' Toby added, laughing.

His mother threw her arms round Katie. 'When will it be? Soon?'

'As soon as I can persuade her,' Toby said.

'But there'll be so much to arrange.' Katie was thinking of all the preparations for Nancy's wedding.

'I can see to some of it. I'd love to,' Mary Frampton said enthusiastically. 'You must let me help. I haven't a daughter of my own to do it for. If your mother wouldn't mind?'

'I don't think she'd mind,' Katie said diffidently, finding the reception of her news better than she'd expected. How could she have been this wrong?

'I had my wedding dress out only the other day. I thought then . . . Well, I'd be thrilled if you'd wear it.'

'Don't go overboard, Mum. Give Katie half a chance,' Toby put in.

'Bridal gowns are so difficult these days. Nobody has coupons to spare for clothes that are going to be worn only once. Were you planning to borrow Nancy's? She had a lovely dress.'

Katie hadn't got round to thinking about her wedding gown. 'Not Nancy's. She's smaller than I am. I wouldn't be able to get into it.'

'Come and see mine,' Mary said. 'I've always been big too, but you can't say until you see it. Perhaps you won't like it.'

Katie climbed the stairs behind her. She was willing to wear anything on her wedding day if it would help Mary Frampton accept her into the family. She was overcome with relief that she was taking so much interest.

Toby's mother took a large box from the top of her wardrobe and opened it on her bed.

'I wore this in 1913.' She smiled. 'It's supposed to be medieval in style. I hope you don't think it too dated?'

'It's beautiful,' Kate breathed. The dress was of rich parchment satin, encrusted with pearls and jewel stones.

'Not all real, I'm afraid.'

'It's absolutely beautiful.' Katie held it against herself. 'You're as tall as I am, so it is long enough. Can I try it on?'

'Of course. Let's see what it looks like, make sure it fits.'

The cloth was cool against her skin. Katie felt like a queen in it.

'You're slimmer than I was, it needs taking in a bit. I'll ask my dressmaker to do it. There's a matching cap that goes with it.' She fitted it on Katie's head. 'Just right for your short curly hair.'

'I'm thrilled with it.' Katie twirled in front of the cheval glass. She was suddenly excited, and delighted too that her future mother-in-law was prepared to lend her wedding gown.

When they went back to the sitting room, Toby winked at her, as if to say, I told you they'd got over all that.

It surprised Amy that weddings could be so different. Katie's was turning out to be rather grand. She'd marvelled at the length and formality of the ceremony.

She and Nancy had been matrons of honour. Sisters had to do these things for each other. Mam had made herself a smart navy outfit for the occasion, and she'd had to make new dresses for them. Pale green parachute silk this time, it was the only material that wasn't on coupons, that looked halfway suitable.

Mam had said the peach taffeta dresses they'd worn for Nancy's wedding would complement the bride's dress very well, and she could take in Katie's to fit Nancy, but Amy's was torn beyond repair, and she was glad. This time they'd chosen a more sophisticated style.

'Our Katie's done well for herself,' Mam whispered. 'The Framptons look very prosperous. Toby will make a kind and generous husband. Better than that Jimmy would ever have been.'

They'd all been driven back to the reception at Henshaw House. Mary Frampton was good at organising this sort of thing. They had caterers in and put on a wonderful spread. Far more splendid than either Amy's or Nancy's had been, despite the fact that rationing and austerity was tougher than ever. It was a dignified, orderly occasion. There'd be no outbreak of fighting here.

Katie was having a dream wedding, but Amy was not sorry she'd missed this for herself. Her simple and hasty ceremony had given her more years of marriage even though she and Paul had not been able to spend them together.

She looked across at him now and saw him smile at her. She was proud of him. He was demobbed now, like all of them, and doing what he loved most. She'd been delighted when he'd found himself a job with a civilian airline.

Katie was a stunning bride in her medieval wedding gown encrusted with jewels. No need to ask if she was happy. It was there on her face for all to see. She was radiant, more beautiful than ever.

A Mersey Duet

Anne Baker

When Elsa Gripper dies in childbirth on Christmas Eve, 1912, her grief-stricken husband is unable to cope with his two newborn daughters, Lucy and Patsy, so the twins are separated.

Elsa's parents, who run a highly successful business, Mersey Antiques, take Lucy home and she grows up spoiled and pampered with no interest in the family firm. Patsy has a more down-to-earth upbringing, living with their father and other grandmother above the Railway Hotel. And through further tragedy she learns to be responsible from an early age. Then Patsy is invited to work at Mersey Antiques, which she hopes will bring her closer to Lucy. But it is to take a series of dramatic events before they are drawn together . . .

'A stirring tale of romance and passion, poverty and ambition . . . everything from seduction to murder, from forbidden love to revenge' *Liverpool Echo*

'Highly observant writing style . . . a compelling book that you just don't want to put down' *Southport Visitor*

0 7472 5320 X

HEADLINE

Kitty Rainbow

Wendy Robertson

When the soft-hearted bare-knuckle fighter Ishmael Slaughter rescues an abandoned baby from the swirling River Wear, he knows that if he takes her home his employer will give her short shrift – or worse. So it is to Janine Druce, a draper woman with a dubious reputation but a child of her own, that he takes tiny Kitty Rainbow.

Kitty grows up wild, coping with Janine's bouts of drunkenness and her son's silent strangeness. And she is as fierce in her affections as she is in her hatreds, saving her greatest love for Ishmael, the ageing boxer who provides the only link with her parentage, a scrap of cloth she was wrapped in when he found her. Kitty realises that she cannot live her life wondering who her mother was, and in Ishmael she has father enough. And, when she finds herself pregnant, deprived of the livelihood on which she and the old man depended, she must worry about the future, not the past. But the past has a way of catching the present unawares . . .

'An intense and moving story set against the bitter squalor of the hunger-ridden thirties' *Today*

'A rich fruit cake of well-drawn characters . . .' *Northern Echo*

'Fans of big family stories must read Wendy Robertson' *Peterborough Evening Telegraph*

'A lovely book' *Woman's Realm*

0 7472 5183 5

HEADLINE